C0028 99380

D0719101

1a

D9
2013
014

1

D12

2

JUN 2013

CASTLES IN SPAIN

An intelligent and engaging romance.

After the death of her lover Venetia Marriott recuperates with her aunt and uncle near Seville. But, far from resting, she is catapulted into village affairs and those of the Quinones family, including brothers Fernando and Felipe. When an old university friend turns up, the two girls are drawn into a web of romantic entanglements – and a bitter feud harking back to the Spanish Civil War.

CASTLES IN SPAIN

CASTLES IN SPAIN

Sally Stewart

Severn House Large Print
London & New York

GLASGOW CITY COUNCIL
LIBRARIES/ARCHIVE

C002600072	
WELF	Cypher
17.03.02	£18.99

This first l   02 by
SEVERN ᴸᴱᴬᴿᴳᴱ ᴾᴿᴵᴺᵀ ᴮᴼᴼᴷˢ ᴸᵀᴰ ᵒⁱ
9-15, High Street, Sutton, Surrey, SM1 1DF.
First world regular print edition published 2001 by
Severn House Publishers, London and New York.
This first large print edition published in the USA 2002 by
SEVERN HOUSE PUBLISHERS INC., of
595 Madison Avenue, New York, NY 10022

Copyright © 2001 by Sally Stewart

All rights reserved.
The moral right of the author has been asserted.

British Library Cataloguing in Publication Data

Stewart, Sally
    Castles in Spain. - Large print ed.
    1.   Love stories
    2.   Large type books
    I.   Title
    823.9'14 [F]

ISBN 0-7278-7126-9

Except where actual historical events and characters are being described
for the storyline of this novel, all situations in this publication are
fictitious and any resemblance to living persons is purely coincidental.

Printed and bound in Great Britain by
MPG Books Ltd, Bodmin, Cornwall.

One

The flight to Seville was delayed, the check-in girl at the Iberia counter explained apologetically; waved towards the departure lounge, Venetia Marriott refused the coffee being offered and considered her fellow-passengers instead: obvious expatriates returning to Spain after Christmas at home, businessmen going back to their incessant round of travelling, and the usual clutch of excited nuns, twittering like sparrows.

One passenger stood out from the rest of them. Registering the fact, Venetia realised something more remarkable as well. Not seen for nearly ten years, this girl was still immediately recognisable. Beauty had marked out Fiona Gilmour from a scruffy raggle-taggle band of women undergraduates, but she was finished perfection now: the flawless face and mane of red-gold hair insisted on being noticed and admired. A magazine on her lap slid down to the floor and the man beside her dived to retrieve it. He was thanked with a dazzling smile, but Fiona's expert glance assessed him and moved on. Then, suddenly, she stood up and walked across the aisle.

'I can hardly believe it,' she said, 'but I don't think I'm mistaken. Aren't you Venetia Marriott?'

Hazel eyes set under brows darker than a neat bob of mid-brown hair regarded her steadily, ruling out the possibility of a mistake. That level gaze was certainly remembered from the past.

'That's me,' Venetia agreed calmly, 'and I recognised you too. That was easier, of course, but it's a long time since we left St Hugh's.'

Fiona waved away a reminder to which there might still be some awkwardness attached. She hadn't been able to help what had happened then, but she knew for a fact of life that other women always blamed her for their disappointments.

'You had Spanish connections, I remember,' Fiona went on hastily. 'I rather envied them for sounding more exotic than the God-fearing Scots I could only lay claim to! I suppose you're going to Seville to visit them?'

'I'm going to a funeral in Jerez,' Venetia said unexpectedly, 'and it's my first visit for years. I hated Spain as a child, and disliked all my Ribera relations.'

'Noble of you to bother with them, then, especially at the beginning of January.'

'I'm going in place of my father. The funeral is his mother's, but he's marooned in Switzerland with an ankle broken in a skiing accident.' She thought she'd explained enough about herself, and asked the question Fiona would be expecting.

'What about you – why is Seville calling *you* in mid-winter?'

'Oh, I'm returning to work.' Fiona smiled, anticipating more surprise; no one ever found it easy to believe that she was a toiler in the academic vineyard. 'I'm on a year's sabbatical, researching a book on the history of Fascism. I went home for Christmas after three months in Italy; now it's Spain's turn. I'm putting off Nazi Germany till last.'

Venetia nodded, reminded of what she'd forgotten until then: the girl beside her could have danced through their student years like a dragonfly skimming the surface of the Isis. Well, dancing there had been, but she'd worked too, and carried off a very good degree. It had seemed unfair to the rest of them; brains *or* beauty should have been enough of a gift from any fairy god-mother.

'I expect you're tired of being told that you don't look like an academic,' Venetia commented, 'but you probably liven up High Table dinners no end.'

Fiona's smile agreed, but it was wry as well. 'I'm not *persona grata* with *all* my colleagues, and I made a very bad mistake in briefly marrying one of them.' She registered the query in Venetia's face and shook her head. 'My choice of husband wasn't the man you and I fell out over, equally disastrous though it proved to be. Only callow youth could have blinded both of us to James O'Halloran's many failings, don't you think?'

'His charm blinded us,' Venetia pointed out, 'though callow I certainly was – the last of the foolish virgins! I was even silly enough to believe that he was a little starstruck with me, until he got *you* in his sights. I recovered from Dr O'Halloran eventually, but I left Oxford still hating you very much.'

A tannoyed announcement rescued Fiona from deciding how to reply. Passengers for Seville could now embark; it was time to gather up hand luggage and straggle to the departure gate.

They found places together on the plane, but Venetia wasn't sorry to see her companion inevitably pounced on by the young man in the seat next door. The meeting had been unsettling; one reminder of the past was like a lit touchpaper to the next, setting off a chain of memories. Fiona's low murmur finally interrupted them.

'Talk, please, Venetia ... this idiot next to me thinks that Francisco Franco is the name of a Spanish footballer! You haven't

10

told me what *you're* doing. I hope a brilliant Modern Languages degree isn't being wasted on a pack of schoolchildren?'

'I did try teaching first, but wasn't very good at it; then I found my true *métier* as a translator, in Brussels of course,' Venetia explained solemnly.

Fiona considered the composed face beside her – ordinary enough as to features and colouring at first glance, but perhaps not ordinary at all in its intelligence and unexpected gleams of humour. 'I hope the *métier* isn't all you found,' she suggested after a moment's thought. 'Even Brussels, *not* the world's most exciting city, must contain *some* personable males.'

'I found one.' It was said with such quiet, sad pride that Fiona waited in silence for the rest of the story. 'He was a Frenchman, distantly related to my stepmother, Arlette. When he died of leukaemia a year ago I struggled on for a bit, but Brussels wasn't bearable without him. I resigned just before Christmas and went back to London. After the funeral I shall be job-hunting again.'

Fiona heeded the note of finality in her companion's voice, and cast about for what it would be safe to say next, but Venetia switched the conversation herself.

'Why have you settled on Seville? I'd have expected you to stay in Madrid?'

'I must go there, of course, but I have a

11

great-uncle still living in Seville, and I hope he'll offer me free board and lodging while I work on my notes. There's only one snag: he and Grandfather Hamish took different sides in the Civil War and never spoke to each other again. I'm relying on my youth and beauty to get me through his rather firmly sealed front door! He's a curmudgeonly old man by all accounts.'

'And if youth and beauty fail, what then?'

'I have an even dodgier string to my bow. My father's brother is somewhere in the south as well. Uncle Ian kicked the puritanical dust of Edinburgh off his feet and made a name for himself in London, not to mention a huge amount of money when several of his books were filmed. Then something went badly wrong and he dropped out of circulation. My father says he's living in some remote corner of the sierras; but even if he is, and I track him down, the truth is that the Gilmours aren't noted for being one big happy family.'

'I doubt if you should count on him *or* your great-uncle,' Venetia observed. 'They both sound unlikely hosts to me.'

'To me as well, I fear; still, I mean to have a go at mending the rifts in the family lute! The alternative is to return home, because my Oxford flat's rented out for a year; but parents at close range are something you and I have now outgrown.' She remembered too late, and quickly apologised. 'Tactless of me – at least I *have* a mother; poor you got landed with the step-variety.'

Venetia was able to smile. 'So I did, and I resisted her tooth and nail to begin with. But even I gradually understood that my father needed a wife, and Arlette has proved a very good one. We rather like each other now, as a matter of fact.'

The rattle of lunch trays being handed out interrupted the conversation, and by the time curried chicken and chocolate custard had been consumed the flight was almost over. They were already above the silver ribbon of the Guadalquivir River when Fiona suddenly reverted to the past again.

'We haven't either of us done very well in the romantic stakes, I'm afraid. Your lover was unkind enough to die, mine turned into a husband I couldn't wait to get rid of. Imagine it – he even put me off men temporarily; thank God I'm here to work, *not* to get seduced by some nicotine-scented Don Juan! It's one of the things I dislike about Spaniards ... they will all smoke like chimneys.'

Smiling in spite of herself, Venetia agreed. Even without having to surrender the quickly unlamented Dr O'Halloran, the truth was that she hadn't ever liked Fiona. It was a surprise now to find that they had anything in common at all, but the

13

unexpected meeting had somehow been needed to smooth away the rough edges left all those years ago. She was glad that it had happened, and was able to sound sincere when they said goodbye on *terra firma* half an hour later.

'Good luck with the book, and with your family-feud-mending. If anyone can charm their way through hostile territory, I'd say it's you for sure!'

'I think so too,' Fiona agreed with pride, 'but I wish you were staying on, Venetia – we could have compared notes about our trying relatives. Well, *adiós, amiga.* My spoken Spanish isn't up to much, so I shall have to smile and look appealing whenever I need help from now on.'

'You can't fail,' she was assured gravely before they parted company, one of them for a taxi ride to her hotel, the other *en route* for the station and a train that would take her to Jerez.

Venetia was there by early evening, installed by her own choice in a slightly less sumptuous room than the one that had awaited her father and stepmother. There had been no message for her from any of her Spanish relations, and the excuses she offered herself for their silence weren't convincing. Arlette had told them she was coming and, however busy they were, however upset by Juanita's death, *one* of them might have had the kindness to get in touch with her. But even as she was deciding this her room telephone rang, and a quiet voice sounded along the wire, speaking in unaccented, mother-tongue English.

'Good-evening, Venetia, this is William Marriott – Uncle William, perhaps I should introduce myself as, even though we've never met. Your father telephoned to say where I could find you, and I told the family here that Edwina and I would look after you this evening. I hope that wasn't too ... too presumptuous of me.'

The occasional hesitation and the diffident voice conjured up a picture of William Marriott that seemed to bear no brotherly relation to her dashing, decisive father. With no more excuse than an amused comment of Arlette's, her imagination provided a contrasting vision of Aunt Edwina as well – William's twin sister, she thought, was likely to be a large, overwhelming lady, endowed with all the amplitude her brother sounded as if he lacked.

'Not presumptuous,' Venetia finally remembered to say, making a mental apology to her Spanish relatives. 'I should very much like to meet you both. Are you staying in this hotel?'

She thought she detected a smile in her uncle's gentle voice. 'No – your father's

15

choice of hotel is a little above our touch! We'll call for you at nine o'clock, if your English insides can hold out that long. The food at the Cocheras restaurant will be very good, but there's no need to dress up – it's a simple sort of place.'

Grateful for the hint, she promised to hold out as long as necessary, and put down the telephone, still smiling – she liked the sound of Uncle William. But, changing out of her travelling clothes, she was suddenly reminded of Fiona's conversation about *her* relatives. The name of Ian Gilmour had, in fact, been celebrated enough to reach Brussels, and although she'd never felt inclined to follow the adventures of his violent, amoral heroes, the books were hugely popular and successful. Something so extraordinary must have happened to send him into retreat in a remote corner of Spain that she doubted even Fiona's chances of being made welcome. But for the moment she had problems of her own to contend with – tomorrow's funeral, and the immediate prospect of meeting her unknown aunt and uncle.

Later that evening, expecting a couple to arrive in the hotel lobby, she scarcely glanced at the tall, thin man who came in alone. But he walked straight towards her as if recognition was no problem, and then she could see some familiarity in *him* – he looked an older, more untidy version of her father. The knot of his tie was slightly askew, and his rumpled tweed suit would have offended Jeffery Marriott, but there was such kindness in the smile he offered her that she thought it might be his defining quality if she ever got to know him better. Even now, to her surprise, there was no awkwardness about this first meeting between them; it was as if they already knew each other.

'Is Aunt Edwina not with you?' she asked at once, holding out her hand. 'I was going to suggest sherry here. My father's instructions were to sign the bill and damn the expense!'

'Kind of him, but Edwina decided to go on ahead to the restaurant – it's very near our hotel,' William explained. 'She wanted to make sure that her favourite *pimientos al pequillo* are on the menu tonight – taking it for granted, I'm afraid, that you would share her passion for seafood! If you can wait a little longer for your fino, I've got a taxi tethered outside.'

Ten minutes later Venetia was introduced to her aunt, and trying not to smile at the accuracy of her prevision. Edwina *was* a large, ungainly woman, with bones that seemed to have been assembled by chance rather than by design. Grace and elegance she couldn't claim, but there was un-

17

mistakable character in her face, and a hint that amusement was often to be found in watching her fellow human beings.

'The child looks too thin, William,' she announced gruffly. 'She needs good food and wine.'

'She looks just like her mother to me,' he answered, sounding pleased. 'I expect that's why I spotted her at once in the hotel lobby.' He delved in his pocket and brought out a photograph to hand to his niece. 'We were on leave in England when Jeffery announced his engagement to Katherine Ingram all those years ago. It was the only time we ever met her, but she had the kind of charm one doesn't forget.'

Venetia studied the faintly smiling face of her mother, seeing in it nothing of herself; but she looked gratefully at William. 'Thank you – my father says she shied away from cameras, so I have few mementoes of her. If you were always away in South America, I suppose you never heard her sing. I have a collection of her records and tapes, but they're too precious to play often. I keep them for the times when my heart needs lifting.' His niece's thin face suggested to William that she'd known such times, but she smiled suddenly and the impression of sadness was gone. 'I'm sorry you weren't ever here when I came to stay with my grandmother. I know you're half Spanish, being Juanita's children, but you both seem thoroughly English, and that would have been a comfort to me then! I found this country too extreme a place – *todo o nada*, as our relatives always seemed proud to say.' Unknowingly she offered them her mother's smile again. 'If you've come here to retire I suppose this country represents home for you. It doesn't for Father – he prefers to live in Paris now with Arlette, and visit London when he has to.'

'I'm not a lover of Paris myself,' Edwina announced flatly. 'We always planned to come back here when William's work in South America was over. Our idea was to settle on the coast, but we were years too late. It had been built over and ruined by the time we got here. No need to ask why that was allowed to happen – the law of greed and gain was operating.'

'And so was the law of desperate poverty,' William reminded her. 'You know as well as I do, my dear, that Andalucía was the most destitute of all Spain's provinces. If these people sold their land to the developers you can't blame them – it's all they *had* to sell.'

It was an old argument between them, Venetia suspected, and she steered them to a safer subject. 'If not on the coast, where *have* you settled?'

A smile transformed her aunt's long, horse-like face. 'It's called Rosario – a *pueblo blanco* in the Sierra de Ubrique, between Arcos and Ronda.'

William took up the tale. 'The truth is that we stumbled accidentally on what seems like the realisation of our dreams – enough paintable wild flowers to satisfy even Edwina, and a million birds to watch for me. We're on the great migration route between Africa and Europe.'

'But best of all it's old Spain still,' Edwina interrupted him, anxious to be the one to explain Rosario's crowning glory. 'The people there work the land as their fore-fathers did, they observe the traditional rules and rituals of the *pueblo*, and they see no reason to change their ways at all.'

Venetia registered the contentment shin-ing in their faces, and understood now why her father reckoned this little-known elder brother and sister odd. Wild flowers and birds and ancient customs were all very well in their way; undoubtedly they should be preserved if possible, that would be Jeffery Marriott's sane and sensible view. But to find them sufficient reason to bury oneself in some remote sierra would seem to him behaviour worthy of the Knight of the Sad Countenance himself.

'I hope Rosario stays as it is now,' Venetia said seriously, 'but isn't it swimming against the tide? Spain is no longer the Continent's most isolated, inward-looking country; on

20

the contrary, it seems to me to be hell-bent on becoming totally Europeanised.'

With obvious reluctance William agreed. 'Well, yes ... I'm afraid it *is* losing some of the old unique flavour. We must hope the busybodies in Brussels make the mistake of banning bull-fights – *that* might annoy the Spaniards enough to swing them back the other way!'

Venetia smiled at the idea, then grew sober again. 'I have to say I hated the *corridas* as a child, and irritated my cousins by refusing to be taken to them. But if I were a Spaniard I'd fight the bureaucrats to my last gasp to keep *anything* that made Spain different from the rest of Europe.'

'*Viva España!*' Edwina trumpeted joyfully. 'No wonder Jeffery said you'd abandoned your Brussels job – your heart wasn't in it, thank God!' Then, glancing in the direction of the door, her expression suddenly changed. 'How very tiresome, William ... some of Juanita's neighbours have just walked in. Now they'll expect to join us, and insist on making a great deal of noise; even on the eve of a burial the dear things can't resist doing that.'

She was proved right, both then and the following day.

Two

On a fine winter morning Juanita's cortège looked impressive, and the requiem Mass was beautiful; but afterwards an air almost of celebration took over the proceedings. At the end of her long life an old and distinctly autocratic lady had been laid to rest; now those present could unblushingly enjoy the funeral feast and get on with the business of living.

Among the guests gathered in the huge room there was much to be discussed and argued about, especially the quality of the past year's sherry grapes, and the prospects for Jerez's great annual Horse Fair. Even nearer to their hearts, would the heir to a rival *bodega* propose to a Ribera grand-daughter or not?

Venetia listened, smiled, and frequently explained the reason for her father's absence but, as in all the years of growing up, she still seemed not to belong among these vivid, exuberant people. Armed with the rasp and vigour of their mother tongue, they engaged in conversation as if going into battle. Born into the sherry-producing dynasties of Jerez, they all had close links with England, but they were undilutedly Spanish still, as Juanita herself had remained throughout her marriage to Edward Marriott, a Bristol shipper's son. Her children hadn't stayed to follow the family tradition, and the Riberas had never quite forgiven these half-English cousins for the treachery of leaving Spain.

Tired of the noise, Venetia eventually found a quiet corner, hoping to be left in peace there, but she was buttonholed by her hostess, Mercedes Ribera, who looked with faint disapproval at her English cousin's simple funeral clothes – a grey tweed suit and white silk shirt.

'*Querida*, you're supposed to be circulating, not hiding in a corner. If you don't know everyone here it's your own fault for staying away from Jerez for so long.'

'I was getting my second wind,' Venetia explained. 'I'll sally forth again in a moment or two. You've provided a splendid farewell for my grandmother.'

Mercedes accepted the compliment calmly, knowing that her arrangements were always splendid. Like almost all the other women in the room, she was a pleasure to look at: exquisitely dressed and perfectly groomed. Her husband, Juanita's eldest nephew, was now the head of the *bodega*,

23

and she was conscious of having a position to maintain. She was also probably aware that, like the others present, he was a less than faithful spouse, but these affairs were acceptable if conducted with discretion, and rarely thought worth disturbing a successful marriage for.

Venetia found conversation with her so difficult that when Edwina's tall figure came into view it was a relief to be able to talk about her instead. 'I'm glad to have met my aunt and uncle at last.'

Mercedes' pained glance lingered on the muddled layers of Edwina's outfit. '*Not* like your father, I'm afraid – always so elegant, dear Jeffery!'

Her guest dutifully persevered. 'It's a pity Grandmother died so soon after the twins came home – I'm afraid she didn't see much of any of her children. But William and Edwina seem enchanted with Rosario.'

This time Mercedes' horrified reaction was entirely genuine. 'It's almost unbelievable; after all, they're not peasants, to be content with the dilapidated stables that belong to someone else's estate. I believe some basic repair work *has* been done since Vicente and I called there, but really ... such discomfort, such confusion! I can see that I shall have to take them in hand, because poor Edwina has *no* idea how to make the place even habitable; but it's very incon-

24

venient when Rosario isn't exactly on our doorstep.' She frowned at the thought, then waved it away. 'For the moment, though, I must still be busy here. Forgive me if I abandon you, Venetia.'

She went away in a rustle of silk skirts. Her idea of what was comfortable and uncon- fused probably didn't match the Marriotts' at all, but even so Venetia felt obliged to emerge from her corner and go in search of William. He'd escaped from the crowded room to smoke his pipe in the sunlit inner patio, and watch the sparkling cascade of water that fell into an ornamental pool.

'The Moors' best gift to Spain,' he said, smiling at his niece, 'the wonderful, ever-inventive use of water!'

'Not to mention their very unsentimental way of dealing with death! I hope my grandmother would have approved of the party now going on indoors.'

William studied Venetia's pale face. 'You look in need of a holiday, my dear. I'd invite you to come home with us, but the truth is that you wouldn't be very comfortable at the moment. Edwina likes to think she can manage it all on her own, but unless I find her some help I suspect that we may *never* get straightened out!'

He made a joke of it, but she detected anxiety as well, and was glad to be able to offer comfort. 'Don't worry – Mercedes

25

means to take you in hand, and I should think she's very competent.'

Instead of comfort, something close to consternation was now written on William's face. 'It's kind of her, but I'm afraid it wouldn't do at all. Even if Edwina *tried* to be tactful, she couldn't keep it up for long, and I doubt if she and her cousin have a thought in common; oh dear ... now I foresee all kinds of problems.'

Venetia hesitated, surprised by the idea suddenly flowering in her mind. 'I'm between jobs at the moment. I could stay and lend Aunt Edwina a hand. Would she mind that? I'm not an expert in putting houses to rights, but two heads are better than one, and I might be able to be useful.'

William's worried frown cleared at once. 'My dear, she wouldn't mind *you* at all, but I shall be devious. She keeps telling me that you need a holiday, so I shall say that's what you're coming for!'

Edwina accepted the suggestion so readily that Venetia suspected her of being aware of needing rescue. They would leave together the following day, her aunt announced at once; the social life of Jerez had worn her out already, and she craved the peace of their own *pueblo*.

The journey to Rosario was a pleasure in itself. Having won a tussle with her aunt over who should occupy the back seat, Venetia settled herself in it, aware of a new-found lightness of heart that was all the more unexpected for making itself felt in Spain. There was no reason now – perhaps there never had been – not to view with an open mind this country that, she had to acknowledge, at least a quarter of her belonged to. Her conclusion might still be that she and it were never going to get on, but at least this time she would have looked at it unblinkered by childhood's resentment and prejudice.

They skirted the lovely white town of Arcos de la Frontera, and branched off there on to the minor road towards Ubrique. This was their nearest shopping centre, Edwina explained briskly, and, Rosario being ten kilometres away, it was a worthwhile morning walk! Reminded by William that there would be no food in the house, they stopped to shop, and Ubrique revealed itself as another *Pueblo blanco* or white town, tucked under a spur of its looming mountain. It was more prosperous than most, William said, having always been a famous leatherworking centre, and its streets still echoed to the tapping of the *petacabras*, the tool used to beat and soften untreated leather.

Rosario itself was tiny by comparison: merely a tight cluster of whitewashed, brown-roofed buildings clinging to terraced slopes above its parent town. But it faced the other way, southwards to the valley of the little Río Majaceite, and ultimately to the coastal plain and the faintly shadowed outline of Africa itself. Above the *pueblo*, olive and almond trees gave way to a forest of cork and oak; above that, a ruined castle dominated the skyline and the village with a useless but still protective air. Gazing up at it all, Venetia understood now why William and Edwina had chosen this spot in which to realise their dreams – it was the real, timeless Spain, untouched as yet by tourism, and still sure enough of itself to ignore the feverish itch to be made into something new.

Their final destination, Las Cuadras, was simply what the name said – a rectangle of what had been stable buildings enclosing a courtyard now mostly carpeted with weeds. A defunct fountain in the middle merely added to the general air of mournfulness. The outside walls showed signs of having been repaired and repainted – Mercedes had been right about that, but nor had she exaggerated the discomfort indoors. Venetia was led into rooms that had the bleak air of a nomadic encampment in which her aunt and uncle's belongings had accidentally lodged themselves. Edwina did her best, enthusing about the convenient layout of a

28

house whose four sides provided them with separate quarters as well as main rooms to share. But at the end of the tour her expression suddenly became despondent and ashamed.

'When William was a British consul we only lived in official houses, with people to take care of everything,' she said with quiet despair. 'I never discovered that home-making is a talent I don't seem to possess. Will's too kind to complain, but I know he hates living in a muddle, and we shouldn't have let *you* come at all ... I'm sorry, Venetia.'

She was given a little hug that took them both by surprise, aunt and niece being equally unaccustomed to such demonstrations of affection. 'I'm not sure about *my* talent, either,' Venetia admitted, 'but you'll have to let me give it a try. There are lovely things here; they're just in the wrong place, it seems to me, or crowded together higgledy-piggledy. We'll make Uncle William comfortable first, and then tackle the rest.'

Though heartened by this confident approach, Edwina still looked doubtful. 'You're supposed to have come for a holiday, not to labour for a couple of old fools you scarcely know.'

Venetia smiled at her, surprised to know that what she was about to say next was true. 'Even if you were fools, which you aren't, it's high time we *did* know each other. Now let's take the tour again and this time we'll make a list of all the things that need doing.'

Edwina could see no objection to so sensible a programme and they set off happily together, stopping to inform William *en route* that his chaotic sanctum was privileged to be the scene of their first endeavours.

A fortnight later the tide of order had flowed even into the main part of the house. One morning, while Edwina and William shopped in Ronda for items Ubrique couldn't supply, Venetia inspected the transformed drawing-room and felt satisfied. Her aunt might be able to see even Mercedes Ribera arrive now without a twinge of embarrassment.

The day was mild and, tired of working indoors, she seized an excuse to move outside. The bougainvilleas in the neglected courtyard would be beautiful later on, spraying the walls with crimson and purple blossom; but at the moment a tangle of bare stems needed to be pruned and tied to the wires that were meant to support them. She was perched on a ladder that wasn't quite tall enough when Encarnita, her aunt's new maid-of-all-work, ushered a visitor into the courtyard. He came across the gravel and stood looking up at her.

'Good-morning, *señorita*. May I help you down – take your place, perhaps, if the work isn't finished?'

His fluent English and pleasant manner gave her a clue to his identity – William had mentioned that his landlord, Manolo Quinones, had two sons living with him at the main house on the estate, and this was likely to be one of them. With the visitor's assistance she descended the ladder more ceremoniously than she'd climbed it, and then smiled at him.

'I'm Venetia Marriott, staying here for a week or two. Did Encarnita explain that my aunt and uncle are out at the moment?'

He nodded and bowed at the same time. 'Felipe Quinones, *señorita*. I live at La Paloma with my father, but we've been away in Madrid. I came only to make sure that all is well at Las Cuadras.'

For the thirty-something she guessed him to be, he had the serious air of an elderly grandee; nor in other ways was he what she might have expected. His untidy hair was no darker than her own, and a slightly worried expression combined with gold-rimmed spectacles all seemed to suggest a university professor rather than one of Andalucía's dashing sons. She'd met such *hidalgos* at Mercedes' funeral party and not taken to them; she liked the look of this man better.

31

'All is very well here,' she finally confirmed, '...except for one last stem up there that was defeating me!'

Watching him climb the ladder, she regretted giving him the task, because it was clear that Manolo Quinones' son hadn't needed to become an experienced handyman. Still, he captured the branch at last and tied it successfully; he was smiling with shy pleasure, and she with relief, when he was safely on the ground again.

'Encarnita will be bringing coffee in a moment, if you can stay,' she suggested. 'When I'm back in London I shan't believe that I was drinking it out here in late January!'

'Our climate is better,' he agreed. 'I'm not sure what else we have to boast about.'

It seemed a surprisingly pessimistic view, especially for someone whose life could scarcely be underprivileged. 'More stability and more prosperity than Spain has known for centuries,' she pointed out, 'aren't those things to boast about?'

He gave a little shrug. 'Visitors certainly see what seem to be improvements, and my father and brother would agree with them. In fact Fernando's law firm helps to bring the changes about. Property developers on the coast are among his most important clients.'

She waited until Encarnita had come with

the coffee tray and left them alone again. 'You sound as if you disapprove of your brother's coastal clients, so I'd better admit that my architect father designs beautiful houses for rich Arabs there!'

Felipe smiled at her. '*Beautiful* houses we perhaps needn't regret! But I'm glad to stay here, trying to write music ... the sort of music that Albéniz and Granados wrote, true Andalucían music, even though, as it happens, they were both Cataláns! It's considered a strange ambition in my family!'

He sounded wryly amused, and she was left to guess that a Quinones was expected to exert himself in making money instead of music, or at least in wanting to. She could see him as the odd man out in his family, and sensed from his diffident manner that he was accustomed to being ignored.

'I thought my father's English tenants here would be like the people Fernando deals with on the coast,' he went on, 'dependent for happiness on expatriate parties, the arrival of the foreign newspapers and a daily round of golf! But when I met your aunt and uncle before we went away they seemed content to have found Rosario. I thought that very pleasant.'

'Their mother was Spanish,' Venetia pointed out, 'so I suppose they're not typical incomers at all. In fact they tried the coast and hated it, but my uncle is determined to be

33

fair: he'd *prefer* Spain to stay as it was, but not at the cost of the hardship it entailed, especially for the people of this poor province.'

Felipe nodded, happily surprised to have found this gentle-seeming girl among his neighbours. Fernando's women-friends frightened him, being all of the modern variety – liberated into views and habits that a music-loving recluse found shocking. Matters were worse, of course, outside Spain, which at least in theory remained faithful to the teachings of the Church, but even here traditions were weakening. Venetia Marriott looked different from the nearly naked girls who thronged the beaches in summer; there was a reticent, spare grace about her that had nothing to do with the voluptuous Spanish beauty of the women his brother chose.

'You look very at home here,' he said shyly. 'I assume you're accustomed to our country.'

'I came quite often as a child to visit my grandmother but, wanting to see myself in dramatic terms, I always pretended I was being sent into exile! I preferred England's greenness and soft light, not the extremes that Spain insists on. My dead mother had something to do with that, of course; I wanted to be *wholly* English, simply because she had been.'

'With childhood behind you, how does it seem now – still a country you don't belong in?' he enquired with a persistence he found surprising in himself. It wasn't his habit to pry into anybody's feelings, least of all those of a young woman he'd only met five minutes ago.

'I haven't made up my mind yet, but at least I'm enjoying myself while I do, and that's a big improvement on the past!'

His face broke into a whole-hearted smile, slightly rabbit-toothed and charming, and she was suddenly glad that William and Edwina would have him as a neighbour. He would probably be kind if they ever needed help; she'd be able to go back to London without worrying about them.

'I suppose you can't help but play the guitar beautifully,' she said next. 'My mother was a singer, and I can remember her saying that northern voices weren't right for Spanish music.'

'She was right,' Felipe agreed; 'the timbre is different. Come and listen to some songs and I'll show you what I mean. I'd suggest a visit this evening but Fernando is due back from Málaga and we never know exactly when he's going to arrive. My father looks forward to his coming so much that everything is made to wait – even dinner becomes a very movable feast!'

'I'd rather come some time when he isn't

going to be here,' Venetia suggested, imagining the Quinones household revolving round its high-powered elder son.

Felipe shook his head, smiling a little sadly. 'You'll like my brother, nevertheless ... women always do.'

He stood up to offer his little bow again and thanked her for a delightful visit. Then he wandered home, leaving her with the impression of a gentle, charming man. His brother sounded neither, but thankfully there was no reason why she should ever meet him.

When William and Edwina returned from Ronda she asked them again about the family living at La Paloma. They'd found Manolo Quinones a pleasant landlord so far, and Felipe a likeable neighbour. Fernando, only briefly seen, had nevertheless made an impression, Edwina was obliged to admit, even though she disliked the aura of success that hung about him. There was something to be said for a man who *was* a man, and about Felipe she didn't seem to be entirely sure in this respect.

Three

Venetia was gradually becoming acquainted with the neighbourhood. She'd met and liked the *párroco*, Don Alberto Segura, who rode over from Ubrique every Sunday to say Mass in Rosario's small, simple church. The gauntlet of the village wives in Consuela's shop had also been safely run, and she'd even survived the ordeal of being too thoroughly inspected by the Mayor, Don Ramón Perez. He was, of course, Consuela's brother, and between them the Perez finger was kept firmly on the pulse of all the *pueblo*'s affairs.

In conversation with the gentle priest, Venetia discovered more about the place her aunt and uncle had come to. At the time of the Civil War his predecessor had still lived at Rosario, next door to the church. He'd been a good man, Don Alberto said, sufficiently loved by his parishioners for the building to be spared – something that had been rare in anarchist-minded Andalucía, where churches and convents, seen as symbols of past oppression, had been

37

enthusiastically set fire to.

From Luís, who kept Rosario's only bar, she learned that the *pueblo*, and Ubrique itself, had famously resisted the Nationalists on their march up from the coast, before being overwhelmed by Franco's barbaric Moorish army. The memory of those atrocious days were fading now, Luís said, but it still hadn't been forgotten that Manolo Quinones' elder brothers had been on the winning side; the family at La Paloma were distrusted by local people even now. Younger generations might be impatient of such memories, but how could they not be etched on the minds of those who'd fought and suffered?

In light of this, Venetia was relieved that the music recital promised by Felipe Quinones hadn't materialised. She explained this to William one morning, saying that the other inmates of La Paloma didn't sound much to her liking.

'But it seems to me,' said her uncle in his quiet voice, 'that Rosario *is* to your liking. You look much less haunted than when you arrived.'

Venetia smiled at him. 'I've loved being here, being useful to you and Aunt Edwina, and feeling that I belong to the Marriott family. It's something I've missed without realising it. My father and Arlette are always kind, but they have each other and don't really need anyone else.' She was suddenly tempted to tell her uncle about Luc, believing that he would understand the greatness of her loss, but before she could make up her mind William spoke again.

'*We*, on the other hand, need you very much, my dear! The house looks beautiful, thanks to you, but another problem is looming for Edwina. She'll never meet the deadline she's been given unless I find her some help, but the sort of assistance she needs isn't easily discovered in the wilds of Andalucía! I suppose you couldn't stay for a month or two and keep her organised and calm? We should have to insist on a proper business arrangement, of course.'

Taken by surprise, Venetia hesitated. She knew by now the extent of her original misconception about her aunt. Far from being a latter-day Victorian lady turning out pretty watercolour sketches, Edwina's reputation was such that she'd been commissioned to catalogue and illustrate the sierra's springtime flood of wild flowers; she was famous for combining botanical precision with painting of the most delicate beauty. But a methodical, organised compiler of material she was *not*, and William was quite right to believe that help would be needed.

The silence had lasted too long, and William spoke again. 'I shouldn't have asked, Venetia. Of course you must want to get back to your own life again. I'm bound to find *someone* my dear Edwina can work with.'

She caught her uncle's eye, grinned, and shook her head. 'Difficult, Uncle Will! Much better leave her to me, I'd say. I can easily stay for a month or two.'

The relief and pleasure in his face would have been enough to make her content, but the truth was that she wanted to be there on her own account, she realised. She needed this odd, charming aunt and uncle at the moment quite as much as they needed her. When she told him so he shyly kissed her cheek and suggested that they must go at once and give Edwina the news in her studio.

It was in Consuela's shop – nerve-centre of the village – that news of a stranger in the neighbourhood began to circulate. Encarnita brought the gossip back to offer her employers one morning.

'Another *inglés, señor,*' she told William, in the happy belief that if two Englishmen met even on Mars they'd be bound to know each other. 'Imagine it ... he's living all alone, up at the old *huerto*, El Perdido – well named if you ask me; lost it *is*, and nearly forgotten.' Eccentric behaviour was clearly implied, and, although she was careful not to say so, what more likely than that it should involve

40

the English, who were famous for it, after all? 'He didn't talk about himself,' she added as a regretful afterthought. 'Not even Consuela managed to get anything out of him.'

William knew enough about the village by now to understand the extent of this failure; the stranger must have met rudeness with unprecedented rudeness to have put the *señora* off the search for information.

The newcomer sounded unlikely to welcome visitors to El Perdido, but William felt obliged nevertheless to call on his compatriot: the man *might* be in need of someone to talk English to. He set out on the walk up the hillside one afternoon, and returned an hour later to report that his reception had been cool.

'No help wanted,' he admitted with a rueful smile; 'no invitations to drink tea or sherry offered or required; in short, our new neighbour doesn't want to mingle! But he looks perfectly capable of managing by himself, so I don't think we need worry about him.'

'What's he *doing* up there?' Edwina asked. 'According to Encarnita, the smallholding has been going to rack and ruin for years, ever since its owner was forced to emigrate at the end of the war.'

'Mr Gilmour almost seems to be trying to restore it with his own bare hands,' William

41

said. 'He was attacking the ground with a mattock when I arrived.'

Venetia stared at her uncle in astonishment. 'Gilmour, did you say? Did you discover a first name by any chance?'

'Ian Gilmour, I think he said – a Scot, I fancy; there was a faint trace of a rolled R, though it may be some long while since he lived in his native land.' William interrupted his musing to register Venetia's expression. 'Why are you looking so amazed? The Scots have always been great settlers abroad, and it's not *such* an uncommon name, surely.'

'No, but I think I know who he is, and it seems to continue an odd coincidence that began on the flight out to Seville. I met a girl called Fiona Gilmour, who was with me at Oxford. She's in Spain, gathering material about the Franco era. As soon as she mentioned an uncle called Ian Gilmour, I knew of him as a man who wrote very successful, rather unpleasant novels that were turned into still more successful films. But, according to Fiona, he'd thrown up his life in London and gone to live in a remote part of southern Spain. She was hoping to track him down, despite a family feud that seems not to have been forgotten.'

'There's no surprise in one coincidence setting off another,' Edwina pointed out. 'It's a natural law in my experience – cause and effect. Having met your friend again, you could have been sure it would be *her* uncle you'd find living on our doorstep.'

'But not on visiting terms – he made that quite clear,' William reminded her.

His sister nodded and lost interest in their neighbour. She went back to poring over her large-scale map of the district, informing them that there was no time to be lost in getting to know the local terrain. Her daily walks were partly aimed at identifying the areas she must soon be concentrating on.

The next afternoon she set out as usual, promising that because the day had turned damp and unpleasant she wouldn't go far. Venetia, busy making cushions for the dining-room chairs, didn't notice the fading light until William came in to say that his sister wasn't back. They stared at one another, both thinking of a darkening landscape that was huge and empty, with more than enough space and pitfalls for one middle-aged walker to get lost or hurt in. They were still anxiously debating where to begin a search when a shabby Land-Rover pulled up in the drive outside.

'It's Gilmour,' William said, peering out, 'and he's brought Edwina home, thank God.'

She was already hobbling to the door that Venetia ran to open. 'No need to fuss,' she insisted at once: 'sprained ankle, that's all. It serves me right for trespassing. This kind man found me on all fours, trying to crawl home!' With a glint of triumph in her eyes, she indicated her rescuer. 'You've met my brother already, Mr Gilmour,' she said to him, 'and this is our niece, Venetia Marriott.'

His brief nod acknowledged the introduction and William's thanks, but no smile was offered to soften the harsh arrangement of his face. Staring at it despite a feeling that it was unfair to do so, Venetia wondered again what had happened to Ian Gilmour. In profile his face was strong and beautiful, nose and mouth finely carved; but when he turned towards her the scars remaining from some dreadful accident were clearly visible. Pale threadlines on the brown skin ran from temple to cheekbone and from cheek to jaw. His dark hair was thickly powdered with silver, making him look older than the age she reckoned him to be. Altogether, he was an alien, intimidating presence in her aunt's drawing-room, and she was glad to leave him to her uncle while she steered Edwina to her bedroom and bathed her swollen ankle.

'I suppose you're feeling pleased with yourself for having winkled a determined hermit out of his shell?' she asked while this work was in progress. 'But I've never seen a more reluctant knight-errant; he would have been happier to dump you on the doorstep and run.'

'I distrust the eager doers of good,' Edwina said perversely. 'Ian Gilmour isn't a very sociable man, I grant you, but I've never liked people who prattle.'

Venetia smiled at the understatement and then bent down to kiss her aunt's cheek. 'You can stay here, and prattle as little as you please! I'll bring you supper on a tray.'

She went back to the drawing-room expecting to find William alone, but their guest hadn't left after all; he was nursing a glass of whisky and, as if to prove her aunt wrong, talking as well. For him, it seemed, Spain still hadn't changed quite enough.

'The old triumvirate is firmly in place,' he was insisting, as though William had dis-agreed. 'The landowners, the Church and the Army – thinly disguised since Franco's day as the Guardia Civil – retain as much power as they ever had. The Republicans who died here fighting for an equal, just society died in vain. The Andalucians had to leave in their hundreds of thousands to find work and a wage they could live on; not many of them have so far been able to come back.'

Venetia was reminded of her conversation with Felipe Quinones, but whereas he'd settled for melancholy acceptance of a state of things he didn't like, this man met it with the flame of anger. Fiona had said her

45

family were a thrawn lot, and now, looking at Ian Gilmour's unsmiling face, it seemed no exaggeration.

'What you said might have been true during the Fascist regime,' she pointed out quietly. 'Don't you make any concessions for what *has* been achieved since?'

He brushed the question aside. 'Making concessions isn't a habit of mine.' Well, *that* she could believe about him, too.

She changed tack suddenly, hoping that the element of surprise might be disconcerting. 'I travelled out to Spain with a girl I knew in Oxford, who said she had an uncle somewhere here. Her colouring is quite different from yours, but I detect a faint family likeness.'

'Imaginary, I'm afraid,' he said curtly. 'I know little about my niece except that it's her mother she unfortunately resembles.'

Fiona had been right, it seemed; the family falling-out had been monumental enough to still blight all their relationships.

'She had research work to do in Seville,' Venetia nevertheless persevered, 'but was feeling rather lonely; in fact she hoped to be made welcome by her great-uncle.'

It was unexpected, and brief enough to miss altogether, but for a moment she could have sworn she saw a glimmer of amusement touch Ian Gilmour's face. 'Fiona is hoping in vain, I fear. Duncan would as soon think of welcoming *me*, and I can't put her chances lower than that.'

He set down his glass and stood up to leave. 'I like your house,' he said to William. 'Clever of you to have turned old, unwanted buildings to such good use; I hate waste. Miss Marriott's free to invade my land again, by the way, when she recovers; I gather she knows rather a lot about wild flowers.'

Without more ado he walked out of the room, and when they heard the Land-Rover being driven away Venetia took a deep breath of relief. 'It feels as if we ought to open all the windows ... let out some of the animus that seemed to come in with that man.'

William shook his head. 'Yes, but it wasn't against us, I fancy. My impression is that Ian Gilmour hates himself ... it's a strange condition for a man who might reasonably think he'd done rather well.'

She didn't share her uncle's opinion of their visitor, but already William's tolerant kindness came as no surprise. It was difficult to remember that she hadn't even known him and Edwina a month ago. If asked to guess, she'd have assumed him to be a man much like her father; an outward resemblance was even there. But she doubted if the success that Jeffery Marriott took such pride in would have meant much to William.

'*You* feel sorry for Ian Gilmour, and my aunt almost seems to like him, but that will have to do,' she pointed out. 'I'd rather steer clear of him in future. Fiona had some idea of tracking him down, but it would be a waste of time. I expect she's realised that by now.'

But the next morning in Consuela's shop there was none of the usual babel of voices mulling over the day's news. The *pueblo* ladies were there in force as always, but something had hushed them for once into listening mode. A stranger was standing at the counter trying to talk to Consuela, and everyone was determined to hear what was being said. How else could they compare notes afterwards about her accent, her clothes, and the mysterious workings of Fate that had brought a woman so different from themselves to Rosario?

Venetia edged her way through the crowd, heard an un-Spanish voice, and saw almost without surprise Fiona's distinctive red-gold head surfacing above the dark ones around her. As Edwina had said, coincidences always came as battalions, not as single spies.

'*Otra inglesa, señorita,*' Consuela shouted, catching sight of Venetia.

Faithful even now to academic exactitude, Fiona was bound to correct her. '*No* ... say *escocesa, señora!*' Then she turned round with a grin. 'How delighted I am to see *you*, Venetia; this good lady thinks she's giving me directions, but they aren't of the clearest!'

'Well, thank her warmly anyway, and then we'll leave them to discuss you to their hearts' content – it's a treat for them to see a visitor from the outside world.'

Venetia led her outside, and crossed the little square to perch on the low wall in front of Don Alberto's church. 'I was thinking you might have gone to Madrid by now – or did Great-Uncle Duncan come up trumps after all?'

'No such thing, although I did my damnedest to look forlorn and greatly in need of nurturing! He gave me a glass of sherry and showed me the door.' Then she stared more closely at Venetia. 'I have to say *you're* looking much better than on the journey out. For a girl who doesn't like Spain, you're positively blooming, and how do you come to be here? I thought the funeral was in Jerez.'

'It was,' Venetia confirmed, 'but there I met my father's brother and sister, recently retired to Spain, who now live near by. Just for a while I'm making myself useful, and enjoying being with them very much.' She hesitated for a moment before going on. 'You obviously know that Ian Gilmour is in the neighbourhood ... I suppose that's why you're here.'

Fiona nodded her bright head. 'I remembered that he did a lot of travelling around Spain during the Franco years; it seemed wasteful *not* to try and talk to him, as well as silly when we're both Gilmours.'

Venetia considered what could safely be said about the elusive relative. 'We can just about claim to have made the acquaintance of your uncle,' she admitted finally, 'but only because Aunt Edwina was caught with a sprained ankle trespassing on his land. I can point you in the direction of his house, but don't expect a warm reception: he seems remarkably determined to dree his own weird, as I believe they say in Scotland!'

Fiona's entrancing smile reappeared. 'Duncan's shaken my usual sunny confidence in my ability to charm, but I comfort myself with the thought that *he*'s too old to be bowled over! That's my hired car parked over there. Why don't I drive you home before I go visiting?'

Now it was Venetia's turn to smile. 'Spare me a short walk by all means, but you'd do better to leave the car with us and avoid a long detour round the mountain. You're in rural Spain now, my dear, where visiting is best done by horse, mule or Shanks's pony!'

'Oh God ... I should have realised it was too much to hope for a road. Well, even the most bloody-minded relation will have to take pity on me when I stumble in footsore and weary.'

Venetia offered no comment about this and a few minutes later simply pointed out the track that led up the hillside. 'Stick to the path and you can't get lost – it leads you almost to your uncle's front door. If he's too mean to offer you lunch, we'll feed you here when you get back. *Adiós, amiga!*'

She waved Fiona on her way, and then went indoors to explain to Edwina the strong possibility that her former fellow-student would be joining them for their midday meal.

Four

The afternoon was half over when Fiona reappeared but, inspecting her face, Venetia decided that nothing more had been forthcoming from Ian Gilmour than a share of whatever he ate in the middle of the day. His niece looked even less her confident self than when she'd set out for El Perdido.

Introductions made, William's apprecia-tive smile cheered her up, male pleasure in her beauty being her chief reassurance that

51

the world wasn't tottering towards its end. Even so, she spoke almost distressfully of the visit she'd just made.

'I thought I knew what to expect but it was much worse ... a desolate place ... horribly lonely and primitive. How *can* a man live there when he was used to being a celebrity in London? In the middle of a huge, empty landscape he's got a house with four poky rooms, and an evil-looking mule outside for company.'

Edwina, who could think of nothing worse than the lifestyle of a celebrity, managed not to say that Ian Gilmour might have made a sensible choice. Instead, she smiled genially at their visitor.

'He can come and see us when he gets bored with the mule, although I believe they're very sagacious animals. In any case I don't think you need fret about him. Even in this effete age there are still men who want to test themselves against deserts or mountains. In deciding to make a small, neglected corner of Spain bloom again your uncle has chosen a more useful challenge, that's all.'

Fiona's expression said so clearly what she thought of this quaintly Kiplingesque view that Venetia hurried into the conversation.

'What will *you* do now ... go back to Edinburgh when you've finished your research?'

Fiona nodded without enthusiasm. 'I shall

have to, more's the pity. My mother and I will fall out in no time at all, but apart from that I'd have liked to work on my Spanish material *in situ*.'

She smiled bravely for William, but he could see that there was puzzlement as well as disappointment to bear – life didn't usually refuse to provide what she so reasonably required. Venetia couldn't help thinking that life had got it right for once, but there was no mistaking her kind uncle's concern. Then, as his expression brightened, she feared she knew what was coming next.

'My dear, are you sure you need go home? We've got space to spare here.' Enchanted with this sudden inspiration, he smiled at his niece. 'It was Venetia's brilliant idea to turn our extra rooms into a separate apartment for summer visitors. You could be our first guest!'

Edwina was also nodding, even though she didn't share her brother's enthusiasm. He was unable to help it, of course; even the most confirmed bachelor couldn't have missed an arrangement of features conferred on Fiona Gilmour that was entirely accidental but entirely flawless. For herself, she could have done without a visitor, but there was Venetia to think of; they must welcome company for her sake.

Not aware of needing company, Venetia struggled instead with something that felt sharply like dismay. The past was over and done with and it was probably ungenerous to wish that Fiona would go away, but instinct – usually reliable – seemed to be warning her that this visit was something she would regret. The trouble was that she could see no way of saying so ... William, looking very pleased with himself, was already being thanked with Fiona's most radiant smile.

'Could I really stay? I'd just *love* it. I'd *promise* not to be a nuisance; in fact I hope you wouldn't even notice me here at all!'

Her disbelief in this statement was clear, but her gratitude and pleasure were charmingly expressed; Venetia reflected that only other Gilmours seemed immune to Fiona's appeal.

'I'd better show you the rooms before you make up your mind,' she pointed out rather brusquely. But her own resemblance to a disgruntled landlady was so strong that she had to smile and, watching her, Edwina felt reassured; she'd been wrong to think their niece hadn't liked William's brilliant idea.

In the unoccupied wing of the house Fiona enthused over the pleasantly furnished rooms, and insisted that she must be allowed to pay some proper rental for them.

'You'll have to argue about that with my uncle,' Venetia suggested, 'but I expect he'll refuse.'

'He's the sweetest thing – well, I mean, they *both* are,' Fiona murmured, happy to stretch the truth a little to include Edwina. 'I can see why you love being here, but I suppose it won't be for much longer. You'll be wanting something else to do.'

Venetia smiled faintly. 'I have a temporary job already – getting Aunt Edwina's wild flower book to the publisher on time! Apart from that, I've a commission of my own to work on: a volume of short stories to be translated into English. They were Luc's, so it's what you could call a labour of love.'

She spoke without emphasis but her face was more revealing. The young Frenchman *hadn't* died for her, Fiona realised; he was still the companion of her mind and heart. Venetia had clearly known pain, but much happiness as well; on the whole, perhaps, she was to be envied for that. Instead of saying so, tactful for once, Fiona changed the conversation.

'You hated Spain, you said. Have you come to terms with it now?'

'Coming to terms with it is part of my object in staying,' Venetia answered thoughtfully. 'I can help Edwina and face my own moment of truth at the same time – it's been waiting for me ever since I was first brought here.' She put the subject aside and glanced at her watch. 'If you're going to drive to Seville you ought to be on your way. When shall we expect you back with your belongings?'

'Would a week's time be all right? I want to dash to Madrid and Burgos first.' Fiona hesitated for a moment. 'What I said to your uncle was true – I'd love to stay and work here. But you don't *have* to be saddled with me, Venetia. I couldn't blame you if that Oxford episode still rankled or hurt. I expect I behaved badly ... I think I sometimes still do even now, although I don't usually mean to.'

She sounded sincere, direct as a child confessing to some impromptu sin. It suddenly seemed possible to like her – and downright unkind not to make her welcome.

'Stay if you want to,' Venetia said cheerfully. 'Hand on heart, I can insist that I soon gave up wearing the willow for James O'Halloran, whose smiling face I can't even recall. I doubt if we shall find anyone here to fight over, and in any case I seem to remember that you've eschewed the opposite sex for the time being! No Don Juans, no seductions, you said.'

Fiona's enchanting smile reappeared. 'Quite right, *amiga*. My book is going to earn me a D.Phil., I hope, but to get it done I must keep my nose to the grindstone.'

She gave her new landlady an affectionate hug and finally drove away, leaving Venetia to realise that in the euphoria of the moment she'd forgotten to enquire whether or not Ian Gilmour was to be informed of his niece's arrival in Rosario.

The man himself, unsettled by a visit that had taken him by surprise, abandoned work for the afternoon and made the stiff climb up to the castle that sprawled across the hilltop. Even in its ruinous state it still provided shelter from the rain and normally a spectacular vantage-point as well. Today visibility was poor, no shadowy African coastline to be seen; but his mind clung to the rim of that huge and different continent hidden by the mist. From there had come the successive waves of warriors, scholars and brilliantly inventive craftsmen who'd transformed Spain for seven hundred years. He would think about *them*, not about the memories stirred up by Fiona's talk of a family he'd left behind.

'*Buenas tardes, señor.*' A man's soft greeting made him spin round. 'Perhaps I should have said "good-afternoon" – I think you must be the Englishman the neighbourhood is talking about, from El Perdido.'

'To be precise about it, I hail from Scotland,' the answer came stiffly. 'My name is Gilmour.'

'And I am Felipe Quinones, from La Paloma. Welcome to Rosario.' Felipe's courtly bow demanded some sort of gesture

57

in return, and this small formality on the top of a deserted mountain seemed absurd enough to both of them to suddenly make them smile.

'Your compatriots are here in force,' Felipe said pleasantly. 'When I called on the Marriotts at Las Cuadras I was told that they have another English guest soon returning to stay with them.'

'I suspect you mean another Scot in that case.' But the smile that had briefly transformed the man's harsh face had faded, leaving Felipe with the certainty that what he had just said was unwelcome. It seemed a strange reaction, but he persevered.

'You have a hard task in front of you, *señor*. El Perdido has been abandoned for so long that we'd given up hope of a new owner.'

'It hasn't got one now – I'm a temporary tenant. Pablo Sánchez intends to come back himself quite soon.'

Felipe considered pointing out that tenants didn't normally labour for their landlords as he was doing, but that also would be resented, he felt sure. A man who invited no conversation at all would certainly object to a comment that seemed to ask for information. It made him an unfriendly neighbour, but Felipe thought he recognised in so uncommunicative a man an inclination that was often in himself; not fitting in with other people, it was easier to reject than wait to be rejected.

'I like to come up here,' he said impulsively. 'My father thinks it a strange pleasure, haunting a ruin that he'd rather see patched up or pulled down. I can't make him understand that it's full of the ghosts of Spain's history.'

'Your father has been a businessman, I believe,' Ian Gilmour answered; 'expect no truck with ghosts from him.'

The unfamiliar English phrase made Felipe smile; he thought he could guess its meaning easily enough. 'You might enjoy meeting him all the same, and he you. Perhaps you'll come to lunch with us one day? There are also the Marriotts nearby for you to get to know – they are very charming people.'

'I've met them already. Thanks for the suggestion, but my days are rather busy. *Adiós, señor.*'

Without waiting for a reply, he plunged off down the hill, aware of having behaved uncouthly to the courteous Spaniard. In different circumstances he might have regretted it, but he doubted if he was mistaken in guessing that it was Fiona who was to be the Marriotts' guest. The ironic gods must be falling about with laughter up above. He'd dropped out of the world for nothing if his own niece was going to be on his very doorstep.

The following morning, sipping coffee in Luís's bar and skimming through the headlines of *El País*, he saw a slender, brown-haired girl walk in. She offered him a brief 'good-morning', and he remembered her as the Marriotts' niece. She'd spoken of knowing Fiona in Oxford, and it was another unlooked-for connection between his past and present life that only a malicious Fate could have devised. If his own niece had already told the Marriotts why he'd gone to ground in Rosario it would explain this girl's cool greeting. He half rose in his seat merely to nod at her in return, then resumed his reading of the newspaper. Uncouthness again, but it was becoming a habit with him.

It seemed that she was there to conduct the purchase of some wine for her uncle; he could hear the conversation, in the sort of Spanish that few English visitors could command. The transaction concluded, her footsteps sounded on the stone floor, but they halted at his table and he was obliged to look up at her.

He found himself confronting a pair of expressive hazel eyes with an unexpected gleam of humour in them, reminding him of Edwina Marriott. She wasn't by any means a beauty but he saw character and intelligence in her face instead. Such women were liable to reckon themselves a match for any man; he would have enjoyed the challenge once upon a time, but not now.

'Two Spaniards meeting by chance in a remote English village would fall on each other's necks with loud protestations of excitement and joy,' she explained solemnly. 'We don't have to go as far as that, but Luís will think it *very* strange if you don't at least invite me to have coffee with you.'

'You're in merry pin this morning.' His hard, unfriendly stare seemed to suggest no pleasure in the fact, but he got up and went to order more coffee – in Spanish as fluent as her own, she realised.

'You aren't a stranger to this country,' she said when he returned and pulled out a chair for her to sit down.

'No more than you are, but *my* antecedents are probably rather less respectable. My grandfather, Andrew Gilmour, helped to run the Río Tinto copper mines of infamous memory. So did his elder son, Duncan, now retired to Seville. But Duncan's brother, Hamish – *my* father, that's to say – hated what the mines stood for, hated his childhood there. He was a half-trained student doctor when he outraged Andrew and Duncan by enrolling in the International Brigade on the side of the republicans at the beginning of the Civil War.' Ian Gilmour stared at her over the rim of his coffee cup. 'Old history, I'm afraid – I don't know why

I bored you with it.'

'I wasn't bored,' Venetia said truthfully. 'Fiona spoke of the feud that her grandfather and great-uncle never recovered from. How very sad ... but then it *was* a sad and bitter war.'

'Wars usually are, but especially civil wars,' Ian Gilmour pointed out. 'My niece should have known better than to think Duncan would make her welcome. I'm not even sure why the old man stays here – he must disapprove of everything about present-day, democratic Spain.'

'You seemed to be telling my uncle the other day that it wasn't yet democratic enough,' she commented; 'in which case the feud between you presumably still goes on.'

The man sitting opposite her seemed so absorbed for the moment in some train of thought of his own that, waiting for a reply, she could safely stare at him. He'd denied any likeness to Fiona, and the darkness of his colouring had presumably been inherited from his mother's family. Venetia was even prepared to credit him with some long-dead Spanish ancestor who'd survived the Armada and been washed up on a Scottish shore! In the bright morning light she could see the fading scars more clearly than before, but other things as well. Deepset eyes and not enough flesh to soften the too-prominent bones beneath gave an impression of hardship endured. It seemed altogether unlikely – the hugely successful Ian Gilmour was scarcely a candidate for any deprivation that she could think of – but the certainty was in her mind that it was still tragedy he was coming to terms with, not success.

He looked up suddenly enough to catch her out while she was still staring at him, and she was flustered into bluntness.

'Fiona hoped there might be a welcome from you, if not from Duncan Gilmour; you *are* her father's brother.'

'And when my welcome wasn't forthcoming she talked the Marriotts into taking pity on her instead, I suppose. They should not have allowed their withers to be wrung,' he said coolly. 'My niece is the very image of her mother, beauty therefore concealing a will of iron that I'd back against any odds. She'll be the cuckoo in your nest, I'm afraid. Now, if you think we've communed long enough to make Luís happy, I'll be on my way. It's quite a climb up to my refuge.'

He spilled coins on the table, then stood up to offer her a small, ironic salute before he walked out of the bar. Venetia felt relieved but also oddly bereft to see him go. Even in his present hostile state he made an impression that wasn't easily forgotten. What had he been like in his London days – arrogant, ruthless perhaps? Some women were attracted to such men, imagining – poor things – that tigers could be tamed.

She said goodbye to Luís and went out into the little square; but, feeling depressed by the encounter, she changed her mind about walking home and went into the church instead. It wasn't often entirely empty – like herself, the women of the village were in the habit of calling in whenever they passed by. There was usually some small prayer or anxiety to be shared with the Blessed Señora whose carved and painted likeness smiled down at them from above the altar.

This morning she was surprised to find the *párroco* himself getting up from his knees at the altar rail.

'Good-morning, Don Alberto ... Have I overlooked a saint's day that brings you out from Ubrique?'

The priest smiled at her, shaking his head. 'Not a holy day, my child, only a change in my duties. Because of age and a slight infirmity I'm being given less work to do. Whether it likes it or not, Rosario will see more of me in future! I'm going to live in the little house next door to the church and confine myself to the *pueblo* in future.'

Had he been giving thanks for that change a moment ago, she wondered, or asking God's help in finding grace to accept it? He was a cultured, scholarly man who might not have expected to end his ministry among the people of a mountain village.

'Shall you mind ... miss Ubrique?' she asked tentatively. 'Much as I love Rosario, I have to admit that the town is livelier!'

His serene smile said that she needn't have bothered to ask. 'I shall have my flock here to care for, and all the beauty of Andalucía on my doorstep. What is there to miss? It's much easier to give up the big, important world than the world likes to think!' He chuckled at the idea, then grew serious again. 'I think your uncle knows the truth of that, and so does another compatriot of yours, who seems content with the isolation of his remote *cortijo* even after what I gather was a busy life in London.'

She could have disagreed with the word Don Alberto had used – surely, whatever he was, Ian Gilmour was *not* content – but she was surprised instead into saying something else. 'I'm astonished that you've met Ian Gilmour, *padre*; he rather shuns the rest of us.'

'It's true that he doesn't attend Mass,' Don Alberto answered calmly. 'But nevertheless he came to see me one day.'

Venetia digested this unexpected piece of information in silence for a moment, then she smiled at the gentle priest. 'Do I need to apologise for a compatriot's lack of old-world charm and grace, Don Alberto, or was Mr Gilmour on his best behaviour the day he called on you?'

'No apology is needed, my dear – I found him very pleasant, an interesting and intelligent man.'

She accepted the statement quietly, supposing that this priest could, if he set his mind to it, shame even the devil into behaving pleasantly.

'May I tell my uncle and aunt that you're coming to live here?' she asked as they reached the church door. 'They'll want to know if they can do anything to help.'

'Tell them by all means, and thank you but no help is needed; I'm told that Señora Perez is taking my domestic arrangements in hand!'

A small twinkle in the priest's eye drew an answering grin from Venetia; then they parted company and she was free to walk home, thinking about the morning's conversations. She found that what stayed with her most insistently was Ian Gilmour's comment on her own frame of mind. His phrase sounded ridiculous when she repeated it but he'd rightly identified a change that she'd scarcely noticed in herself. Grief for Luc still kept her company, but she found herself content to have come back to Spain; with so little softness and compromise about it, at this moment in her life perhaps it was the best place she could have chosen to come to. The discovery led her to another surprising thought – perhaps that was what had brought Ian Gilmour here as well?

Five

She got back to Las Cuadras to find Felipe Quinones there, explaining to her aunt and uncle that a touch of fever – something he was prone to – had kept him indoors for several days. He smiled shyly at Venetia and reminded her of her promise to listen to some music with him; would she, please, come to La Paloma that evening? Assuming it to mean that his brother was no longer there, she gladly agreed. In their walks together, she and Edwina had been careful not to stray near the main house, but she was curious to see whether her imagined picture of it was correct.

It turned out to be more attractive than she expected: white walls and old, pantiled roof fitted happily into the landscape, even if the garden surrounding the house was too formal and fussy for her English taste. But inside luxury reigned; by fair means or foul Manolo Quinones had made himself a rich man, and saw no reason not to advertise the fact. He was tall for an Andalucían and, though running to fat, still handsome. His eyes hadn't lost the habit of thoroughly examining women, and it was a relief to Venetia when he left her alone with Felipe in his music room. There, a grand piano and several guitars strewn about indicated a serious musician, not the enthusiastic amateur she'd suspected him of being.

'This room is for pleasure,' he explained with a smile; '*work* is done in my sound-proofed studio next door.'

She was given a glimpse there of another grand piano, many more instruments, microphones, a battery of computers and a sophisticated recording console – all the present-day necessities of a working composer. A row of tapes and CDs labelled 'Felipe Nuñez' finally made matters clear.

'Now I know who you are,' she said, almost apologetically. 'I have some of your recordings, and most beautiful they are.'

His shy bow acknowledged the compliment. 'I used my mother's name – it's part of my own anyway. She died ten years ago and after that I decided that I wanted to write music, not just perform other people's. It's taken me a long time to discover my own "voice", but I'm getting there now. I'll risk playing you some when we get to know each other a little better!'

He played for her instead de Falla's *Piezas*

Españoles until, reluctantly, she said it was time she went home. He escorted her back along the drive and held her hand for a moment when he said good-night. She didn't misunderstand the gesture – he was a shy and lonely man expressing gratitude for having unexpectedly found a friend.

By the time Fiona arrived, Felipe had become a regular visitor to his father's tenants, and Venetia found that she increasingly enjoyed her friendship with him; the companionship of someone much the same age was the only pleasure life at Las Cuadras had lacked until now.

She waited curiously for a shy, diffident man's reaction to their new house guest, and was surprised to discover that they seemed not to take to each other. Felipe was courteous, of course, but obviously not bowled over; Fiona was openly critical of him after a day or two, and refused to go with Venetia on her next evening visit to La Paloma.

'I'm not being tactful,' she said candidly. 'Flamenco heart-searchings poured out in Arabic semi-quavers and quarter-tones may speak volumes to you, but they do nothing at all for me!'

'A wonderful synthesis of Moorish, Indian and gypsy influences – *that*'s what you're missing,' Venetia explained with a smile, but she went on more seriously: 'I think it's Felipe himself you don't appreciate. I can't see why. He's charming, gentle and intelligent – a rare sort of man altogether, it seems to me.'

'Very true. But no adult male, however rare, should allow himself to be despised while being kept by his father. Manolo Quinones *does* despise him.'

'Only because they don't value the same things. Felipe must be very comfortably able to keep himself, but he needs the technical set-up that he has at La Paloma. It's worth putting up with his family for that, and I value him all the more for not caring what an overweight, over-loud and disreputably roving-eyed old adventurer thinks of him! Manolo may be respectable enough now, but he hasn't always been; his fortune began with black-market dealings after the war, and his elder son keeps up the good work by conniving with the people who despoil what remains of a beautiful coast!'

'Go and enjoy your Moorish music,' Fiona recommended, blinking under this onslaught, 'and the company of your gentle friend, who – I prophesy – wouldn't mind becoming your lover as well, given a little encouragement! My own evening's entertainment will be to beg another backgammon lesson from William instead. I'm determined to beat him before I go home.'

70

Venetia smiled and went away, dismissing from her mind the suggestion that Felipe was falling in love with her. When it came to a man and a woman, Fiona thought only in those terms, but the truth was that Felipe needed affection and friendship, not the more unsettling risks involved in a passionate affair.

With this quite clear to her, she smiled sweetly as usual when he met her at La Paloma's door. But then the comfortable pattern changed. Without warning she was suddenly pulled into his arms and kissed, and it was no friendly peck – his kiss was warm and lingering. Even more disconcerting from Venetia's point of view was the discovery that this unexpected development had been observed by someone else. She didn't need to be told who the man was who stood watching them; he was a younger version of Manolo Quinones – leaner, fitter, smoother, still more arrogantly self-assured ... the man she had hoped not to have to meet.

Felipe, now smiling but a little flushed and flustered as well, made the introductions. Venetia held out her hand, Fernando bowed over it, and she could swear from the amusement twitching his mouth that he perfectly understood the reason for the scene his brother had just enacted.

'The charming neighbour I've heard so

much about from my father?' he suggested, raking her with bright, dark eyes. 'But I must have been mistaken ... I thought he mentioned richly coloured hair!'

'Then he spoke of my friend, Fiona Gilmour,' Venetia said, trying not to sound ruffled. 'She's staying with us at the moment and her hair *is* very beautiful.' With that established, she could turn away from him and smile at Felipe. 'Music was promised – I rate it higher even than the pleasures of Don Manolo's table!'

He shook his head, looking regretful. 'A different programme this evening, Venetia. Fernando has brought us visitors from Madrid – my sister Blanca and her son. Juan has been ill and the doctors insisted that he should escape the rest of the capital's harsh winter.'

'Then you should have put me off,' she said quickly. 'Your sister won't want to be troubled with a guest when she has a sick child to look after.'

It was Fernando who answered first. 'Juan has already been put to bed, and Blanca is waiting with my father ... eager to meet you, *señorita*.'

'But not, I hope, also confused as to the colour of my hair.'

For a moment she thought she might be wrong about Fernando Quinones ... a gleam of pure amusement seemed to be greatly

72

improving his face. But before she could be sure, Felipe stepped between them.

'Dear Venetia, don't talk of leaving ... of course you must stay and meet Blanca.'

He took her hand – again, it seemed, to underline an intimacy they hadn't enjoyed before – and led her into the over-furnished salon next door. Manolo looked briefly disappointed, not to find the luscious Fiona with her, Venetia suspected; but he put down the sherry decanter he was holding and surged towards her, always ready to be an exuberant host.

'*Señorita*, meet my precious daughter, Blanca Esteban y Quinones. We are allowed to keep her here for a while instead of having to go all the way to Madrid to see her.'

'Because your son is unwell, I understand. I'm sorry, *señora*.'

Venetia held out her hand, thinking that had she been warned about this meeting she would have made more of an effort with her own appearance. No one looking at Blanca – a younger, more beautiful version of Mercedes Ribera – could have guessed that she'd just arrived after a long journey, or that she had a maternal care in the world. She had the lustrous black hair that seemed to be every Spanish woman's birthright, and the same olive complexion and dark eyes as her elder brother. Felipe's softer, northern colouring had come, along with his gentle ways, from the Asturian mother who'd died.

Aware of being inspected, Venetia supposed that an elegant *madrileña* wished to gauge her brother's degree of interest in his neighbours' niece; it seemed that neither of his siblings expected him to have any at all.

'Juan will run wild here and get very spoiled,' Blanca said with a rueful smile. 'Pity me instead – I must miss my husband, who is in New York, and the dear friends I've had to leave behind! I'm delighted to find you and your friend here, *señorita* – one doesn't want always to be talking to men, don't you agree?'

'My aunt is here as well,' Venetia pointed out, wondering in what terms Edwina had been described to her. 'She and my uncle have settled at Rosario; Fiona and I are simply visiting.' Then she spoke to Felipe. 'There's another incoming male that your sister *will* enjoy talking to. I expect you've heard that Don Alberto is moving into the little house next to the church.'

'And there's also the Englishman up at the old *huerto*,' he reminded them. 'No, a Scot, he insisted when I bumped into him, and of the same name, strangely, as your guest, Venetia.'

'Not strangely at all,' she admitted; 'they happen to be uncle and niece!' She smiled at Blanca Esteban. 'Not really another

74

neighbour to avoid, however – Mr Gilmour isn't socially minded!'

'Then perhaps we shall make him so,' Blanca suggested. 'It will be something to do, and Rosario doesn't offer many social challenges!'

She was like Fernando – a chip off her father's block, Venetia reflected: competitive and used to success. With nothing to say about Ian Gilmour, it seemed safer to ask what took Blanca's husband to New York. Again Fernando answered the question before his sister could.

'American investment in this country is Rodrigo's speciality. He's a corporate lawyer, required to watch over Spanish interests when high-level horse-trading is going on among multinational companies.'

'More foreign infiltration?' Venetia suggested lightly. 'Even if it's unavoidable, it seems a pity.'

Manolo smiled at her, managing to wipe most of the impatience out of his voice. '*Not* a pity, my dear ... highly desirable in fact! You've been listening to your aunt and uncle. Señorita Marriott, especially, disapproves of progress – the old, isolated, primitive Spain is what her romantic heart craves!'

Venetia thought he made Edwina sound not only a dreamy-eyed romantic but a fool as well. About to take up the cudgels on her

75

aunt's behalf, she was forestalled by the bright-eyed man who watched her as a cat watches a mouse.

'*Padre*, here is a different sort of romantic, I think. Señorita Venetia is seduced by the travel posters' views of Andalucía – handsome men lean as whippets, gorgeous women in polka dots and flounces, and glossy horses more beautiful than both! She can't help it, of course; I'm told her antecedents are in aristocratic Jerez. The Quinones origins are much more humble!'

A small silence followed this speech which, though delivered with Fernando's flashing smile, seemed to have amused no one. It was a relief to have Manolo's man-servant come to the door to announce the serving of dinner.

It was still more of a relief to Venetia when the meal came to an end and she could exchange the luxury of the overheated house for the cool darkness of the night. She would have preferred to walk home alone, but Felipe insisted on going with her, holding her hand – in case she stumbled, he said. The evening had been a strain, parrying Fernando's deliberate provocations and Blanca's small, sharp challenges, but she cared very little what either of them thought of her; her relationship with Felipe was of much more concern. Had there really been the change in it that he seemed intent on insisting upon? If so, was it important enough not to be ignored?

She was silent as they walked along the drive, and Felipe also found nothing to say until her door was reached. Then he turned her round to look at him, and the light of a nearly full moon beautifully illuminated her face.

'Did I make you angry this evening, Venetia? I think I did. I should have liked to kiss you before, but never did because I always felt you weren't *wanting* to be kissed. Tonight, because my brother was watching, I forgot about that, but it was unkind as well as foolish. He likes challenges and always wants to win; I haven't cared in the past, this time I do!'

Venetia reached up to touch his cheek in a fleeting, reassuring gesture. 'Fernando can see it in any way he likes; it makes no difference to me.' She smiled at her friend, inviting him to look less anxious. 'There won't be any challenge. Your brother only has to catch sight of Fiona to forget about me – I suspect she's much more to his taste!'

Even Felipe, she could see, thought this might be true, but he returned unexpectedly to what he'd just touched on. 'Was I right, Venetia ... something happened in the past that you haven't forgotten yet?'

She nodded, trying to decide what to say. Their friendship was warm, and growing warmer, and she liked him enough to trust him with the truth. 'I've had my precious adventure,' she admitted finally, 'but the Frenchman I loved so dearly fell sick and died much too young. I decided then that I'd had enough of Brussels and went back to London. It's how I come to be here ... footloose and free, but still just a little sore at the moment!'

'I thought so,' Felipe said gently. 'Thank you for telling me ... I shall take care of you, Venetia, and *not* be a nuisance. *Buenas noches*, dear friend.' He smiled at her with great sweetness and walked away, looking pleased with the knowledge that the evening had unexpectedly deepened their relationship.

At breakfast the following morning she had scarcely mentioned the new arrivals at La Paloma when Felipe walked into the courtyard with a small, thin boy at his heels.

'Forgive me, Venetia ... I was foolish enough to talk about your uncle's photographs. Juan has been waiting for me to bring him ever since.'

Introduced first to Edwina, Juan Esteban, all of ten going on eleven, bowed as he'd been taught with all the punctilio of an old Spanish hand. With eyes too large for his face, and the shadows of ill-health still under them, he wasn't for the moment a handsome child, but he had a shy, engaging smile.

'My uncle said the *señor* has many bird pictures ... Could I see, please? There are few birds to watch in Madrid.'

Venetia led him away to William's study and returned smiling five minutes later. 'The talk is of eagles, kestrels, peregrines and all the rest. It will be some time before we see Juan again, and I predict that he'll be calling quite often in future!'

'He lives in a large and beautiful apartment in Madrid,' Felipe explained. 'The apartment has a large and beautiful balcony with a great many flowers growing in pots. Juan, I'm sorry to say, despises them – things should grow in the earth, he thinks.'

'The child is right, of course,' Edwina said firmly. 'No wonder he looks peaky, brought up on a balcony.'

'Rheumatic fever is responsible for the peakiness,' Venetia felt obliged to point out. 'He's better now, he tells me, but let off school until after Easter, so he's feeling rather pleased with himself.'

'He's happy at Rosario,' Felipe agreed. 'Blanca refuses to admit it but he's a throwback to our mother's ancestors in the north; they farmed land there for generations.'

Now ready to smile favourably on a small boy who had the sense to look at birds instead of blinding himself with computer games, Edwina sailed away to join the conversation in the study. Felipe smiled at

Venetia. 'We all seem to like coming here, but Juan mustn't become a nuisance.'

'Don't worry – Edwina will be quite capable of shooing him away, even if William isn't.' She thought again of the previous evening, and decided to ask the question in her mind. 'I take it that your brother won't be staying? I don't quite see *him* feeling at home in rural Spain.'

Felipe gave a little shrug. 'No, but with modems and faxes, his office is as much at La Paloma as on the coast. He'll want to keep Blanca company while she's here – they've always been close – but I think he's got business to discuss with my father as well.'

'Do you feel outnumbered?' Venetia asked gently. 'They make a formidable trio, the rest of the Quinones!'

His charming smile shone for a moment. 'I know, but at least I have a reinforcement – Juan is on my side.'

'We'll send him home in time for lunch,' she promised, 'but now I must go back to work.'

Felipe accepted the dismissal, but as he turned to leave remembered his other reason for coming. 'I was supposed to deliver an invitation from Blanca. She would like you *all* to dine with us tomorrow evening, Fiona as well of course.'

Having no excuse to offer – the social life

80

of Rosario scarcely made hectic claims upon them – Venetia agreed that the Marriotts and Fiona would look forward to an evening out.

There was some discussion the following day about what they should wear, but having proposed to unearth a much-worn velvet smoking-jacket, William thereafter lost interest in the subject. Edwina dithered between beige and black lace, and was finally persuaded by her niece to set off in what became her best – a severely cut shirt and long skirt. Venetia herself settled for silk jersey in a subtle celadon green and, looking at the simple perfection of her dress, Fiona had a moment's fear that her own black velvet outfit was overdone. But, arrived at La Paloma, she was reassured: sophistication was what a man like Fernando Quinones demanded to see in a woman. They were still waiting to go in to dinner when two more guests arrived – Don Alberto, whom Venetia was happy to see walk into the room, and, quite unexpectedly, their neighbour from El Perdido.

Fiona gave a small, astonished exclamation, and Edwina, having already had enough of Manolo, looked pleased to see him. Blanca greeted the *párroco*, and then offered the other newcomer a smile that suggested she'd done her best to rescue the evening from tedium.

'I needn't introduce you to your own niece, of course, *señor*, and everyone else is known to you, I think, except my father, Don Manolo Quinones, and my brother, Fernando.' Turning to the rest of them, she then explained, 'Señor Gilmour found Juan wandering up the hillside this morning and was kind enough to bring him home.'

'He was looking for eagles – he called them *your* eagles,' Ian Gilmour said, turning to William.

'Oh dear ... I'm so sorry,' William began to apologise, but Blanca shook her head.

'Nothing will keep my son within doors here, Señor Marriott ... your eagles, someone else's mules or donkeys ... Juan will be out looking for them. But it's what he's here for – to get fresh air and exercise.'

Venetia watched with interest as Fiona greeted her uncle; like all her performances, it was nicely judged: amused surprise combined with the right amount of pleasure at finding him there. The sincerity of his response was even harder to judge, but, having decided to endure an evening among his fellow human beings, he had at least resurrected from his former life some neatly conventional clothes and an adequate ease of manner. He might even, Venetia thought, be aware of the speculative glance that Blanca occasionally sent in his direction.

Manolo Quinones was a generous host –

he offered his guests excellent food and wines fine enough to lull them into harmony. No disagreement occurred at all until they were back in the salon after dinner, drinking coffee and French brandy. Then Blanca made some casual reference to the Spanish royal family and mentioned, for the benefit of her guests, that her husband had often been a sailing companion of Juan Carlos and his son. Manolo seemed eager to explain the connection.

'Rodrigo's father was a very young officer serving with General Franco, you understand. They flew together from the Canaries to Morocco in the plane chartered in London by Luís Bolín, the *ABC*'s correspondent there. The rest is history that you probably already know – Franco brought back to Spain the Army of Africa that enabled him to win the Civil War for the Nationalists.'

It explained, Venetia thought, how families like the Estebans and the Quinones had prospered – by staying close friends of the Caudillo, and of the monarchy that had followed him. Even then the subject might have been allowed to lapse but Fernando, patience tried by some of Edwina's more outspoken pronouncements, suddenly decided to bait a guest whom Blanca had been paying too much attention to.

'Of course, even now not everyone agrees

83

that a Nationalist victory was what Spain needed or the Republicans deserved. Do *you* have a view, Señor Gilmour?'

'Yes, I have a view – it was my father's view, in fact.' The words came slowly, in Ian Gilmour's deliberate voice. 'He'd been brought up as a child at Río Tinto, and what he saw of the miners' lives there left him in no doubt as to which side to support. He volunteered as a medical orderly and served with the International Brigade. He went back to England afterwards but never forgot the Civil War, never quite got over the things he saw, and never forgave Franco for the treatment the defeated Republicans received from the regime.'

There was silence in the room for a moment, and it seemed to Venetia that they all looked to Don Alberto, depending on him to relieve the moment's awkwardness. To give him the responsibility was unfair, but so had Ian Gilmour's simplistic 'view' been, too.

'This is Spain,' she felt impelled to say herself, 'where even now no one wants to admit that the madness and inhumanity infected *both* sides. You speak of atrocities against the Republicans, but it wasn't the Nationalists who crucified good priests, and burned nuns alive in their churches.'

She received for that a frown of cold distaste from Ian Gilmour, but it seemed no worse than that Fernando should now be watching her with interest and approval. To her great relief, Don Alberto finally asserted himself and brought the conversation to an end.

'Evil begets evil, and so it always will until we learn to break the vicious circle by simply renouncing it.' He shook his head at the expressions on their faces. 'You think it can't be done. My faith in God Almighty says that it can. But first we have to discover how to forgive each other for the wickednesses of the past.'

He stood up, smiling serenely at his hostess as if it was on just such an unworldly note that her Madrid dinner parties were in the habit of ending. Ian Gilmour got up too, offering to shepherd the priest home before beginning his own journey. The night was brilliantly moonlit, but even so the thought of his having to return alone to the isolation of El Perdido sent the others back to Las Cuadras wrapped in a silence that no one seemed to want to break.

'Remarkable man, your uncle,' Edwina said finally to Fiona.

But it was agreed to absent-mindedly and, understanding her better now, Venetia thought she could guess the reason. Fiona required people, especially men, to respond to her. Even William had passed this essential test, but Felipe had failed it, and Ian

85

Gilmour had simply ignored it. With Fernando, however, she had felt on reassuringly firm ground ... surely no mistake there about the impression she'd made, and it was on this memory of the evening that she intended to dwell. Her uncle's defence of an unpopular view, or even his probable loneliness, were merely faint echoes in her ear while she recalled the promising glint in Fernando's dark eyes.

Six

February brought the winter's final onslaught of rain – days of it, to flood every gulley and irrigation channel, and transform the little Majaceite into something that could properly be called a river. While the women of Rosario splashed their way into Consuela's shop to complain about the weather, their menfolk congregated in Luís's bar to talk and smoke and argue about the weight of the downpour. Every drop of water would be needed when the summer heat came; meanwhile there was nothing to do but enjoy a respite from work that heaven itself provided.

At Las Cuadras William received a visit

every morning from the small, dripping figure of Juan Esteban, determined to watch and wait with his mentor for the first arrivals across the Straits from Africa. He still had much to learn, although he now knew the English names of orioles, cuckoos, finches and the dozens of other visitors who would need to be identified among the eagles and vultures and goshawks patrolling the sky above them.

Beyond observing occasionally that some of La Paloma's inmates might as well move their beds into the stables, Edwina paid little attention to Juan, and none at all to Felipe, who also now called every day on some pretext or other – there was exotic fruit to be raided for them from his father's hothouses, or magazines the Marriotts might enjoy. Venetia had given up wishing that he would come less often, and a day when they didn't meet now seemed to lack pleasure and completeness. The slow, steady deepening of their friendship pleased them both; it might one day become something more, when Luc was a less bright memory, but the day was distant yet, and neither of them felt inclined to hurry.

Content herself, working on the translation of Luc's stories, Venetia couldn't help noticing a change in her guest. Fiona went frequently to Seville to consult archives there, and otherwise read and wrote in her room; but something she'd expected hadn't gone according to plan. That evening at La Paloma, Fernando's glance had held out the promise of a splendid seduction being very close at hand. But it hadn't happened, and the failure was both puzzle and bitter disappointment combined. Fiona was aware of always needing most what it seemed she couldn't have.

Then, one morning, the skies cleared. She danced in to breakfast, becomingly flushed, to announce that Fernando had telephoned; a weekend on the coast, he'd suggested, would be good for both of them. Venetia inspected the radiant face across the table and held her tongue. Fiona was old enough, and surely experienced enough, to know what was on offer; she didn't need well-meant, impertinent advice.

The morning had dawned dry for once, with a hint of soft spring mildness in the air; there was no longer any risk in planting up the tubs in the courtyard. Venetia hadn't been at work long when Fernando sauntered in under the archway from the drive to collect his passenger. As usual he was elegance itself, but informally so this morning. 'On pleasure bent,' Venetia suggested for something to say, wishing that he wouldn't stand watching her.

'Not altogether, although I hope pleasure will come into it,' he admitted with his gleaming smile. 'I've some useful friends for Fiona to meet. I would have invited you and my dear brother as well, but something tells me that Señorita Marriott would have turned me down. I have the strong suspicion that she disapproves of me!'

The provocation was deliberate, she knew. Fernando wasn't interested in small-talk; his conversational darts were carefully aimed when he was talking to a woman. She had to be made aware of him – if impudent but undeniable charm failed, then by open assault. Those who refused to join in the game were pursued if he thought them worth the effort, or ignored if not, and Venetia suspected him of not being sure which category she came into. She would have been astonished to know that she was wrong. He could analyse precisely the reactions she aroused in him: anger at her unreasonable preference for his brother was mixed with astonishment at himself. She wasn't his sort of woman at all, but he wanted to keep looking at her. He didn't like quiet, stubborn girls, but he couldn't allow her to ignore him.

'You have beautiful hands ... why grub in the earth with them like a labourer?'

The sharp question succeeded in its aim of making her look at him. 'Why not? The earth washes off. In any case I have the feeling that plants don't like to be handled with gloves, and I want them to thrive, not sulk!'

He came to stand beside her, and at close range it was impossible *not* to be aware of him. Fernando Quinones wasn't a man to be overlooked: bright, intelligent eyes, white teeth against the brownness of his skin, and the clean fragrance of a perfectly turned-out male – they were merits any sensate woman would be a fool to despise. But Fiona was clearly subjugated even before the weekend started, and Venetia felt suddenly anxious for her. It was one thing to keep a flock of tame academics safely leashed at home, but this man was something else – as attractive as a marauding leopard, and just about as incalculable. Fernando Quinones was the end result of centuries of ethnic couplings that Oxford knew nothing about – Greek, Roman, Visigoth, Moor and Jew could all have been involved in this Andalucían corsair's ancestry. An exciting lover he no doubt was, but there would be little gentleness or generosity on offer, and Venetia feared for the impulsive optimist getting ready for him across the courtyard. She did her best to put her anxiety into not too offensive words.

'If Fiona has told you about her broken marriage, you'll know that this sabbatical is a chance for her to get back on an even keel again. She may always seem as gay as a lark, but she's still vulnerable at the moment.'

The intention to warn was obvious, and it got the reaction that she supposed well-meant interference always deserved.

'Why not let Fiona fight her own battles? She's well equipped to do so. When a man is talking to *you*, you're not supposed to remind him of another woman. Most of your sex find no difficulty at all in concentrating on themselves – why not you, Venetia?'

'Your experience is very wide, I'm sure,' she said politely, 'but we still come in all shapes and sizes. Now, if you don't want me to go and hurry your passenger up, I'll get on with my planting.'

She was glad there wasn't time for him to answer before Fiona herself appeared – flushed and breathless, as if there'd been several panicky changes of mind about what to wear. But the final choice of tartan skirt, cashmere sweater and buckled shoes earned from Fernando a compliment that made her blush. She was able to smile with a kind of complacent pity at the girl being left behind. Poor dear thing ... remembrance of times past was all very well, but what she should be doing now was burying old memories, good and bad, and rousing Felipe to some kind of more than musical activity. He wouldn't be able to match the performance Fernando offered in Málaga, but she doubted if her friend would have been quite up to that in any case. In certain important respects a convent education was probably very hard to live down.

Venetia watched them drive away, thinking that Fernando had been right: it was point-less to worry about Fiona. She was an experienced player in the game of sexual warfare, and probably had nothing more serious in mind than a weekend's escape from the calamities of twentieth-century European history.

'You're ramming that poor geranium into its pot as if you hated it; you won't get it to grow like that,' Edwina's voice suddenly remarked behind her. 'I point that out in passing – it isn't what I came to say. Your father's just telephoned from Seville – he and Arlette plan to arrive this afternoon and stay the night. They're bringing what you asked for from London ... clothes and books.'

'*Very* kind of them,' Venetia said with pleasure. 'But I hope this isn't a special journey they've been talked into – I asked my father's secretary to be kind enough to send some things by freight.'

'Not a special journey – Jeffery's on his way to Marbella, where one of his sheik friends needs a new mosque or minaret or some such thing. I shall chide him for it: the Arabs are recapturing al-Andalus quickly enough without his help. Look at Granada ... it'll be more Islamic than Christian before long!'

Venetia smiled at her aunt's affronted expression. 'Uncle William thinks rather highly of the Moors' civilising contribution to Spain in the past, so why not welcome it now?'

'The dear man thinks highly of anyone who doesn't slaughter migrating birds – which, I'm bound to say, rules out a great many Frenchmen and Italians, not to mention our own brave hunters here!' Edwina was tempted to pursue this promising red herring, but there were pressing domestic matters to consider as well. 'Encarnita's getting a room ready, but supper's got to be thought of – Jeffery won't greatly enjoy a potato omelette, I fancy, however lavishly Will pours our best Rioja.'

'Well, there's nothing wrong with Consuela's *serrano* ham, and we could follow it with saffron rice and *mariscos* – delicious enough to please anybody.'

'Prawns, shrimps, clams and perhaps just a few succulent mouthfuls of tiny squid!' Edwina breathed the words like a litany. 'Dear Venetia, shall you go to the fish stall in Ubrique, or shall I?'

'I'll go – you're better at talking Consuela into parting with her best ham than I am.'

'That I *can* do,' Edwina agreed. 'Impress

Arlette in any way at all I cannot; she'll arrive groomed to the last eyelash, say something very kind about my paintings and wonder yet again how her elegant husband came to have such a mad old frump for a sister!'

Venetia smiled, but shook her head. 'Dear Aunt, my stepmother is a kinder woman than you're pretending. She's been good to *me* at any rate.' Fairness demanded that it should be said, but she was already aware of the gap that separated Edwina from her worldly Parisian sister-in-law. This prompted another suggestion. 'Apart from having the *mariscos* to look forward to, you could spread the entertainment load by inviting someone else – what about Don Alberto?'

'Excellent,' Edwina agreed thoughtfully. 'I doubt if it would hurt Jeffery *or* Arlette to pay a little attention to their immortal souls; I'll call with an invitation on my way home.'

Venetia set off for Ubrique feeling that a potentially thorny evening had been cushioned as best they could. It was a shock to get back an hour later and discover that William had taken precautions of his own. Ian Gilmour, met in the course of his morning stroll up the hill, had also been talked into joining the dinner party.

'The man is supposed to be a recluse,' Venetia complained. 'Why can't he at least behave as we expect him to?'

William sounded unexpectedly firm. 'He doesn't invite sympathy but I believe he's lonely. That's why I said, rather cunningly I thought, that he'd be doing *us* a favour by coming.'

Edwina was now looking so much more cheerful that Venetia abandoned protest and smiled at them both instead. 'All right – I shall go and beat the squid into submission before Encarnita gets to work on it.'

The most that could be said for the evening in prospect was that it looked interesting: her sophisticated father and stepmother confronted by a saintly priest and a man who, if he hadn't renounced the devil, had certainly turned his back on the world.

Arlette and Jeffery arrived in the late afternoon – she as wonderfully groomed as Edwina had predicted and he, though walking with a stick, insisting that his broken ankle had nearly mended. They'd come, Venetia thought, warned by Mercedes Ribera to make allowances for the hospitality they were about to receive; but Las Cuadras took them so agreeably by surprise that Jeffery commended his brother for a shrewd find, and Arlette's tour of inspection finished in the drawing-room with a generous award of praise.

'It's charming ... really charming,' she admitted, looking round, 'and clever of you to put these colours together – mixing blues and greens can be perilous, but against these whitewashed walls and the dark wood of the furniture they work beautifully.'

'Venetia's choice,' Edwina said honestly. 'We were in a terrible mess until she arrived. I'm inclined to think it's what she ought to be doing for a living – sorting out poor fools like me who don't know where to start putting themselves to rights.'

Arlette smiled kindly, not quarrelling with her sister-in-law's description of herself. 'You paint your flowers, *ma chère* – let that be enough.'

Venetia saw her aunt's grin of pleasure at a comment she'd been expecting, and decided it was time to separate the two ladies before Edwina could enquire sympathetically about the misery of living in Paris.

She led Arlette back into the guest wing of the house, thanking her for what she'd brought from London. 'I *was* running rather short of clothes, and one or two of the reference books I need aren't even in Uncle Will's considerable library.'

Arlette considered her stepdaughter for a moment, aware of changes that were too elusive to be easily pinned down. Years ago, in Brussels, Venetia had introduced them with a mixture of pride and despair to the ill-looking man they knew had died soon afterwards. Beyond that brief report she had never mentioned him again – because she couldn't bear to, her stepmother realised. Now there was a change, at least on the surface. The girl looked well, and extraordinarily content seeing that she'd chosen to make herself useful to a dear but very odd couple.

'We didn't imagine you were going to *stay* here,' she began by saying; 'you were just supposed to attend Juanita's funeral, not get trapped by your aunt and uncle! William is a dear man, I grant you, but of Edwina's awkwardness there is no doubt.'

Venetia couldn't help smiling even while she shook her head. 'Awkward or not, I love her as she is. I'm enjoying Spain as never before, and I've got translation work that can be done here as well as anywhere else. It's a pleasant new sensation, feeling wanted ... I've been on my own too long!'

Arlette nodded, but offered a word of warning. 'Even so, *ma chère*, don't forget, please, that Rosario is the backwater your aunt and uncle have chosen to *retire* to; at your age it's necessary that you go back to the real world.'

Venetia was tempted to suggest that Rosario was real enough to the men who worked the difficult, steep land, and to the women who tended *them* and raised their families. But it was a point of view that Arlette would be unable to understand. She would see Rosario life as a subsistence-level existence, and miss altogether the kinship and shared tradition that made it irreplaceable.

'The real world is with us even here,' it was time to insist. 'Uncle William's landlords at the end of the drive are as successful and worldly as even *you* could wish, and one of them – the least worldly of them, I'm bound to say! – has become a very dear friend.'

Arlette left this interesting statement uninvestigated and they rejoined the others in the drawing-room, but her glance was drawn almost fearfully to the immense view they looked out on – high Spanish sky and a landscape of valley, hill and mountain that seemed to go on for ever. Suddenly she seemed impelled to revert to her conversation with Venetia.

'I don't mind short visits – there's a lot to enjoy – but I couldn't live here,' she insisted. 'There's no moderation about Spain, just altogether too much of *everything* instead!'

For once Edwina could look at Arlette with a touch of pity. 'It's exactly what aficionados like Will and myself love – the sheer excess that makes it different from anywhere else.'

William smiled at his sister-in-law, seeing that she still looked unconvinced. 'Never mind, my dear, we have one very unexcessive dinner guest for you this evening – our priest, Don Alberto; but I'm bound to say the other one, an author called Ian Gilmour, is a less certain quantity.'

'Less certain indeed, if we're thinking of the same Gilmour,' Jeffery observed, 'although the man I met once or twice lived in London. I don't know what became of him after his fall from grace, of course.'

It was Edwina who broke the silence. 'I suppose he foolishly ran off with someone else's wife and then regretted it; he lives alone here now.'

'Nothing like that, I'm afraid – he faced a manslaughter charge after he was released from hospital. Two joy-riding teenagers were killed when they crashed into his car. As far as I remember, he got a suspended sentence, but he *had* been drinking ... might have been able to avoid them otherwise.'

The long pause this time was finally ended by William. 'We shan't refer to it, of course; Gilmour hasn't yet decided to trust us by referring to the past.'

'You and Venetia were abroad at the time, but he was well enough known for the case to get a lot of coverage in the press,' Jeffery pointed out. 'He may assume that I remember it.'

'There's also *our* problem,' Edwina said quietly. 'How do we conceal what we now know from an intelligent and perceptive man? Should we even try? Might he not feel less intolerably isolated if he knew that

99

we *did* know?'

She glanced at her silent niece, but Venetia stood up, brushing the subject of Ian Gilmour away with an abrupt gesture.

'Encarnita can manage perfectly well, but she doesn't think she can. Excuse me while I keep her calm in the kitchen.'

She knew it to be a cowardly escape from the conversation, but she couldn't go on with it. The man's story was dreadful enough in itself, but how could it not remind her of her own mother – lovely, gifted Katherine, killed, as those boys had been, by a drunken driver? She could understand now why he'd told William that he hated waste; it must seem to be the ultimate tragedy of his life, just as it had been that of the Frenchman she had loved. But Luc had lost a battle against disease, not thrown his future away in a moment of reckless misjudgement. Reclaiming a wilderness by gruelling hard work might be Ian Gilmour's way of trying to salvage something from the wreckage of the past, but she doubted whether it would be enough.

The evening they'd hoped to make convivial now seemed likely to become an endurance test instead, but, in the way of ordeals dreaded beforehand, it turned out to be quite bearable in the event. Don Alberto was his serene and civilised self, and

Jeffery and Arlette put forth such efforts to charm and entertain that Ian Gilmour might have been forgiven, Venetia thought, for wondering why William had pressed him to come at all. But she was aware of being too silent herself, even on the provocative subject of whither Spain, whither Europe, that engaged the rest of them. When their visitor's speculative eye occasionally fell on her she supposed she knew what he was thinking: she was a poor jealous creature who'd never come to terms with a step-mother not much older than herself but a great deal more scintillating!

It was a relief when the evening came to an end and, dearly though she loved them, she wasn't sorry to see her father and Arlette drive away the following morning. Neither of them had quite understood how deeply pleased she was to be included for the time being in her aunt and uncle's contented company, and to feel that she belonged with them. Now the house would be quiet and peaceful again, at least until Fiona burst in, bringing with her the different air breathed by people who, like Arlette, considered that what *they* inhabited was the real world.

But the recollection of Fiona started up a different train of thought. In keeping the secret of her uncle's tragedy, she'd been anything but the extrovert, indiscreet chatterbox she sometimes seemed. Did Ian

101

Gilmour know that, or simply assume that she would have told them his story? It was another worrying complication, but for the moment Venetia was determined to put it aside – the morning was fine, and the almond trees were beginning to throw a veil of white blossom over the hillside. When Felipe arrived she would insist that they go out and look at them together. But she found herself hoping that the man at El Perdido might see their beauty too, and even find in the return of spring the possibility of his own redemption.

Seven

Fiona's weekend on the coast prolonged itself by an extra day, leading the Marriotts to tell each other that the excursion was obviously proving a great success. William sounded so pleased when he said it that Venetia merely agreed, wondering what he imagined a weekend with Fernando might involve. William was a charmingly unworldly man, but even he must surely guess that Fiona hadn't been invited just to inspect the beauties of Málaga.

She walked in the following day while they were sitting over the remains of lunch. The offer of coffee was accepted very cheerfully but, watching her face with care, Venetia thought she saw the effort needed to produce such gaiety.

Not interested in Fernando, Edwina sounded surprised that Málaga itself had been so much enjoyed. 'Richard Ford was right as usual – "One day will suffice. It has few attractions beyond climate, almonds, raisons and sweet wine"! And I'm quite certain it won't have improved since *his* day.'

William smiled at his sister. 'My dear, our friend here didn't look at it with cantankerous old Ford! She had a more persuasive companion altogether.'

Fiona brightly agreed, and there the subject rested; but when she got up from the table Venetia followed her along the corridor to her own quarters.

'Do you want to tell me how the weekend was apart from Málaga ... or not?'

She thought Fiona was about to refuse, but suddenly the cheerful façade cracked to reveal what lay underneath.

'Yes, I'll tell you, *amiga*, confession being good for the soul; isn't that what you Catholics believe?' She managed a bitter little smile that wavered on the edge of tears, then began her story. 'At least I can now confirm that Fernando is the world's most exciting lover – any woman's dream companion in bed!'

'Even so, he doesn't seem to have made you very happy,' Venetia suggested quietly.

Fiona's hands suddenly clenched themselves into tight fists that banged the table in front of her. 'I thought I understood; that first evening at La Paloma we'd recognised one another. He avoided me for a while afterwards; I thought he was afraid of committing himself, but he was sure to give in because we needed each other. That's what I *thought*, and the time we had together bore it out. But on the way back Fernando explained it to me – wonderful experiences were best not repeated because, alas and alack, the novelty always wore off! That's all an unforgettable weekend amounted to for *him*, a change from his usual Spanish lovers!'

Her tormented face revealed how differently she'd seen it herself; genuine pain was being struggled with, as well as wounded pride and the fear of having shown herself to be a gullible fool.

'So you played your part, I very much hope,' Venetia suggested after a moment; 'you smiled and gaily agreed that he was right; a regular diet of even Fernando Quinones wasn't *quite* what you were looking for! Fiona, please promise me it's what you said to that ... that atrociously self-confident,

104

unprincipled villain.'

'I did my best,' Fiona admitted with a faint clutch at pride, 'though it seems to me *you*'ve learned a thing or two since the days of James O'Halloran. You wouldn't have said *that* when you first arrived in Oxford, with wisps of the dear nuns' incense and piety still clinging to you!'

'I've grown older,' Venetia agreed, 'and we *are* expected to learn from our mistakes. A Spanish charmer like Fernando Quinones is harder to resist than most, I grant you, but you have a very susceptible heart; try hating him, please – it's what he deserves.'

Fiona nodded, torn between the desire to smile at the advice her convent-reared friend gave so calmly and to weep for a delight that had been brutally short-lived. 'I'd have stayed with Fernando for ever if he'd asked me to,' she confessed; 'that's how good it was. But you won't see me pine and fade away; I shall smile and smile whenever he's around.'

Venetia put out a friendly hand to pat her arm, aware that this time, at least, Fiona had come off worst; she'd wreaked havoc herself in the past on other people's hearts, but never wantonly. Fernando's cruelty was of a more deliberate kind, a Spanish kind that she probably wouldn't have come across before and hadn't recognised.

Venetia halted on her way to the door. 'I've

just remembered something else that needs talking about. It's upsetting, but at least it might take your mind off Fernando for a moment. While you were away my father and stepmother called in on their way to Marbella. The subject of your relative cropped up – in fact they even met him, because William invited him to dinner. But my father remembered his story and told us about it before he arrived.'

After a small silence Fiona found something to say. 'I suppose you think I should have told you.'

'No ... you were right not to; there was no reason for us to know.'

Fiona swung round to face her companion. 'Were William and Edwina very shocked? A supposed manslaughterer as their near neighbour can't be what they're accustomed to.'

'After a working career in the capitals of South America I doubt if they're shockable at all,' Venetia pointed out. 'Now that they do know they won't treat your uncle any differently.'

'What about you – brought up as you were and probably *not* much exposed to the brutalities of life?'

'I left the convent ten years ago, and haven't exactly been in close confinement since then. Ian Gilmour and I will continue to do what we've done until now – more or less ignore one another – I expect. But at least it explains why he's here; that had me puzzled before.'

'I knew how terrible his story was, of course, but it didn't become real until I went up to El Perdido. Then I saw what he'd been left with ... what he'd lost. It's also haunting *you*, I think, more than it should,' Fiona suggested, looking at her friend's face. 'You aren't your neighbour's keeper; my uncle must find his own salvation.'

Venetia nodded, thinking that the suspicion she'd had about Ian Gilmour had been right. He'd chosen Spain deliberately, and the lonely isolation of El Perdido was something he felt obliged to endure. Expiation for a sin was a strange and unfashionable idea, but she could believe that that was what he was engaged in.

Later that day, expecting Felipe to stroll down as usual to share what her aunt always referred to grandly as their pre-prandial glass of fino, she was surprised to see Blanca walk in under the archway instead.

'Apologies from my sickly brother,' she announced as Venetia met her at the door. 'Influenza is developing, which he insists he mustn't share with anyone else, so he is keeping to his own room. My father and Juan are watching some dreadful American film, and that leaves *me* going quietly mad with my own undiluted company!'

'Then come in,' Venetia said quickly. 'My aunt and uncle are shopping in Ubrique – Consuela ran out of cumin and paprika this morning, which Encarnita insists our supper can't do without – but they'll be back at any moment.'

She led the visitor into the drawing-room and turned to smile at her. 'Which do you prefer: fino, manzanilla, or – tell it not in Gath – Gordon's gin?'

Blanca's bored face suddenly quivered with amusement. 'Since you ask, I'm *sick* of sherry! A stiff gin would make me feel less of an exile from Madrid.'

Venetia produced a drink of the required stiffness and poured fino for herself. Then, though wary of her guest, she made an effort to sound cordial. 'You're bound to be missing your husband and friends, but don't you find anything at all to enjoy in Rosario? I know it's tiny and remote, but...'

'It's tiny, remote, extremely boring, and smugly convinced that it can ignore the outside world,' Blanca interrupted her sharply. '*You* enjoy it for the moment, knowing that you can leave whenever you want to. I only find it bearable when Fernando is here to make us laugh and talk about something other than village gossip, but he had to leave again after bringing Fiona back.'

'Well, you aren't here for ever yourself, and Juan is looking better every day – that must make the tedium worthwhile.'

Blanca's nod seemed to agree, though not enthusiastically; then she looked round the room, comparing it to its disadvantage, Venetia suspected, with the ornate luxury of La Paloma.

'Felipe likes coming here, and I suppose I can see why – he's a man of simple tastes!'

However viewed, the remark seemed intentionally double-edged, and it took Venetia a moment to decide what to do with it.

'We have tastes in common then,' she finally said. 'He's a very welcome guest, and we should all miss him if he didn't come.'

'I'm sure.' Blanca inspected her hostess's guarded face before going on. 'I'm very attached to my brothers – one must be, of course – but they are *both* my father's sons, Venetia. In Fernando's case it's easy for any intelligent woman to know what to expect, and I hope Fiona does ... a great deal of pleasure and perhaps the risk of a little heartache! With Felipe both pleasure and risk might be less, but the principle is the same: like any Quinones, he arranges life to suit himself.' She smiled at an expression she *could* now read. 'You don't believe me, because he's gentle and sweet-mannered; but nevertheless what I say is true.'

'True or not, thank you for the warning ... which is what I seem to think that was.' Venetia hesitated for a moment. 'I take it you didn't warn Fiona what to expect from Fernando?'

Blanca repeated her familiar shrug. 'Yes, I did, and I should have expected the answer I got: she agreed that what I said might be true for the rest of the women Fernando knew, but not for her.'

'Perhaps she knows him better now,' Venetia suggested quietly, just as a commotion outside signalled the return of the Marriotts. Edwina smiled at a visitor she hadn't expected. Felipe was the usual caller, and she'd grown to like him well enough, but he was too content to sit and smile at Venetia. With his sharper-tongued sister Edwina could be sure of an exchange of barbed compliments that gave a spice to social visits. She lost no time now in enquiring tenderly after Fernando's business activities.

'No unforgiving moment being wasted, I trust; there must still be an inch or two of coastline left as God made it, for your brother to help some barbarian to sell.'

William attended to the replenishment of Blanca's glass, and calmly suggested to his sister that she should reserve her fire for Fernando himself.

'Very true,' Edwina had the grace to admit, 'and I'm also obliged to say that our own dear brother is contributing *his* mite to the ruination of this unique and beautiful

110

country. Fernando's clients buy up land; Jeffery designs the concrete carbuncles that increasingly disfigure it.'

William smiled at their guest. 'As usual, Edwina spoils her case by exaggerating it! Like her, I might prefer to see a simple, beautiful church being built to the glory of the God *we* believe in, but the mosque my brother designs for his Muslim friends will be beautiful, and no doubt they'll worship in it as devoutly as we do.'

'But this is *Spain*, Catholic and apostolic!' Venetia protested in support of her aunt. 'The Moors were evicted five hundred years ago. The Muslims have their own countries to worship in – let them do it there.'

She saw Blanca's pitying smile, and knew what she was thinking: how quaint they were, these supposedly hybrid creatures whose Spanish blood had made no difference to what they remained – English to their hearts' core, pragmatic, sentimental and deeply resistant to change; nothing would alter them from being island people, unable to feel part of any continent at all.

'You should listen to my father and my husband,' Blanca recommended kindly. 'Progress no longer stops, as it did for centuries, at the Pyrenees! Instead of being proud, backward and extremely poor, we're becoming rather prosperous and glad to be part of Europe, even at the cost of a carbuncle or two!'

For once Edwina didn't rise to the bait. 'The pass has been sold by the politicians, here as everywhere else,' she said sombrely. 'Now the speculators and the profiteers move in. Well, thank God we found Rosario.'

She nodded to Blanca and walked with telling dignity out of the room, leaving the rest of them to digest her parting speech and conclude that, at its most generous, it lumped Fernando in with the speculators. Casting round for something safer to break the silence with, William hoped he'd found it.

'We look forward to Juan's daily visits. He's a credit to you: charmingly behaved and intelligent, and very happy not to be in Madrid!'

'Which is where he nevertheless belongs,' Blanca was quick to point out. 'We shall go back after Easter when my husband returns from New York, and then Juan must forget this nonsensical notion he has of wanting to live in the country. We are city people, not simple-minded rustics.'

'But your father chose La Paloma,' Venetia wasn't sorry to be able to point out.

'He liked the idea of finally becoming respectable, and a country estate unfortunately necessitated living in the country,' Blanca explained with cool honesty. 'Juan is an Esteban, therefore *not* a would-be farmer. He's simply a child enjoying the freedom from discipline and schoolwork; he'll be happy enough when he gets used to being back in Madrid.'

With that matter settled she stood up to go, insisting that as soon as Felipe had shaken off his illness they must dine at La Paloma again – if only so that the Señorita Edwina could learn to come to terms with modern Spain! It was said with another slightly condescending smile, but while William escorted Blanca to the door Venetia was left to hope that another invitation wouldn't be forthcoming soon. Maddened by Manolo's view of progress, there was no telling what lengths of rudeness Edwina might feel obliged to go to in order to contradict him.

'We have to remember that you're tenants here, do we not?' she asked pointedly when her uncle came back into the room.

'We do indeed,' he agreed with a rueful smile. 'It might be wiser to plead the pressure of Rosario's social life than risk a knock-down, drag-out fight between Edwina and our host!'

'Pity, though, because I think she might win.' Venetia pondered her next remark and approached it carefully. 'Blanca also seemed anxious to shed light for me on her brothers – she reckons they're much more alike than

113

they seem.'

'Well, she's quite wrong about her son, so why not about them?' William suggested, and saw his niece's frown relax into a grateful smile.

'That's exactly what I think, too,' she agreed.

The following morning, sent out by Edwina to search for a specimen of an evergreen laurestinus known to hide itself in the sierra, Venetia wandered far enough to discover that she'd lost the track she'd climbed up by. Matters weren't desperate – the day was fine and suddenly rather warm, and following any water-course downhill must eventually bring her to a spot where she could get her bearings. But the remains of some once-careful stonework made her realise that what she was following was not a natural stream but an ancient irrigation channel. It led her eventually to dilapidated outbuildings sheltered by a copse of ancient olive trees. Beyond them a small house tucked into the hillside promised at least the possibility of a welcome drink of water, but a moment or two later she understood what her round-about route had led her to. The small grubby figure climbing out of the ditch ahead of her, smiling a welcome, unexpectedly belonged to Juan Esteban – but, like Edwina before her, she was trespassing on El Perdido's land.

'The *señor* is inside the house,' he explained, 'but only for a *momentino* – he hurt his hand.'

She might even then have cravenly beaten a retreat, but Ian Gilmour was now standing in the doorway of the *cortijo*, no doubt watching her hesitate. There was nothing to be done but walk towards him.

'I was hoping for a drink of water,' she said briefly. 'It's thirsty work tracking down plants for my aunt and getting lost in the process. Can I fix your hand for you?'

He smoothed a strip of Elastoplast over the cut and shook his head. 'All done, thanks. You can have lemonade outside with Juan.'

She wasn't to be encouraged to help or to linger inside, it seemed ... perhaps to see how simply and uncomfortably he lived there. But the house itself offered no welcome, and she was glad to return to the warmth and brightness outside. Juan came to sit beside her on a stone wall, and began to explain that he and the *señor* were rebuilding an irrigation channel first dug into the hillside by the Moors, so very *long* ago, a gesture of his small brown hands indicated.

'The water is needed to make things grow,' he explained gravely, '... the *moros* knew that very well because they came from the desert, poor things.'

Venetia agreed that this was so, but, looking at his absorbed face and contented muddiness, she felt a twinge of pity for Blanca. Esteban or not, all the signs were that this single-minded child would one day kick over his city traces for good and become the countryman she refused for the moment to accept.

A lesson on the age of olive trees was in progress when Ian Gilmour appeared with tumblers and a jug of lemonade. Venetia pulled out Edwina's rough sketch and explained what she'd been sent to look for – vibernum tinus, whose berries later in the year would be extremely poisonous.

'Ask this chap here,' Gilmour suggested. 'He won't know its name but he has an eagle's eye for vegetation and the memory of an elephant.'

Juan missed most of this tribute but, having frowned over Edwina's drawing, jumped down off the wall and disappeared.

'Will *he* get lost now?' Venetia asked anxiously. 'Shouldn't we call him back?'

'He has a compass which he knows how to use, he's quite sensible for his age, and he's familiar with the hillside. We don't need to interfere at all.'

She said nothing more, determined that if there was to be any further conversation he would have to start it. When her lemonade – deliciously tangy and cold – was drunk, she'd get up and leave. But for the moment she was tired, and content to sit and rest in the sun, looking at the immense view spread out in front of her.

'You think Juan shouldn't be here.' Ian Gilmour's deep voice suddenly spoke beside her. 'I'm not safe to be in charge of a child ... that *is* what you're thinking, isn't it?'

She felt suddenly cold despite the warmth of the sun. It was the moment they had wondered how they would deal with when it came; sprung upon her now, she was still unprepared for it. The emptiness of the landscape all around them echoed the desolation that she sensed in this solitary, hostile man, and she had no idea how to answer him.

'We know your story, if that's what *you're* thinking,' she admitted in a low voice.

'Fiona told you, of course,' he went on as if she hadn't spoken, '...I suppose she was bound to.'

It was pleasure and relief combined to be able to contradict him. 'No – all she said was that you'd come here because something had gone awry with your life. It was my father who remembered the ... the press coverage of what happened.'

She glanced at the gaunt profile of the man beside her and looked away again ... impossible now to imagine him as a care-free, celebrated lion of literary society in

London. But the question he'd begun by asking was still left unanswered, hanging in the warm scented air; whenever she smelled wild thyme and rosemary in future she would be reminded of this agonising moment.

'Juan looks entirely happy to be here,' she finally insisted. 'He wouldn't come if he felt unsure of you.'

'Very tactful! How do *you* feel, *señorita* ... rather pleased with yourself for behaving so nicely to a man with children's blood on his hands? I should have gone to gaol if those two boys hadn't been high on some filthy drug or other. I *was* condemned for not being entirely sober myself, so you mustn't be too sweetly forgiving!'

The derision in his voice stung her into honesty, and anger. 'My mother was beautiful – not just in looks but in herself; she was also a very gifted singer. When I was fourteen *she* was killed by a drunken motorist. Sweetly forgiving is the last thing I'm inclined to be, to him *or* to you.'

The silence that followed felt as heavy as death itself; even a nearby cicada seemed to have been hushed into sudden quietness. She prayed for Juan to reappear; it was more than she could bear to be left in the huge empty landscape with only this man who sat beside her so motionless that he might have been carved out of stone. She wasn't afraid of him; as William had said, his battle was within himself. But she wanted more space between them than there was, even at the risk of seeming to run away.

'I wouldn't have jeered at you if I'd known about your mother,' he said at last in a ragged voice, 'but I don't suppose it made things *very* much worse. I can't alter what has happened to either of us, though I wish I could, and you needn't try to pretend that I can. I got used to being cold-shouldered by most of my so-called friends; the syrup of pity poured over me by a few well-meaning "Christians" was what I really couldn't bear.'

'Have a little pity on *us*,' Venetia suggested quietly. 'Understand that it's difficult for us to behave in *any* way that you wouldn't find intolerable.'

He turned to look at her, seeing clearly now what he'd scarcely registered before – lovely eyes more green than hazel in the bright morning light, delicately carved nose and mouth. It would have been a pleasure to touch her hair and the softness of her skin. He hadn't allowed such a thought to enter his mind for a long time; it seemed another punishment that he should think it now, about *this* woman, set apart from him by the appalling accidents of Fate.

Disturbed by some anguish in his face, Venetia struggled to find a subject that would haul them on to safer ground.

'You were doubly wrong about Fiona, by the way; not only did she not talk about you, but we've grown very attached to her. I expect she told you that she's researching the history of Fascism. It's a weighty enough task.'

'Another unread doctoral thesis to gather dust on library shelves?' Ian Gilmour suggested after a moment, making an effort to sound his usual calmly sardonic self.

'Well, perhaps; although I wouldn't be altogether surprised if the Great Work never got completed. One part of Fiona genuinely wants an academic career; the other part knows perfectly well that no red-blooded male can help trying to distract her from it.'

'Difficult for her,' he agreed carelessly. 'But I told you once before not to worry about my niece.'

'Of course ... she's a Gilmour, so no family feeling need be considered, no sympathy offered for likely hurt! It's a harsh view that you all take of life.'

'Not harsh, realistic. Shared blood isn't enough to make us like one another. You're too sentimental, if I may say so – your own upbringing was probably in a web of cosy family relationships!' But even as he spoke he remembered her dead mother, and the elegant stepmother he'd met. 'Then again, it wasn't cosy at all, of course,' he amended

120

swiftly. 'I'm a tactless fool, and you're just a natural patsy!'

Disinclined to comment on that, Venetia was about to point out instead that it was time to go looking for Juan when the child reappeared round a bend in the track. Face alight with pleasure, he cradled a small green plant in his hands which he assured them resembled the sketch in his pocket in every particular. In future, he suggested kindly to Venetia, if the *señorita* needed something else she couldn't find, she had much better send *him* to look for it.

She promised to relay this helpful message to her aunt, and got up to leave, saying that she must deliver the specimen at once. It was a good enough reason, but she knew that her true need was to escape from El Perdido. Its silence and loneliness might always have been intimidating; now they laid more stress than she could bear on Ian Gilmour's ruined life.

But some way along the path she suddenly turned to look back. Man and boy were squatting on the ground, absorbed again in the task of repairing the *moros'* ditch, and their contentment at what they were doing together was clear. She'd been right to say that Juan was happy with Ian Gilmour. There was no desolation after all in that sunlit landscape; the exclusion and loneliness she felt were in herself.

121

Eight

With her elder brother away, and Felipe keeping to his own room for fear of passing on the *gripe* to Juan, Blanca had to resign herself to boredom as best she could; she understood and admired her father, but he was scarcely an adequate companion. When Fernando arrived sooner than expected one evening she greeted him with smiling relief.

'Thank God – I was nearly desperate enough to inflict myself on the Marriotts again, despite the touch of frostiness I detect in Venetia's manner! Does she disapprove of your attentions to the gorgeous Fiona, I wonder, or merely envy them?'

Fernando shook his head. 'Not envy, *querida*, that's for sure. I can make very little headway with the splendid Edwina, but none at all with her niece!'

'I think you're irritated by that,' Blanca suggested, eyeing him more closely. 'Why? She's not your usual type, so I suppose male vanity is piqued!'

A faint smile touched her brother's mouth. 'All right, we'll call it that. You must admit that I don't often have to watch Felipe cut me out completely with an attractive girl!'

It was true, of course, but Blanca knew her brother too well not to be aware that she'd been fobbed off. His usual attitude to a woman foolish enough to resist him was to move on to more profitable material; it seemed that he wasn't merely irritated by Venetia Marriott.

She considered her next question more carefully. 'I hope Fiona understood what was on offer last weekend – she *is* staying on our doorstep after all, and I suspect her friends of seeing things differently from us. I offered Venetia a word of warning about Felipe, but she didn't believe what I said. She prefers an idealised version of the truth – for her he's a gentle, artistic dreamer who inhabits a different world from the rest of his ruthless family!' Having frowned over this, Blanca went on to another matter. 'Juan spends too much time with the Marriotts, but also with that strange creature up at El Perdido. He comes back tired and dirty, but always determined to go again.'

'You could ask Gilmour to send him away,' Fernando pointed out. 'I'll ask him for you if you like – I have to go up in that direction.'

This time she stared at him in astonishment. '*You*? My dear, when did you last feel the urge to go scrambling about the hills? It's Felipe who's discovered the delights of the countryside – thanks to Venetia, of course. The English have this strange passion for walking about in it.'

Fernando's most attractive smile was offered to his sister. 'Not your scene, is it? I see *you* in a previous incarnation as the lazy, pampered favourite of someone like Haroun al-Rashid!'

'I expect I was,' Blanca decided, 'and I should have been very good at it – more beautiful than most, and intelligent enough to be *au fait* with all the seraglio intrigue. I should have been indispensable to my lord and master.'

Fernando's nod agreed, but he repeated his question. '*Do* you want me to call on Gilmour?'

'No; pampered and lazy as I am, I still might manage to walk that far myself. The man is something of a mystery, and God knows *that* makes a welcome change in Rosario society.'

'All right – in any case my own first call has to be on Don Ramón Perez.' Blanca made a grimace of distaste and he smilingly explained. 'It's not a social visit; Father and I have a matter of business to discuss with him.'

'I should hope that's all it is,' Blanca said firmly. 'The man is as brash and vulgar as

124

that dreadful new house his son has built for him. God forbid that I should sound for a moment like Edwina Marriott, but I still have to admit that the *pueblo*'s traditional buildings have a certain fitness and decency about them, whereas the Mayor's monstrosity has none at all.'

'Our friend at the stables would have the poor Serranos still living in whitewashed caves hewn out of the hillside! But time isn't going to go backwards even here, however much an eccentric Anglo-Spanish lady would like it to.'

Blanca stared at her brother, recognising the air of excitement that he was keeping under firm control. 'You're as keyed up as a hunting dog about to be let loose! If this is the start of some new venture, and Perez is involved in it, I hope you'll keep a sharp eye on him.'

Fernando's smile flashed again in the brownness of his face. 'There's an English saying I could offer you: "Set a thief to catch a thief"! If I couldn't handle the Ramóns of this world we should be in a poor way by now.'

She nodded, knowing it to be true, then suddenly reverted to where the conversation had begun, hoping to take her brother by surprise.

'You didn't say anything about your Málaga weekend. I hope Fiona enjoyed it.'

125

Fernando smiled, knowing his sister quite as well as she knew him. 'The weekend was *very* enjoyable; but what you really want to know is whether it's likely to become a habit! The answer is no, my dear. I was offering Fiona the good time we had together, not a lifetime's devotion.'

He spoke lightly, but Blanca knew when she was being told to leave a subject alone. She weighed her words and proceeded delicately.

'All the same, I can't help feeling that our relationships here are getting rather in-volved; we seem to be taking part in some complicated dance – ourselves, the Mar-riotts, Fiona, and even the mysterious man who turns out to be her uncle.'

'All invented for your entertainment, *querida*, while Juan's convalescence keeps you here!' Fernando suggested cheerfully. 'Count your blessings, and leave me to worry about upsetting our neighbours ... if that *is* what you're now doing.'

Blanca lifted her hands in a little gesture that conceded she would ask no more questions about Fiona Gilmour.

The subject of calling at El Perdido didn't have to be mentioned again because one morning Blanca found herself unexpectedly overtaken by the man himself, on the road home from Rosario. He'd almost loped past before he acknowledged that in courtesy he must trim his pace and walk beside her. Glancing at her, he thought she cut an incongruous figure there, but at least she remained true to herself, and for that he silently awarded her a good mark: no deliberately countrified outfits for Blanca Esteban, no pretence; she looked what she felt herself to be – an exile from metropolitan life.

'All La Paloma's cars broken down, *señora*?' he suggested hopefully. 'We don't normally see *you* footing it back home from Consuela's emporium.'

'It is the housekeeper who shops, not I,' she corrected him. 'I've merely been to call on her elderly mother who is unwell. A large foreign car at her cottage door would have seemed to stress our different situations rather unkindly, I thought.'

'Very commendable.'

She could gather nothing from the bland statement, nor from the expression on his face. As a rule she was able to judge quite precisely the effect she was making on a man, but this one, subtle and wary as he was, defeated her. Confident that she couldn't not be making any effect at all, she allowed him to be a sophisticate like herself, adept at self-concealment.

'Between you and the Marriotts, we see very little of Juan,' she pointed out next.

127

'I don't encourage him to come to El Perdido, but I enjoy his company.' After the briefest pause Ian Gilmour felt impelled to add something that would make the matter clear. 'He's only a bit younger than my own son.'

'Who isn't here, obviously.'

'Who is living in New York with his mother.' Had he managed to sound casual enough about that? Longing for a child he hadn't seen for two interminable years couldn't be allowed to show, but why in God's name had he mentioned the boy at all? After a moment he had his voice under control again. 'You don't like Juan coming to see me, or spending hours with William Marriott?'

'He must have something to do while he's here, I realise that,' Blanca admitted. 'But he doesn't understand that it's a holiday game, not an introduction to a future for him at Rosario. How can there be one, when every year still more people leave these villages to look for an easier life in the towns?'

'And every year a little more land that could be tended and made fruitful reverts to wilderness. Even now your son has the good sense to think that's wrong ... I'm afraid you'll have to let him make his own choice when the time comes.'

She wanted to ask the man beside her

what had made El Perdido *his* own, strange choice. A neglected smallholding clinging to the side of a hill was as inappropriate a setting as she could imagine for the city dweller she guessed him to be. A solitary, monastic life seemed even more unnatural for a man whose personality was so insistently magnetic. He was a challenge because he was a mystery.

'You speak excellent Spanish for a foreigner,' she suggested. 'Is it because of the family connections with Río Tinto that you mentioned at dinner the other night?'

'I never lived there as a child, but some fascination with Spain was probably bred into me. I spent every college vacation walking about the country by myself. It was the best way of learning the language, but I came to understand the people as well.'

The entrance to La Paloma's long drive was in view now, the conversation nearly over, but she was aware of wanting it not to end; with only the smallest encouragement she'd have gone on with him, up the lonely hillside. The truth was that she was lonely herself.

'There's a lot we don't understand about you,' she said suddenly. 'It seems rather a pity.'

He stood staring at her for a moment, ready for a moment to join the game her glance invited him into. He wasn't blind –

she was vividly attractive, and bored enough by *pueblo* life to welcome whatever overture he might offer. It seemed a pity in a way that he wanted to offer nothing ... not even an explanation for a lack of response that probably left her surprised as well as resentful. But in the end he had at least to answer her.

'One of the nice things about your son is that he understands how little it's necessary to know, and what he doesn't know never troubles him! *Buenos días, señora* ... I think this is where our ways divide.'

With one hand lifted in an ironic salute, he headed up the track, and she could almost feel the relief with which he lengthened his stride as he moved away from her. She walked on up to the house pretending that she was only puzzled by the paradox he represented. He was struggling up on his lonely hillside to reclaim good land from wilderness; but in more personal terms the opposite seemed to be true: he was deliberately reverting to wasteful isolation himself, and rejecting what human contact could offer. Her own approach had been clear enough, but not sufficiently tempting. It hadn't, to her own surprise, even been made entirely selfishly – she would have liked to entice him back into normal life again.

Back at the house she merely explained to Fernando that there was no need for him to go looking for Ian Gilmour – she'd already met him herself.

'And he was charmingly conversational as usual, I expect,' Fernando suggested, '... ready to remind you that the Quinones and the Estebans fought on the wrong side in the Civil War, and have managed to do very well for themselves ever since.'

'We didn't talk about politics, thank God – it's the dreadful Spanish habit that keeps the past alive when it's much better forgotten. It's not just a Spanish habit, either – even Venetia Marriott, who doesn't seem to care very much for her aristocratic Jerez antecedents, became rather passionately anti-Republican, I remember.'

'Because she's a devout Catholic, convent-reared ... what did you expect?' Fernando considered the question and answered it himself with a hint of irritation. 'Though what you expect isn't necessarily what you get with Venetia Marriott.' He brushed the memory of her aside, almost impatiently. 'So, no politics; what *did* you talk about with Gilmour?'

'Juan, of course – he said that he doesn't encourage the child to visit El Perdido.'

'So now *you*'ll tell Juan not to go?'

Blanca shook her head. 'No ... I have the strange idea that it would be unkind – to both of them.' She half smiled at the expression on her brother's face but, remembering

131

the muffled pain in Ian Gilmour's voice, found herself not wanting to repeat what he'd said about his own son.

A moment later Felipe brought the conversation to an end by reappearing downstairs. He looked pale and listless after several days in bed – a contrast to Fernando's lithe fitness, and a frail wraith compared with the man they'd just been discussing.

'You've been missed at Las Cuadras,' she said, intending to be kind, 'especially by Venetia.'

'*Only* by Venetia, I suspect,' Felipe suggested with a flicker of amusement. 'William Marriott asks nothing more of life than his books and birds and strolls about the countryside; and Edwina looks tolerantly at me, wondering why I don't do something more manly and profitable than compose the sort of music she doesn't like – my own family's view, of course, and probably the only point on which she agrees with you!' He smiled pleasantly at his brother and sister, and went on to surprise them still more. 'It doesn't worry me. As long as Venetia likes what I do, nothing else much matters.'

'Which puts *us* in our places, *querida*,' Fernando observed wryly to Blanca. 'I get the impression that an acquaintance with the Marriotts is proving instructive all round!'

He smiled at their puzzled faces, then walked out of the room.

'What did he mean by that?' Felipe wanted to know.

'Don't ask – you know Fernando likes to be inscrutable. By the way, he's got some deal brewing with Ramón Perez that I can't help feeling even we might disapprove of. I shall pump Father about it, because he's involved as well.'

Not much interested, Felipe asked a different question. 'Are our friends along the drive all right? I was afraid I might have passed my wretched germs on to Venetia.'

'She seems in perfect health – they all do, except that I can't speak for Fiona Gilmour, who wasn't visible. I feel slightly uncomfortable about *her*. If Fernando took her away just to bring Venetia to heel, which I now strongly suspect, then it was a wickedly unkind thing to do. The poor girl probably won't have come across such behaviour before.'

Felipe gave a little shrug; then, tired of his Spanish family, let himself out of the house and walked through the garden to the stables. He had a present for Venetia – some verses of Antonio Machado's that he'd set to music because she'd said how beautiful they were, and for once he was almost sure that his song did them justice. She was having a wonderfully liberating effect on his music, he'd noticed. In fact her effect was liberating altogether, but he'd been careful to stay within the bounds of their quiet companionship. Fernando would judge him a fool not to hurry things along, but he didn't mind the slowness of the love affair – he was good at being patient.

He walked under the archway and into the courtyard; the tubs and urns weren't blazing with colour yet, but evidence of Venetia's loving attention was everywhere. The fountain had been persuaded to play again, and a tracery of new leaves was already throwing shadows on the whitewashed walls. The early evening was soft and fine, and he found the Marriotts sitting in their favourite, sunlit spot, in the sheltered angle between two sides of the house. Venetia got up at once to greet him, and he wanted to wrap his arms about her, but what came naturally in front of Fernando seemed harder with her uncle and aunt looking on.

'Dear Felipe ... you're better at last. What a beastly bug it must have been,' she said warmly.

He bowed over Edwina's hand with his usual grace, and she examined him critically but with kindness.

'Rather wan, even now! Forget the sherry, William,' she commanded. 'Pour the boy a glass of good red wine.'

While this was being done Felipe offered

134

his rolled-up sheet of manuscript paper to Venetia. 'I was feverish, but determined not to be entirely idle!'

She glanced at it with a flush of pleasure in her face. 'Oh, what a pity I can't hear it straight away, but Fiona will be out in a minute, and she's rather in need of company. A diet of Fascists is getting the poor girl down!'

But Felipe was less keen to see Fiona. Instead of the lovely ease he knew with Venetia, this other girl aroused a different, disturbing current of emotion – three parts dislike mixed with something he recognised as unfamiliar excitement. Fiona Gilmour had no interest in him; he knew that. But still she asked of him what she required of every man – that he should recognise her beauty. Her faint smile now invited him to look at her and be pleased with what he saw. He sat as far away from her as he could, and clung to Venetia's hand beneath the table. It felt like a life-line amid the danger Fiona Gilmour represented.

The following morning he called again, earlier than usual. He had an errand in Ronda and wanted Venetia to go with him. She reluctantly refused, determined to finish her translations of Luc's stories before Edwina's spring flood of work began.

'If you want a passenger, why not take

Fiona?' she suggested. 'All the weeks she's been here, she's never seen the famous Tajo Gorge.'

His expression said that he was about to refuse, and she took hold of his hand in a little gesture of pleading. *'Please,* Felipe – an outing would do her good at the moment. Your wretched brother, whom I *don't* much wish God to preserve, has hurt her rather badly, but she can't stop hoping he'll change his mind and suddenly come back to sweep her off again. If he did show up, I'd love to be able to tell him that she's out having a happy time with you!'

Felipe touched her cheek gently. 'You make a good friend, Venetia, and I'm not at all sorry that my handsome brother hasn't made his usual impression on *you* at least. I doubt if Fiona will think much of me as a substitute, but I'll invite her if you think she'll come.'

She went to knock on Fiona's door, explaining that it would be a kindness to make up for her own failure to go with Felipe on the drive to Ronda. She waved them away at last, discovering that the only reward for so much virtuous effort on other people's behalf was to leave her strangely discouraged and extremely tired.

At intervals throughout a day spent grappling with the beautiful complexities of Luc's French prose, she found herself wondering how the excursion to Ronda was going. It was a lovely enough place for anyone to enjoy, and Felipe would be a charming guide, provided Fiona didn't make it clear with every breath she drew that she was wishing to be there with someone else.

They arrived back later than expected, the road being always a dramatic one to negotiate even when tackled in broad daylight, and Venetia concluded from that with some relief that the outing had been a success.

Puzzlement only came afterwards, from the terms in which they separately described it. Fiona seemed to have encountered a Felipe Quinones Venetia didn't recognise – bold and dashing at the wheel of a car, and charmingly forceful in his arrangement of the day. Bemused by this unlikely picture, she later heard Felipe making no mention of his passenger's beauty or bright spirit; instead it was her gentleness and docility that had taken him so pleasantly by surprise! Still, the odd excursion seemed to have worked – Felipe had quite forgotten that he'd set out a convalescent invalid, and Fiona had begun to smile again, as if recovery from Fernando might be possible after all.

Nine

Looking back afterwards, it seemed to Venetia that Felipe's drive to Ronda with Fiona had been the single event that set in motion everything that subsequently happened. At the time she was merely aware of them all being in suspense: William impatient for the first signs of his visitors from across the Gibraltar Straits; Edwina almost willing the early trickle of colour that would signal the arrival of spring; and Fiona still hoping that Fernando would admit to needing her. Restlessness, quite unlike the usual serenity of Las Cuadras, seemed to be in the air, and as if he'd noticed it himself Felipe made a suggestion one day that Venetia reckoned was exactly what they needed.

'Why don't we arrange a visit to the Coto Doñana? Easter or Pentecost will mean huge crowds of pilgrims – combining in a way only known to Spaniards, I'm afraid, genuine religious fervour with days and nights of riotous carousing in the open air!'

She knew that people came from all over Spain to attend the Rocío there – though

William's personal pilgrimage would be not to the Virgin's shrine, but to the great bird sanctuary nearby, in the delta of the Guadalquivir.

Felipe's idea was debated over supper, and pronounced very good. The excursion began to take shape, and Juan had to be warned that the Marriotts would be away from home for several days. From then on he took to watching William with huge, imploring eyes, unable to believe that he was going to be left behind. At last, resistance crumbling under this silent pressure, William went to call on Blanca and wrung from her permission to take Juan with them. But the following morning brought a startling development: Manolo Quinones had decided to take charge of the expedition. His English tenants, not always impressed no doubt by the way Spaniards did things, should be impressed *this* time. He would play the part of host himself, aided by Blanca as well as Felipe, and the Marriotts and Fiona need do nothing but prepare to be his guests.

Edwina made no objection to the extended party – not sure of being able to distinguish a shrike from a booted or any other sort of eagle, she rather welcomed the prospect of pleasure that didn't entirely depend on birds. It was left to William and Venetia to exchange rueful glances.

'Not quite the visit we had in mind,' he said sadly. 'Manolo means to be kind, of course, but he'll insist on bringing La Paloma's luxury with him. We shall live like lords in the *hostal*, thanks to his cook and his catering arrangements, and his Range Rover will thunder through the reserve, disturbing every bird for miles.'

'We could call it off ... there's still time,' Venetia suggested.

'And then be found to have gone anyway by ourselves? No, I'm afraid that would be intolerably rude. We shall just have to enjoy what we can, and slip off again later on, without announcing it to anyone next time.'

But even William looked more cheerful when Manolo decreed that cars would take them no further than Sanlucar; after crossing the river there they would travel by methods that were traditional in the Coto – on horseback or in horse-drawn carriages. All the necessary arrangements were being seen to, he said with a sly smile at Edwina – even down to the supply of chilled fino that his dear friends would require *en route*!

With Juan's excitement at fever pitch and the rest of them anticipating varying amounts of pleasure, an early hour was fixed for setting off on the day. But in the pre-dawn darkness Venetia was awoken by unmistakably familiar symptoms. Blurred vision, a stunning headache and bouts of sickness were the certain onset of a severe migraine, something not experienced in all the weeks she'd been at Rosario. She was returning, white-faced and shaking, from her third visit to the bathroom when Edwina came to find out why she wasn't up.

'I don't think I can go ... it's hopeless,' she muttered. 'I couldn't even get as far as Sanlucar without being sick again and again, and after that ...' She closed her eyes, unable to contemplate the carriage ride that was to follow.

'Of course there's no question of it,' Edwina agreed at once. 'Bed's the only place for you, my poor child ... I'll tell William. Fiona must still go, of course, but we shall stay here.'

'*No*, my dear aunt.' With a huge effort Venetia focused on her concerned face and managed to speak firmly. 'You can't help by staying, and I shall recover best on my own. In any case we can't reduce Manolo's party by a half. Just make my apologies, please, and especially insist to Felipe that *he* mustn't feel he ought to stay behind.'

After consultation with William, Edwina agreed that she was right. She was consigned to Encarnita's devoted care, and thankfully heard them set off an hour later. For the moment it was all she asked of life: to be left alone in the merciful dimness of her room.

By the following morning, still frail but recovering, she was glad to move outside and sit in the gentle warmth of the sun. In the rather pleasant lassitude that followed the previous day's torment she was sorry to hear Encarnita's voice talking to a visitor. It was worse when she opened her eyes to see who it was that loomed above the small, dumpy figure of the maid.

'I was in Consuela's shop yesterday evening,' Ian Gilmour said briefly. 'Everyone had heard – from Encarnita I suppose – that the Señorita Venetia was not only *muy indispuesta* but was here alone, for some reason. I thought I'd better take a look-in.'

It was such undreamed-of thoughtfulness that she had to struggle not to give her astonishment away. 'Not alone – Encarnita's been looking after me like a mother. It's only an ill-timed migraine, and I managed to persuade the others to go to the Coto without me. You must have heard about the trip from Juan – he's been unable to think of anything else for days.'

'And so has his grandfather, I gathered – no cheese-paring for Manolo Quinones. No nonsense, either, about the simple life, even in the middle of a wetland wilderness.'

A gleam of amusement stole into Venetia's pale face. 'Poor Uncle Will ... it's exactly what he feared! But I'm bound to say my aunt was preparing to let rip and wallow in Manolo's luxury!'

Her smile was full of affection for her relatives – and it was an illuminating smile, Gilmour noticed. In the course of their acquaintance she hadn't yet smiled at him like that; he would have remembered if she had. Unlike his niece, or the women he'd known in London, she made no gift of herself in casual encounters; strangers were made to work for the pleasure of getting to know her. Wanting her to give something away, he chose a question carefully.

'I rather liked your father's wife, but stepmothers are traditionally unpopular, so perhaps you *don't*?'

'I like her very much,' she contradicted him. 'We didn't take to each other immediately, but that was because after losing my own mother I didn't welcome the idea of a replacement. Arlette proved patient and kind – in practical ways, not being at all sentimental. I was even taught what French women seem born knowing ... the right clothes to wear!'

She broke off to smile at Encarnita, who came bustling out with a tray of coffee for the *señor* and a glass of mineral water for the *señorita* – who, she said approvingly, had been *muy valiente* the day before.

'That was a very Spanish comment,' Gilmour pointed out when she'd retired into the house again. 'They still respect

143

courage here.'

'Hence the undying tradition of bull-fighting!' Venetia observed wryly. 'But there wasn't anything very brave about putting up with a headache.' She glanced at his with-drawn expression, and decided that she *would* give courage a chance now.

'Was it your view of Spain that brought you back here?' He would either, she thought, administer a brutal snub or decide that he'd been neighbourly long enough and walk away. Instead, slowly and deliberately, he began to talk about himself.

'I suppose you could say that Spain itself was the cause of my troubles. I always remembered it as having clung, at great cost, to old ways and old values. By com-parison, my life in London seemed to have no value at all ... I was a celebrity, God help me ... a gimcrack, tinsel thing surrounded by the sort of people who live to fawn on the famous. It wasn't an upbringing that I wanted for my son.'

He fell silent, but his expression as he looked back into the past was so haunted that, unable to leave him confronting it alone, Venetia prompted him quietly.

'You wanted to bring your son here?'

He nodded and finally went on. 'My wife had a different idea. Even London was becoming too slow for the successful New York woman she was, so Andalucía was

144

bound to sound to her like the end of the world. We quarrelled once too often and too bitterly over dinner at a friend's house. I walked out and drove home when I shouldn't have done. On the way I met two drug-hazed joy-riders in a stolen car, head-on. They were killed and I spent the next three months in hospital having my face put together again.'

There was another silence which she finally managed to break. 'What happened … to your wife and son?'

'They eventually went back to New York. I expect I was impossible to live with, and Elaine asked for a divorce. Ranald was ten then; I haven't seen him since. He's a bit older than Juan.' The brief sentences fell on her like blows, and felt just as painful. Then, as if the past had been dealt with, he spoke in a different tone of voice. 'Have you enjoyed my books … or *not* enjoyed them … or, worse still, perhaps not read them at all?'

'Not read,' she admitted. 'I'm afraid you're talking to a woman who even prefers what Jane Austen actually wrote, and rages at the costumed travesties of the real thing on the box!'

'I should have guessed, of course.' A glimmer of amusement transformed his face, showing her the different, relaxed man he must have been. 'Don Alberto, who occasionally beats me at chess, says that you're giving English lessons to some of his flock. Does that mean you're intending to stay here?'

'Not for ever, but until the summer at least. What about you?' They were suddenly getting on so well that it seemed possible to ask.

'Not for ever,' he repeated unhelpfully. 'I've seen you out walking with Felipe Quinones. Does that mean you like him?'

A hint of derision in the way the question was asked made her hackles rise; they couldn't get on well for long, it seemed. 'I like him very much,' she said fiercely, '... very much *indeed*.'

'You've made it clear; no need to shout. Does it also mean that you could stomach a connection with the Quinones family?'

Anger put colour back into her face and a spark of hostility in her eyes. 'You're like everybody else here – whatever happens, don't let the blood-soaked past die! Why not judge Felipe for the man he is, instead of despising him because *his* uncles and *your* father were on different sides in a war that tore Spain apart? I can stomach *him* easily enough, and the rest of his family don't concern me.'

'If you decided to partner him, of course they would concern you.' But it was said quietly, almost sadly, as if he was talking to an unthinking child. '"No man is an island

146

entire of himself" – didn't someone say that?'

'Someone did, but it's an unfair way to end the argument.'

There was no doubt about it now – his smile was warm and sweet when he meant it to be. She could see easily enough the charismatic celebrity he'd once been.

'You're right ... it *is* unfair; and I've also remembered that I came to enquire after your health, not to set you all on end! If there's nothing helpful I can do instead, I'll leave you in peace.'

She shook her head, made helpless by the change in his manner. It was one thing to hate the fact of what he'd done, quite another to cling to that lack of forgiveness when she knew how it had come about. Now, she was more inclined to grieve for the ruin of his life, and for those few minutes of time that he could never hope to cancel and live differently.

'Thank you, but Encarnita is very happily in charge,' she finally muttered.

On an impulse that she couldn't explain she held out her hand and after a moment's hesitation he took it in a firm, warm grip. It was a mistake to be touching her, even as impersonally as this; he'd forgotten how soft her skin would feel, and how delicate the bones of her hand. She was released immediately, and the next moment he was gone, without even bothering to say good-bye. For no good reason that she could think of, she suddenly wanted to weep, and had to blame the after-effects of her migraine for the fact that the courtyard seemed empty without him and the morning not as warm as before.

She explained to Encarnita that she would take a little stroll and, accustomed by now to this strange habit, the maid only recommended her earnestly not to go far, since she was in a weakened condition and not yet at all *vigorosa*. The advice was good, Venetia discovered. She'd got no further than a vantage-point overlooking the valley before she was glad to rest on the seat conveniently provided by a fallen tree. Watching a kestrel lazily quartering his territory, she wondered how the Coto expedition was going; but the immense view spread out before her brought Ian Gilmour to mind again. It was easy enough to see why this harshly beautiful land had ensnared him in the dream of a different life, but the appalling result had been death, and the destruction of his own happiness.

'*Buenos días, señorita!*' On the soft ground she'd heard no one approach, and the unexpected greeting made her spin round.

It came from a man she would have preferred *not* to meet on a deserted hillside; she didn't like Rosario's mayor at any time, but found his inspection of her now particularly objectionable. There was no danger: he had a wife, and a reputation to maintain, and she wasn't – she felt almost sure – voluptuous enough to inflame a man whose taste was reputed to run to the sort of fleshy women that Rubens had liked to paint. All the same, it was a relief that he showed no signs of coming to sit beside her.

'I can escort you down the hill, *señorita*, but not linger here,' he explained regretfully. 'I'm late already for an appointment.'

'Thank you, Don Ramón, but I *shall* linger a little longer, enjoying the view.'

His full lips curved into a smile that she perfectly understood – hard-working Spaniards couldn't spare time to sit and admire the scenery, and anyway they'd certainly find more profitable things to do with its seclusion. He gave a mock-humble bow and set off down the track, leaving her to wonder why he'd been there at all. He was urban man personified, from his smoothly swept-back hair to his expensive Gucci loafers; she would as soon have expected to see Manolo Quinones tramping about the countryside.

She walked home, and was being welcomed by Encarnita as if from some perilous expedition, when the third surprise encounter of the day began to unfold. An antiquated car drew up outside, and a moment later a tall, elderly, but still upright man walked through the archway into the courtyard. He spoke in English, but almost hesitantly, as if it were a language he hadn't occasion to use very often.

'Miss Marriott? My name is Duncan Gilmour. My great-niece wrote to tell me that she is staying with you.'

Venetia crossed the space between them, holding out her hand. 'Yes, but you've called at a bad time, Mr Gilmour – Fiona is with my aunt and uncle and some friends in the Coto Doñana until tomorrow evening.'

'You didn't care to go with them?' he asked with a directness that reminded her of his nephew.

'I wasn't able to.' She decided to take a leaf out of his book and simply ask what she wanted to know. 'Have you driven here specially from Seville?'

'I was on my way home from a visit to Granada – this was an alternative route and I dislike motorways. I called merely on impulse; it's no matter that Fiona isn't here.' He raised his tweed hat as if to say the visit was over, but with the sunlight striking his silver head and time-worn face she saw him only as old and vulnerable, not the inhospitable curmudgeon that Fiona had described.

'It's nearly lunchtime,' she said impulsively. 'Won't you stay, or at least join me in a *copa* before you go? I'm by myself for the moment except for the maid.'

'I'm not alone either – my servant is driving the car, being a little less ancient than I am myself!'

Venetia smiled at the dry humour, finding him altogether less forbidding than she'd been led to expect. 'Sit down then, please, while I ask Encarnita to look after him.'

When she returned, with chilled wine and glasses, Duncan Gilmour was staring at a flare of gold where a mimosa was just coming into bloom against a sheltered wall. He hauled himself punctiliously to his feet until she sat down, and asked permission to serve the wine for her. Altogether, she thought, with his formal clothes and speech and manners he belonged to a fast-disappearing age, and she was reminded of what Ian Gilmour had said about his life in present-day Spain. But presumably he stayed because he would now be still more out of place anywhere else.

'Fiona mentioned that the two of you were at Oxford together,' he observed when he was back in his chair again. 'Perhaps it's a foolish thing to say, but you don't *look* as if you would have been my great-niece's close friend.'

She could see what he probably meant, but acquitted him of any desire to wound, and gave an honest answer. 'We weren't close friends then – Fiona was *much* more of a dasher than me! But I've got to know her better here, and my aunt and uncle and I have grown very fond of her.'

He didn't comment on this, and sipped his manzanilla before he spoke again. 'She was hoping to stay with me, I think, but one grows selfish in old age, Miss Marriott. Afterwards I realised that I should at least have made sure she was all right. I can see now, of course, that she's much better off here with you.'

'She blamed her difficulty with you on a family quarrel,' Venetia pointed out with a glimmer of amusement, 'not on the selfishness of old age!'

A faint answering smile lurked in the depths of Duncan's neatly trimmed beard. 'Well, yes, there was *that* as well. My brother Hamish – Fiona's grandfather – and I didn't dislike each other as children, but as we grew up he came to hate everything I valued about Spain, and our differences of opinion were made worse, of course, by the Civil War.'

'It's changing, though, isn't it ... Spain, I mean?' Venetia suggested. 'Even my uncle, who loves it deeply, says so. That's why he and Aunt Edwina came to Rosario – the changes seem less here.'

'I ignore the changes,' Duncan said truthfully, 'but in any case they're more superficial than people think. The essence of the place is in its magnificent, untameable terrain, which *can't* be changed, thank God, and in its extraordinary past, which is already written. The froth of hideous development along the coast won't last; nor, I suspect, will today's slightly reckless enjoyment of democracy and prosperity – neither of these things being very traditional Spanish attributes!'

She had a vision of Duncan Gilmour matched against Manolo Quinones: immovable object and irresistible force; the battle would be fascinating but the result uncertain. It was tempting to mention his nephew in the hope that one old rancour might at last have been allowed to melt, but Duncan was speaking again.

'Fiona mentioned Holy Week ... talked of bringing a car into Seville. I doubt if I dissuaded her enough – the truth is that it would be nearly impossible then.'

'Thank you for your advice – I'll tell her that we must travel in and out by train to see the processions. The ones I watched in Jerez as a child were memorable, but probably not to be compared with Seville's.'

Duncan nodded but refused her repeated offer of lunch. 'Kind of you, but we should be on our way, if my Sancho Panza can be prised away from your Dulcinea in the kitchen! I don't encourage chatter in the car, and the poor fellow gets very bored just turning the steering wheel. It's one of the few things I'd change about a Spaniard if I could – his need to always be talking!'

Venetia retrieved the chauffeur and led him back to the car. Then she smiled warmly at Duncan Gilmour. 'Fiona will be disappointed to have missed you, but it was an unexpected pleasure for me.'

He bowed over her hand in a way that spoke of a lifetime spent in Spain, but continued to hold it for a moment while he stared at her. She was so little like his great-niece – so 'right' and 'charming', were the words in his mind – that he found himself tempted to change his mind about leaving. Instead, something equally surprising framed itself in words.

'Provided that I'm not expected to entertain you both, you and Fiona are welcome to stay with me during the Semana Santa,' he heard himself say. 'I live in the Santa Cruz area, conveniently close by the cathedral.'

She thanked him gratefully, and he was driven away, still trying to explain to himself the reason for that rash invitation. It had something to do with her quietness, he thought, but something also to do with a smile that reminded him of a girl he'd known long ago. Laura had been already married to another expatriate before he met her, and in those long-ago days one simply didn't consider stealing another man's wife.

154

He'd stayed lonely instead and grown selfish, and forgotten until Venetia Marriott had smiled at him what a pleasure it could be to look at a woman's face.

Ten

It was so late the following evening when the Coto adventurers returned that they all went straight to bed. Venetia had to wait until her aunt appeared at the breakfast table the next day to ask how the expedition had gone. Edwina sounded enthusiastic about the wildlife, and very appreciative of Manolo's hospitality, but she seemed to lack her usual gusto.

'I hope Uncle Will and Juan had the lovely time they expected,' Venetia had to suggest, when for once her aunt seemed to need prompting.

'Oh, seventh heaven, both of them: more geese of every known variety than even Will had seen in his life, and – the *ne plus ultra* – a sighting of an imperial eagle! My brother can die happy now.'

'What about the rest of you ... I hope you didn't just loll about, consuming Manolo's food and wine?'

155

'I studied the flora, as is my wont,' Edwina said with dignity, 'and very remarkable it is. The others amused themselves I know not how – well, it probably took all Manolo's time deciding what we were going to eat next. And I believe there was some talk of Felipe and Blanca teaching Fiona to ride a horse.'

'Felipe would have been good at that,' Venetia suggested: 'patient and kind.'

Edwina's nod seemed to agree, then she applied herself to buttering her toast. 'You're better, I can see – we rather hated going off and leaving you.' She heaped more sugar in her coffee than usual and stirred it vigorously. 'How much longer are we to have the pleasure of Fiona's company, by the way?'

Faintly surprised by the sudden question, Venetia stared at her. 'I don't know; she's not in any hurry to move on to Germany, but she'll have to go before long.'

Still stirring, Edwina stared at the coffee in her cup as if she hadn't seen it before. 'She's a pleasure to look at, very lively and engaging in her ways ... seductive, I suppose, is the word a man would use. All the same, I shall be rather glad when she leaves.'

Venetia digested this in silence for a moment. 'It would be difficult to *ask* her to go,' she suggested finally.

'I dare say it would be impossible; she's

156

not some housemaid who's been caught filching the family silver.' Edwina glanced up at last, and suddenly her face looked so old and anxious that Venetia understood her anxiety.

'You wouldn't mind a bit if our lodger and Fernando were wrapped up in each other,' her niece observed. 'So what *is* upsetting you ... was Fiona getting on too well with Felipe? Dear aunt, she needs bolstering up at the moment and Felipe knows that his brother has treated her cruelly. I *wanted* him to be kind.'

Edwina examined her niece's serene face and couldn't bring herself to say that Felipe's kindness had been noticeable enough for his sister to comment on with her usual barbed amusement.

Venetia walked around the table and kissed the top of her aunt's grey head. 'Stop worrying,' she suggested gently. 'Fiona has been hurt by Fernando; she isn't planning to hurt Felipe or me, just to make up for it.'

This ended the conversation, but its subject didn't appear, and finally Venetia went to knock on her door.

'You've been learning to ride, I gather ... painful?' she enquired with a smile.

Fiona grimaced and agreed. The visit had been enjoyable, she said without any notice-able enthusiasm – the Whitsuntide pilgrim-age, of course, would have made it more exciting. 'What about you? Everyone missed you, of course, even Manolo.'

'Most unlikely – he and I fight shy of each other! Now, I can see that you're trying to work but I must just tell you what happened while you were away – a surprise visit by your great-uncle!'

Fiona's pale face flushed with sudden colour. 'Duncan Gilmour came *here*? I can't believe it ... I thought he was like some medieval anchorite, never to be winkled out into the light of day.'

'Well, at least he broke a journey home from Granada. I think he was concerned about you ... even admitted he'd been selfish! As a matter of fact I liked him very much – he has charming manners and a nice, dry sense of humour.'

'None of which can I say, hand on heart, that I observed myself. You aren't a Gilmour from the wrong side of the family fence, of course – perhaps that made the difference.'

'Well, he's prepared to have us *both* for Semana Santa, as long as we don't make a nuisance of ourselves, and try to park a car outside his house; if we go we must go by train.'

Fiona's dazzling smile finally reappeared. 'Well done, Venetia! Of course we want to go. We can't miss the high point of the Spanish year.'

Venetia reminded her kindly that between

now and then there was still a little time in which to catch up on work. Then she went away to interrupt William in his study. To him she described the brief meeting with the Mayor up on the hillside.

'I still can't imagine what he was doing there – up to no good, prejudice is inclined to say,' she admitted with a rueful smile, 'but that's only because I don't like him.'

'For once prejudice might be wrong, my dear. I found a note from Ian Gilmour waiting for me this morning – he says he's sure a pair of eagles are nesting at the top of the sierra; if so, it's going to be necessary to keep the wretched weekend sportsmen from disturbing them. Perhaps Don Ramón had gone up to see for himself. I shall go and call on him later on. It's wonderful news ... almost more exciting than going to the Coto!'

He was so entranced that she resisted the temptation to mention Ian Gilmour's visit. However much he liked the man, for the moment the eagles were a more urgent matter.

'You still look washed out, my dear,' William nevertheless managed to notice. 'You must rest, not work, today.'

'I'm afraid it has to be work,' she insisted. 'All the signs are that Aunt Edwina is about to go into action, and I still haven't quite finished translating Luc's stories.'

'They've taxed all your skill, I think,' William suggested gently, 'and perhaps all your fortitude as well. My impression is that they mean a great deal to you.'

She nodded, reluctant to talk about the poignancy of hearing Luc's voice for the last time in his beautiful, succinct prose. Instead she spoke of something that had unexpectedly disappointed her. 'I gave Felipe the stories to read ... I wanted to share them with him. He tried to sound generous but I don't think he really enjoyed them.'

'The vagaries of human behaviour observed by a Frenchman's realistic but compassionate eye? They should have appealed to him, surely?'

Venetia shook her head. 'I worked it out in the end: even dear Felipe wanted something more extreme! It's a very Spanish reaction – the death-or-glory tradition of the *corrida* breeds a craving for high drama in these people.'

She left William without mentioning a different disappointment: she certainly hadn't wanted her gentle Spaniard to stay behind with her instead of going to the Coto, and of course he would have felt obliged to look after Fiona. But all the same she'd expected him to hurry to enquire about her this morning. The omission seemed so strange that she wondered if he could be unwell again himself.

Instead it was Juan who appeared, later in the morning, to give her a shy hug and hope that she was properly *recuperata*.

'Tío Felipe hasn't come with you today,' she said, smiling at the grave little boy. '*He*'s not sick, I hope?'

'No, Venetia, he's in his music room ... I went in and heard him playing the guitar, and then the piano, very loud!'

Now she could explain it to herself. He'd been separated from his precious instruments for several days. If a piece of composition in his head insisted on being written down, it was what he would have to do first.

He came at last, just as she went outside to join her aunt and uncle, already entertaining Don Alberto on the terrace before dinner. He kissed her hand and cheek, and enquired tenderly after her health.

'We *all* missed you, Venetia ... even my father! This is his gift of special wine, chosen to help you recover strength, he says.'

She was about to thank him, but in the same moment Fiona came out of the house and walked towards them. The evening sunlight struck her red-gold hair, making her extravagantly beautiful. Venetia saw Felipe's face change as he looked at her, and knew that nothing on earth could have prevented him from giving himself away. Beyond the slightest doubt she knew now what had

161

been keeping him away all the long day. With a meaningless smile that he didn't even see, she murmured that she would take the wine indoors.

When she eventually rejoined them outside Felipe was in control of himself and talking calmly to Edwina, and Fiona was pretending to listen to Don Alberto's account of Consuela instructing him to give his house its spring-time coat of whitewash. The scene looked normal ... nothing had changed; they were the usual pleasant gathering of friends watching the sun set and the first evening stars appear. But Venetia knew that another significant milestone in their lives had just been reached and no amount of wishing would take them back to where they'd been before. Ian Gilmour had been right after all, and she'd been quite wrong to believe that this time there was no harm Fiona could do her.

The company broke up, and a rather silent supper was eaten before Fiona went off to her own room, to write letters she said. William took the little stroll that he always insisted on before going to bed, and only Edwina was left with her niece, apparently immersed in a book.

'I find Henry James fairly impenetrable myself,' she finally said, 'but you haven't turned a page for the past ten minutes. Shall we both admit that what we're really doing is thinking how much we'd like to send our guest packing?'

Looking at her aunt's face, Venetia registered again the resemblance to a kind, sagacious horse, but it would have been dishonest as well as pointless to deny what she'd just said.

'It's too late, I'm afraid, even if we could bring ourselves to do it. Felipe's reaction to Fiona is worse for being delayed; she's like a germ he's been slow to catch. He's simply helpless in the face of so much beauty. But if Fernando beckoned, she'd run, and it would be Felipe's turn to be devastated.'

'What about *you*?' Edwina asked fiercely. 'I don't care what *they* do to each other.'

Venetia managed a little shrug. 'I think Felipe is very fond of me, as I am of him; that hasn't changed, but it isn't enough compared with the force of nature that Fiona represents!'

'Well, forgive our guest if you can, and Felipe if you must,' Edwina snapped, 'but at least try to hate Fernando! I've never seen why we should be expected to love those who deliberately trespass against us – I'm not even sure that God should.'

It made Venetia almost smile as she tried to explain. 'I tried hating years ago, because I loved someone whose life was being eaten away by illness. Before he died he made me understand that hating achieves nothing at

163

all, except more destruction. I've no right to hate Felipe because he finds he doesn't love me quite enough to blot Fiona out of his mind. If she'd set out to hurt me I might try to hate *her*, but she works by instinct, not reason.'

There was a moment's pause, then Venetia spoke in a different tone of voice. 'What about you, dear aunt … no misread signals in your past, no one taken for granted who wasn't yours to take?'

By Edwina's reckoning Felipe's signals had been clear enough, but she could see that she wasn't meant to say so. 'No signals at all,' she said regretfully instead. 'I hadn't the looks for them, of course, but in any case I made up my mind at an early age that I was going to stay with Will. There was a girl once that he seemed taken with, but I knew she wouldn't do.'

Venetia spared a thought for the man who'd perhaps wanted a different life and then abandoned it because it couldn't be made to include his twin sister.

'I suppose he and I both missed experiences we might have had,' Edwina was reflecting now. 'There's this much to be said for being a Buddhist – at least we could have looked forward to coming back for another chance.'

Venetia attempted to cheer them both up: 'Risky, though – suppose you came back as

Don Ramón's next wife!'

'I should give him a very bad time,' Edwina pointed out with pleasure. 'Will went to see him this afternoon, to remind him that, deplorable as Spain's conservation record has been in the past, it's required to mend its ways now that it's a member of the EU! The Mayor nodded a lot and promised nothing, smiling villain that he is. I expect we shall have to watch over the eagles ourselves.'

With this new problem now occupying her mind, she said good-night and went to bed, but Venetia stayed where she was, knowing that it was time come to terms with what she now knew. At the heart of it was her own mistake – she simply hadn't given a shy man the encouragement he needed because she hadn't been sure enough of wanting to. It was sod's law operating as usual that, when it was too late, she knew how much she'd come to count on Felipe Quinones.

The following morning Fiona appeared as she was arranging mimosa in a green Manises pottery jug for the breakfast table.

'Hello,' Venetia greeted her calmly. 'Are you eating with us this morning?'

'Thanks, but no – I've had coffee.' Fiona was making an effort to seem unconcerned but a flush of bright colour gave her away. 'Felipe insists on showing me Arcos de la

Frontera – he says it's the most beautiful of all the white towns.'

'I'm sure he's right,' Venetia agreed, pleased to see that her hands weren't trembling; then she put down the plate she'd aimlessly picked up. 'Shall we be honest with each other? He's suddenly woken up and *seen* you, and now he can't see anything else. You aren't to blame for that, but I *shall* blame you if he's just being used to remind Fernando that you still exist. Felipe deserves better than that.'

She spoke quietly, but Fiona felt the underlying prick of steel, as she was meant to. It goaded her into sounding flustered for once. 'You're angry, of course, and you've every right to be, Venetia. But I promise you I didn't set out to snare him. Don't you remember? I used to rather pour scorn on him. Now, of course, I know how very sweet he is ... so different from his brother.'

Venetia's gaze held hers steadily across the table. 'What happens if Fernando discovers and decides he doesn't like the new arrangement?'

Looking more sombre than usual, Fiona shook her head. 'He won't care; he might even be rather amused by it; Felipe can have what he couldn't be bothered to keep himself.'

There was silence for a moment, each of

them lost in unprofitable thought. Then Venetia made a little gesture with her hands, pushing it away.

'What a mess we've all got into. Go and enjoy Arcos, for heaven's sake; but you might remind Felipe, and yourself as well occasionally, that you came to Spain to advance your academic career!'

Fiona walked towards her and planted an apologetic little kiss on her cheek. 'Don't hate me, please, even though we've lost our way a bit. We were going to do without the men who complicate our lives so dreadfully, but I suppose the truth is that we *can't* do without them, poor fools that we are.' She managed a tremulous smile as she thought of something else. 'Do you re-member saying that we weren't likely to find anyone here to fight over? Famous last words! Why do feminists forget that it's in our blood and bones to fight over the nearest male?'

Venetia shook her head. 'I thought the males were supposed to fight over *us*. In any case, let me tell you, I'm not fighting – *you* can have the entire Quinones clan, with Manolo thrown in for good measure. Now on your way, *amiga* – my aunt and uncle will be wanting their breakfast.'

She managed a faint smile and, after a moment's hesitation, Fiona took the hint and left. The worst was over; Venetia told herself she could manage now quite well. Acceptance, not hatred ... she hoped the ghost of Luc was smiling at her; it was what she surely deserved.

Eleven

The tempo of *pueblo* life was speeding up. It was already mid-March and any day now the full flowering of spring would burst upon them; no hour of daylight could be wasted. The men had begun setting out soon after dawn, mules clip-clopping beside them. Tractors were all very well, but only these intelligent animals could safely work the sheer slopes of the sierra. At the end of the day men and mules returned to the safety of the *pueblo* – that was how it had always been, how it still was at Rosario.

But for how much longer? William wondered as he watched the daily ritual. For every country-minded child like Juan Esteban, there were a dozen others whose only ambition was to escape the labouring life their parents had known. It was a saddening thought to take with him up the hill each morning, but there was comfort on the walk as well; the great birds *were* nesting

– he'd seen their majestic flights about the summit often enough to be sure of it. The wonderful Spanish landscape and the creatures whose rightful habitat it was were not yet so very changed after all.

As he made his way home one morning Ian Gilmour came out and hailed him as he passed El Perdido's door. 'I was hoping to see you. Join me in a glass of beer.'

The kitchen of the *cortijo* was as bleak as it was spotlessly clean. William doubted if a woman would be content with such spartan simplicity, but the question didn't seem to arise. Thanks to Encarnita, they were well abreast of all the *pueblo* gossip, and there'd been no hint of any female visitors to soften this strange man's isolation.

'I've been up the hill,' William said while his beer was being poured; 'everything seems as it should be.'

'Not necessarily, I'm afraid,' his host answered curtly. 'If you want to know what's going on here, patronise Luís's bar! Hints were being dropped that sent me to see the Mayor. Perez wasn't telling what he knew, but I still have friends in Madrid, and they found the information for me. The old *duque* who owned much of this sierra, including the land the castle stands on, died last year. His family in Madrid, with no interest in it themselves, finally agreed to sell.'

'Not to Don Ramón, surely – can he

169

possibly have that kind of wealth?'

Gilmour smiled at William's anxious expression. 'Not the Mayor – the new owner is Manolo Quinones! A worse or a better prospect, would you say?'

'Quinones *couldn't* be worse.' But it sounded so harsh that William apologetically explained: 'Sorry, but I'm afraid my niece and I have agreed *not* to like the Mayor!'

'Sensible of you both, I'd say, although I'm not enchanted with your landlord either. Your niece would reckon that I'm prejudiced against a family that supported Franco in the Civil War and afterwards.'

William thought it was exactly what Venetia would reckon, and cast around for encouragement to offer instead.

'Manolo was kind enough to take us to the Coto Doñana recently – I think you know that. He wouldn't spring to mind as a man with a burning interest in natural history or conservation, but he's too clear-sighted not to see the folly of destroying what makes this country unique. Perhaps more to the point, he lives here himself; he can't want to spoil the treasures on his own doorstep.'

Remembering what Felipe Quinones had once said of his father's attitude towards the hilltop ruin, Gilmour didn't look convinced. 'You may be right,' he answered finally; 'let's hope you are. But you're on better terms with him than I am, so I'll leave you to persuade him not to try to tart up the castle into some sort of tourist attraction.'

'I shall do my best,' William promised, 'and so will Edwina and Venetia ... though on second thoughts my dear sister's intervention might do harm rather than good. You may have noticed that she's sometimes a trifle outspoken!'

'Not Edwina then,' his host agreed with a grin, 'but I don't suppose your niece will mind concentrating her efforts on Manolo's sons.'

William was unable to commit himself on this, but he thought about it on his walk home. Even *he* hadn't missed the change in Venetia from the pale, thin girl they'd met in Jerez, and Edwina had been definite about it – they had Felipe to thank for the improvement. But now, confusingly, his sister had taken to muttering darkly about *both* Manolo's sons and seemed inclined to think she should hate them equally. More awkwardly, she'd withdrawn some tacit approval previously given to Fiona; there was tension in the air now instead of their old happy companionship, but all William knew was that the inmates of La Paloma were involved in it.

He put the worry aside with a faint sigh, determined to concentrate on a matter that he *could* do something about. Ian Gilmour had entrusted him with the delicate task of talking to Manolo and this, too, needed thinking about.

With the landscape beginning to burst into brilliant flower, Edwina was painting furiously, and turning over to her assistant a flood of material to be catalogued and captioned. But Venetia was thankful to be busy, as she didn't have to notice how rarely Felipe now came to call on them. When he did, still with awkward, apologetic traces of his old affection, it was only when he could be sure of finding all three Marriotts together. She thought it would have been less painful if he hadn't come at all. Their walks and music recitals were a thing of the past, and so was their shared partaking of Communion on Sundays in Don Alberto's crowded little church. Alone of his family, Felipe had gone with them to this, and Venetia understood what it now cost him to stay away. He was infatuated, enslaved almost, by Fiona's physical appeal, and helpless to resist it – but he wasn't happy.

It was harder to know about Fiona herself, usually only met now crossing the court-yard. She was polite, but no longer talkative, only anxious to explain that she couldn't linger because she was working very hard. But one morning, tired of pretending that they could hide for ever behind evasions and small talk, Venetia repeated the question she'd asked before.

'What happens when you *have* finished your work here? Are you still planning to go to Germany, or is the D. Phil. beginning to look less attractive?'

A faint, sad smile touched Fiona's mouth. 'You'll think I'm a fool, or a selfish cow, but the truth is that I'm not sure *what* I want to do. Felipe would like me to stay, of course, and in a way I'm fond enough of him to want to. If Fernando would only leave La Paloma for good ... but he doesn't; he *enjoys* reminding me of our visit to Málaga. I think he does it just to upset Felipe, but it makes me feel I've set brother against brother.'

Her voice trembled a little with the enjoyable complication of it all. Not aware of being out of her depth, she was pleasantly sure that this Andalucían drama had the tepid academic rivalries of Oxford beaten hollow, and she was where she always wanted to be – in the thick of it.

'Fancy yourself as Carmen if you must,' Venetia suggested unkindly, 'but Felipe is no Don José, about to run a dagger through his brother. He's an unhappy, troubled man, that's all. Go or stay, Fiona, but make up your mind, and give a thought to someone else beside yourself for a change.'

A little silence followed, and Venetia waited for her companion to wrap herself in offended dignity and stalk away. Instead, when Fiona replied at last she spoke simply, with a sadness that sounded genuine.

'I'm very fond of Felipe – who couldn't be? – but staying here with him for ever simply wouldn't work. I'd have to stay if *Fernando* asked me, but he never will. I don't know why it's all gone so wrong, but it has.'

Watching her, Venetia knew she spoke the truth; what was more, just as it had gone wrong before with her failed marriage, so there might always come this recurring moment in her life when things went wrong without her knowing why. As if she suddenly understood it for herself, tears gathered in Fiona's eyes and overflowed as fast as she tried to wipe them away.

'Sorry – I'm a stupid bitch, and you're the one who has cause to feel sorry for herself.'

Venetia abandoned any hope of staying angry with her. It even seemed, however absurdly, necessary to try and help her.

'We've rather lost sight of Semana Santa in Seville,' she pointed out while Fiona mopped her wet face. 'I can't afford to be away for long because Aunt Edwina is working too hard – but we could escape for a night or two.' Fiona's tears began to flow again and the suggestion was retracted hastily. 'Not if you don't fancy the idea – a Scots presbyterian might well choose death rather than watch an Easter procession!'

'It's not *that*,' Fiona wailed; 'of course I want to go; but I was afraid *you* wouldn't. I thought you'd just be waiting for me to leave Rosario.'

Venetia shook her head, smiling wryly. 'You've been with the Quinones too much – you're getting very intense and Spanish, my dear! Telephone kind Duncan Gilmour and ask if we can stay two nights.'

The visit was duly arranged; on the afternoon prior to their departure Venetia set out in search of the purple viper's bugloss Edwina swore should now be in bloom. Its flowering season was very short and a specimen *had* to be tracked down. Successful at last, and feeling pleased with herself, she scrambled back on to the path, meaning to turn for home. In the stillness of the afternoon sounds carried easily, and, although what was visible of the track was empty, she could hear the sound of voices higher up the hill. It was rare to find others there at this time of day, but she felt no twinge of unease when the two figures appearing round a bend in the path turned out to be Fernando Quinones and the Mayor's unlovely builder-son. She bade them *'buenas tardes'* calmly enough, waiting for them to overtake her and go on ahead. Instead Fernando murmured something to his companion and, after offering her an unpleasantly knowing smile, the younger man swung off by himself.

She would have preferred to see Fernando leave as well, but only because they were unlikely to find anything to say about which they didn't disagree. All she was considering, in fact, was whether or not to reveal that Ian Gilmour had told William about the new ownership of the castle. But the silence was threatening to grow significant in some way she couldn't understand, and she had to make an effort to sound unconcerned.

'Don't wait for me, please ... I tend to amble about, looking for plants for my aunt.'

Fernando still didn't hurry to reply, content to know that he could overtake her if she tried to walk away from him. The afternoon was fine and warm, and she wore no jacket. He could see that the colour of her skin was already gaining a faint warmth from the sun; she would tan quickly and beautifully, he thought, and it would suit her very well. Everything about her, unfortunately, seemed more and more desirable – even the slender, boyish figure that he'd always found unappealing in other women seemed thoroughly right in her and made the rest of them look overblown. He acknowledged it to himself with the usual unsettling mixture of irritation and delight. It wasn't fair or reasonable or even remotely understandable when she hadn't any of Fiona's stunning beauty – only her own elusive charm and grace. Taking her to bed would be delight enough, but she would delight him in other ways as well, keeping boredom at bay. He could imagine passion intoxicatingly mixed with laughter for once ... she might even teach him to laugh at himself.

Venetia supposed from his silence that he had nothing to say, and lifted her hand in a small farewell salute. But the gesture was a mistake, making him feel dismissed; she had no right to be merely waiting for him to go away.

'You're the one who's supposed to leave,' he suggested with a glinting smile: 'you're trespassing on what is now Quinones land!' But if he'd hoped to disconcert her even that small ambition failed.

'I doubt if the old *duque* would have minded,' she said calmly. 'If your father does mind, he must tell us so. I can't deny that my aunt *is* rather making free with his wild flowers at the moment, but we pick them carefully; no damage is done.'

She was disliking the meeting more and more, but Fernando now blocked the way downhill and she didn't care to try pushing past him. He looked at ease standing there, but she felt certain that he wasn't; tension was like a charge of electricity leaping across the space between them now, setting her nerves tingling.

'You and Fiona are going to Seville together, I understand,' he said next. 'Felipe wanted to go too – to look after you both, he suggested; but even Fiona seemed to think there might be a certain awkwardness in that and instructed him to stay at home.'

Venetia stared at the handsome, smiling face in front of her, shaken by a longing to slap it very hard. It was more than twenty years since she'd given in to a similar desire, but she still remembered the pleasure of assaulting a small Ribera cousin who'd taunted her with being an English heretic, not a true Catholic at all. It would probably be an imprudent move now, though, and instead she spoke as coldly as she could.

'It amuses you, doesn't it, to watch other people going through idiotic hoops and getting hurt in the process? *You* don't get hurt, because their stupid involvements are merely a game to you. I should like to think that you might get snared yourself one day, but it won't happen; your next business deal will always be more important than people, so inconveniently made of flesh and blood.'

Colour touched his cheekbones, as if the slap had been administered physically after all, but he spoke quietly and she had to acknowledge his extraordinary self-control.

'If you're referring to Fiona, we had a

good time together; that's all that was ever promised, whatever she may say. Felipe, besotted by mere beauty, imagines he sees virtues that she *doesn't* possess, but I can't help it if my brother is a fool. I should be sorry if *you*'d been hurt by their antics, but I can't believe it's likely – you're too intelligent not to see him for the nice, ineffectual dreamer he is.'

'That's your estimate of him, not mine. It isn't Blanca's estimate either – she thinks you and Felipe are much alike; but I'm glad to say she's wrong about that.'

This time she'd gone too far for even Fernando's self-control. He closed the gap between them in a couple of strides and pulled her roughly into his arms. Instinct warned her that it would be a perilous mistake to struggle, and she forced herself to submit to a hard, insistent and very practised kiss. She refused with all her strength to respond, even though her body wanted with craven suddenness to give in to the pressure of his arms and mouth. She knew what it was to have been loved, knew what she now missed; but she couldn't permit the surrender, and finally Fernando had to release her, unsatisfied and angry.

'Blanca was wrong,' he said unevenly, 'but so were you, Venetia – you see, I *did* get snared after all!' Then with a small gesture she didn't know how to interpret – of

179

apology, regret, farewell? – he turned and strode away down the hill.

She stayed where she was, too shaken and uncertain of herself to move. Her lip bled a little from his rough treatment, but she was unaware of it. Had she heard his last sentence correctly? Could he have meant what he seemed to be saying, or was Fernando Quinones still playing games?

Too distraught to notice that she was no longer alone on the path, she wasn't aware of the newcomer until he spoke behind her and she had to turn and face him.

'Not wanting to interrupt that touching little scene, I waited further down,' Ian Gilmour explained with inhuman detachment in his voice.

'C ... considerate of you,' she managed to mutter.

'I thought so too, but I'm afraid I wasn't careful enough; your ... admirer must have caught sight of me.'

She smiled a sad little smile, because it seemed preferable to bursting into tears, but it catapulted him into a sudden flare of anger.

'I got it all wrong ... imagined Felipe was the Quinones you were after; but perhaps you like to keep both of them dangling on your string – one gentle lover, one more demanding!'

Contempt edged his voice with ice now,

stinging her into pulling herself together. 'You don't have to imagine anything at all,' she said with heroic steadiness. 'Just go on your way, Mr Gilmour; I'm quite anxious to get home myself.'

Her derisive little gesture of farewell invited him to walk away, and at last he accepted dismissal and went on up the hill. She was alone, thank God, unless of course the Mayor put in an appearance now; he was all the afternoon's misery lacked. The thought propelled her into a fit of sobbing, hysterical laughter, but the sound of it shocked her into rationality again. She commanded her legs to move, and then she saw what had been trampled in the dust – the tattered remnants of the plant she'd come looking for. She gathered the useless pieces up, weeping in earnest now, but no longer knowing who she wept for. Fernando, it seemed, had strangely to be included among the people who'd got hurt, but his image was blotted out by the anger and disgust she'd seen so unmistakably in the face of Ian Gilmour. It was time to get away from Rosario; thank goodness for Seville.

Twelve

Duncan Gilmour's house was, as he'd promised, in the heart of the city. They found the Calle San Isidoro in the *barrio* of Santa Cruz – its maze of alleyways and black-grilled, whitewashed houses as much of a tourist attraction as the great Gothic cathedral nearby. Picturesquely pretty, overflowing with greenery and flowers, the neighbourhood seemed altogether an unlikely spot for an austere Scot to have come to roost in.

At dinner, having made them more welcome than Fiona expected, Duncan explained that it was the history of the district that had caught his fancy. It had been the Jewish quarter until *los reyes católicos*, with a bigotry ominous for Spain's future, had expelled its inmates and gone on to install the Inquisition. Both policies had been disastrous, Duncan said severely – indeed, were scarcely recovered from yet. Isabella and Ferdinand should have been cursed for many of Spain's subsequent ills; instead, their reputation rested on evicting the

Moors, whose culture had done so much to enrich the country.

'My uncle, though a Catholic, would probably agree with you,' Venetia said honestly. 'My aunt would not – she's very anti-Islam! I'm afraid I veer one way and then the other, unable to make up my mind.'

'That's Oxford for you,' Duncan pointed out with sly pleasure. 'Does it teach its students *anything* positive, I wonder?'

Fiona would normally have felt obliged to protest, but it was more important at the moment to stay on amicable terms with her great-uncle. He didn't know it yet, but he was required to invite them again for the Feria in two weeks' time. She had no intention of being left behind at Rosario while Manolo and his family shared in Seville's great annual revels.

Each day of Holy Week, elaborate processions organised by the religious brotherhoods, the *cofradías*, had threaded through the streets of the city. But Good Friday brought the great culminating drama, when Seville's most treasured image of the Virgin – La Macareña – was carried to the cathedral. Priests, dignitaries, pilgrims and bizarrely hooded and gowned penitents accompanied their Lady through the silent, watching throng. They walked to the muffled beat of drums, and the occasional heart-stopping sound of a *saeta* – flamenco singing in its purest form – being winged to heaven by someone in the crowd.

Still gripped by the emotions of the day, Venetia returned to the Calle San Isidoro tired but content.

'Well – high expectations met?' Duncan wanted to know.

She smiled at him, thinking that he already knew the answer. 'I should like to be here again another year, but it won't matter if I'm not – at least I shall have today's experience to remember.'

The shimmer of amusement on his face reminded her of fleeting moments when she'd almost caught Ian Gilmour out in a smile. 'We have to remember you're a papist, of course,' he pointed out with pleasure. 'It's a different matter where I and my great-niece hail from. Prejudices are very strong there against bedizened images of the Virgin Mary, and ordinary citizens got up in fancy dress pretending to be penitential sinners hoping for salvation!'

'Prejudiced or not, Fiona managed to look rather moved herself from time to time. I left her with some Americans we met in the crowd, by the way, but she'll be back soon.'

He busied himself with pouring their pre-dinner sherry, but his long, thin hands, not quite as steady as they'd once been, reminded her of his age and accentuated his frailty. She was enjoying her friendship with him very much, but the pleasure was sharpened by the knowledge that it wasn't likely to last very long. Instead of an ill-tempered recluse, she'd found a friend – a congenial and drily humorous man whose formal manners hid warmth that had been too little called upon. With the glass of wine put beside her, Duncan settled himself back in his chair.

'Fiona drops hints that you both want to come back for the Feria,' he said next. *'Does that appeal to you?'*

Trapped by a question she hadn't expected, Venetia did her best to combine honesty with the answer her friend would require. 'I have work to do for my aunt at Rosario, but I'd certainly like a glimpse of the goings-on, and they wouldn't be much fun for Fiona to watch alone. That's not to say that you're obliged to put up with us again, though!'

His face broke into a charming smile. 'I know, but I find that I should rather like to. There isn't time now to put pleasures off!'

They were still deep in conversation when Fiona arrived back, anxious to be an appreciative guest: it was her turn now to entertain her great-uncle with some brilliant impressions of the day. But on the journey back to Rosario the following morning she was generous in acknowledging where credit for the noticeable change in Duncan Gilmour was due.

'All *your* doing, my friend – I didn't even crack the ice when I went calling on my own, but he couldn't stop smiling at *you*.'

'There's no ice, only shyness and the habit of solitude,' Venetia answered, 'but he looks frail – I suspect that he begins to wish for the first time in his life that he was among his own people. Ian Gilmour should at least get in touch with him; it's unkind not to.'

'He has,' Fiona said surprisingly. 'Duncan told me that much, but didn't say how they'd got on and I wasn't quite bold enough to ask.' She abandoned the subject for one that interested her more. 'It's all fixed, you know – our Feria visit – and I didn't even have to suggest it. We shall have the time of our lives – something to remember, whatever happens afterwards!'

It was impossible not to share such whole-hearted zest – Fiona was at her most engaging when she was hot on the scent of the next great experience. Only if expectation wasn't met would she be equally cast down into despair.

'We're going to watch a lot of beautiful people enjoying themselves,' Venetia risked pointing out, '... great fun, but I'm not keen to do it for long. Even if I thought Edwina *could* manage on her own, I'd soon get tired

186

of looking at vain men in skin-tight trousers prancing about with polka-dotted beauties on pampered horses!' Her smile admitted that this was a rather harsh view of the proceedings, but Fiona was shaking her head.

'My dear girl, we're not just going to *watch*,' she finally announced with a mixture of pride and embarrassment. 'I shall expect us to be right up there among the pampered beauties ourselves! Manolo has his own private *caseta* all arranged and we're to be among his guests. All the family will be there, but it's largely for *our* benefit – he very sweetly says it must be a week we shall never forget.'

There was a long silence while Venetia struggled to overcome a sudden spurt of rage. In her imagination Manolo Quinones appeared, however unfairly, like a large, fat spider sitting in the middle of his web, waiting to gobble up any foolish fly that might pass by. What she would be ready to consider kindness or generosity in someone else only seemed in him an intention to manipulate their lives; it amused him, as it did Fernando, to pull the strings and watch them dance.

'If you'd told me that at the beginning I should have said no at once,' she said coldly at last. 'Who am I supposed to entertain – Manolo himself, while you and Blanca cavort with his sons? I was coming to keep *you* company, I thought; now there's no need.'

'There *is* a need,' Fiona insisted with more gravity than usual. 'If you don't come Felipe will feel worse than he already does, and so shall I. We've both behaved badly; we know that. But if you could ... could just seem not to mind ... show everyone that you're not hurt or angry ... though of course I do admit that you've every right to be – oh God, I think I've lost the beginning of this sentence ... Dear Venetia, *please* come, just for a little while, and make everything seem normal again.'

'For one night,' she agreed slowly; 'but after that I shall go home. Anyone who isn't sure by then that I'm as merry as a singing lark will have to stay unconvinced.'

She picked up a copy of *El País* and pretended to read, but the words made no sense; instead, a sequence of images flicked across her mind's eye as she wondered which of them might seem 'normal': Felipe waiting at the bottom of the ladder the first time they met; his hand just touching hers when they were out walking; his smile when the music he was playing for her went well? He was changed now, made more taut, certainly more resolute, by his attachment to Fiona; but he was also less content than before. To make him not feel guilty about her she would endure his father's hospitality at the Feria long enough to reassure him, but no longer. She would even smile politely at Fernando, and somehow pretend that, between both brothers, Fiona and herself, there was nothing but the most untroubled friendship.

Aware that Fiona was still watching her, she glanced over the top of the newspaper. '*One* of Seville's all-night parties, and then I'm leaving,' she repeated firmly. 'And even to please you, Manolo Quinones or the King of all the Spains himself, I'm damned if I'm going dressed up in frills and flounces, with a carnation behind my ear!'

'Not your style at all,' Fiona agreed, beginning to smile again. The future might be painfully uncertain, but for the moment it could be ignored. The exhilarating gaiety of the Feria lay just ahead, and from its week-long whirl of events might come the next nudge from Fate that her life now seemed to require. It was something she'd learned in Spain: things happened as they must; all she had to do was wait, as patiently as she could.

Given the choice of going to Seville with the family or staying with his friends at Las Cuadras, Juan didn't hesitate. He almost had to be reminded to wave goodbye when left with them, Blanca complained tearfully to her brother.

'He's an unnatural child. His father will be arriving back from New York after months away but even that wasn't enough to make him want to come with us.'

Fernando's smile for her, full of amused affection, was one that other people rarely saw. '*Querida*, it's a week's visit, not a lifetime, and although it's only to the end of the drive, to go away on his own is an adventure. Rodrigo won't mind; he'll be too happy seeing *you* again.'

Blanca agreed that this would be true; then, with a glance at her brother's face, she risked a question he might think an intrusion. 'You're not looking forward to the Feria as you usually do – is something wrong?'

'I expect I'm getting too old to cut the right sort of figure in a *traje corto*!' His tone of voice said that he didn't believe this himself, but her expression trapped him into speaking again, this time with a kind of bitter honesty. 'The trouble is that I made a mistake – not something I'm in the habit of admitting to – and instead of putting it right, I made matters worse.'

Blanca shook her head, glad to be able to give comfort. 'Not permanently worse, my dear – Fiona just wants you to suffer a little. I'm sure she's not in love with Felipe.'

Fernando didn't correct her misunderstanding, but managed a faint smile instead.

190

'Never mind – it's Feria time; we shall talk and drink and dance the nights away, and spend the days making sure we're seen with all the loveliest people! It will be good for business at least, and I'm told that's what I care about.'

'Do I hear the trumpet note of Edwina Marriott?' Blanca asked, going wrong for the second time. 'You needn't take any notice of our opinionated neighbour, you know.'

'I never do,' he agreed sweetly and walked away, leaving her more puzzled than before.

They left for Seville the following morning, Felipe taking their guests from Las Cuadras in his car. When he explained that Manolo was already there, with some of La Paloma's staff, Fiona looked pleasantly surprised.

'Servants? I imagined a week-long picnic in a glorified tent!'

'That's more or less what it is,' Felipe agreed solemnly, 'but the "tent" will have imported sofas and chandeliers, a specially laid dance-floor, and a few other such refinements! My father never likes to skimp when it's a question of offering hospitality.'

Venetia smiled but left Fiona, sitting beside him in the front, to keep the conversation going. She was more occupied herself in regretting with every passing mile that she'd been manipulated into coming at all.

Even so, walking through the *barrio* of Los Remedios on the western side of the river that evening, she admitted to her host that no one could wish not to be there. The transformation was complete and entirely entrancing – a large, bleak space had become a fairy-lit wonderland of temporary pavilions filled with music, laughter and elegantly dressed people. Excitement and pleasure were in the flower-scented night air. With Seville in this enchanted mood there was nothing to do but join in the gaiety and smile at whomsoever next drew her into the dance.

In Manolo's beautifully decorated *caseta* she met Blanca's husband, just arrived back from New York. Rodrigo Esteban was older than she expected, a man who looked preoccupied and tired after the long flight home, but he grinned very pleasantly when she admitted that the entire Marriott household was as putty in the hands of his son.

'Even my formidable aunt soon caved in, and not only because Juan is better than I am at finding the rarer plants she wants to illustrate!'

'And there are birds to be watched, I gather, and stars to be identified – in fact a whole collection of delights that don't come his way in Madrid,' Rodrigo commented. 'Blanca warns me that we shall have to drag him home, kicking and screaming every inch of the way!' He fell silent for a moment, watching his beautiful wife dancing with a friend who'd strayed in from the *caseta* next door. Then his glance moved on to Felipe, arms encircling Fiona as they moved slowly round the floor.

'I've come back to a brother-in-law I scarcely recognise. He used not to ... to...' Rodrigo halted, remembering too late what Blanca had said; the girl beside him was supposed at one point to have been involved in the making of this new Felipe.

'He used not to dance?' Venetia suggested calmly. 'I don't know why not – he's doing it rather well, if a non-Spaniard is allowed to judge.'

Her companion's considering eye was now turned on her instead – not dazzling like Felipe's partner, he judged, whose appeal was of the instant but unsubtle variety. Venetia Marriott's charm was potent nevertheless, because even a connoisseur like Fernando was making a poor job of pretending not to notice it. Her own pretence seemed to be that she was enjoying herself and, sharing her difficulty, Rodrigo smiled at her kindly.

'If you haven't survived a Feria before you're probably wondering whether it's possible to endure six more nights like this! I can promise you that a second wind kicks in, and by the end of the week you're convinced that any night spent merely sleeping is a waste of time!'

Venetia shook her head. 'It would be a comfort if I were staying long enough to test your theory, but I'm going back to Rosario in the morning ... Fiona, on the other hand, is determined to have the full Feria experience – unless her staying-power crumbles before the end.'

He examined her face and made a guess. 'Are the contrasts here too much for you? All this surface gaiety and extravagant show of wealth on one side of the coin, and Seville's starker face on the other – high unemployment, drugs, and an unenviable reputation for crime?'

'It's an uncomfortable mixture,' Venetia admitted, 'but I can't claim that it doesn't occur elsewhere. I never intended to stay more than one night – I've a lot of work waiting for me at home.'

She watched Fernando and his sister coming towards them, and guessed what was likely to happen next. Blanca smilingly pulled Rodrigo into the throng of dancers; Fernando held out his hands to Venetia but she shook her head.

'Thank you, but I'm afraid I've shot my bolt. Evening sandals chosen for their elegance turn out to be murderously uncomfortable for all-night dancing. I'm already reduced to limping from chair to chair!'

She had protested too much, and his sharp bright glance said that he didn't believe her.

'I'd prefer you to admit the truth,' he said quietly. 'You don't approve of me at all, but you're afraid of finding that hard to remember with my arms around you. I'm everything you dislike in a man, but you might forget that if I were to make love to you. It's time to live dangerously, Venetia, and let what *ought* to happen, happen.'

There was – she knew it by the sudden racing of her heart – some truth in what he said. Fernando Quinones could probably convince almost any woman that she'd be a fool not to go to bed with him. He seemed to promise excitement and delight, and, as he'd said, he made good his promises.

'I tried living dangerously once before; that was enough,' she said finally. The gleam of malice was in his smile and she braced herself to be hurt because she had hurt him.

'So you thought you'd settle for a quiet life with my brother instead. Bad timing on your part, Venetia – the sleepy dormouse suddenly woke up and discovered excitement for himself! Are you waiting for him to recover from Fiona? I doubt if he will.'

'I doubt it, too,' she said calmly. 'I hope he doesn't need to; we might find that he offers *her* excitement enough.'

Before Fernando could reply there came a

change in the evening's entertainment. The musicians were laying aside their instruments and it was the turn of Felipe himself to sit down in front of them with his guitar. The recital was brief but beautiful: an artist communing with his instrument, trapping his audience in a web of sound that held them hushed and content.

Afterwards, reluctant to have the memory of it spoiled, Venetia stepped outside. It was cool in the night air after the heat of the crowded room, and in comparative quietness she could watch a bright star fall down the purple darkness of the sky. Then a voice spoke beside her.

'There hasn't been a chance to talk to you. I'm glad you came, but I'm afraid you aren't enjoying it very much.'

She turned to smile at Felipe. 'I enjoyed your contribution just now, but the truth is that I don't thrive on large parties. The night will end too soon for Fiona – she's determined to prove that as long as a Spaniard can keep going, so can she!'

'She's dancing with Fernando now, and looking as if the music should never be allowed to stop.'

His quiet voice laid no stress on what he'd just said, but she knew what he was remembering; Fernando had been before him and taken possession of Fiona himself. There was no moderation in these Spaniards, she thought with bitter humour – they were either suicidally resigned to Fate or, like Fernando, convinced of being able to out-jockey it.

'Fiona has danced with a lot of men to-night, your brother included,' she said with some sharpness. 'You'd do better to go in and claim her, instead of hiding out here with me.'

'You sound tired of us all,' he replied simply. 'I don't blame you.'

'I *meant* to sound as if I wanted you to be happy,' she insisted.

He watched the moonlight touch her face and reflect itself in her eyes. She was gener-ous and lovely, but it came as no surprise; he'd recognised that at their first meeting in the stable courtyard. He'd chosen instead the feverish delight of loving her friend, and although he couldn't quite regret it, he couldn't feel much pride or security in his choice.

'Venetia,' he blurted out, 'I'm sorry it's all such a mess. I haven't said that before, but I should have done.'

'Not a mess,' she said with a determined smile. 'We end as we began, I hope – true friends.' Perhaps it wasn't the note of high drama his Spanish temperament craved, but it was the only one she found bearable. 'When the moment comes to leave Spain I shall be sorry for the first time in my life –

childish nightmares finally forgotten, and taking away with me the certainty that I'll want to come back often to Rosario, hoping to find it blessedly unchanged.'

Felipe accepted this with an unsmiling nod. 'But you aren't staying here now, I gather – not even for tomorrow's parade.'

Venetia smiled more easily. 'This morning's display of glamour, human and equine, was enough, but I shall while away the bus journey home imagining how beautiful you all look! Now isn't it time we went back inside?'

The parties ended as dawn was breaking, but even then the click of castanets and sudden bursts of song charted revellers' homeward journeys through the city. Venetia woke later than she meant to and it was mid-morning by the time she went downstairs. There was no sign of Fiona or of her host, but Josefa smilingly announced that the *señorita*'s breakfast was laid on the patio. Señor Gilmour, long since up, was occupied in his study with a visitor.

The two weeks since their previous visit had strengthened the morning heat, and persuaded the shrubs that climbed the arcaded pillars of the patio to burst into flower. It was a beautiful, secluded spot – a beautiful home altogether that Duncan Gilmour had found and created for himself. She felt no surprise that he preferred not to leave it for the hurly-burly outside.

Packed and ready to leave after breakfast, she said goodbye to Fiona, who was just waking up, and came downstairs again hoping to find that Duncan's visitor had gone. Instead, two men stood up as she approached them – her host and Ian Gilmour. Taken by surprise, it was a moment before she greeted them.

'*Buenos días, señores!*' Then she smiled at Duncan. 'Josefa's been kindness itself, and so have you. Thank you for letting us come.'

Even in old age he was a tall, upright man and she had to reach up to kiss him on both cheeks. 'Now I'm off to the bus station – for a cross-country ride home.'

'My car's outside, and I'm driving back to Rosario,' Ian Gilmour said briefly. 'But there's no need to spare my feelings if you'd prefer the bus.'

She agreed to the suggestion reluctantly. Tired of people, tired of smiling and being sociable, she'd have preferred to go home alone, but there'd been a challenge in his offer that it seemed necessary to accept.

They were settled in his car a few minutes later, but he didn't immediately drive off; instead, he turned to look at her.

'Sorry – I needled you into coming, but I should have remembered that you might be nervous. There's no need to be: when sober, I'm a competent enough driver.'

She wasn't sure whether he meant to disconcert her with that reference to his crash, or to reassure her. 'I'm not nervous,' she said coolly, 'only so tired that, unless you happen to collide with something again, I shall probably go back to sleep.'

A different smile, warm and amused, suddenly changed his face. 'Slumber away then. If we don't talk even *we* can't fall out!'

Thirteen

She was roused by the sudden change from motion to stillness, and awoke to find that they were parked in the lovely square at the centre of Arcos de la Frontera.

'This is where we eat,' Ian Gilmour's voice announced beside her. 'I normally avoid *parador* restaurants, but this one happens to be good, and its décor is mercifully unpretentious – scarcely a suit of armour or a tattered battle flag in sight!' Then, as she turned to look at him, a rueful grin changed his face. 'Living alone has made me careless! I should, of course, have asked where you'd like to be given luncheon, here or somewhere else.'

Her mouth twitched but she answered

solemnly. 'Here by all means, but I'd better warn you that I've woken up ravenous after my little nap; luncheon will be expensive!'

A few minutes later, washed and neat, she joined him in the dining-room, where the *parador*'s usual welcoming gesture of a glass of fino was waiting for her on the table. When her companion got to his feet – manners perhaps not so careless after all – she was reminded of Duncan Gilmour's old-fashioned courtesy.

'I like your uncle very much,' the memory prompted her to say as she took her place. 'You suggested once that he must find present-day Spain uncongenial, but I don't think he does. What he treasures about it hasn't changed, and the rest – froth, he calls it – doesn't worry him.'

'Ignore what you can't do anything about, in other words – it's an old man's sensible philosophy,' his nephew agreed. 'I suspect he was more of a firebrand in his younger days – Gilmours aren't noted for being sweetly reasonable.'

She smiled at that, but the conversation was suspended while they chose gazpacho and *fritura de pescados*. The waiter brought white wine and good Spanish bread, but when he'd gone away again Venetia reverted to the subject of Duncan Gilmour.

'He *is* old, and looking even a little more frail than when he called in at Rosario a few weeks ago. I'm afraid he's unwell, so it's all the nicer that you got in touch with him.'

Her companion glanced wryly at the ceiling. 'If you're imagining a sickly reconciliation scene in which we fell on each other's necks, let me tell you that it's no more Duncan's style than it is mine! I wanted his help, that's all.'

'And I expect you asked for it with your usual finesse and charm of manner!' But with his enquiring glance now fixed on *her* she had the grace to blush. 'It's my turn to apologise. Don Alberto told me once that he found you not only intelligent but pleasant as well. Your uncle's impression might have been exactly the same for all I know.'

'And, struggling with disbelief, you've also just remembered that I'm being generous enough to give you lunch!'

'There's that too,' she agreed, trying not to smile. She sipped the cold, tangy soup that had been put in front of her and risked a question likely to earn a snub.

'Am I allowed to ask what sort of help Duncan was needed to provide?' She saw her companion frown, but the expected rebuff wasn't delivered.

'My uncle's been in Seville a long time: I reckoned he'd know how to contact the people I want to reach, the Conservation Officer of the province in particular.'

She was reminded of her encounter with

Fernando on the hillside at Rosario. The unpleasantness of it had almost driven something else from her mind – the memory of him walking down in the company of Don Ramón's son.

'Is it to do with the castle?' she asked anxiously. 'My uncle is half afraid that Manolo might think it worth trying to restore. He keeps remembering the Alhambra in Granada – enough of a tourist draw to tempt anyone else who can lay claim to a Moorish ruin.'

'What Manolo remembers is the hotel inside the Alhambra. My information is that he dreams of converting his own castle into a small, exclusive and no doubt murderously expensive hotel!'

She found nothing to say for a moment, feeling sick now rather than hungry. 'But he can't just *do* it, surely?' she asked finally. 'Even here there must be restrictions on the use of historic places. How do you know what he plans, in any case ... or can't he resist boasting about it?'

'I got the Mayor's son rather drunk in Luís's bar one night – it was *he* who couldn't resist boasting. Since then I've made more official enquiries. There's no doubt about it – the Quinones' application for permission to make the conversion has already been filed.'

Venetia considered this, frowning a little.

'Will the application be judged fairly, or *not*, simply because Manolo is rich enough to bribe the people who matter?'

Her companion answered with a gleam of amusement in his face. 'Working in Brussels has made you cynical, I fear! Bribery isn't as easy as it once was, even here. The castle itself won't be a problem for him – Spain's got more ruins than it knows what to do with, and officials are rather in favour of private individuals taking them in hand. But the sierra is a different matter. There are European conservation rules affecting that which can't be flouted openly.'

But Venetia had no faith at all in Manolo Quinones abiding by rules that didn't happen to suit him. 'Poor eagles,' she said sadly. 'Does William know?'

'The eagles will be safe for this season, and we can delay things further with protests and petitions. In fact, your uncle's already hard at work – "the mildest-mannered man that ever scuttled ship or cut a throat"!'

The vision of William as Lord Byron's corsair made her smile, but only briefly. 'Yes, but I'm afraid it presents another problem. William and Edwina's new home, which they love, is only rented; Manolo is their landlord.'

'Difficult,' Gilmour conceded. 'Your uncle should have told me. The opposition must be seen to be coming from me.' He stared at her for a moment before changing the subject. 'Fiona wasn't ready to quit the jamboree in Seville?'

'No, she's having a lovely time. Felipe will bring her back at the weekend.' She sipped her wine calmly, leaving him to hesitate before he plunged across more difficult ground.

'I've seen them driving about together recently. Not trusting my niece, I wonder where that leaves you?'

'I suppose where you warned me it might,' she said slowly, then shook her head at the expression on his face. 'If you think Fiona set out to snare Felipe, you're wrong; it came about quite accidentally. I encouraged him to help her get over Fernando, so it was my own fault in a way.'

'Not exactly the reward that virtue ought to have had,' he suggested drily.

'My fault was being in a muddle,' she explained simply. 'I loved someone very much but he died a young man. When I came to Rosario I was playing safe, not wanting to get hurt again. Cowardice reaped the reward it deserved: I lost Felipe to Fiona.'

While the waiter returned to remove their plates they sat in silence, but she wasn't troubled by it; for the first time in his company she felt at ease. They knew enough about each other now for wariness and the scoring of points to seem merely silly, and although she doubted that she'd have liked what he once was, it wouldn't be hard to like the man he'd become.

'I'm sorry I offered you a stupid taunt up on the hillside that afternoon,' he said at last. 'I suspected almost at once that I'd got the wrong end of the stick, but I doubted if you'd want me to come back and say so. Does Fernando Quinones make a habit of pestering *you* – as a way of getting at Fiona?'

She shook her head, reluctant to say that the situation was more complicated than that. However tempting it was to point out that she'd managed to rouse a ladykiller's interest all by herself, it would have sounded unpleasantly like boasting.

'Fernando likes to play the field,' she said instead, 'but one rejection is enough. I'm sure he always has other options lined up.'

'Probably, strange though it seems to another male. But we have to admit that women *are* very strange when it comes to choosing men, if I'm allowed to say so without your feminist hackles rising.'

'By and large I agree with you,' she said with a rueful smile, then grew sober again, remembering that his own choice had been a woman who'd left him to face tragedy alone, and taken his son away to America. It wasn't a wound anyone else could touch, but she risked a subject associated with it.

'Just supposing that Manolo *is* allowed to go ahead with his hotel, what difference will it make to you?'

'None at all in the long run; I'm going to oppose him on principle. I'm not planning to spend the rest of my life hacking away at El Perdido, and in any case its owner will be arriving before long.'

Of course he was bound to leave, sooner or later, but she realised it with a strange, sharp feeling of regret. The life he'd known, the wife and child he'd lost, hadn't been given up for good. He would set about recovering them when the moment seemed right, and meanwhile a battle with Manolo Quinones would serve to get him in fighting trim again.

'I hope my aunt and uncle will like their new neighbour when he comes,' she said, 'though perhaps I should ask whether Manolo Quinones will like him.'

He was saved from answering by the arrival of the waiter with the bill, and nothing more was said until they were back in the car again. Then, before a silent journey was resumed, he turned to look at her.

'If I promise to keep an eye on Duncan, will that comfort your soppy heart?' She nodded, and saw him smile. 'Good – now you can go to sleep again; it makes you a remarkably restful passenger!'

★ ★ ★

At Las Cuadras Juan Esteban was carefully attending to one of the duties he'd been given – watering Venetia's urns and tubs – and an unfamiliar car was parked at the entrance to the courtyard.

'You've got visitors apart from Juan by the look of it,' Ian Gilmour said. 'I'll call and talk to your uncle tomorrow.'

But as he was getting ready to drive away William came hurrying out. 'Don't rush off. My brother's here unexpectedly – you met him once before. We should pick his architect's brains about our problem.'

Venetia left them there and went indoors to find the others in the drawing-room, lingering over tea; Edwina always served it at five o'clock, on the un-Spanish principle that something other than a siesta was needed to fill the long afternoon pause.

'Lovely to see you,' Venetia said, kissing Arlette and then her father, 'but you should have warned us – I could easily have missed you. I only got a lift back with Ian Gilmour by accident. He's still outside, and Uncle William thinks some professional advice might be helpful.'

Jeffery sauntered to the door, followed by his wife's plaintive injunction to remember that they must be in Seville in time for a late dinner.

'We're spending a couple of nights with the Villanuevas,' she explained. 'You left too soon, Venetia – we could have seen you there.'

It seemed unlikely to her stepdaughter, even given the Estebans' friendship with royalty. She doubted if Manolo had yet scraped acquaintance with the Marqués de Villanueva.

Instead of saying so, she asked, 'Where have you come from – Marbella?'

'Yes, your father had some problems to attend to there. Then it seemed sensible to stop here on the way to Seville and settle the matter of Juanita's house. Thank God William and Edwina have finally agreed that it should be sold. None of us would ever want to live in it.' Arlette registered her stepdaughter's change of expression and looked surprised. 'Don't tell me *you*'d have liked it kept – I thought you hated your visits there.'

'I did!' But, true though that was, Venetia found she disliked the idea of one of Fernando's clients getting his hands on it. It would either be demolished altogether or parcelled out in apartments swept clean of all past associations. In the process, not only her grandmother's life but some of her own would be lost. The thought made her shiver slightly, but she smiled at Arlette's puzzled face.

'A ghost walking over my grave,' she explained cheerfully.

'The result of a night's Feria carousing,

more likely,' Edwina suggested. 'You need to be a true-born Spaniard to stand up to it.' Then she added a genial afterthought for her sister-in-law. 'And preferably under the age of twenty-five!'

'We shall do what we can to keep up,' Arlette promised sweetly – coming off best as usual, Venetia thought, in these spirited exchanges.

'I don't suppose you've been shown what my clever aunt is doing, so you'd better come and look,' she decided it was time to insist.

Edwina's recent work was spread around her studio, waiting to be captioned and catalogued. Arlette examined it in silence, not blind to the quality of what she looked at. Each small flower painting captured its subject with such precision and perfect delicacy that honesty compelled her to say so.

'She's good, isn't she, my maddening sister-in-law; opinionated and disorganised though she is, she can still do *this*!'

'Your adjectives sometimes fit,' Venetia agreed, smiling at her stepmother, 'but she's a lot of other things as well – valiant and funny and very kind.'

'You know her better than I do,' Arlette conceded. 'Nevertheless, listen to me, *ma petite*. If you're staying here in order to be kind yourself, it may be no such thing – William and Edwina must learn to manage without you. You needed a breathing space after Brussels but it's lasted long enough. You must begin a new life, unless of course you expect one to offer itself here.'

It was the viewpoint of an intelligent, clear-sighted woman, and it had been helpful often enough in the past to the muddled adolescent Venetia knew she'd been. She liked her stepmother too much not to be honest with her in return.

'It did seem possible, began to look probable even. I didn't expect to recover the sort of happiness I had with Luc – that doesn't come twice – but I thought Felipe Quinones and I could make a contented life for each other.'

'So what went wrong?'

'He's very fond of me, but he fell head over heels in love with the girl who came here to stay. History repeated itself – she filched a man from me in Oxford years ago!'

'She sounds a bitch – you should have been warned, my dear.'

'She sounds it, but isn't; she's even very torn herself, so we shall probably all end up with no one getting what they want.' Arlette's expression said what she thought of this and made Venetia smile. 'These things are managed better where you come from, you're thinking!'

'On the whole they are. Abandon this place, my dear, and give Paris a try. You could get a job there easily enough; your French is up to native standard.'

'I've already been offered one, by a French publisher,' Venetia confessed. 'I'm thinking about it, but I want to stay and help my aunt for the time being.'

With that Arlette knew she must be content. Her stepdaughter gave, as all quiet-voiced people did, an impression of malleability, but it was entirely misleading in her case.

Back in the drawing-room they found that William and his brother had returned indoors. 'Gilmour wouldn't come in,' William was explaining to Edwina. 'He'll walk down tomorrow to discuss our protest campaign. Jeffery's been very helpful.'

'But my best advice is *this*,' their brother said seriously. 'Think of yourselves, for God's sake, as well as the local flora and fauna. You *like* living here, so if there's ill-feeling to be stirred up with your landlord, let Ian Gilmour do it. He seems willing enough – more than willing. I'd say he rather relishes the prospect of a fight with Manolo Quinones.'

William nodded without committing himself; looking thoughtful, Edwina for once said nothing at all; and Venetia refrained from pointing out the smallness of the chance that her aunt and uncle would step aside and leave this particular fight to someone else.

Arlette broke the silence to remind her husband that it was time they left, and ten minutes later they were being waved on their way.

'So how was the Feria?' William asked as they strolled about outside, inspecting Juan's labours.

Mindful that the small boy had come to listen, Venetia answered carefully. 'Very exciting, very beautiful, and *very* exhausting for a non-*sevillana* like me!'

'But you saw Papá, Venetia?' Juan asked anxiously. 'He came home from America?'

'He did indeed. I think he was disappointed you weren't there, but I explained that you were needed here, to help my aunt and uncle.'

His look of worry melted into an entrancing smile. 'It's true – Señorita Edwina says so; and I still have much work to do.'

He bustled happily off to his next small task and Venetia gave a regretful sigh. 'I'm afraid he's going to hate Madrid, but at least Blanca's warned her husband. *He*'s a very nice man, by the way; not what I expected at all.'

'Which means that your expectations were not high! I read your account of the Feria visit correctly I hope – modified rapture, and no regret at leaving so soon!'

'Quite correctly,' she agreed, smiling at

him. 'What I enjoyed most was getting to know Duncan Gilmour. I'll take you to meet him one day. I think the two of you would like each other.'

William's quiet glance rested on her face for a moment while she inspected an early rose just coming into bloom. Even allowing something for partiality, he thought that by any sane man's reckoning she was surely beautiful – soft brown hair, smooth, suntanned skin, expressive eyes, neat nose, lovely mouth. If Edwina was right, there'd been a good chance of having her always close by, and he was to blame for that chance being lost. William regretted it for themselves but feared much more what his invitation to Fiona had cost his niece. She didn't look heartbroken or even angry but that was only – again according to Edwina – because she had too much proper pride.

'Arlette thinks you're wasting precious time here,' he murmured, taking her by surprise. 'She doesn't say so, but we catch a hint now and then that we should be urging you to rejoin the rough-and-tumble world of high endeavour and rich reward!'

'Urge if you *want* to, but not otherwise,' Venetia said after a moment or two. 'If you aren't tired of me, I'd like to stay a bit longer.'

William smiled happily. 'There you are, you see – even a clever Frenchwoman *can* be wrong, though she will seldom think so. Leave when *you* want to, my dear, but otherwise never go away at all.'

They strolled contentedly in silence until he spoke again – bravely grasping the nettle, he thought. 'What about Fiona? We've seen so little of her lately that we don't know what she plans.'

'She hasn't quite known herself, but I suspect she's hoping that this week in Seville will settle her future.'

'You're ... you're still friends?' William asked tentatively.

Smiling at him, Venetia agreed. 'Rather surprisingly, all things considered, I think we are.'

And being a sensible man William left the subject there.

The rest of the week passed peacefully, with their small guest from La Paloma making the fourth member of a congenial quartet. Juan's only regret seemed to be that he couldn't stay for ever; but when Saturday arrived and it was his father who delivered Fiona back, he hurled himself into Rodrigo Esteban's arms and there was no more talk of not going home.

When they'd driven away a pale and unsmiling Fiona announced that she craved sleep and could think of nothing except a long siesta. Half an hour before suppertime

Venetia knocked on her door, and then went in. Caught in the middle of what looked more like packing than unpacking, Fiona turned to stare at her.

'Are you eating with us this evening?' Venetia asked, 'or up at the house?'

'Not eating at all, thanks; I need to recover from a week of Manolo's rather excessive hospitality.'

Venetia considered her face for a moment. 'Are you going to tell us what's been happening? My aunt and uncle shouldn't be expected to guess whether you're staying or leaving.'

The reproof brought a tinge of colour into Fiona's white face. 'I'm leaving tomorrow – I'll go home and work out my German trip there.'

It seemed that she'd said all she was going to say and, reluctant to go on dragging information out of her, Venetia turned to leave the room. Suddenly Fiona's ragged voice halted her at the door.

'After you left, Fernando decided to remember that I existed. I tried hard to keep my head, but I could as well have tried to stop the tide coming in. We were together for almost all of three delirious days and nights. I was alive again, and for me Felipe had ceased to exist. Then came the last night of the Feria, the best, the most enchanting of all. Fernando smiled and said hello, and ... and just moved on! After that he didn't leave the side of a girl who was a guest at the *caseta* next door. She was beautiful, need I say, and now it was my turn not to exist. I smiled a lot, danced with men whose names I don't remember, and wished I could die on the spot.'

Silence fell while Venetia struggled to find something to say. 'I'm sorry,' she muttered at last. 'It's late in the day to point out that, since Fernando is one part *hidalgo*, three parts Moor, cruelty is bred into his very bones.' She hesitated a moment, then went on. 'I hope you realise that Felipe will have been hurt, too.'

'I *know* that,' Fiona cried out. 'Even then he tried to look after me again. His heart wasn't in it, but he knew that I was close to falling apart.'

Venetia stayed silent now, watching Fiona's mouth twist into a bitter smile. 'Now comes the bit you'll enjoy. I'd been feeling guilty about *you* as well, but Blanca put me wise. What a laugh you must have been having. It was never *me* Fernando wanted; it was you all along. Well, I'll return good for evil and give you a word of advice: don't overplay your hand – he won't hang about for long.'

White-lipped herself now, Venetia struggled to speak calmly. 'I've never felt like laughing at you, and nor am I interested in playing any sort of hand with Fernando. My only mistake with him was to make that too clear.' She lifted thin brown hands to push the subject aside. 'What shall I tell my aunt and uncle?'

'I'll tell them myself in the morning that I've had enough of Spain; it has the merit of being true. I've got a reservation on an afternoon flight from Seville.' She folded another garment with hands that trembled slightly. 'I shall leave hating you quite as much as you left Oxford hating me – fair, wouldn't you say?'

'Symmetrical at least,' Venetia agreed unevenly. 'I hope the hating won't last long – mine didn't.' But there was no reply, and at last she turned and walked away.

Fiona appeared at breakfast the following morning, able to announce quite calmly that it was time she went home. She thanked William and Edwina for their kindness but explained, without a glance at Venetia, that after the Feria anything else would be an anti-climax. She would need to recover from so rich an experience, and then buckle down to work again.

It was a very brave performance, Venetia thought, and the only thing wrong with it was that she'd spoken to William and Edwina as if their niece wasn't there. With embraces and promises to stay in touch, Fiona drove away straight after breakfast as

218

suddenly as she'd arrived, leaving the Marriotts silent and thoughtful. She'd been an intimate part of their life there and her departure had been too abrupt for them to feel easy about it.

William thought better of mentioning Felipe. 'She smiled too much, didn't you think?' he said instead. 'The poor girl wasn't happy.' Getting no reply, he wandered off sadly to his study, while Edwina eyed her niece, then barked a question.

'Are you going to tell me what happened in Seville?'

'I don't think so,' Venetia answered. 'It doesn't matter now.'

'Well, I shan't pretend I'm sorry Fiona's gone. This isn't where she belongs. For one thing her colouring's all wrong for Spain. She couldn't survive an Andalucían summer.'

It was probably true, Venetia realised, and it might as well stand as a slightly inadequate epitaph to Fiona's Spanish adventure: her colouring had been all wrong for it.

Fourteen

No one had walked down the drive from La Paloma to intercept Fiona's departure; no one had come afterwards to express regret or even surprise. Her part in their lives was over. Only a sad-faced Juan appeared, to say his goodbyes to Las Cuadras while his family were still recovering from their exertions at the Feria. Then he climbed the hill to see his friend at El Perdido.

As so many times before, he and his host sat outside on the wall to talk. The morning was beautiful and clear, and perhaps by looking very hard he could commit the precious surrounding sweep of hills and valleys to memory. Above them the outline of the Moors' castle fretted the intense blue of the sky, and he thought he glimpsed the wing-beats of one of the great birds that made their home up there – even the eagle seemed to be saying goodbye to him too. Tears were not manly, not Spanish, his mother always said, and he mustn't weep for what he was being made to leave behind. But it was very hard not to, and the tears in his throat made talking difficult.

Ian Gilmour glanced at the small, set face beside him and broke the silence himself. 'Señor Marriott tells me you're taking the high-speed train home tomorrow – very exciting, I believe; I've never travelled on it.'

'The train is well enough,' Juan managed to answer; 'the rest is not: school, Madrid, and stupid people who don't know about important things.'

'They know about things *they* reckon are important,' Ian Gilmour pointed out. 'It's tempting to think that everyone who disagrees with you is a fool, but for the moment you must at least listen – with *cortesía* if you can manage it – to what they say.'

'I don't see why, when they only speak stupid things,' his companion said stubbornly.

He was offered the truth, softened by an understanding smile. 'Because you're eleven years old, my friend, and you haven't got all the answers yet!'

Juan acknowledged it with a small, reluctant nod, then clutched at a nearer future. 'I shall ask to come back for the summer holidays. There'll still be work to help you with, won't there?'

His huge, dark eyes were fixed on his friend's face. A lie now was tempting but had to be resisted. 'The holidays are several months away. I don't know what might have happened by July. If I'm still here we shall certainly be able to find work to do. If not, you must come up anyway and see how the olive and almond trees we've planted are doing.'

A long pause followed, then a brief, choked question. 'El Perdido is not your real home?'

'No, it belongs to a friend of mine called Pablo Sánchez. He's not in Spain at the moment, but he hopes to come back quite soon.'

Staying manly and Spanish was becoming harder by the minute. Nothing in this world – unfairly left to adults to run – could be depended upon not to change. Even his dear bird friend at Las Cuadras had been unable to promise that everything would be the same in two months' time. He turned his face away so that the man beside him could see only an averted brown cheek, but Ian Gilmour knew the distress he struggled with. Juan looked a different child now after weeks of running wild in the open air; he was convalescent no longer. But he was troubled and torn, knowing that even the people who loved him couldn't be relied upon to understand the things that he understood himself.

Their conversation was becoming difficult for once, and his host went indoors in search of lemonade. But when he returned with it the wall was empty; a small, desolate figure was already trudging down the hill-side, leaving him with another sense of failure.

The Estebans left La Paloma the following morning – Juan silent but stoically calm; Blanca respecting his grief to the extent of concealing her own relief at going home; Rodrigo wondering whether they could escape before the hostility simmering between his brothers-in-law broke out into open warfare.

Lunch for those left behind was a silent meal, no one making any pretence at conversation now that it was no longer necessary. But at last Fernando found something to say.

'I'm afraid it's time I left as well. I've been neglecting affairs on the coast while Blanca was here.'

Manolo looked relieved; the same thought had occurred to him. Their competitors were hard men, only too ready to seize any opportunity. He said an affectionate good-bye to his son and went away to his afternoon siesta in a more contented frame of mind. Left alone with his brother, Felipe knew that the moment he'd both dreaded and longed for had come.

'I called on the Marriotts this morning,' he

began quietly. 'Fiona had already left for England.'

'Just as well, don't you think?' Fernando answered carelessly. 'She's supposed to be determined on an academic career.' He glanced at his brother's pale face and smiled faintly. 'If you're making up your mind to quarrel, shout or knock me down, for God's sake get on with it – it's very unnerving to have you sitting there like some stern, avenging angel!'

'If I could manage it I'd *like* to beat you into the ground,' Felipe said in a voice that shook a little, 'but we aren't supposed to be savages, settling our differences with fists and bloody noses. Fiona went away hurt and humiliated. What did she do to you to deserve that treatment?'

Fernando gave his usual graceful shrug. 'She did nothing to *me* except take too much for granted. But she used her friend badly, and she treated you even worse. Does that make her someone who shouldn't be taught a little lesson?'

'*You* were the cause of the mess we were caught up in,' Felipe almost shouted. 'Fiona couldn't help herself, but *you* never meant anything but harm. You couldn't even resist the last refinement of cruelty, by telling her that it was Venetia you'd wanted all along.'

'Not I, dear brother; Blanca must have decided she needed to be told. At least she'll get over imagining that she's in love with me and hate me instead – *much* more useful!' He stared at his brother for a moment, then went on in a different tone of voice. 'It had to happen, I suppose – one day you were bound to meet a girl who'd wake you up too suddenly to the intoxicating pleasures of the flesh. But you left it later than most of us, and made things worse by endowing her with every improbable virtue you could think of. All I did was show you the truth about her. Fiona will recover, I promise you, from whatever punishment you seem to think I've meted out. I'm less sure about you – for a Quinones you're hopelessly sentimental!' His smile for once was not unkind, and Felipe was left with the helpless feeling that yet again he'd been out-manoeuvred by his brother. 'Don't lose too much sleep over Fiona – she enjoyed Spain, but the novelty would have worn off soon enough,' Fernando said almost gently. 'Be sorry for what *you* might have had instead. With deplorable lack of taste, Venetia refused to like me at all!'

He laid no stress on what he'd just said but Felipe heard its hidden message; perhaps for the first time, his brother had emerged a loser.

'What happens to the castle project when you're away?' he asked, to change the subject. 'Is Father looking after it or are you leaving it to the Mayor's shifty son?'

'He's not clever enough to be shifty,' Fernando said with a trace of regret, 'but he's a very adequate builder. Nothing will happen immediately – we're stuck in bureaucratic delays, stirred up by the people you like so much – the Marriotts and Ian Gilmour.'

'You can't assume they're not speaking for other people here as well. It's not everyone who shares your view of progress.'

His brother gave a little shrug. 'I'm prepared for some kind of public debate, but it's an unnecessary nuisance; we shall get what we want in the end.'

The certainty in his voice goaded Felipe to argue. 'You might *not* win; you might find yourself ranged this time against people who can't be bought or intimidated – people who believe that what *they* are doing is right.'

Fernando smiled faintly. 'You have a charming idea of my business methods, I must say! At least I haven't *your* dilemma of choosing which side to support – your own flesh and blood, or the eccentric friends who have little reason to feel pleased with you. Now I really must be off – *hasta la vista, amigo!*'

He gave an ironic little salute, left the room, and presently drove away. Felipe sat there alone, considering the dilemma that his brother had rightly identified. He couldn't bear to think about Fiona or Venetia, and his only coherent hope was that Fernando might find himself defeated for once, by the very people he seemed to despise.

It was a change that needed getting used to – walking into Consuela's shop and hearing the babble of harsh Spanish voices dwindle into something as near a silence as the *pueblo* ladies could bring themselves to observe.

They still offered a courteous '*Buenos días, señorita*', but the cheerful demand for information that normally prolonged every purchase was missing now. Rosario was on edge, knowing that battle-lines were being drawn. The men would be the ones to decide, the writ of female emancipation having scarcely begun to run in the high villages of the sierra; nevertheless, the women talked among themselves in hidden courtyards and secluded alleyways. They knew how matters stood, and in Consuela's shop they didn't need reminding that her brother, the Mayor, was in the pocket of Manolo Quinones and his elder son.

Feeling depressed by the alteration in the atmosphere, Venetia hurried through her shopping and then walked across the square into the church. It was empty for once; in its quietness she could kneel and find rest. As usual someone had left a fresh posy at the foot of the Virgin's statue, gathered from the May flood of wild flowers with which every roadside was now awash. She lit candles in memory of her mother and Luc as usual, then turned at the sound of footsteps on the stone floor. Don Alberto had emerged from the vestry and come to stand beside her.

'Concepción will have the coffee pot on,' he suggested; 'come and join me.'

She walked with him to the little house next door, blindingly white in the sunlight under its fresh spring coat of lime-wash. Inside it was neatly kept but austerely furnished; a lifetime of service had provided the priest with few of the comforts most people, now took for granted.

When the coffee was poured and Concepción had bustled away again Don Alberto inspected his guest. 'Shall I ask what brought you into church this morning looking troubled, or would you rather talk of other things?'

She answered the question honestly. 'Anxiety drove me in – it's usually what does, I'm afraid, instead of the gratitude we *ought* to be offering.'

He didn't look upset by this admission. 'I suppose you're worrying about what is going to happen here?'

'*Is* happening already,' she corrected him. 'Consuela served me in the shop this

228

morning because nothing would allow her sound business instincts to turn away trade, but it was made clear that she was doing me a favour!'

'Does that trouble you?' he asked gently.

'Not very much, but other things do. Rosario is uneasy with rumours and uncertainty. People who have accepted each other without question now wonder which side they're on ... where does safety or advantage lie? I'm not sure it isn't *more* destructive than just allowing Manolo Quinones to run amok up on the hilltop; but my uncle wouldn't agree with that, and nor would Ian Gilmour.' Her dark eyes were fixed for a moment on the priest's silver head. 'You must have been a small child at the time of the Civil War, father, but I doubt if you've forgotten the horror of it. I know this is a small, local matter, but it's enough to re-open old wounds and make them bleed again.'

'The danger is there, of course,' Don Alberto agreed, 'but we cannot run away from every test of how adult we've become as a nation. With only God knows what suffering along the way, Spaniards now hope they've learned to disagree without bloodshed and bitterness; Rosario is to have its own chance to prove it. We must be glad about that, not fearful.'

She smiled at an optimism that sounded

reasonable only because *he* put it into words; but she couldn't help feeling that all their prayers would be needed if Rosario wasn't to disappoint him.

'After this morning I'm not sure whether to go on with the English conversation lessons,' she said, remembering another anxiety. 'Perhaps my pupils won't turn up!'

'They *will* turn up, and you mustn't disappoint them,' he insisted firmly, and in that at least he was proved right the following day; or perhaps he'd made sure himself that her 'class' would assemble in the church as usual.

She supposed that Manolo knew very well how the opposition to his scheme was being orchestrated. In times gone by she might have expected that Felipe would be against it as well, but now there was no knowing what he thought; it seemed another sadness to add to the poignant beauty of this strange spring.

No small part of its strangeness was that Ian Gilmour had now become a frequent visitor, with such an easy friendship growing up between him and her uncle that it was hard to remember a time when he'd avoided them. She took no part in their discussions, but one afternoon, returning home with a butterfly orchid Edwina had requested, it was Ian Gilmour who fell into step beside her. She didn't know that he was reminded of another occasion – in a different season, with a different woman. Unlike Blanca Esteban then, this girl looked content to be where she was, entirely at ease with her surroundings. The sleeveless pink dress she wore was simple, and her bare legs and face were already tanned by the sun. Even so she possessed a certain style that would have seemed exotic on a country path at home; here, paradoxically, he thought he would have recognised her at once as being English. He pointed to the orchid in her hand, its stem carefully wrapped in damp moss.

'One of mine, or does it belong to your landlord?'

'Yours, I think,' she admitted without embarrassment. 'It's a rarity in less favoured places, but not here.' A sudden smile lit her face. 'My aunt will give fulsome acknow-ledgements, of course, to anyone whose land she steals from!'

'Edwina, fulsome?' The disbelief in his voice made her laugh out loud and, although his own face remained thoughtful, she knew with a mixture of surprise and pleasure that somehow he'd been liberated from the bitter isolation of the past. The guard he kept on himself had been dis-mantled – perhaps by his growing friend-ship with her uncle, or else by the prospect of the battle ahead. She could see him easily enough as a man who relished being in the thick of a fight.

'I gather the *pueblo*'s public meeting to debate the hotel has been fixed now,' she began hesitantly. 'We shall soon know how Rosario feels about a tourist attraction on its doorstep.'

'And *you* can't decide what to pray for,' Gilmour suggested with a glance at her face. 'A win for us would mean that the sierra is kept safe; but what if it causes Quinones to boot William and Edwina out in a fit of pique?'

'There's yet another worry – Rosario itself,' Venetia pointed out. 'Elderly people with even the faintest memories of the Civil War believe they have good reason to distrust Manolo. The younger ones only want to bury the past. Don Alberto thinks that divisions can be managed now without tearing the *pueblo* apart, but compromise still doesn't exactly spring to mind as being the guiding genius of this lovely place.' She brushed the anxiety aside and spoke of something else. 'Perhaps you know that Fiona went back to Edinburgh – rather unhappily, I'm afraid. The Feria proved a disappointment after all; perhaps Spain itself did.'

'Because she didn't get what she wanted?'

'I doubt if she was even sure what that *was* in the end – it might have been what troubled her most.'

'You mean she played her admirers off against each other and finished up losing them both? Foolish of her – Spanish men still like to believe *they* call the tune. Only we emasculated northerners have been taught that this isn't the case any longer!'

An echo of the old bitterness sharpened his voice, but she stopped in her tracks to consider him and then shook her head. 'No – I can't see you as a shorn Samson, nor Felipe as a full-blown macho warrior! He just wanted to be allowed to love Fiona. It's been pain and muddle all round, not the game of trivial pursuits you seem to suggest.'

'Then I stand corrected,' he said. 'But with my well-known lack of tact and finesse I'll predict that, much sooner than Fiona would like, Quinones will recover from his madness. He'll wake up "with clear eyes and sharpened power", as a poet said, ready to see *you* again!'

She imagined that she saw derision in his smile and was stung by the foolishness of thinking they'd reached a kind of understanding.

'You can't help despising both of us, can you? Felipe is a weak-minded fool, ready to fall in love with whoever happens to come along; I'm at my last gasp, desperate for another chance to make a grab at him! Well, even if I wanted it, the chance won't come – I can tell you now that he'll just go on grieving for Fiona.'

She'd scarcely finished her speech before Gilmour's hands clamped themselves painfully on her shoulders. Expecting to be shouted at or shaken, she was stunned by the discovery that there was sadness in his face, not anger.

'I did mention the lack of finesse,' he said quietly, 'but no contempt was intended, Venetia. I don't even despise Felipe for being trapped by a girl who can't help exploiting her looks as naturally as she breathes – I've been down that humiliating road myself. I'd have liked something more than waste to come out of it.'

It was a conviction she'd heard him put into words before: waste was a sin, a denial of life's possibilities. Not sure that she could trust her voice to say that she agreed with him, she merely nodded instead, and saw a faint smile soften the harshness of his face.

'Now, having got that straight, we'd better resume our walk before Edwina's plant dies in your hand.'

They moved on in silence, but when they came to a piece of rough ground he took hold of her hand to lead her over it. His grip felt warm and strong, fashioned to offer a woman comfort or the sheer pleasure of being touched. More waste, surely, that his

234

hand should be used so seldom.

'You and Uncle William face Manolo and Fernando – is it an even contest?' she asked after a pause.

'I think so,' he said calmly. 'They have more fire-power, but I hope we're faster on our feet!'

Neither of them had taken Felipe into account, but Ian Gilmour would have no doubt, she thought, about whose mast *his* colours would have to be nailed to.

'Having to take sides is obnoxious,' she suddenly burst out, 'and, no matter what Don Alberto says, it's what everyone here will have to do.'

Gilmour shook his head. 'He believes they can now disagree without the destructive violence their ancestors would have required. Blood won't run through Rosario's alleyways, Venetia, on account of our dispute with Quinones; and it won't do the good citizens any harm to have to decide what they value most.'

'You make a fight sound positively desirable,' she protested.

'It's a touch of the old Adam – it comes out in all of us from time to time,' he agreed gravely.

She smiled because he wanted her to, but she was reminded again of Duncan Gilmour – sharing the same rock-like strength and solidity, they were men to have on one's side in time of trouble.

A few minutes later they walked under the archway into the courtyard, only to be halted in mid-stride by the very thing she'd assured him a moment ago wouldn't happen. Felipe was there, interrupting a conversation with William to smile hesitantly at her. She couldn't help looking at the man beside her and saw what she feared – a grin that made its own sardonic comment on her belief in a disappointed but faithful lover. It was Gilmour who spoke to him first.

'Hobnobbing with the enemy, Quinones?'

Colour tinged Felipe's face but he answered quietly. 'I came to call on my *friends*; at least, I hope I may still call them that.'

William suddenly decided to take charge of the conversation. 'I've got some ministry papers for you to see, Ian – shall we discuss them in my study?'

He marched away, leaving Gilmour no choice but to follow him. Alone with Felipe, Venetia struggled with an unruly mixture of emotions in which pity for the sadness in his face finally overcame the shameful regret that he should have timed his visit so badly.

'It's lovely to see you again, Felipe,' she managed to say, 'but I'm afraid I can't stay and talk to you. Wild flowers, though beautiful, don't last and I *must* deliver this long-suffering specimen to my aunt.'

He nodded, but still stood staring at her;

her own glance enquired why he wasn't wearing his usual gold-rimmed spectacles.

'I don't really need them,' he confessed. 'Fiona told me that I was only using them to hide behind. She ... she made me see quite a lot of things clearly.' It seemed an ambiguous statement, and Venetia was still wondering how to reply when he spoke again. 'Gilmour seemed to think I shouldn't be here. If it's what *you* think as well, I won't come again.'

The simple directness of it touched her more than any apology or appeal would have done, and suddenly she could smile at him without any effort.

'Of course, come again. Shall we agree here and now that it needn't make any difference to *us* if your father owns fifty Moorish ruins he wants to turn into hotels!' It left aside the difference that Fiona had made, but she could see no way of touching on that, and she supposed that Felipe would prefer it *not* touched on anyway.

His unhappy, strained face still didn't relax, and she felt ashamed that he might have sensed her own reluctance to find him there. She had a vivid recollection of his very first visit, and of her impression then of a gentle, lonely man at odds with his family. That isolation from his father and brother was almost certainly made worse now, by his dislike of what they wanted to do, and by the knowledge that, but for Fernando, Fiona might have stayed with him for always.

Venetia moved near enough to hold out her free hand. 'I said something silly just now. What your father and Fernando want to do with the castle *does* matter, of course, but I don't see why we shouldn't still make our own choices. My choice would be for you and the Marriotts to stay friends, whatever Ian Gilmour thinks!'

Felipe's troubled expression melted at last into almost his old, sweet smile. 'Dear Venetia, you must go and see to that poor flower, but I shall come again, feeling less nervous next time!' He lifted her hand to his mouth, then gripped it tightly for a moment before releasing her.

She watched him walk away, gave a little sigh for she knew not what, and finally went indoors to see Edwina.

Fifteen

Edwina had been dropping hints for several days that the paper and paints she was running short of couldn't be found in Ubrique or even Ronda. At breakfast one morning, hopeful that William would spare the nerves of other motorists on the road by offering to take her, she supposed wistfully that she would have to undertake the drive to Seville herself. Venetia answered before her uncle could.

'I can do your shopping for you, and invite myself to lunch with Duncan Gilmour at the same time, if Uncle Will doesn't want to use the car.'

Edwina beamed at her brother. 'There ... you see how nicely things work out provided one is patient and not inclined to make a fuss! Venetia will enjoy a day out and I shall get my materials.'

William smiled at his niece, and retired to his study; the public meeting was looming and he must plan his speech. Venetia set about her own morning's work and emerged from it at lunchtime to find Felipe there again, listening to her aunt's description of the next day's planned visit to Seville. Even as he smiled at her she knew what was coming next.

'I offer myself as the chauffeur, Venetia. May I not take you, please? It's a tiring journey to make on your own.'

He meant to be kind, but she was reluctant to be helped, had even rather looked forward to going alone.

'Thank you,' she began, trying to sound grateful, 'but you're probably deep in composing something, and I have a luncheon appointment with Fiona's great-uncle. He's very elderly and very frail – I couldn't wish a strange extra guest on him.'

'Of course not; I would merely collect you when you were ready; not even that – just meet you somewhere if you prefer.'

'I intend to leave *very* early,' she warned him. 'Doesn't that put you off?'

On the contrary, he was ready to depart at whatever hour she liked. She had to give in, acknowledging to herself a subtle change in him. In the earliest days of their friendship she would have expected him to withdraw, like a snail into its shell, at the slightest hint that he wasn't wanted; but this new Felipe was altogether more resolute. It added a touch of strength or obstinacy missing before, and suggested that there might after all be some truth in Blanca's insistence that the Quinones brothers resembled each other.

The following morning he was already waiting outside with his car when she hurried under the archway. The early-June dawn was fine and beautifully cool, and her lingering resentment was washed away by the perfection of the morning. It was impossible to feel anything but grateful for the privilege of being alive in this exquisitely beautiful corner of Spain.

'You're very prompt,' she said as she was helped into the car.

'I've also been very busy! I know exactly where we need to go in the Calle de las Sierpes for artists' materials; and if we make good time with the journey and Edwina's shopping there's also a treat in store. Had you forgotten that today is the Feast of Corpus Christi?'

She thought for a moment that he was suggesting attendance at a special Mass in the cathedral; then light dawned. 'Of course – the Dance of the Seises! Oh, Felipe, how splendid! But I'm afraid nothing will convince Edwina that *she* didn't plan it all herself – my dear aunt has no doubt that she's mysteriously involved whenever some lovely unexpected thing happens!'

Her pleasure was at last so unmistakable that Felipe's confidence, a little shaken by her obvious hesitation the day before, finally returned. He'd been right to insist on coming; he might count it as his first small step along the road to redemption with her, and being useful was infinitely better than flaying himself at home with thoughts of Fiona.

'Now, no conversation, if you'll forgive me,' he said almost gaily. 'I must concentrate on driving fast instead.'

She nodded and turned to stare out of the window, but found herself thinking of another car journey, and a different driver who'd once commended her for being a silent passenger.

Edwina's needs successfully dealt with, they were still in good time for the Corpus Christi ceremony in the cathedral. Six choristers, in seventeenth-century satin knee-breeches, plumed hats, and jackets swinging elegantly from one shoulder, performed a stately dance before the high altar, to the unlikely sound of castanets – the last relic of Spain's once-popular religious dancing.

'It isn't my favourite cathedral by a long way,' Venetia admitted when they were outside the huge Gothic pile afterwards; 'it's altogether too dark, too large, too overladen with treasure. But we couldn't have watched *that* enchanting tradition anywhere else.' She glanced at her watch, then smiled at Felipe. 'Now we part company for a while.

Shall I meet you here in front of the Giralda Tower at four o'clock? Duncan Gilmour will have had enough of me by then.'

Doubting it, Felipe agreed and watched her walk away – a slender, long-legged girl who moved differently from Spanish women and seemed unconscious that the men she passed felt it worth inspecting her with care.

She threaded her way through the labyrinth of alleys and tiny squares to the now familiar house, to be greeted by Josefa with the warmth of an old friend. The *señor*, she said, had been looking forward to the visit with *mucho satisfacción*; feeling the cold now, he was waiting for her in the sunlit patio.

She found him there, watching the daily watering of the plants. Besides being Josefa's husband, and Duncan's chauffeur when required, Aurelio was also the indispensable man about the house and garden. He offered Venetia a smiling greeting while Duncan slowly hauled himself to his feet. It was less than a month since her visit at the time of the Feria, but the change in him was distressing. His face and frame were now skeletally thin, and his skin was parchment-pale despite the climate he lived in. Nevertheless, his smile welcomed her, and so did his opening words.

'I'm so glad to see you, girl. My people here smother me with kindness but I miss

English conversation. Tell me what's going on at Rosario – I hear Ian's interpretation when he telephones, but it may not be the same as yours.'

'Well, the opposing sides are limbering up, I suppose your nephew would say. He and my uncle are full of confidence, while I am full of dread, and Aunt Edwina paints flowers so frantically that I know she's anxious too. She and William have a great deal to lose, you see, if Manolo Quinones decides to punish them for opposing him.'

Duncan nodded, and sipped from the water glass beside him to keep her company while she drank golden Montilla wine.

'Of course they must fight, but I'm afraid Quinones will win if all he requires is a majority vote from the people of Rosario.'

'Because they're too poor, you mean, and too tired of working hard, to turn down the promise of an easier way of earning a living?' she asked. 'My uncle would be very disappointed, but he wouldn't blame them, being wonderfully fair and tolerant. I'm not sure I can say the same of your nephew, though!'

'Nor I – we have to remember the family he springs from!' Duncan agreed with a faint smile. 'But it isn't only a matter of money, and the people of the sierras are accustomed to working hard; what they're *not* yet used to is the idea that their magnificent countryside is anything but the arduous setting of their lives. Preserving it, protecting it, is a concept they've still to come to terms with.'

'And in that they're not so far different from some of our own struggling farmers at home,' Venetia observed sadly.

'Exactly – it's the foreign in-comers who have the time and money to worry about inessential things!'

'Except that they *aren't* inessential,' she objected, then broke off as Josefa reappeared, bringing a tray of food.

'A tapas lunch, the *señor* asked for,' the housekeeper explained, setting out a selection of small dishes with pride – prawns fried with garlic, *serrano* ham, home-cured olives, stuffed artichokes, broad beans, and rings of aubergine cooked in olive oil. Venetia ate with relish because she thought her host wanted her to, and made no comment on how little of the food he took himself. Afterwards, with coffee on the table, he asked about her own plans for the future.

'I could easily drift into staying for ever at Rosario,' she admitted with a smile. 'It's very tempting, and I know it's what my aunt and uncle would dearly like. But my clear-sighted French stepmother warns me from time to time that I must bestir myself and rejoin what she is pleased to call the real world! She's right, of course; I need to find a home of my own, and a settled job.'

Duncan accepted the news calmly and didn't, rather to her relief, feel it necessary to comment on his great-niece's sudden departure from Spain. Instead, she asked about his life at Río Tinto, and only when it was almost time for her to leave did she pose a different question, more abruptly than she intended.

'May we, please, stop pretending that nothing's wrong? Will you tell me why you eat next to nothing and look so thin?'

He didn't answer for a moment, but stared at a crimson rose against the wall as if the need to note its beauty petal by petal was much more important than a discussion of his failing health. Then quietly, indifferently almost, he admitted what she'd begun to fear.

'Cancer of the liver leaves one very little appetite, I'm afraid!' But her shocked face made him stretch out a thin hand to cover hers. He even smiled, and she could have sworn that it needed no effort. 'My dear girl, don't look sad. I've lived long enough, and I'm quite ready for the next "awfully big adventure"! Being a Scot, like Barrie, I have to believe in that, while you must certainly believe in it as a good Catholic.'

Venetia said nothing for a while, afraid of weeping. 'Will you ... will you stay here?' she finally managed to ask.

'Yes, I should prefer that. Josefa, Aurelio and my good doctor friend are prepared to keep on taking care of me, even when I become a nuisance!'

She looked at him with pleading in her face. 'You won't mind if I ask Josefa to ... to keep in touch ... just so that I know how things are?'

'No,' he agreed gently, 'I shan't mind at all.' As if he'd forgotten that he still held it, he didn't release her warm hand. 'We haven't met many times, but that never matters in true friendships. The girl I would have married fifty years ago I only met twice, when she was already someone else's wife, but I can still see her in my mind's eye. Her name was Laura, and you remind me of her.'

Venetia blinked away a mist of tears that Duncan Gilmour would certainly despise and tried to smile instead. 'It's time for you to rest, I think, and for me to find my chauffeur. It's Felipe Quinones who is kindly driving me home this time, not your nephew.'

'One of the opposing side? Poor fellow – I can see *his* predicament!'

She shook her head but, warned by Duncan's exhausted face, merely kissed him goodbye and left him to sleep. Inside the house she had a brief conversation with Josefa, kissed her warmly as well, and then walked back to where Felipe was waiting. The journey home was quite as silent as the outward one had been but, apart from an occasional glance at her sad face, he was kind enough to leave her alone with the thoughts that kept her company.

The public meeting had officially been called by the Mayor, but, since the only building in Rosario large enough to contain the expected turn-out was the church, Don Alberto and Don Ramón had agreed on its use.

The day was carefully chosen: a Saturday, when even a discussion late into the night wouldn't have to be followed by a dawn rising for the men. They appeared, freshly washed and even shaved for so special an occasion, and took their seats. The march of progress allowed the wives, with Edwina and Venetia among them, to range themselves along the sides of the church, but they were there as onlookers, not participants. Remarkably for a gathering of Spaniards, there was so little buzz of conversation before the proceedings began that Don Alberto's reminder of where they were seemed almost unnecessary. Nevertheless, he wished them to remember that they were in God's house, where he could allow nothing to His dishonour to be done or said.

Invited by the priest to open the discussion, the Mayor launched into the speech he'd been practising for days past in Luís's bar. An appeal to local pride came first: thanks to their resident benefactor, Rosario now had the chance to be on the tourist map – part of the famous route of the white towns in its own right, instead of Ubrique's poor relation. Next, the economic carrot: with the conversion of the castle into a hotel, and the building of a new road up from the river valley, there would be months of immediate work for anyone who wanted it, and future prosperity for ever more once the hotel was open. In short, Rosario had every reason to be grateful to Don Manolo Quinones, and none at all to block his magnificent proposal.

William Marriott rose next, to make his own quiet but no less impassioned plea. He spoke well, Venetia thought with pride; but, surveying the intent faces watching him, she feared that she could guess the working of their minds – the *inglés* meant well and they respected him, but it was known to all that *he* could sit watching birds all the time while they had to toil for a living. How could his viewpoint be the same as theirs?

Then came the conservation officer from Seville, primed by Ian Gilmour to stress the obligations of Spain's EU membership without harping too much on where the laws that they were supposed to be observing originated. Madrid was reckoned distant and daft enough by most Andalucíans; Brussels, being still more remote, was bound to seem infinitely worse. The official was listened to in a silence that was polite but unconvinced; he pitied the foreigner now getting to his feet.

Ian Gilmour cut an impressive figure, easy but authoritative, and Venetia couldn't help agreeing with her aunt's loud aside that it was a pity it wasn't the women who were voting. With a deceptive gentleness much enjoyed by some of those present, he went straight for the Mayor's throat: the prosperity Don Ramón looked forward to would belong, as well as to the proprietor of the new hotel, mostly to himself, as the only garage owner for miles around. The initial work that Rosario was to be grateful for would be navvying and bricklaying. Did this appeal to men whose great, inherited skill was in tending the land and making it fruitful? Afterwards, for the six months of each year that the hotel would be open, they could have the pleasure of turning themselves into waiters and bell-hops, and their wives into chambermaids. Was *this* a proper ambition for proud men and women who were still the respected owners of their own land? This was the decision they were really being asked to make, Ian Gilmour said – not what would become of Rosario, but what they themselves would become.

There was still no applause as he sat down, but Venetia thought the audience's reaction indicated something more interesting – it was aware of having been given serious matters to think about. Then came the final speaker, Fernando Quinones, also experienced and very much at ease. He courteously thanked the *forasteros* among them for their concern and sympathised with the official whose thankless task it was to make Brussels legislation popular. His acolytes in the audience duly led an appreciative snigger, but Fernando waved this away and moved to the attack. The people who *belonged* there, unlike the foreigners, knew that the world wouldn't come to an end if the crested coot, or the lynx, or a daisy called oxalis pescaprae disappeared from the Sierra de Ubrique. The protection of this or that animal, flower or bit of pastureland wasn't at the heart of the argument, nor was the argument about themselves, as the previous speaker had tried to suggest. Simply, it was ancient Spain versus new – their corner of Andalucía left to its age-old poverty and backwardness while their neighbours followed the rest of Spain into ever-increasing prosperity. Fernando agreed that they might cling a little longer to the ways of the past, but it was certain that their

251

children wouldn't. The next generation wanted a different life, and if it wasn't on offer in Rosario they would go elsewhere to find it. *That* was the essence of the matter: progress and a bright future, or the backwardness of the past.

He sat down with a small, confident grin at Manolo, knowing for sure, Venetia thought, how thoroughly the compass needle of mood had swung in his direction. They now waited for Don Alberto to announce that voting would begin, but suddenly it seemed that the speeches weren't over after all: someone else, white-faced but determined, was getting to his feet. There was a murmur round the packed church, hushed by the priest's lifted hand. Then Felipe swallowed the obstruction in his throat and began to speak.

'My friends,' he managed to say clearly and slowly, 'you've heard the arguments for and against my father's hotel, but there's one viewpoint you haven't heard, and I promised my nephew, Juan Esteban, that you *would* hear it. He is one of today's children that my brother speaks of, but he *doesn't* want things to change. If the argument is between old and new Spain, he knows which he prefers. He can't wait to be as you all are – old enough to own a small piece of Spanish land that he can work with love instead of greediness. He wants this landscape, and the animals and birds and flowers that belong to it, to remain unspoiled so that *his* children may still know them when the time comes. He is too young to say this for himself, so I have come to say it for him!'

Felipe sat down in a silence so complete that the entire audience seemed to have stopped breathing. Edwina clutched her niece's hand, and Venetia stared at Felipe across the nave of the church, wondering what it had cost him to make that declaration. Then Don Alberto rose for the last time to say that voting must begin. Each man present was to mark a slip of paper he'd been given and hand it to one of the Guardia Civil officers borrowed from Ubrique. The result would be announced outside as soon as the counting was completed.

The women left first, still under some strange spell of silence, while the men laboriously marked and folded their papers. Let out at last, they made as one for Luís's bar across the square where wine – supplied by Manolo, though this was *not* made known – was being freely offered.

Uncertain what they should do next, but determined not to go home, the *pueblo* ladies huddled in groups, whispering among themselves. Manolo and Fernando were already installed at one of the tables Luís had set out, but there was no sign of Felipe. Leaving Edwina proudly reunited with her brother, Venetia went back into the church, almost empty now except for the Guardia Civil men counting votes under the watchful eye of Don Alberto.

She found the man she'd come looking for, but didn't interrupt him – Felipe was kneeling before the altar in the little side-chapel used for baptisms. She turned to leave and almost bumped into Ian Gilmour, propped against the wall by the door.

His withdrawn and sombre expression prompted her to offer comfort. 'Whatever happens, it went in a very orderly way. I should have had more faith in Don Alberto's estimate of these people.'

'Have as much faith as you like, but don't be optimistic about the result,' Gilmour suggested.

'I'm not, but I didn't sense hatred in the air and that's what breeds violence. All the same, it's a pity you didn't speak *after* Fernando.'

'True, but someone else did. If we *should* win, which I doubt, the evening's hero will be the traitor in the Quinones' camp.'

Her face lit with sudden pride. 'It was splendid of him, I think. Fernando and his father may have hated every word of it, but I doubt if they'll feel able to ignore Felipe in future.'

Ian Gilmour glanced over at the solitary kneeling figure she was looking at. 'No doubt, you want to stay and wait for him. I shall mingle bravely with the opposition outside.'

'You mustn't blame yourself if you fail,' she said impulsively. 'When I saw your uncle recently he predicted the result you're obviously expecting, but he said we couldn't despise these people for it – their lives have been too hard for Manolo's offer not to be tempting.'

'I'm not in a position to despise anyone. I told you that once before, but I'm afraid you don't listen to me as raptly as you do to Felipe Quinones.'

He went with his usual abruptness, leaving her discouraged, oppressed by a feeling of loneliness that seemed absurd given the crowds outside. She found her aunt and uncle and they stood together without talking until Don Alberto appeared on the church steps, flanked by his official entourage. A sudden hush fell over the crowd the moment he raised his hands.

'Here, my friends, is the result of your vote. Five voting slips were discounted because they were blank, two because both choices were ticked. Of the remainder, one hundred and seventy votes were cast against Don Manolo's conversion of the castle; two hundred and ten were for it. The scheme must therefore be allowed to proceed. We must *all* accept the result now, my dear people, without rancour on one side or gloating on the other. In that way Rosario will derive nothing but good from this development.'

Don Alberto's appeal was immediately lost on the Mayor, whose grinning face proclaimed that he was ready to gloat with anyone who cared to join him. But Manolo – following a plan that Venetia suspected him of having had ready for the occasion – got up and walked over to where the Marriotts were standing. He held out his hand and, watched by everyone present, William had no option but to take it in a brief, friendly clasp. To loud applause and cheering, Manolo then returned to the centre of the square, and thanked Don Alberto for the use of the church and the people of Rosario for their well-behaved participation. *This* was the changed country Fernando had talked about, peaceable, democratic and forward-looking; let them all congratulate themselves on being part of modern Spain!

More applause broke out, led by the Mayor, and under cover of it William murmured to his companions: 'Let's go home. At any moment now we shall have Don Ramón on his feet again and, even at the risk of disappointing our priest, I cannot listen to *him*, or shake his greasy hand.'

They edged their way round the outside of the crowd and walked home in silence. The night was soft and warm and they sat outside, watching the stars come out – William naming them as usual in an effort to insist that the evening had its pleasures still. But his face looked sad, and Venetia felt obliged to offer what comfort she could.

'It's *not* the end of the world. Most of what we value here *can't* be spoiled. Duncan Gilmour said that to me one day and it's true. Juan will realise it too, I hope; he'll be able to find a place where old and new Spain don't have to fight each other for the upper hand.'

'I hope he also discovers that his uncle spoke bravely for him this evening,' Edwina said.

'I shall make sure he knows,' William agreed briefly.

Edwina nodded, then thought of something else. 'Dislike of the Mayor propelled us out of the square too fast; we should have found Ian Gilmour and brought him back with us.'

Again it was William who answered. 'I saw him leave before we did – I expect the sight of me shaking hands with Manolo was more than he could bear.'

'Understandable,' Edwina acknowledged sadly.

A little silence fell, until Venetia suddenly

got to her feet and said an abrupt good-night.

'She's worried that Felipe has cooked his goose with Manolo,' Edwina observed when she was out of earshot. 'If I'm honest I suppose I can't help feeling we've done the same thing ourselves.'

William smiled faintly at her. 'My dear, you'd have had cause to be nervous if we'd won; as it is, Manolo is determined to be magnanimous. Even *he* couldn't shake hands with me watched by most of Rosario and then kick us out.'

'All the same, does it spoil things for you here?' she asked anxiously.

'It makes it a little more like the rest of the world, therefore a little less perfect than before, but we should have known it couldn't stay entirely unchanged.' He stopped talking, apparently to observe Orion moving into position above their heads. Then, after a moment, his quiet voice broke the silence again. 'Something has changed for Venetia too, I think, but we shall have to wait to be told whether it makes Rosario more or less perfect for *her*.'

Sixteen

There was no sign of their neighbour the following morning, but William wasn't surprised – Ian Gilmour would have no taste for chewing over the dregs of failure. Felipe did appear just before lunch, looking remarkably as usual, and again William asked himself what else should have been expected. A bloodless battle had been fought and lost, and the way to behave now was as this civilised Spaniard was doing; life would go on as usual if they allowed it to.

Felipe deposited on the terrace table the basket of fruit he was carrying. 'Picked for you personally by my father,' he explained with a faint smile. 'It seemed churlish to refuse to bring it.'

William nodded, liking a generosity of attitude in both father and son that he hadn't been prepared for. 'Thank Manolo for us – Edwina is very partial to white peaches! She and Venetia are both hard at work at the moment, but they'll be out to join us soon; stay for lunch, won't you?'

Seated at the table with wine poured,

259

William embarked on what needed to be said next. 'We left after your father's speech last night. Your own contribution was greatly appreciated by *us*, but I expect it's made things very awkward for you, putting forward young Juan's point of view.'

'It happens to be my view as well, but it seemed more telling to let it come from him.' Felipe rumpled his already untidy brown hair still more. 'The result at home isn't what you might expect. My brother thought I was merely paying off a personal score, which strikes him as a reasonable, Spanish thing to do. My father, even more strangely, has decided that I was doing some good – convincing the people who still mistrust us that we're fair and impartial after all! I had neither of those motives in mind at the time, but my standing in the family seems to have gone *up*, not down! Life takes surprising twists and turns, don't you find?'

'Quite often,' William agreed, trying not to smile. 'You might, of course, have met with a different reaction if you'd helped to sway the voting in our favour!'

'I think so too,' Felipe answered, getting to his feet to bow to Edwina, who was just arriving.

She grinned at him with more approval than usual. 'I'm relieved to see you – we thought you might have been locked away in a cupboard by now! Are you making matters still worse by coming to call on the trouble-making foreigners?'

'Not at all,' William drily answered for him. 'Manolo has forgiven us to the extent of sending you your favourite peaches.' But what his sister might have replied was mercifully forestalled by Venetia coming out to join them.

Over lunch, by mutual consent, they left alone the vexed subject of how and when work on Manolo's hilltop ruin would begin. But Felipe raised it before he left:

'I've warned my father and Fernando that I shall continue to interfere in their castle project! It's all I can do – try to contain the damage – but *you*'ll have to tell me what to protest about.'

'It will be a pleasure,' Edwina said with a light in her eye. 'We'll make a start tomorrow.'

And start they would, Venetia realised, making a mental note that she must warn Felipe when she got a chance. Her aunt said nothing that she didn't mean, and he would find himself hauled up hill and down dale, being instructed to protect this or that plant with his very life.

When he'd gone home Edwina considered Manolo's peaches with a regretful eye. 'It would be more principled *not* to eat them, I fear.'

'It would also be rather silly, seeing that we

261

continue to live on the man's property,' Venetia pointed out.

They looked at William and he smiled at them with rueful affection. 'You're both right, of course! Perhaps we should enjoy the gift, and also try to persuade our landlord to treat the hillside with respect. We'll flatter him, if need be, into seeing himself as a born-again conservationist. If we couldn't beat him at the ballot-box, we must defeat him by guile!'

On this cheerful note he set out to thank Don Alberto for conducting the previous evening's proceedings, but Edwina explained that his brightness was for their benefit. 'Poor Will is discouraged,' she said sadly, 'and I don't doubt that Ian Gilmour is not only discouraged but angry. He would take failure personally, and he's not inclined to see *any* redeeming feature in the family at La Paloma.'

'He appreciated what Felipe did last night – he said so,' Venetia insisted. 'But he seemed to expect that we should lose – no doubt in the cynical belief that the Mayor had been allowed to bribe his supporters beforehand.'

'Well, don't let's pretend that it isn't *exactly* what Don Ramón had been doing,' Edwina snapped. 'And if Ian Gilmour *is* cynical it's because the experiences of the last few years have made him so.'

Venetia smiled at her indignant aunt. 'I'm not arguing with you! You like him very much, and so does Uncle Will, and I hope you'll go on doing so. He may be angry after last night, but he's not nearly so hurt in spirit as he was, and that's largely due to you two.'

Edwina was tempted to ask how she knew about this alteration in a reticent man she took little notice of, but thought better of it. Her niece, though gentle, was not soft, and the 'retort courteous ... the reproof valiant' were well within her armoury if she reckoned them justified.

Left alone, Edwina stayed where she was, disinclined for once to return to the comforting atmosphere of her studio. William was doing his best to pretend that nothing was amiss, but he was whistling in the dark. Their idyllic life was showing signs of strain now, and Edwina slowly traced the disturbing sequence of events back to Fiona Gilmour's arrival. *She* had been the catalyst changing the lovely, ordered contentment of their days. Now there was never any telling what would happen next, except that it was soon likely to be the worst thing of all – Venetia's departure from Rosario. She might have stayed for ever without Fiona's disastrous meddling, but it wouldn't happen now. Deep in painful thought, Edwina was slow to register the arrival of another visitor.

'You look like "Patience on a monument, smiling at grief",' Ian Gilmour said, coming towards her across the courtyard. 'I hope you're not still mourning last night's outcome.'

Edwina gave a hurried sniff and managed to sound almost her brusque self. 'I can't always be merry and bright – I *try* to put a brave face on it, but we live in a depressingly awful world.'

She sounded so far from bright that he smiled gently at her. 'Why aren't the others here cheering you up?'

'William's gone to call on Don Alberto; Venetia is working in the studio; and Encarnita is I know not where, probably picking over the public meeting's bleeding remains with her cronies in the village.'

'Dear me, it *has* put you out,' he commented. 'We did our best, you know – no fools can do more!'

'I know that, but please do *not* tell me that I must love Fernando and smile at the Mayor! You needn't even pretend, as William's trying to do, that nothing's going to change. Rosario *will* change, if only because the new Spaniards Fernando Quinones represents are determined that it should.'

Her long fingers, paint-stained as usual, trembled slightly on the table, and Gilmour covered them with his own warm ones in a rare demonstrative gesture. 'I grant you the changes, Edwina, but you must remember something else. There was a lot wrong with the old Spain that you revere – injustice, hardship, poverty for men and women caught in the bind of ruthless landowners and a too-powerful Church. That's why Anarchism flourished in Andalucía almost more than anywhere else. Some of the present changes were long overdue.'

She accepted what he said with a good grace, knowing it to be true of a complicated country with a long, tormented history. Then, achieving a watery smile, she confessed to something else.

'I was feeling depressed about Venetia as well. She's got to think of her own life, I know, but we shall miss her dreadfully. She's like the daughter neither of us had.'

'Well, cheer up – she's coming now,' he said, looking over Edwina's shoulder.

He watched Venetia cross the courtyard, and saw her hesitate at the sight of him before she recovered herself enough to smile. 'You missed a very conciliatory speech from Manolo by leaving early. And Felipe, egged on by my aunt, is now promising to keep a careful eye on the castle work. So perhaps we needn't be too pessimistic about it.'

'*You* needn't be,' he agreed politely, 'but the eagles will have to find another breeding-place next year, and it remains to be seen whether the *pueblo* can live happily with a fancy hotel on its doorstep, siphoning off labour that's needed elsewhere. We shall know then how far a ruthless businessman is ready to let anyone else's interests outweigh his own.'

She inspected his expression and shook her head. 'I couldn't see the Mayor taking much notice last night of Don Alberto's plea for tolerance, and you seem equally determined to ignore it as well. Why assume that Manolo can't be persuaded *not* to siphon off anything the *pueblo* needs?'

'Because I lack your touching faith in human nature, I expect.'

'No, because you're still bound hand and foot in the bitter animosities of the past,' she contradicted him swiftly. 'Compromise is simply a sign of weakness – you said something like that the very first time you came to this house.' She regretted admitting that she remembered it, and hurried on. 'In any case you're forgetting that we've got Felipe on our side – he's been here this morning, promising to help restrain his father.'

She saw Ian Gilmour smile, but not with the real amusement or warmth that had occasionally given her pleasure. This time his expression said clearly what he thought, even before he put it into words.

'Last night's hero to the rescue again,' he

remarked thoughtfully. 'Why didn't I expect that?'

The rest of his message needed no words at all. He understood her willingness to give Manolo the benefit of the doubt because, with Fiona gone, she was to be taken back into the Quinones fold. Felipe was busy redeeming himself, and she would soon be convinced that all was sweetness and light at La Paloma. She *wanted* to be convinced, against all reason and all probability.

Venetia saw all this in his face; she was being judged by a man who would allow nothing for forgiveness, for tolerance or compromise. Their friendship had wavered like a candle-flame, usually flickering uncertainly, but sometimes giving out a life-enhancing glow of warmth and light. It had failed altogether now – she could smell the acrid whiff as it guttered in the still air.

With nothing left to say to him, she spoke only to her aunt. 'I've got shopping to do for Encarnita in Ubrique ... I shan't be long.'

They watched her walk away with her free English stride. Edwina, he thought, would see it as a reminder that she didn't belong there, but his own certainty was that she would go no further than the end of the drive. Even Felipe couldn't try again with her and fail, and there seemed no doubt that he *was* trying. The thought of her among the Quinones at La Paloma felt strangely like an outrage, but he managed to rationalise his sense of shock – even a man who didn't greatly care what became of this one of his neighbours didn't like to see her make such a desperate mistake.

Gilmour had survived the long nightmare that had followed his crash by mastering the lonely art of detachment. Learning to step outside his wincing flesh and tortured mind, he'd been able to endure as an observer the suffering of a man he could think wasn't himself. But when he was finally free of it and out in the world again the habit had stuck – until he came to Rosario. Its kind, gentle priest had insisted on becoming a friend; Edwina and William had simply ignored the past; and young Juan Esteban had walked clean through his defences, shattering the pretence that he didn't still ache for his own son. His mind allowed Venetia Marriott no part in this demolition process that had left him vulnerable again; she just happened to be there. He told himself that he simply disliked the idea of her being entrapped in the robbers' cave at the end of the drive.

'I think you've forgotten me,' Edwina's voice reminded him gently. 'As a rule I'm too large and noisy to get overlooked!'

He emerged from his dark train of thought to smile at her. 'Not overlooked – as it happens you figured in my meditations! I was remembering the past and considering the future – both of them things I've preferred to avoid until now.'

'Today's what counts,' she said firmly. 'One of the few blessings attached to growing old is discovering that the past no longer matters very much, and the future may not matter at all. "Present mirth hath present laughter" – it's as true now as the day Shakespeare put it into words.'

'So is everything else he said; we modern-day hacks have to eat our hearts out over that fact!'

She considered him for a moment, with interest and affection. 'Is *that* your future – going back to writing?'

'I think so; it's my *métier* after all, and I should soon tire of my battle with the reluctant soil of the sierra even if El Perdido belonged to me, which it doesn't. *That* rather dished me with Juan when he knew, by the way.'

She smiled at the memory of Blanca's son, but grew serious again. 'He won't be happy about Rosario's vote. I hope it doesn't mean that we shan't see him again. With a gap of nearly sixty years between them, he and my brother became friends.'

'Then they'll remain so. Juan may be a child still but he has a constant heart.' Ian Gilmour glanced at his watch and then stood up. 'I shall have to give William up.

Will you ask him to call in if he's out walking tomorrow? *Adiós*, Edwina.'

She watched him walk away, thinking sadly of their conversation. It would be another loss when *he* left El Perdido – expected, but now perhaps having to be faced quite soon. Her brave words about living for the moment had been a lie; like everyone else, what she really prayed for was a future that securely contained everything they cherished about the present.

Seventeen

After the excitement of the public meeting, Rosario returned to normal more easily than Venetia expected. There was, if anything, a little extra air of satisfaction as people greeted one another; they were pleased with themselves for having managed things so well. She also detected the same recovered contentment in Felipe, once he'd insisted on telling her what had happened at the Feria.

'I knew all along that Fiona wouldn't stay with me if Fernando glanced her way. It was almost a relief when it happened and I was *made* to see how hopeless it was.' He stared at Venetia, looking for some clue to what she was thinking. 'Are you still hurt ... still angry with me?'

She shook her head, smiling a little because he suddenly reminded her of Juan hoping that some misdemeanour might have escaped notice. 'Neither, I can truthfully say ... only sorry if you're missing Fiona.'

'I'm *not*, and that's the truth as well. She was like a fever that I've recovered from. I even missed you when I *was* caught up with her; she pretended to enjoy things to please me, but I could always tell when she was bored. Venetia, will you come and listen to some music again ... be my dear friend again?'

She hesitated, saw the pleading in his face and smiled at him. 'It's what I said we were, if you remember.'

From then on her visits to La Paloma were resumed. Manolo seemed to bear her no grudge for being a Marriott, and she told herself that he showed more Christian tolerance than the bigoted Ian Gilmour had done. She hoped *he* noticed that she now went out walking again with Felipe.

There remained, though, the question of the future. Each day's increasing warmth was a reminder that Edwina's work would soon be over. The explosion of colour along every path and roadside was already dwindling; soon the heat of early summer would bring the wild flowers' brief life to an end for another year. Her own help would no longer be needed, and she must tear herself away from what now felt like home. Arlette's advice confirmed that the decision she'd all but taken was good; she would settle down in Paris and accept the job Luc's publisher friend had offered her. It was time to break the news to William and Edwina.

But before she'd plucked up courage enough to upset them with it, William broke some more bad news himself at the breakfast table.

'I found a note had been delivered this morning. Ian Gilmour has left El Perdido.'

Edwina glared, angry with her brother, it seemed. 'How *can* he have left? He hasn't said goodbye.'

'Nevertheless his note says that he's on his way to New York – a sudden change of plan, apparently. He asks to be remembered to you, my dear.'

To her aunt, Venetia registered through a sudden stab of pain that held her speechless. It wasn't regret for *him*, she tried to tell herself. She was seeing El Perdido in her mind's eye, left empty again and desolate.

William didn't add to what he'd just said, but sought refuge in his study, unwilling to discuss a man he'd come to look upon as a friend.

'It's churlish behaviour,' Edwina said reluctantly. 'I can see Will's disappointed in him; we were going to keep Manolo in order *together*.'

Venetia found her voice at last and made a huge effort to sound unconcerned. 'Ian Gilmour's ex-wife and son are in New York. I think he's missed them very much, and hopes they can become a family again.'

Her aunt accepted this but clearly continued to struggle with a sense of hurt, and Venetia managed not to point out that it was unfair to blame a man who'd done so little to make them like him. They waved William off to an appointment in Ronda and had settled down to work in the studio when Encarnita called Venetia to the telephone. The faltering voice at the other end of the line belonged to Josefa in Seville, tearfully explaining that she was making good a promise to the *señorita*. Her dear *patrón* was growing very weak; they feared that he wouldn't live much longer. Venetia said at once that she would come, and only after the brief conversation had ended remembered that her uncle had driven off for the day in the car.

She told Edwina that she must somehow hurry to Seville, then made up her mind to ask for help and rang La Paloma. It wasn't a servant or Felipe who answered but, rather to her dismay, Fernando Quinones, explaining that Felipe was driving his father to visit cousins on the coast.

'Silly of me,' she murmured unevenly... 'I'm afraid I forgot ... he *did* mention it.'

'You sound agitated, Venetia. Is something wrong?' The question, asked so calmly, steadied her.

'Nothing here, thank you – I just want to get quickly to Seville to see a sick friend, but Uncle Will's got the car. It doesn't matter – I'll take a train instead.'

'Stay where you are. I shall be with you in five minutes.'

The line went dead, and she was left to tell herself that being under an obligation to Fernando mattered much less than reaching her friend.

In less than ten minutes they were on the road, and she was obliged to sound grateful. 'I'm being a great nuisance, I'm afraid, but I felt sure Felipe wouldn't mind being asked.'

Fernando's glance flicked over her, then returned to the road. 'I don't mind, either; it's a novel sensation – doing something Venetia Marriott approves of!'

She didn't reply, and his car swallowed up another kilometer or two before he spoke again. 'Has your friend no family, that *you* must rush to help?'

'None nearer than Scotland that I know of. He's Ian Gilmour's uncle, but Ian himself has flown to New York. Duncan Gilmour is old and dying ... I can't allow him to die alone.'

Fernando made no comment, and she was left to wonder whether he'd have gone to his present trouble if he'd known who it was for. Then he asked a different question.

'Are *you* encouraging Felipe to revolt over the castle venture, or is he under the thumb of your awe-inspiring aunt?'

Venetia could answer this easily enough. 'My impression is that he isn't under anyone's thumb now, not even your awe-inspiring father's.'

'Perhaps true,' Fernando conceded, 'but I can certainly blame the Marriotts for that. Our family life was quite harmonious until they came to rent the stables.' He smiled as he said it, and she was obliged to concede something herself: Fernando smiling like that was a very attractive man.

As if he read her thoughts, his next question went to the heart of the matter. 'If I'd offered to quench my father's enthusiasm for the hotel, would it have made any difference – to you and me?'

She hesitated for a moment and then answered truthfully: 'No, it wouldn't have done.'

'That's what I thought.'

'I hadn't finished,' she insisted quietly. 'I also wanted to say that I was mistaken about you ... I didn't realise that you were vulnerable, like the rest of us.'

His mouth twisted in a wry smile. 'I'm sure I can hear your dear aunt saying that it's high time I found myself wanting something I couldn't have – so character-building!'

'She might,' Venetia agreed, 'say something along those lines ... she's the last of the Victorians.'

His hand touched hers for a moment, then she was released, and while he concentrated on driving fast, she thought how strange it would be if she ended up liking Fernando Quinones after all.

There were tourists about, making their dutiful round of the sights – cathedral, Torre del Oro, Plaza de España, and the university housed in the famous one-time tobacco factory – but after the drama of Holy Week and the hectic gaiety of the Feria, Seville was sinking back with relief into drowsiness and summer heat. The *barrio* of Santa Cruz, blindingly white or deeply shadowed according to whether its narrow lanes happened to lie in *sol* or *sombra*, seemed all but deserted. She imagined its inhabitants withdrawn into the shaded, fountain-cooled quietness of their inner patios until it was time to *'tomar el fresco'* in the usual evening stroll with their friends. It seemed, given the Andalucían climate, an ideal way to live – a perfect combination of privacy and neighbourliness. She said this to Fernando and saw him smile.

'Maybe, but give me Madrid; I find Seville a narcissistic city, always looking at itself.' He drew up outside the house she indicated, and turned to look at her. 'What happens now?'

'I'm not sure; but I shall stay for a night or two in any case. You've been very kind, but I can certainly take the train home. Thank you again for bringing me here. Will you tell Felipe what has happened?'

He nodded, then leaned towards her and lightly kissed her mouth. 'Pretend it was from Felipe, *querida.*' Then, much to her relief, he drove away.

Inside the house she was greeted first with tears, and then with the sad warning that she would find the *señor* much changed.

'The doctor promises us that he doesn't suffer,' Josefa explained brokenly, 'but our dear *patrón* pretends, I think; he hides the pain for our sake.'

It was what Duncan Gilmour would try to do, Venetia felt sure. He came of a race and a generation that, in his own Scots word, tholed in silence, because suffering was a private matter. He was lying on a day-bed in

277

a room on the ground floor, but the door was wide open, enabling him to see the greenness and the blossom outside. Instead of sickness, the room smelled of the summer jasmine and climbing roses that swagged the patio's arches. His face was skeletally thin, and he tried to sound displeased at the sight of her.

'I told Josefa *not* to telephone. You mustn't stay long, Venetia – too depressing for you.'

'I'll leave when you get tired,' she said, sitting down beside him. She took hold of his hand, bone-white against her brown fingers, as if the contact could transfer to him some of her own warmth and strength. But his life, she sensed, was ebbing away; only a still-unclouded mind and stubborn spirit refused to be diminished by approaching death.

'Josefa couldn't find my nephew,' he murmured, 'but it doesn't matter. Everything's in order ... the lawyer knows what to do, and Josefa and Aurelio are well taken care of.'

'Uncle William received a note from Ian Gilmour to say that he was on his way to New York. That's why Josefa's message didn't reach him. He'd have come otherwise, I'm sure.'

'Perhaps,' Duncan agreed, 'but perhaps not! He owes me no favours. My brother reared him to see me as being on the Fascist side – the wrong side, in Hamish's view.

Spain made extremists of us all, I'm afraid.'

His voice faded into silence, his small reserve of stamina exhausted for the moment, and Venetia brought out of her bag one of the books she'd borrowed from William's library.

'You're to stop talking now and rest for a little while,' she insisted. 'I thought you might like to listen to Mr Pickwick and friends arriving for poor Bob Sawyer's disastrous party!'

His tired face suddenly smiled at her. 'Did I seem not pleased to see you? I was only pretending, Venetia.'

'I know,' she said, and began to read. She went quietly on until she was sure he'd fallen asleep; then, outside in the shaded coolness of the patio, Josefa brought her food and wine.

'No need to worry,' the housekeeper said softly. 'The *señor* has a little bell within reach, and Aurelio is always listening. It still troubles the *patrón* to have a woman attend to him, so it is better this way, I think.'

'He's blessedly lucky to have you both,' Venetia told the small, sad-eyed woman, 'but he knows that very well.'

Josefa's tears brimmed over, but she mopped them away with her apron and tried to smile. 'What better master could we have had? Aurelio got into a fight once with the servant next door who said that Río Tinto had been a dreadful, inhuman place, mostly run by the *ingleses*.'

'Life *was* hard there for the miners – cruelly so,' Venetia felt obliged to suggest.

'So it was for my father, a day-labourer on the land, and for the men who had no work at all,' Josefa pointed out. 'It wasn't rare for Spaniards to be close to starvation then, *señorita*.' She put away the subject of the past with a heavy sigh and returned to the anxious present. 'The doctor will be here soon ... he calls every day. But there's time for you to eat a little *colación* before he arrives.'

Enough was eaten to satisfy Josefa and Venetia was drinking coffee by the time a small, grey-haired man walked in, introducing himself as Dr Casals. He shook hands briskly then went into Duncan's room and closed the door. When he emerged she was still sitting there, praying that her friend might die without pain, or the indignity he would hate.

'I read him to sleep with Charles Dickens. Was that a good thing to do?' she asked anxiously.

'Of course ... now that he's awake I expect he's hoping for the next instalment.'

Venetia studied the doctor's face for a moment before asking her next question. 'I'm not a relation, you know, only a friend. On a previous visit Duncan Gilmour said that he had cancer of the liver. Are you allowed to tell me any more, seeing that the only members of his family I know about are a long way away?'

'I can confirm what you've probably already guessed – he is dying, *señorita*, because the tumour is inoperable, and he can eat almost nothing. Had he not been a man of great physical and mental strength, he would be dead by now. The reserves are almost gone, but he will probably survive a few days more – it's impossible to be precise.' The doctor hesitated before approaching his own question. 'Self-sufficiency has always been his watchword, but it's been taking all his courage to die alone. He speaks of you with love, like a father speaking of his daughter, but he's a proud man and he won't *ask* you to stay. Perhaps you aren't able to anyway, have commitments of your own?'

There was a little pause. 'Nothing that can't wait,' she said at last. 'I can stay for as long as I'm needed.'

The doctor inspected her face for a moment, as if still in doubt. 'Your being here will only help if you can conceal your own distress. It won't be easy – you're not a professional nurse.'

'I know, but I shall do my best.'

His nod accepted it as being enough, but there was one last anxiety to air. 'Josefa and

281

Aurelio have spent their working lives in his service...'

'I know,' she said again, 'but they won't mind my being here. They'll understand that we are taking care of their dear *patrón* together.'

Dr Casals' expression relaxed into a transforming smile. 'I shall tell my friend tomorrow that he is a fortunate man, although he seems to think that himself already. *Adiós, señorita*; we shall be seeing more of each other.'

With Duncan awake again, she said firmly that she'd come to stay, being bored for the time being with Rosario. His worn face looked distressed and she grasped his hands, offering all the reassurance she could. 'I'll go if you don't want me here; otherwise *please* let me stay, if only to help Josefa.'

He slowly lifted her hand to his mouth, and then he managed to smile at her. 'Stay, girl, but only if you promise not to get upset. There's nothing unnatural about an old man going to meet his maker.'

The next day began watching Aurelio at his daily task of watering out in the patio while she breakfasted there, the scent of freshly damp earth and greenery mingling with the smell of Josefa's coffee. It ended in her watching Duncan released at last into sleep by the pain-killing drugs he resisted during the day. In between they spent the long, slow hours together, and Venetia knew that when this strange interlude was over what she would value it for most would be its tranquillity. He talked about the Andalucía of eighty years ago, with its still-unravished coast, its beauty and its terrible poverty. When he grew tired, he listened to her own much briefer story; heard, as no one else had done, what she had lost when Luc died, and understood why she still sometimes seemed to be waiting for a voice that no one else could hear.

That evening William telephoned to say that he was coming to Seville in the morning; he wanted to see for himself that she was all right. She met him at a café nearby but gently refused when he suggested that she ought to drive home with him.

'No ... Duncan refuses to let us be harrowed; even Josefa has to shed private tears because he won't be wept over. His only regret is that he won't now have the chance to argue with you and Don Alberto – he claims to be an atheist, but I only half believe him.' She took a sip of coffee, then moved the conversation to a subject she could manage more easily. 'How is my dear aunt?'

'Resuming normal life,' William said with thankfulness. 'Now that the spring flood of bloom is drying up we're sailing into calmer waters. She's only checking that everything she's done is up to standard, which of course it is. In this one area of her life Edwina is a relentless perfectionist.' William hesitated, not sure how his next piece of information would be received. 'Felipe came with me, and I promised not to use up all your free time. The poor fellow is anxious to see you, so I shall disappear when he arrives and attend to the little matter of Edwina's shopping list instead. Why is it that even the best of women discover a dozen things they can't live without the moment one is going anywhere near a shop?'

'It's the acquisitive streak in us, I expect,' Venetia suggested with a smile. 'Give her my love when you get home.'

William nodded, then, as he spotted Felipe walking towards them, got to his feet. 'Well timed, my boy. Venetia and I were just about to say our goodbyes.' He leaned down to kiss her, gripped her hands in his own for a moment, and then delved in his pocket for Edwina's list. 'Now for the tedious business of the day. If the awnings aren't out across the Calle de las Sierpes I shall probably get sunstroke as well!'

He lifted his ancient Panama hat, grinned at them and walked away, reinforcing for Venetia the impression she always had of

284

him – there went Chaucer's 'parfit gentle knight' crossed with not a little of Cervantes' Don Quixote. Then she smiled at the man who stood watching her.

'It's lovely to see you, Felipe. I can't stay much longer, but we've just time to share some more coffee.'

He signalled to the waiter, then took William's place at the table while she registered the fresh perspective that absence gave – or perhaps she simply hadn't got used to seeing him without the spectacles Fiona had forbidden. The shy neighbour of their first meeting had certainly been a misleading concealment; he seemed now as much to be reckoned with as Fernando was.

'Am I being a nuisance wanting to see you?' he asked quietly. 'I was worried about you, but also missing you very much. It was kind of Fernando to bring you here, but it should have been me.'

The directness with which he spoke was something new as well; and the small span of time she'd been away from Rosario had made a difference to them. Previous knowledge of each other was still there, but now this fresh acquaintance seemed to promise different discoveries as well. The combination of old and new made conversation both more difficult and more interesting.

'It's kind of you to feel concerned,' she answered at last, 'but there's no need to be.

285

Duncan has wonderful servants who insist on taking care of us both, and kind Dr Casals calls regularly.'

Felipe examined Venetia's face, then stretched out a hand to touch the hollows beneath her cheekbones. 'You've got thinner, and I can't help wishing you weren't here. A hospital, surely, is the place for Señor Gilmour now.'

'He'd hate it,' she said gently. 'We want him to die where *he* chooses – in his own home. I wouldn't stay if there were relatives here to keep him company, but there aren't any nearer than Scotland, and he doesn't want them sent for.'

'Ian Gilmour *was* here,' Felipe pointed out. 'Perhaps he should have been the one to stay.'

She frowned at the mention of someone she'd tried hard to banish from her mind – without any success at all. She shared to a degree that seemed unreasonable Edwina's disappointment in a man *none* of them was able to forget. But, with sufficient effort, she thought she could at least now sound unconcerned about him.

'He and Duncan were virtual strangers, accustomed to thinking rather ill of each other. Ian Gilmour was taught to see his uncle as an intolerant defender of the old, reactionary Spain.'

'It might even be a fair description of a

man who once helped to run the Río Tinto mines,' Felipe suggested, and saw Venetia shake her head.

'It doesn't in the least describe a wise and generous lover of this country, which is what Duncan *is*.'

His hand covered hers in instant apology. 'Then forgive me for my mistake ... You know him; I don't.'

Her smile excused the offence, but she glanced at her watch. 'It's time to go, I'm afraid. Give my greetings to your father. I expect he's longing to start on his new venture.'

It was Felipe's turn to smile. '*Querida*, he *is* starting. There are a lot of technical problems to solve, but surveyors, architects and designers are commanded to beat a path to our door – my father doesn't like the word "delay"!'

They got up to leave, but as they fell into step together Venetia turned to smile at him. 'All the same, you said that as if you admired Manolo.'

'I do,' Felipe admitted, almost ruefully. 'I take risks in my music, and I can see that my father is adventurous in his own way, just as Fernando is in his.'

'Quinones one and all!' she agreed. 'No wonder Blanca said as much.'

They walked in silence after that until the door of Duncan's house brought them to a halt. 'Here's where we part company,' she said. 'Thank you for the escort home.'

He stared at her for a moment, trying to frame his next question tactfully. 'Do you know how long you'll be here? Has the doctor said?'

'Perhaps a few more days, he thinks.' She tried to say it firmly, but her voice shook a little, and, instead of keeping to his resolve to smile and walk away, Felipe suddenly wrapped his arms about her. His body felt warm and strong, and she rested against it for a moment, grateful for the reminder that life would go on after she'd said goodbye to Duncan Gilmour. Then she gently released herself and managed this time to sound calm.

'Don't be anxious. Even now my dear friend is the most considerate of men.' She unlocked the massive, iron-studded door, then turned to kiss his cheek by way of goodbye. 'Drive carefully back to Rosario.'

He nodded without answering, and waited until the door had closed behind her before he walked away.

Eighteen

The following morning, on her way back to the house after listening briefly to Mass in the cathedral, a figure Venetia recognised came towards her from the opposite direction.

'This is silly,' she insisted, stopping in her tracks. 'You can't spend your life driving between Rosario and Seville – or have you been out all night, sleeping standing up, as horses are supposed to do?'

'Something requiring much less effort! I invited myself to stay with the friends you met at the Feria.' But her frown of worry deepened, and Felipe spoke less confidently. 'Do you mind my being here? I should have thought of that, I'm afraid.'

'I only mind the waste of time for *you*; I'm sure you've got work to do. Promise me you'll go home this afternoon ... *please*, Felipe.'

Reassured again, he shook his head. 'I've nothing more important to do than look after you. There are more dangerous cities than this one, but even so the park's no place for you to wander about in alone.'

She knew that to be true, having been stopped when she last walked through it by a drug-hungry youth desperate for money. Carrying none, she'd been forced to surrender her watch instead, and had gone back home feeling both angry and sick at heart.

'Not the park today,' she suggested abruptly. 'Let's walk by the river for a few minutes; then I must go back.'

They went in silence for a while until, afraid that she must have seemed ungrateful for his kindness, Venetia spoke cheerfully again.

'What is the news of Juan?'

'He's counting the days until school ends for the summer; then he's quite certain he's coming back to Rosario.'

'He'll be disappointed to find El Perdido empty.' It was something she hadn't intended to say. If Ian Gilmour refused to fade from her mind, she could at least not conjure the man up more vividly by talking about him.

'Juan may be disappointed, but not surprised – Gilmour warned him, apparently, to expect things to change. But my single-minded nephew is still determined to look after the trees they planted together.'

In her mind's eye Venetia saw Juan's small figure trudging up the hillside, valiant but lonely, and unable to change the course of events that governed his young life. 'Has anyone told him what may have become of the landscape he thinks of as his – if not this summer, certainly next?' she queried slowly.

Felipe took hold of her hand. 'If there's any need, I shall tell him,' he promised, 'and we'll plant more trees somewhere else.'

She thought he would, and found the certainty comforting. When they parted company outside the house she was grateful to know that he was there; Fiona's disruption to their friendship had done no lasting damage after all, and she was content now to know that he cared enough about her to want to remain in Seville.

Duncan was awake when she got back, and alert enough to register a change in her that made his wasted features sketch a smile. 'You look better, either for the walk or the prayers!' he murmured.

'The friend I saw yesterday – Felipe Quinones – is still here. It's useless to tell him I don't need looking after ... he's determined to be helpful instead of going home.'

'Good; that sets my mind at rest,' Duncan admitted – rather strangely, she considered. She adjusted the blinds so that the brightness of the late-morning sun filtered more softly into the room, and he watched her with the pleasure that her movements always gave him.

'What shall it be today?' she asked as she came to sit beside him, '...Norman Douglas wandering about in old Calabria, or a traveller closer to home?'

His head moved slightly against the pillow. 'Not just yet ... I want to say something first. Your friend probably thinks you shouldn't be here, and he's right – you ought to go home.'

She took his thin hand between her own warm ones. 'Are you still worried about Josefa and Aurelio? They don't mind my being here – at least, I don't think so.'

He frowned because she'd misunderstood. 'Of course not – they love you. It's *you* I worry about. I don't want you upset.'

'If I promise not to get upset may I stay?' she asked gently. 'I might be frightened if *you* were, but you're not.'

He didn't answer at once, and she thought the effort of talking had exhausted him; then another smile lit his ravaged face. 'Manuel Casals says I'm the happiest dying patient he knows! It's true, Venetia; for me the best was saved till last.'

She blinked away sudden tears and smiled instead. '*Gracias, señor* – the loveliest compliment I shall ever receive! We should remember Fiona *very* kindly; without her we wouldn't have met.'

She hesitated on the verge of asking again whether she should contact his relatives in

Scotland, but he'd made it clear that Ian Gilmour was the only one of them he would have liked to see.

She rested in her room after luncheon, and when she came downstairs she was immediately aware of a change in the atmosphere of the quiet house. The glass doors of the patio were open as usual, but Aurelio wasn't there, busy about some task. Instead, with his head against one of the pillars, he was silently weeping, and without being told she knew that Sancho Panza had finally lost his master – the *don* was dead.

She went to stand beside him, not speaking, just clasping his hand until it was time to begin doing what needed to be done.

Duncan made good his promise. His departure had been methodically arranged and the instructions given to Abogado Morena were precise – brief announcements locally and to the Gilmour family in Edinburgh, and a simple funeral and interment.

While these arrangements were being made Venetia remained, at the lawyer's request, to help Duncan's grief-stricken servants. For the funeral itself Felipe returned, bringing William and Edwina. She was grateful to see them, but their presence seemed to accentuate the total lack of Gilmours; one of them in particular *should* have been there to say goodbye to Duncan.

But as the service was about to begin there was a small and unexpected commotion. Relatives *had* arrived after all, in the persons of Fiona and a middle-aged man she hastily introduced as her father, the elder of Duncan's nephews. She'd found time, Venetia observed, to change into elegant mourning – black dress, gloves and a wide-brimmed, black straw hat. Probably aware of looking very beautiful, she glanced pityingly at her former friend's white cotton jacket and skirt – under-dressed, of course, but perhaps it didn't matter in someone who wasn't family.

Afterwards, it was Venetia who suggested a return to Duncan's house, knowing that Josefa would be too shy to do so; but when they were back in the Calle San Isidoro Fiona seemed determined to take charge. With becoming hat still in place but gloves removed, she managed a few words of thanks in Spanish to the servants for their care of her great-uncle, and then switched more fulsomely into English with the doctor. Manuel Casals bowed politely, Aurelio looked at his feet, and Josefa's glance at Venetia asked if it was time to start serving wine and the tapas already carefully prepared.

Watching them do this, Fiona spoke approvingly to Edwina beside her: 'They're very good. My great-uncle might have been a confirmed bachelor but he trained them well.'

Edwina nodded, in no hurry to offer the information she was keeping in reserve. 'William and I came to make up, as we thought, for a dearth of Gilmours; we didn't expect to see you and your father.'

'Blood relatives are obliged to put themselves out,' Fiona pointed out sweetly, 'though my uncle certainly hasn't done so – it was left to the lawyer to telephone us.'

'Ian isn't here, that's why. As far as we know he's still in New York. We miss him – we liked having him as a neighbour.'

'Not Venetia, I think – she told me once that they preferred to ignore each other.'

'It wasn't *my* impression,' Edwina insisted, looking down her long, thin nose. 'I'd have said they liked each other very well.'

Fiona abandoned the subject, being more concerned to watch Felipe. His greeting to her had been very brief, but she couldn't miss the care with which he hovered near Venetia while she talked to the guests who had been Duncan's neighbours.

'Dear Venetia – putting me to shame by being *very* busy,' she next observed sweetly.

Edwina smiled her crocodile smile. Well, after all, she knows these people – she stayed here while your great-uncle was dying.'

There was small pause before Fiona

recovered enough to fire back. 'He should have let *us* know he needed help.'

Miss Marriot was now admiring the sky-blue blaze of Aurelio's morning glories on the wall beside her. 'He seemed not to want to do that – he was very content, I believe, with Venetia and his servants.' She moved away to inspect something else, and Fiona resurrected a smile as Felipe edged towards her.

'Kind of you to come,' she said with all her old warmth of manner. 'I didn't realise you knew Duncan Gilmour.'

'He wasn't well enough for me to meet, I'm afraid. I'm only here to support Venetia.'

Felipe studied her face beneath the sweeping hat brim, bemused by the idea that it had once dazzled and tormented him. He could see its perfection even now, but without the smallest flicker of excitement in his blood. She was beautiful, but she couldn't destroy him again, and gratitude for that knowledge made him smile kindly at her. 'What happened to the research – is it going to earn you the laurels you expected?'

'Well, I begin to feel confident!' Irritatingly, she noticed that his glance had strayed in Venetia's direction again. 'What about you?' she asked, '...still hoping to overtake Rodríguez in the guitar-concerto stakes ... still perhaps hoping to redeem yourself with our *amiga* over there? Poor girl – between us we did treat her very badly!'

The 'poor girl' looked lovely, he thought, talking to the doctor across the patio. Sunlight had gilded her hair, and the white dress that so flattered her tanned skin was dappled with light and shadow. Aware of Fiona's inquisitive eyes on him, he managed another smile. 'I can't make any claims about Venetia, I'm afraid, but my music is coming along nicely; in fact, it's rather in demand at the moment!'

Then, as the neighbours began to drift away, the lawyer called the rest of them to order, suggesting that they should return indoors while he made known the contents of Duncan Gilmour's will.

Seated round the table in a little-used dining-room that felt cold after the heat outside, they waited for Eduardo Morena to begin. He spoke in Spanish for Josefa and Aurelio's benefit, and then translated into English. The intentions of his old friend were clear and simple, he said: items of family silver and jewellery were to go to the Gilmours in Scotland, together with his precious historical archive of the Río Tinto mines: there would be no difficulty in sending these things out of the country – the necessary permits would be obtained by the time the estate was wound up. Next, Duncan's small but choice collection of paintings went to his old friend

Dr Manuel Casals.

The lawyer glanced at his papers again, and then smiled at Josefa and Aurelio. Señor Gilmour had intended *them* to be well looked after, and money from the estate had already been earmarked to provide them with a pension which would ensure them a comfortable life; it was their *patrón*'s way of thanking them for years of faithful service.

Venetia clasped the weeping Josefa's hand and hoped that, somewhere, Duncan might be aware of his servants' wordless gratitude. She was scarcely listening when Eduardo Morena began to speak again, but suddenly it was her own name that was being mentioned. Duncan's remaining assets, and the house at 15 Calle San Isidoro, together with all the contents not separately bequeathed, were left to his beloved friend, Venetia Marriott. At this point the lawyer drew an envelope out of his briefcase and passed it to her, not seeming to notice the sudden heavy silence in the room.

Venetia sat there a moment longer, but the pressure of things not being said began to weigh on her unbearably. Still without speaking, she got up and walked out, clutching the envelope she'd been given. Outside, the air smelled sweet, and she stood for a while breathing it in with a kind of desperate gratitude. At last, she opened Duncan's letter.

My dear girl,

When you read this you'll know of the small gifts I've made you. Don't be in a fuss about them; they're nothing compared with what you've given me. You must do with the house exactly what you please. Sell it if you like, but I remember you saying that a home of your own would be needed. Josefa and Aurelio are well taken care of, and I expect they'll want in any case to return at last to their own *patria chica* – Seville isn't where they hail from, and they've put up with it for my sake long enough.

I have only one regret – that our friendship didn't last longer. *Vaya con Diós*, my dear – whom I'm glad *you* believe in even if I do not.

Adiós y gracias,
Duncan Gilmour

She folded the sheet of paper carefully and put it in the pocket of her skirt. Nothing now seemed real except the warmth of the sun on her face and cold hands. Her only conscious thought was that her friend should be there to listen to the music of the fountain and smell the fragrance of the roses Aurelio tended so lovingly. These things still seemed to be inseparably his, and it was all wrong that he was never going to be there again to enjoy them.

A quiet voice spoke beside her – William Marriott, of course, come to share her distress.

'Aurelio asked me to say that they'll do whatever you want, my dear – go at once or stay. It's what the *patrón* would have wished, he said – that they should follow *your* instructions now.'

She nodded, helpless to check the tears that Duncan was no longer there to forbid. 'I doubt if they have anywhere else to go, immediately; their parents are dead. Of course they must stay here for as long as they need to.' She mopped her wet cheeks and tried to smile at him. 'Shouldn't we be thinking of Fiona and her father – offering them some more hospitality before they leave?'

'I already have but they refused.' William hesitated a moment, choosing his next words carefully. 'I'm not sure what they expected of Duncan's will, but perhaps not quite what they got. There's a whiff of resentment hanging in the air, I fancy, but I forbid you to be upset by it.' He smiled at her suddenly anxious face. 'They'll be gone soon, and in any case had no right to expect Duncan's will to please *them*. Just come and say goodbye.'

Venetia followed him indoors, to find Donald Gilmour shaking hands with Edwina and Felipe, obviously eager to go. Fiona smiled brilliantly at Venetia.

'Well done, *amiga* ... You seem to have been remarkably far-sighted – you've quite swept the board, in fact!'

Even if the knife-edged malice of it could have been missed there was no mistaking the blaze of hostility in her large blue eyes. She might as well have spelled out in words the conviction in her mind that an old, sick man had been influenced and battened on. An accusation could have been denied; the unspoken innuendo was much harder to deal with.

At last Venetia simply held out her hand. 'Uncle William says you're anxious to get home, so I won't press you to stay.'

But her gesture was ignored and she didn't repeat it to Donald Gilmour, who was looking flushed and uncomfortable. Instead she shook her head at Edwina, who looked ready to intervene, and heard with relief Eduardo Morena's offer to deliver the Gilmours to their hotel on the way back to his office.

When they and the doctor had gone Venetia managed an unsteady smile at her aunt and uncle. 'I once claimed that Fiona and I had been able to remain friends – wrong, I'm afraid!' Her voice wavered and broke, and Edwina gave her hand a little pat.

'Forget her, child; just come home with us – you badly need a rest.'

Venetia smiled again, more easily, but shook her head. 'Forgive me if I stay here. Looking after *me* will give Josefa and Aurelio something to do, which *they* badly need at the moment. But apart from that I have the feeling that I must do some thinking about the future here. I'll come back next weekend, I promise.'

With William's glance telling her that she mustn't argue, Edwina was bound to agree, and the two of them set off with Felipe an hour later. Venetia remained resolutely cheerful until they'd gone, but then sat for a long time out in the patio, deciding nothing at all. She was only conscious of loneliness and of the oppression of knowing herself hated. It was what Fiona had meant her to know, and the message had been made very clear.

For as long as Eduardo Morena was with them Fiona's sick anger had had to be contained, but it burst out the moment she was alone with her father at their hotel.

'We should have contested it. *You're* the lawyer ... why didn't you say something?'

'What was I to say?' Donald Gilmour asked calmly. 'That we didn't like the way Duncan had left his possessions? My dear girl, there was nothing wrong with that will – it was a perfectly legal, competently drawn-up document.'

'Of course – they would have made sure of that! But Venetia Marriott and the servants she was – how do lawyers like to put it? – colluding with, spent the last weeks of Duncan's life persuading him to part with his goods in *their* favour. Isn't that something we should challenge?

Donald Gilmour inspected her flushed face, thinking that when she was in pursuit of something she believed should be hers she reminded him most strongly of his wife.

'It would be, if you could prove undue influence,' he pointed out. 'But even if it did take place, I'm quite sure you can't.'

'Then the law *is* an ass,' she said fiercely.

'Quite frequently, I'm afraid – it was framed by us, not by the Lord God Almighty.' Her coarse exclamation of disgust wasn't one that her mother would have used, and he stared at her with a mixture of shock and curiosity. 'It isn't just a matter of the will, is it? You didn't tell us what happened during your stay in Spain, and we thought it better not to ask. But from being the friend you were indebted to for her aunt and uncle's kindness, Venetia seems to have become the wicked witch of the piece. I'm bound to say it isn't what she *looks*.'

He expected another outburst, but this time Fiona answered with such quiet conviction in her voice that it was harder not to believe what she said.

'I know how she *looks*, but you have to remember that she's clever, very good at ingratiating herself with everyone she meets – even a canny Scot like *you*, trained to doubt people! All I'm certain of is this: Duncan's will would have been different if *we'd* been told he was dying, but Venetia made sure it didn't happen.'

'His money has gone mostly to the servants,' Donald pointed out. 'She gets little of that.'

'The house was what she wanted. When we stayed there I could see how much she coveted it. At the time it seemed rather useful that she was getting on so well with Duncan – I even congratulated her, fool that I was! How she must be laughing about it now.'

Donald Gilmour registered again the fact that his daughter's angry turmoil was disproportionate to the loss of a house she couldn't seriously have expected to get and probably didn't really want. It had more to do, perhaps, with the agreeable Spaniard who'd kept closely beside Venetia during the funeral.

'You knew the man we met this morning, I suppose,' he ventured.

'I knew him very well, and his brother more intimately still!' she admitted with a flash of pride. 'I could have had either of them, and for as long as I was here Venetia didn't get a look-in. But I outgrew the Quinones family – she's welcome to them.'

Knowing that his daughter protested too much, Donald retreated on to firmer ground by producing the list the lawyer had given him.

'Our share of my uncle's estate. Why not be grateful for it? He had no need to leave us anything.'

'Some bits of silver and his mother's jewellery? Old-fashioned and probably quite unwearable!'

'Perhaps, but still far from valueless. The family papers will be of more interest to my brother than to me, if he ever gets in touch with us again. They probably *should* be looked at by someone qualified to piece a story together from them.'

'Well, Ian Gilmour is the last person to do it if you want an impartial view of Rio Tinto's history. If he ever had any family feeling at all, it didn't survive his disgrace and our far from loving reaction to it!'

She watched her father's face flush uncomfortably at the memory. 'How *could* it be loving?' he asked sharply. 'I was a Scottish procurator-fiscal; my brother was being tried for drunken manslaughter. Your mother was right to insist that we distanced ourselves from the whole tragic business.'

'Mother is always right,' Fiona agreed. 'If we listened to her we should never make mistakes at all.' There was irony in her voice, but bitter regret as well.

'That worthless creature you married was a mistake, I grant you, but it's the only one *you've* made,' he said, hoping to give comfort. 'You're the most beautiful, successful daughter a man could have.'

She blew him a wry kiss, re-establishing their usual harmony. 'I must remember that the next time someone *much* less beautiful and clever walks off with every prize! Now, unless you want to be shown the sights of Seville in the blistering afternoon heat, you'll have to forget your Presbyterian upbringing and sleep away the hours until it's time for dinner.'

'I shall read the *Scotsman* instead,' he said with a faint smile, 'and thank God we're going home tomorrow. I can't say this is a country I feel comfortable in.'

Nineteen

While they were driving home with Felipe in the car Edwina managed not to talk about the day's events, but she could scarcely wait for him to get back to La Paloma before she began.

'That charming house was a generous gift from Duncan Gilmour,' she said immediately, 'but Venetia's bound to sell it, I suppose.'

'I don't think so,' William answered after a little pause. 'My guess is that she'll decide to live there.'

'Will dear, how *can* she?' Edwina asked, torn between astonishment and hope. 'Mr Gilmour didn't also leave her a fortune; the child has to live.'

'I realise that; I'm only telling you what I believe. Duncan's house is something she will be very disinclined to part with – it's important to her.' He smiled at his sister. 'I'm afraid Fiona didn't like the way things were left; her father may not have done either, but he concealed his chagrin better, didn't you think?'

Edwina nodded, looking pleased now. Then her expression changed again. 'It's a pity Ian wasn't there; he should have been.'

William agreed, but saw no point in bewailing what they could do nothing about. 'I'm going to take a stroll,' he announced instead, 'see what's going on up the hill.'

When he got back it was obvious that he had news to share, but he didn't mind teasing his sister by producing it for her slowly.

'El Perdido isn't empty any more,' he began mysteriously.

'Do you mean Ian's back?' Edwina almost shouted at him.

'No, but the door was open so I walked in.'

'To pass the time of day with a burglar, I suppose, and get hit on the head! Really, Will – anyone else would have had more sense.'

William smiled at her over the pipe he was lighting. 'I passed the time of day with someone who had more right to be there than I did – El Perdido's owner!'

'Well, go *on*,' she insisted. 'Is he young, old, fat, thin, bald or bearded? Is he even Spanish, for heaven's sake?'

'Oh, I'd think so, wouldn't you, with a name like Pablo Sánchez? I asked him down for a drink tomorrow; you can make up your mind about him then.'

She was obliged to wait but, as soon as he

arrived the following day, liked the look of Señor Sánchez – a sensible man who'd taken the trouble to dress just formally enough for this first meeting. In his early fifties she guessed him to be, and out of the same middling social drawer as Manolo Quinones had originally been; but he bowed over her hand very correctly and she bestowed on him in return her friendliest smile.

'Welcome to El Perdido, *señor* – we haven't liked to see it empty since Ian Gilmour left.'

'He told me about his friends at Las Cuadras,' Pablo Sánchez said. 'He described you with much ... affection!'

The hesitation over the last word wasn't lost on Edwina, but she admired the visitor's tact and let it pass. There was information to be obtained, and she allowed William to seize the conversational ball now that wine was poured.

'You own the *huerto*, I think Ian said. He did a lot of work up there in the hope that it would be lived in permanently again.'

'He knew I meant to live there,' Pablo said in answer to the question William had baulked at asking outright. 'I'd been working abroad long enough: it was time to return to my *patria chica* and settle down on the land my father was driven from at the end of the Civil War. He would never come back while Franco was still alive, and then it

309

was too late; he was dead himself, in London. I'm here for him, as well as for myself, reclaiming the place we belonged to.'

Emotion roughened his voice, reminding them once again that past griefs still weren't forgotten. How could they be, William thought, when they had been so terrible?

'The *pueblo* hasn't been spoiled,' Edwina said after a pause; '...it's still a nice place with nice people, give or take an exception or two.'

'My sister doesn't care for the Mayor,' William explained with a smile. 'Nor, to be truthful, do I; but we're very polite to each other!'

The lines of Pablo's ugly face rearranged themselves in an unexpectedly attractive grin. 'I think I see the picture. Ian told me about the public meeting – I expect you were *too* polite then.'

'We were rightly seen as *forasteros*,' William answered calmly; 'it was for the *pueblo* people themselves to decide, and they were tired of scraping a living. The Quinones scheme seemed to offer them a richer and an easier life.'

'Seemed,' Pablo agreed, 'but it's already illegal in certain respects, and will probably become more so. I shall be watching what they do up there, and I'll make sure the men in Luís's bar hear about it.'

'Good – they're more likely to listen to

you. I'm known as the mad Englishman who likes to watch birds fly back and forth across the Straits!'

Pablo grinned again. 'That *is* something very strange, I admit, but my friend warned me about it!' Liking his new neighbours, he revealed a little more. 'I first met Ian in London years ago – he was a young man then, just becoming famous. He was a good friend to my father when I couldn't do anything to look after him myself, and I can tell you it's not easy to help a Spaniard without hurting his pride.'

'And you, in turn, have helped Ian, I think,' William suggested gently.

'He needed to get out of London. When I offered him El Perdido he decided that hacking its stony ground would work some anger out of him!'

'We think it did,' Edwina put in. 'We also grew to like him very much.'

Unsurprised, Pablo merely nodded. 'What about your neighbours at La Paloma – do you like *them*?'

'We disagreed, of course, about the castle. Otherwise we have to say that Manolo Quinones has been an amiable landlord,' she admitted.

'Neighbours are one thing, landlords another,' Pablo said thoughtfully.

'True,' William agreed with a smile, 'but that won't stop my sister berating Manolo if he destroys the sierra's precious flora.'

Their visitor advanced on her so enthusiastically that Edwina feared she was about to be kissed, but Pablo confined himself to bowing over her hand, and promising as he left that they would soon be seeing him again.

'Nice man, but tough,' Edwina said when he'd gone. 'Fernando and his father won't get things all their own way – I wonder if they realise that.'

William concerned himself with realising something else: as yet, Manolo's hotel seemed very slow in taking any kind of shape, but sooner or later work would have to start. With a man like Pablo Sánchez keeping watch, skirmishes would probably be inevitable, and they could soon develop into an all-out war. William could see himself and Edwina firmly in Pablo's camp, but what about Venetia? He would have needed to be blind to miss Felipe's care of her yesterday in Seville. The Spaniard seemed determined to make up ground lost over Fiona, and William could unhappily foresee a time when their niece might find herself having to choose whose side to be on.

She came back to Rosario the following weekend and announced that she'd decided to make her home in the Calle San Isidoro.

'You don't look surprised,' she said, smiling at William.

'I'm not! Duncan's house seemed to suit you beautifully. Your aunt is bursting to ask a question, but I shall phrase it more delicately. Will you be able to manage there on your own?'

'I think so – I've even got a job, thanks to kind Dr Casals. He introduced me to the head of the Languages Department at the university, and I'm to start in October, teaching English and French.'

Edwina's nod approved an arrangement that seemed so providential all round that she was only surprised she hadn't had a hand in it herself.

Later in the day it was Felipe's turn to hear the news. He didn't comment on it for a moment or two, and for once she couldn't guess what he was thinking.

'My aunt and uncle looked pleased when I told them,' she finally pointed out.

'I'm pleased that you're staying in Spain – that of *course, querida*.' He rumpled his hair, hesitated, and then rushed headlong at the hurdle in front of him. 'It's too *soon*, Venetia ... I know that. You've got to learn to trust me again, forgive me. But if you're not going to be here I can't do things for you ... show you how much you mean to me.'

It was a typical speech, she thought. Most men would have tried to pretend that Fiona hadn't mattered; some, especially Spaniards, would have reckoned they'd done well to return so faithfully to their first love. But Felipe was determined to deserve reinstatement, and it made her smile very warmly at him.

'Couldn't we move on from the forgiveness bit, and just enjoy each other's company when we can? I know you must work at La Paloma – all your instruments and equipment are there; but when I don't come to Rosario at weekends you could come to Seville. That sounds to me a very nice arrangement.'

'To me too,' Felipe said earnestly. He took hold of her hands and kissed them, and then gently kissed her mouth. It seemed a promise of some kind, and she didn't mind that it was so. Without haste and without unnecessary striving, a future that they'd seemed to have given up on might be available after all.

The following weekend she stayed in her own house, with the intention of testing two things at once: the first that, as her stepmother had said, she must let William and Edwina get used to doing without her; the other that the journey to and from Seville would prove to Felipe whether he was determined to be with her or not. But he came eagerly, bringing his guitar, so that she could hear a newly completed song cycle: six settings of his favourite Machado poems. The songs were beautiful, Josefa and Aurelio seemed delighted to have a guest to look after, and the experiment all in all turned out to be a huge success.

A week later she went back to Rosario, to find Edwina looking shame-faced as well as pleased.

'I was telling myself you'd given us up,' she confessed; 'I should have known better. Now Will's asked our new neighbour, Pablo Sánchez, down to meet you.'

'I hope *he*'s going to stay, not just plant a few trees and drift away,' Venetia suggested.

Her aunt frowned over this. 'Of course he'll stay; the man's an *andalúz*, thankful to be back where he belongs. He'll be a real addition to the *pueblo*. I haven't got him to call on Don Alberto yet – his father fought on the side that shot priests during the Civil War – but I'm working on that.'

'Do I guess that he won't visit La Paloma, either, in that case?'

'Not as a friend, I'm afraid. Pablo's keeping a close eye on developments, and already things are happening that he doesn't like.'

Venetia brushed away a faint shiver of alarm, and heard herself ask instead about Ian Gilmour.

'We've heard no word,' Edwina said

regretfully, 'but I ought to mention that it would be a brave soul who spoke ill of Ian in front of Pablo Sánchez.'

'I'll remember,' Venetia promised. She abandoned the subject with a smile as William Marriott came in to greet her, and then the talk was only of her new home until Encarnita ushered their luncheon guest into the room.

He was a stocky, powerfully built man, unlike the usual small and wiry Andalucían. He was also widely travelled, opinionated and articulate, and Venetia could easily see why Manolo might not like him; there were ways in which the two of them were much alike. For a present-day Spaniard he was an outspoken critic of what went on in Brussels, and had even more to say than Venetia herself of the jobbery and corruption among the Commission's staff. She was getting on well with him until the conversation led him to speak of Manolo; then she had to point out firmly that she considered herself a friend of the Quinones family. He looked disappointed for a moment, but saw no reason to soften what he was about to say.

'There's been some illegality already, you know. They're beginning to lay out the new road up from the valley – a private road, mark you, leading only to the hotel. But it uses the route of one of the old *cañadas*

316

reales, so how can it be private? It's common property to the people of Spain!'

'The EU conservation officer didn't mention that at the public meeting,' William said with a frown. 'I suppose he assumed that no one would be very concerned.'

'They probably wouldn't have been then, because Spaniards can only think of one thing at a time, and at that moment nobody was wanting to move livestock along a drove road; they were *talking* instead, which, God knows, is their greatest weakness!' Pablo saw the expression on Venetia's face and had the grace to grin. 'And mine as well, the *señorita* is too polite to say!' But he grew serious again and came to the nub of the matter. 'I've been up there, you know, scouting around and talking to the men. The issue we shall *have* to fight is water; if not, the *pueblo* people will grow nothing in future.'

Edwina stared at him. 'My dear man, water comes from heaven in the form of rain, and the rain in Spain falls mainly on the mountains, of which we have all too many here.'

'Exactly, and its purpose is to pour down the hillsides, swell streams and rivers, and fill reservoirs and irrigation channels. But I can tell you this: in future El Perdido will get none of this surplus, and nor will the men who work the slopes below mine –

317

because the intention is to steal it higher up!'

'Everyone is entitled to a share,' William said sharply. 'That's how this land has been farmed from time immemorial.'

'Exactly,' Pablo agreed again, 'a *share*! But Manolo Quinones doesn't understand that. His beautiful hotel will need a lot of water, and his men are already looking for places to sink tanks and cisterns to see that he will get it. They even want to divert the Maja-ceite itself so that their precious new road doesn't get washed away when it floods.'

Forgetting that her niece was there, Edwina turned a stunned face to her brother. 'Without water the men who wanted to go on farming and voted against the hotel will have to give up ... is *that* what he's counting on?'

'He's thinking only of what *he* needs,' William answered. Then he saw Venetia's expression and spoke gently to her. 'I'm sorry, my dear – you can't be enjoying this conversation. But Manolo must be made to understand that whatever prosperity his hotel brings will be cancelled out if he ruins the *pueblo* in other ways.'

She tried to smile at them. 'We should ask him to read Lampedusa's *The Leopard* – it has a lot to say about water stolen from the Sicilians by the Mafia! But this is *now*, not the nineteenth century, and Manolo isn't a villain. The trouble is that he's not a countryman either – that's why he doesn't understand. Will you let me talk to Felipe and ask *him* to help? I realise that it's urgent, because the autumn rains will be starting soon.'

She didn't wait for them to agree, merely stood up and walked away; but William broke the silence round the table.

'You needn't fear that my niece won't do what she promises,' he said to their guest.

Pablo accepted this with a little bow. Then, with more delicacy than she expected, he apologised to Edwina for putting them on the horns of a dilemma. 'My opponents say I'm always looking for a fight, but the truth is that I came to Rosario only thinking of the peaceful life I've dreamed about for years, working my own land.'

'Which you won't have, unless we can get Quinones to change his plans,' William pointed out as their neighbour got ready to leave.

Alone again, brother and sister looked at one another. 'It's all very unfortunate,' Edwina announced, more inadequately than usual, and William nodded, not knowing whether their shared regret was for Pablo's belligerence, Manolo's greed or their niece's unfortunate connection with his family.

Venetia chose to attend early Mass alone the following morning, and couldn't decide whether it was good or ill fortune to bump into Manolo himself on the way home. He smiled at her benignly, on the whole not sorry that his younger son's relationship with her was developing so promisingly. A man needed women in his life, but Felipe had seemed determined not to understand this. Now Venetia was persuading him to change his mind, and Manolo prided himself on recognising quality when he saw it – as Rodrigo had done, she would add something to his family.

Aware that she must seize her chance, she smiled at him: 'You're very busy, we hear, starting work up on the hill.'

'Of course – we must do what we can before the weather forces us to stop.'

'There is some anxiety in the village,' she said, unable to find a more tactful way of introducing the subject. 'I'm sure it's a misunderstanding, but the men are afraid that the water they depend on won't be available in future.'

Manolo still smiled, but less lavishly than before. 'The trouble-maker has been busy here, I see – I recognised the type immediately. He won't be welcome on my land in future.'

She swallowed her anger, knowing that a shouting match would end in defeat. 'If you mean Pablo Sánchez, he's anxious for his own future, of course, but concerned for others as well.'

'The *pueblo* voted for the hotel,' Manolo reminded her testily. 'Sánchez wasn't here.'

'Others *were* here who also didn't vote for it,' she said with firmness.

Though so gently mannered, she was just like Edwina Marriott, he realised – last representatives of an awkward breed of woman England hadn't quite given up producing. In a way she would be the sort of daughter-in-law he could take pride in, but not if she interfered in what were men's affairs.

'I shall be truthful with you, Venetia, but you must listen to *me* and not to some hot-head with a chip on his shoulder from the past. The farmers will receive the water that falls on their land – I could do nothing about that even if I wanted to. But I shall make use of what falls on mine, and *they* can do nothing about *that*. If what they receive is not enough they must find a different occupation ... I will even help them do it.'

'They are men of the land, not waiters,' she said steadily, 'and the hillsides should continue to be dressed in what grows there naturally, not turned into pretty tea-gardens and car parks.'

She expected a roar of rage, but with a great effort Manolo contained himself; he even managed a courteous farewell bow. 'You share your aunt and uncle's view, of course. But you must remember that I do what I am entitled to do, and I am a businessman, not a sentimentalist.'

She looked so upset when she repeated this conversation at home that Edwina tried to rally her forces.

'Don't despair ... that was only the opening shot. We all live to fight again, and finally find some compromise.'

'This is Spain,' Venetia reminded her sadly; 'no prisoners, no compromise! I expect I did more harm than good, and I've no idea at all what to try next, except to leave it to Felipe.'

'It's not your problem, my dear girl,' William said. 'Nor is it even his. You must think of *your* future and leave Rosario to fight its own battles with Manolo.'

She seemed to agree, and left for Seville that evening with the subject having been carefully avoided for the rest of the day.

Twenty

Ian Gilmour's meeting in Seville was nearly over. His uncle's precious archive material had been handed over; there was nothing left to do but thank the lawyer and leave. Instead, he found himself lingering because a question needed asking.

'By the way, what happened to my uncle's house ... I suppose Miss Marriott decided to sell it?'

'I thought that might be her intention, *señor*, but all I can tell you is that she is still there.'

His visitor accepted the information with a nod, and went away. But out in the street he stopped, and then swung round in a complete change of direction.

The house in the Calle San Isidoro looked as he remembered it – blindingly white, its wrought-iron-grilled windows wreathed with flowers and greenery: a delectable piece of property in the most sought-after *barrio* in Seville. There was no doubting the value of what Duncan had bequeathed to Venetia Marriott; his brother and niece had been right about that, and the likelihood was that the rest of what they'd said had been accurate as well.

He'd come on a fool's errand almost certainly, and felt more than half inclined to walk away. Then it was too late: the heavy old door swung open and the servant he remembered was standing there smiling at him.

'I saw the *señor* arrive,' she explained almost gaily; 'come in, please. The *señorita* is at home.'

He was led into the hall, still sparsely furnished as he remembered it with an old oak chest and chairs standing on the black-and-white-tiled floor; but crimson roses in a copper jug scented the air and brought the room to life.

'I didn't expect to find *you* still here,' he said to Josefa. 'I remember Aurelio telling me that you both came from Huelva province.'

'We are not *sevillanos*,' she agreed, 'but we stay for as long as the *señorita* is here ... the *patrón* would have wished it.'

A telephone rang in another room and Josefa hesitated until he said, 'Don't worry – I can find my way outside.'

She smiled and went away, leaving him free to stand in the shadow of the arcade, watching the girl who sat working at a table in the patio. If he'd expected her to look changed, she didn't – he remembered very well the tanned face, and soft brown hair noticeable in a land where women liked to flaunt their elaborately dressed dark heads; altogether, there was nothing showy about Venetia Marriott. For a moment he could imagine that Fiona was wrong, that Venetia *was* what she seemed: a girl who even looked a little lonely there by herself. Only, of course, she *wasn't* what she seemed, and certainly wasn't lonely; she was firmly in the Quinones clan.

There was a sound behind him, and when she looked up to see him and Josefa he could see nothing in her face except the stillness that might come of complete surprise. Then she offered the maid a smile of thanks for the drinks tray that was being set down on the table and Josefa went away, leaving silence behind. Finally, with hands hidden in the pockets of her skirt, Venetia stood up and found something to say.

'Will *you* pour the fino? Your uncle always insisted that it was the man's job.'

He did it clumsily, and the spillage of some wine on the tray infuriated him because she had no right to seem calm when he was not.

She examined his face, sensing in its tautness some anger that, although under control, was directed at herself.

'You must have been told about your

uncle's death,' she suggested more calmly than she felt. 'It's a pity you weren't here.'

'My brother and niece agree with you – when I saw them recently in Edinburgh they told me what had happened. I came to Seville to collect the material Duncan left us.'

She nursed the glass he handed her, grateful to have something to clutch. 'I expect you share Fiona's view that he didn't leave you very much and that I'm not entitled to *my* inheritance.' There was no need for him to answer – she could guess his opinion easily enough. 'So I'll just say one more thing about it,' she added. 'Fiona wasn't here at the time to know that Duncan chose to suffer rather than cloud his mind with drugs. For that reason I have to believe that the arrangements he made are the ones he wanted. It's Abogado Morena's view, too.'

Ian Gilmour gave a little shrug, leaving his own acceptance of what Duncan had done unanswered for. 'He seemed surprised that you hadn't sold the house. I came in the hope that you might agree to sell it to me.'

It was the last thing she'd expected, and for a moment she struggled to find a reply. 'It's my home, for the time being at least,' she said at last, 'not an asset to dispose of.'

'And meanwhile Josefa and Aurelio also stay, because they think Duncan would have expected them to look after you?'

Her eyes suddenly locked with his across the table. 'In other words, I keep them here simply to suit my own convenience? Wrong, Mr Gilmour – I haven't been able to *drive* them away! I don't even pay them because they won't allow me to. They stay because this is their home, and they assure me that Duncan's pension pays their salary. I suspect I know how Josefa's daily prayers are phrased in the cathedral.' She felt in control of the interview now, even able to make an attack of her own. 'My aunt and uncle can't know you're back or they'd have told me. Edwina was disappointed when you left El Perdido so suddenly. William made allowances of course, but *she* thought it a shabby way to treat a friend.'

'Then let me tell you why I went,' he said savagely. 'My lawyer telephoned to say that my ex-wife was about to marry a man I knew and thoroughly disliked. That was her affair, but she proposed to have my son's name changed to that of her new husband. I needed to know how Ranald felt about that before it was too late.'

Ian Gilmour's face warned her that the subject was perilous, but it couldn't be left hanging in the air.

'Are you going to tell me what he said?' she asked quietly.

'My son thought that anything would be an improvement on the name of Gilmour!

His mother had made a rotten choice the first time round, but everything looked fine from now on; he seemed glad of the chance to make that clear.'

In the long silence that followed he stared at the little bronze figure in the pool as if all that mattered was his careful observation of the myriad tiny prisms the sunlight struck from the piper's cascading drops of water. But Venetia knew that what he was looking at he didn't see at all – with stubborn hope finally killed by that journey to New York, he was saying goodbye to a child who'd been taught to despise him by the woman he'd once loved.

'What happens now ... are you going back to Edinburgh?' she managed to ask.

'Never again, unless dragged by a team of runaway horses. We have to accept, my brother and I, that we must go the way of Duncan and *his* brother. You met Donald at the funeral, but you were spared the pleasure of meeting his wife. Elspeth is Fiona writ large, twenty-five years from now. We agree not to tolerate each other.'

'The Gilmour family curse,' Venetia said quietly. It was occurring to her now that his offer to buy the house had been genuine after all, but before she could refer to it he spoke again.

'For the moment I'm going back to Rosario. I might discount Pablo Sánchez's bulletins, but not Don Alberto's alarm when I telephoned him. There seems to be real trouble brewing, which perhaps your uncle has been careful not to mention.'

She frowned over that, suddenly wishing that she hadn't been so anxious to stay in Seville, studying the syllabuses she was soon going to be teaching. 'I asked Felipe to see what *he* could do; he promised to try,' she said anxiously.

Her visitor looking unimpressed, and was probably about to remind her, she thought, that despite Felipe's contribution at the public meeting all Quinones were much the same under the skin. She was getting ready to fly to his defence when Josefa came out of the house to deliver a message.

'Señor Felipe will be here at the usual time this evening, *señorita*; he said not to disturb you now if you had a visitor.' Confident of having brought welcome news, she smiled and went away, leaving silence behind.

At last Ian Gilmour spoke. 'Silly of me to imagine you were content to be here alone; even sillier to think you might sell me the house. It must make a charming *pied-à-terre* for you both away from Rosario!'

The implication brought a flush of colour to her face, but she pinned a careless smile to her mouth. He could make what assumptions he liked; she was damned if she'd insist that Felipe came as a guest, not a lover. 'I enjoy his visits,' she agreed calmly. 'It can't have been her intention, but Fiona did us a service in the end. We got ourselves sorted out very nicely!'

She was suddenly afraid of having gone too far in provocation, but if rough handling *had* been in her visitor's mind he managed not to give way to it. Instead, his smile flicked over her with the icy touch of a rapier across her skin.

'I thought it was where you'd finish up, in the enemy camp, with Felipe not trying *very* hard to keep his charming father in check!' He gave her a small, ironic bow of farewell. 'Don't trouble Josefa; I can see myself out.'

A moment later the front door slammed. Now she could breathe freely again and tell herself there was nothing to regret. It was only in her imagination that the world felt cold, as if the sun had suddenly decided to abandon its universe. Ian Gilmour had believed much too readily his relatives' interpretation of events. But, even disapproving of her as he did, he might have *tried* to be fair. Yet that sounded so ridiculous when she said it out loud that she bundled it to some hidden corner of her mind and went to telephone William instead.

It seemed that the situation at Rosario was volatile – her uncle's carefully chosen word – but nothing for her to worry about. She was to stay where she was and not feel alarmed about them. For once he didn't prolong the call, and nor did she, even though it felt strange not to have mentioned to him the fact of Ian Gilmour's return. They would soon hear about it from Pablo Sánchez, and the conversation hadn't been something she could bear to recount to William. She could discuss some of it, at least, more easily with Felipe.

But he arrived that evening brimming with some news that *he* wanted to talk about.

'Forgive me, Venetia, but I can only stay one night – I must leave for Madrid tomorrow. I've wanted to keep it as a surprise for you.'

'A *nice* surprise, I hope,' she said, mindful of the day's other discoveries.

'*Querida*, the best of all. Listen! You know that it's twenty-five years since Juan Carlos came to the throne. Well, there are all kinds of celebrations, including a gala concert on Saturday. I've known for ages that I'm to play the Castelnuovo-Tedesco guitar concerto, and Pilar Berganza is to sing 'La Maja y el Ruiseñor'. What I didn't know is that she's preparing one of *my* Machado songs as an encore ... I can scarcely believe it even now!'

'The *very* best surprise,' Venetia agreed, smiling at him. 'I'm so glad ... she'll be the perfect performer for you.'

Felipe grabbed her hands and kissed

them. 'I knew you'd be pleased, but *you*'ve got to be there. I shall need to know you're in the audience. Dearest, will you come? Blanca insists that you stay with her.'

Venetia nodded, not stopping to think. It was going to be the most important night of his life; of course she had to be there.

She caught the high-speed train the following Saturday morning, in a jumble of emotions that she spent the journey trying to sort out. There was the excitement of the evening to look forward to, of course, mixed with proud and nervous anticipation of Felipe's share in it. But something else tugged at her heart and she finally confronted it – she was anxious about what was happening at Rosario, and all too well aware that this visit committed her to more than an attendance at a concert; she had publicly thrown in her lot with the Quinones family. Everybody knew that now, and it was time to accept the fact herself. It made what was to happen next seem pre-ordained, inevitable.

She was greeted at the Estebans' sumptuous apartment by Blanca, explaining that they wouldn't see Felipe before the concert began. Any awkwardness was put to flight by Juan, anxious to hear news of his friends at Rosario. Then she was led away by her hostess to the room she was to sleep in. It looked charming and comfortable, and the only surprise was that it was obviously the room that Felipe was already using.

With dismay ironed out of her face, she hoped, she tried to smile at the woman watching her. 'You don't mind this ... this arrangement?'

'Why should I mind?' Blanca answered with her slow smile. 'I'm delighted – relieved in fact! I was beginning to fear that Felipe might never discover joys that have nothing to do with music. I congratulate you – he looks quite transformed now, a truly happy man at last.' She examined Venetia's face for a moment, then spoke again with more hesitancy than usual. 'Perhaps you *aren't* quite sure yet about being part of our family. We aren't as black as we're painted, you know, and I doubt if Felipe is black at all – in fact he's probably the best we can offer in terms of general niceness!'

'I agree, even if it sounds offensive to my kind hostess to say so!' Venetia's smile would have been enough to soften the offence, but she could see only friendly amusement in Blanca's face, and decided that it might be easier than she'd supposed to like Felipe's sister. 'I assume you're coming to the concert,' she said next. 'I've already heard Felipe's songs, of course, and even sung by him instead of an exquisite mezzo voice they're very lovely.'

'I shall *look* beautifully attentive,' Blanca promised cheerfully, 'and my dear Rodrigo will really listen and be able to say something appreciative afterwards.'

'A perfect combination,' Venetia was bound to agree.

Blanca smiled at her with something resembling affection. 'If you're feeling nervous about meeting Juan Carlos and Doña Sofia, there's no need to be – they're the most informal of royals. But Rodrigo will steer you through what little protocol there is. Now, drinks and tapas when you're ready. We shall dine even later than usual, so you must eat something before we leave.'

Left alone, Venetia did nothing about unpacking her dress for the evening – cream silk organza, uncrushable, she hoped; there were more important things to think about. She stared at the large bed she was to share with Felipe, aware that she wasn't surprised at the way this visit was turning out. It seemed, in fact, to have been neatly pre-arranged by whatever Fates were now in charge of them. The long open windows drew her to the balcony outside, still bright with flowering shrubs; but she was remembering Juan's face aglow with the pleasure of finding one of Edwina's wild flowers growing where it belonged. That moment seemed a long time ago, when she'd sat beside a hostile man and looked at Spain spread out below them.

She could scarcely chart the route that had brought her from that moment to this, but she refused to think that it wasn't the one she should have been on. She was committed to Felipe now, and about to confirm the fact by sleeping with him. The coldness in which she seemed to have been wrapped since Ian Gilmour's visit would go away when she was loved again, belonged again to someone she wanted to make happy. With her future mapped out, she could kiss uncertainty and loneliness good-bye.

The concert was a huge success. Felipe's performance of the concerto was rapturously received, and Berganza's singing of his song so beautiful that he was called back to the platform to share her applause. Watching him kiss her hand, Venetia saw a man who had finally found himself. He was confident of his worth at last, no longer inadequate when measured against Fernando. Everything was possible now.

Blanca's supper party, attended by all Madrid's rich and famous, set the seal on the evening's success. Feeling uncomfortably out of place Venetia smiled, drank and talked as required. She occasionally caught sight of Felipe and it was plain that he reckoned the evening marked some defining moment in his life. It would soon be a defining moment also for herself and him, she realised, and assumed that he must be understanding that, too.

The guests seemed reluctant to leave, but when the last of them had gone Venetia thankfully said good-night. Felipe still lingered – out of thoughtfulness or shyness, she wasn't sure which.

She was already in bed when he came into the room. The evening's intoxication hadn't entirely worn off, but the contentment in his face was now mixed with acute anxiety. Laughter seemed out of place, but she tried a little teasing instead as an antidote to the embarrassment that threatened them.

'You're supposed to look eager when coming to the couch of your lady-love,' she suggested solemnly. But it was a mistake; he seemed to think that lightness didn't suit the moment they were faced with.

'You have to forgive me, Venetia,' he said pleadingly. 'I expect I rather boasted to Blanca about my visits to you in Seville, but she just assumed I meant that we slept together. When I came earlier and saw your things in here I should have explained, but I was afraid she'd tell Fernando and they'd laugh at me. My dearest, I'll sleep on the floor ... anything you like, as long as you don't mind having me in the same room.'

She was silent for a moment, struggling with the disappointment of realising that for her reluctant lover it didn't seem to be a defining moment after all. But they'd passed the point of no return now; at least she was certain of that.

'I'd like you to sleep in the same bed,' she said deliberately. The sudden mixture of doubt and shock and delight in his face made it easier to smile at him. 'Dear Felipe … Blanca's only forced our hand a little. Don't you think it's time we took the plunge?'

'Yes … *yes, querida,* of course it is, and it's exactly how this wonderful evening should end. Oh Venetia, do you have any idea how much I love you?'

'You're about to prove it to me,' she said serenely.

It was consideration, she told herself later, that made him an ineffectual, apologetic lover, and many women would be only too grateful for a man so seemingly afraid of taking his own pleasure. In time she would banish the memory of nights spent with Luc, and in time the passion that Felipe poured into his music would be offered to her. They would manage very well together.

With this sensible decision made, she lay wide awake while he slept beside her,

337

happily exhausted by the various exertions of the day. At last she crept out of bed and went to sit by the window. A nearly full moon washed the balcony in silver-green light; it was beautiful but unreal, having form but no substance. She shivered, fearing that it resembled her own life ... fearing, too, that the night's failure might have been entirely hers after all. What if she could never put aside the memory of a man whose dying wish had been that she should find happiness with someone else? She was unaware of weeping until the cool night air flowing against her face made it feel stiff. At last she went back to bed and slept, only to dream that she was a child again, being dragged to a hated *corrida*. She hauled herself out of it with relief, to find Felipe already up and dressed. He came to sit beside her, looking content to know that he'd earned the right to be there.

'*Buenos días*, my dearest! How beautiful you look. But will you promise not to mind when I tell you my news? Miguel Alvarez offered me last night the most exciting commission I've ever had – an entire film score! I can scarcely believe it, or anything else that happened yesterday!'

'All deserved, richly deserved!' she said, smiling at him.

His joy dimmed a little. 'Well I *hope* so, but it means staying here longer: I have a lot of work to do with Miguel. *Querida,* do you mind?'

'Of course not, but I can't stay with you. I've an appointment at the university to-morrow.'

His eyes examined her face anxiously. 'It's important, Venetia, otherwise—'

'I know it's important,' she interrupted him, 'and it's settled that you must stay.'

But he still thought something was wrong, and forced himself to say what troubled him most. 'Did I ... did I hurt you, frighten you last night? If so, I won't ever again – I only want to make you happy.'

'And to fill your life with music,' she pointed out gently, not answering his question.

'Of course, but you *are* my music, Venetia. You're in everything I do.'

She kissed him for the compliment, hoping it wasn't true, and he went away reassured again, leaving her to get dressed.

There was time after breakfast for a brief visit to the Prado – the most wonderful picture gallery in the world, Felipe claimed – but after lunch they had to part company, and at the railway station his high spirits suddenly deserted him.

'I hate you going off alone,' he said miserably. 'Promise to keep loving me, at least until next weekend!'

She agreed that she would do her best,

339

and reminded him that they must spend it in Rosario, not Seville. 'I've all Juan's messages to deliver to Uncle Will and Edwina, and I must make up for not seeing much of them recently. *Hasta luego*, my dear; don't let Alvarez bully you – remember that he probably needs you more than you need him!'

He smiled at her from the platform and she knew that he would remain there waving until the train was out of sight. She was blessed among women – he was good and charming, and he would probably love her faithfully all his life. But as the achingly empty spaces of the Castilian plain flashed by she found herself thinking of two different men. Compared with Felipe last night, Fernando's performance as a lover was probably something any normal woman might regret refusing, but her mind scarcely considered it. She was remembering instead a scarred warrior whose only joy in life now seemed to come from fighting for lost causes. Ian Gilmour, embittered by his own unfortunate choice of woman, had labelled *her* as well: Venetia Marriott had manipulated a dying old man, and now enjoyed her ill-gotten gains with a family that any right-minded creature would have had the good taste to leave alone.

She blinked fiercely, telling herself that she was becoming far too prone to weep; but

340

still tears seeped through her eyelids and trickled down her cheeks. Then someone touched her hand and she opened her eyes to see the woman opposite smiling anxiously and offering her a neatly folded tissue. She accepted it, mopped her cheeks and smiled at her companion.

'Thank you, *señora*! I wasn't born here, but I consider myself very lucky to live in Spain.'

And it was true, she thought – but not for the dramatic grandeur of the landscape outside; not even for the flowering beauty of her small, secluded patio at home. It was for the people she found herself among, like Josefa and Aurelio and this kind fellow-traveller, that she now so properly valued Spain.

Twenty-One

The summer was ending early; there was even a shower of rain falling when she arrived back in Seville, reminding her of the ever-present Andalucían concern with water. Soon the autumn rains would begin in earnest, and her overwrought imagination pictured Pablo Sánchez prowling the hillsides with sticks of dynamite in his hand. He wasn't a man to mind what weapons he used as a means to an important end.

A worse anxiety concerned her aunt and uncle. She couldn't see either of them joining an armed band, but there was no doubt where their sympathies would lie, nor that Manolo Quinones would realise this. The only faint relief came from knowing that Ian Gilmour was back at El Perdido. There wasn't any doubt about *his* sympathies either, but she couldn't see him allowing his friend to behave rashly.

She was only just indoors, being greeted by Josefa and Aurelio, when her aunt telephoned.

'How was the concert?' Edwina wanted to know.

'A triumph – even the King himself said nice things!' Venetia was able to report proudly. 'And Blanca and Rodrigo were welcoming and kind. Juan sends his love to you and Uncle Will and swears that he'll be back for Christmas.'

'*Nice* child,' Edwina observed approvingly. 'Now, I've got news for *you*. Who do you think is back in Rosario? Our dear friend Ian, staying with Pablo. It's rather a relief to us, as a matter of fact, apart from the pleasure of seeing him.'

Distracted by the realisation that their dear Ian hadn't mentioned his Seville visit any more than she had, Venetia was slow to ask the obvious question: 'Why a relief, Aunt Edwina?'

'There was some trouble here ... a scuffle that got out of hand. Will didn't mention it when he spoke to you, in case you put off your trip to Madrid.'

'I think you'd better tell me about it now ... *all* of it, please.'

'Well,' Edwina began slowly, 'it's becoming clear to the people here what the cost to them of Manolo's scheme is going to be. Even the ones who voted for it are starting to feel uncomfortable, but rather than admit it they're swaggering into Luís's bar at night and infuriating the men who see their livelihood at stake. Rosario is not the happy, peaceful place it was, and for that I find it

343

hard to forgive Felipe's father. Forgive me for saying it, my dear, but I'm afraid it's the truth.'

After a little silence Venetia spoke again. 'Felipe is still in Madrid; I had to come back because I report for work at the university tomorrow, but we'll both be at Rosario for the weekend ... would you and Uncle Will mind if he stayed with me at Las Cuadras?' She made a huge effort to sound cheerful. 'I can't quite see myself installed in La Paloma's luxury!'

Edwina considered the implications of this little speech and, in her turn, tried hard not to sound depressed. 'He'll be welcome of course, my dear ... I think we rather expected that the two of you had become an item, as they now say; though why you can't be called a couple, I quite fail to see.'

'Cheer up, dear Aunt – it's something called progress,' Venetia said rallyingly. 'Give Uncle Will my love, and pray for me tomorrow, please, embarking on my new career!'

She put the telephone down, and ate the supper Josefa had lovingly prepared, but went to bed miserable, and apprehensive about more than the next day's ordeal.

In the event, her inauguration at the university went smoothly; her students seemed likeable and disposed to like her, and she began to feel optimistic that she could teach them well. But beneath that satisfaction lay disquiet. She felt lonely, too, and very much in need of a companion.

It was several days later that she approached the house one evening and saw a man standing at the door. She ran eagerly towards him, then stopped, betrayed by false hope; it wasn't Felipe who stood there. Instead, Fernando smiled at her, with raindrops running down his brown face.

'There's nothing wrong with Felipe?' she asked anxiously.

The urgent question made him smile. 'Nothing wrong except, from your point of view, that I'm myself, not him! I'm in Seville with an evening to kill, but I can go away again if you'd rather I did.'

She recovered herself enough to shake her head. 'Don't be silly – come inside and share whatever Josefa is cooking. I shall be glad not to dine in state alone – she and Aurelio are sticklers for not letting me eat with them in the kitchen!'

She had the impression that she was talking too much; it was the effect he always had on her, simply because he watched her too closely. But indoors, wet coats hung up and wine poured, in the small, comfortable room that had been Duncan's study, she relaxed enough to behave more naturally.

'Have you been working too hard? You look tired.' He was seven years older than

345

Felipe, she knew, and now began to look it, with the first frosting of grey showing on his dark hair. An air of weariness humanised him, she thought, making him vulnerable like the rest of them.

'I'm envying my brother his good fortune,' he said, too blandly for her to be sure whether he meant it or not. 'Blanca reports that Felipe is a changed man. She seemed a little less certain about *you*, however.'

It was his usual tactic, but she'd forgotten it – the sudden unsettling comment that his opponent didn't expect. 'She needn't have been. I'm not at all uncertain myself.' Venetia felt his glance on her again, but she was determined to be what she claimed – certain and serene. 'There hasn't been quite enough time to ... to get used to things. I shall be very glad when Felipe returns from Madrid; we've a lot to talk about.'

'Are you going to stay in this nice house? If I'm allowed to say so, it suits you better than La Paloma does!'

'It's rather what I think, too,' she agreed, suddenly rewarding him with a smile for that perception. 'In any case I've just started a new job here. Have you been to Rosario recently?'

'I've just come from there, so yes, I know about your little difference of opinion with my father.'

'I doubt if it can be called little,' she

corrected him, frowning now. 'How *can* it be, when people's livelihoods depend on it?'

'True – the word was badly chosen.' He poured more wine for them and for once seemed content to sit and admire its golden colour in the lamplight. This was a reflective, thoughtful Fernando she hadn't encountered before.

'You must also know about El Perdido's owner – Pablo Sánchez,' she went on. 'Manolo thinks he's just a trouble-maker; he's not. The man is realising the dream of a lifetime and doesn't want it spoiled, but he's thinking of the *pueblo* as well, not only of himself.' She could read nothing in her companion's face, and longed suddenly to convince him. 'Fernando, those men *can't* grow food without water, and why should anyone, however rich and powerful, say that what their ancestors have done for centuries, they must no longer do?'

She was beautiful in her passionate pleading, and he had to deal with that sharp awareness before he could answer her. He wanted more than anything in life to be allowed to love her, but instead of wrapping his arms about her he must sit quietly in this chair, discussing irrigation! After a moment or two he managed it.

'You reminded my father that not everyone voted for the hotel – true enough. It's also true that Pablo Sánchez has the right to try to protect his smallholding. But it's not the whole truth, Venetia. The crops they grow at Rosario with so much anxiety and effort are more easily grown elsewhere; the men still prepared to labour from dawn to sunset will be followed by a generation expecting a different life – whatever my nephew believes! Spain is changing – *must* change, or be hopelessly left behind in a world that recognises only success, not idealistic failure.'

'I *hear* the force of what you say,' she admitted, 'especially when you say it so quietly and reasonably. The trouble is that I can't quite bring myself to believe it. There *has* to be room for people who aren't hell-bent on change and what you call progress.' She sipped her wine, then framed the only question that mattered. 'What is going to happen about the water?'

'What you'd expect, I'm afraid. My father will build his tanks on his land – it's what he's entitled to do.'

'By legal right perhaps, but not by long tradition. Isn't there an alternative? Can't he, *please*, build his hotel somewhere else, where pipes galore could be laid to his door by a grateful local council?'

Fernando smiled at her, and she registered again the tiredness of his face and its attractiveness. 'You don't understand him, my dear. He wants it on the top of that damned mountain just because it *is* difficult and different. He sees it as the last challenge of his life; it's *his* dream, just as an unchanged *pueblo* fits the dream of your aunt and uncle. I shan't dissuade him from it.'

She could find no answer, but was saved from saying so by the arrival of Josefa. While she wandered in and out with food they talked of Madrid, and music, and Venetia's own childhood visits to Jerez. It was pleasant and all too easy in the lamp-lit intimacy to forget disagreement and simply enjoy not being alone. But a different tension slowly grew in the quiet room, and she knew its danger when his hand brushed hers on the table, making her heart race. The evening could easily end in a way that she had to remember was unthinkable. She must drink no more wine, keep her head and somehow, please God, remain convinced that Fernando had arrived by chance, *not* to prove to her that her body couldn't be content with what his brother offered.

Suddenly his voice broke the silence that had fallen. 'I should like to stay – more than anything else in life that I can think of – but I'm terribly afraid you have principles that get in the way of the pleasure we could undoubtedly find together. So I shall leave when I've finished my coffee – if that's what you want.'

She looked across the table at him. 'Yes –

it's what I want.' But it couldn't be left there; they must find an easier, less charged air to breathe before he went. 'It would help a great deal,' she said, trying to smile, 'if you'd find some beautiful, glamorous girl to settle down with – you're rather a danger on the loose! Wouldn't Fiona have done very well?'

'She wouldn't have done at all,' he answered after a pause, 'but I shall have to see if I can find someone who will, if that would make you happy.'

The silence grew heavy again, and it was a relief to hear a disturbance out in the hall. A moment later Felipe walked into the room, and halted at the sight of his brother. Venetia forced herself to smile warmly at him.

'My dear, what a lovely surprise! The second one this evening – just as I was expecting to eat all alone, Fernando arrived and kindly kept me company.'

Felipe kissed her hands, and then her mouth. 'I suddenly couldn't stand Madrid a minute longer without you, but if I'd stopped to telephone I should have lost the train, and I've missed you too much to risk that.' Then he turned to the man who was watching them. '*Buenas noches*, brother dear – what brings you to Seville?'

'Business meetings tomorrow morning. I'd expected you both to be here.' The lie was told casually, sounding almost bored; a danger was over, and Venetia knew she could safely ask him if he needed a bed for the night. His eyes held hers for a moment, then he smiled a little. 'I think not, thank you; the Alfonso XIII will put me up.'

He stayed long enough for Felipe to share the last of the wine and coffee with them, and talk about his doings in Madrid. Then, after courteously sending his thanks to Josefa for her delicious dinner, he stood up to say good-night.

'Early for *you*,' Felipe commented, smiling at him. 'Old haunts to be revisited, perhaps?'

'I think not,' his brother said again. 'I'm getting old, *amigo*, and I've been told it's time I settled down!'

A moment later he was gone, and Felipe looked questioningly at Venetia. 'Something different about him, did you think, or was it just my imagination?'

'Certainly something tired about him ... and probably about *you*, too, but there *are* things we need to discuss.'

He stared at her pale face, thinking that it was she who looked tired and strained. 'I shouldn't have stayed away,' he said with sudden anxiety. 'I'm sorry, my dear one; it seemed better than having to go back, but I won't leave you alone again.'

She shook her head. 'Starting my new

career has been a little nerve-racking, that's all. To save you asking, it's going rather well!'

'I *should* have asked. Oh God, I shall keep making mistakes,' he said humbly. 'Forgive me, please.'

She smiled at him, aware of errors of her own but determined that he should be made to think of what so closely concerned them, not only of his own affairs.

'I've told Edwina we'll be at Rosario this weekend. Will you mind very much if we stay at Las Cuadras?' His face clouded over, and she hurried on. 'You know already that I don't feel at home in La Paloma, but also your father might think our arrangement a little too informal! My aunt and uncle are prepared for it.'

'I want to do whatever makes you happy,' he said with a little more reserve than usual, 'but we must consider Father as well. He and I are getting on much better now, and he'd be lonely and hurt if we just abandoned him.'

She nodded, aware that she was the one who sounded selfish, if not downright silly; but something in her face led him to make a guess at what might really be troubling her.

'You think I shouldn't depend on him so much! I don't, *querida*. My music earns what I need. You don't have to work at all unless you want to … in fact Father would certainly think that you *shouldn't* work!'

'Then I must disappoint him,' she said firmly, 'because I'm going to enjoy what I do and become quite good at it.' She shelved the discussion of where they would sleep at Rosario, knowing what else she had to tackle. 'I'm afraid there's a more serious problem concerning your father – listen while I tell you what's been happening.' As impartially as she could, she described the developing battle, and rounded it off with an account of what Fernando had said earlier in the evening. 'Your brother insists that right, and progress, and common sense are all on Manolo's side, but even if it's true there are still other things to be addressed. Have we any chance *together* of convincing him of that?'

She read Felipe's opinion in his face before hc answered her. 'No chance at all, I would say.' He gripped her hands as if the contact between them would help her to understand. 'It's not what you're thinking, Venetia, not just pure greed. Ever since he bought La Paloma he's been dreaming about that hilltop ruin, planning what he could do with it. He can't bear to see such a wonderful possibility being wasted. I understand that better about him now.'

'But he *can* contemplate people in the *pueblo* being ruined,' she said coolly.

'That's only this man Sánchez's exaggeration, my love – they *will* still get water, though perhaps not as much as before.'

There was some truth in that as well, of course, and she knew that she was being trapped as usual between opposing arguments – forced, because this was Spain and not a country bred up to compromise, to choose the side she must belong to. But the worst of her trouble was that even Felipe seemed to be coming round to the Quinones' side. She forced herself to smile at him, knowing that if they were to survive together they must be adult and sensible; it was, as William had insisted, Rosario's problem, not theirs, and their chief responsibility now was to each other.

'I shan't change my view that Manolo is morally in the wrong,' she said quietly, 'but I *will* agree not to get involved. I'll tell Uncle Will that we aren't in the battle – on either side. In return, *you* must try to be calmly English for once, instead of the dyed-in-the-wool Spaniard that you really are!'

He smiled sweetly, relieved that the discussion seemed to be over, and, when the time came to go to bed, went with her to her room. But he made no attempt to make love to her. They shared a bed and it seemed to be all he needed for contentment. On the whole, she was thankful; the oddity of their relationship would need facing later on, but

354

she couldn't tackle it now. The man who'd aired his nephew's view at the public meeting now seemed altogether less sure where his conviction lay. Manolo was a wily, wickedly manipulative old man, but although she had no intention of being manipulated herself she hadn't the right to destroy Felipe's new-found harmony with his family. Somehow it must be reconciled with her loyalty to the Marriotts and to what she believed in herself. But their next visit to Rosario looked fraught with difficulties, and she would have to pray that they didn't get there to find Pablo Sánchez and Edwina patrolling the sierra with shotguns.

The owner of El Perdido still avoided the priest, but that didn't stop Ian Gilmour going to call on him. Don Alberto welcomed him as a much-missed friend, and smiled at the offered bottle of whisky with which it was suggested they should celebrate their reunion.

'A rare treat, my dear man,' he admitted with a smile. Then he examined his visitor's face. 'Some grief gone through since I saw you, I think. I hope it can be survived.'

Ian Gilmour nodded. 'Yes, it can be; but that's not why I'm here.'

'Taking us by surprise too! Or if the Marriotts knew, they didn't mention it.'

'No, I asked Pablo Sánchez to let me slip

355

in unannounced.' He took a sip of Perth Royal, then began to explain. 'When my uncle died he left us a priceless archive of material about Río Tinto, where he and his father before him had worked all their lives. I never went there as a child, because of a bitter family quarrel, but the history of the place fascinates me. The minerals are exhausted now, with the mines on the verge of closing down, but I want to make a visit there before they do.'

'There are mixed feelings about them, I believe,' Don Alberto suggested gently.

'As about everything in Spain! All the more reason, perhaps, to find out the truth.'

'*That*'s not why you're here, though.'

Ian smiled, accepting that Don Alberto was more interested in his present troubled parish than in the past events of a different province. 'I made the mistake of telling my friend, Pablo, that I was coming back to Spain. He admitted there was a worsening problem here and, knowing him, I thought I'd better come. He can take care of himself well enough, but he may not understand the sort of gentle but unyielding man that William Marriott is.'

'Or the sort of unyielding woman that Edwina is!'

Pure amusement suddenly made Ian Gilmour look young again. 'Pablo will make no mistake there! I'd bet my life they're thick as thieves already.'

The priest grew serious again, cupping long, thin hands round his whisky glass. 'We're talking of the water problem of course. The villagers think of nothing else, and who can blame them?'

'After the public meeting,' Gilmour said slowly, 'it seemed that Rosario *could* disagree without tearing itself apart, but I doubt if that's still the case. There's been violence already and there'll be more before we're done.'

Don Alberto nodded sadly. 'The men who lost the vote assumed that it wouldn't affect their lives: they would go on as before, while those who wanted to could join Manolo Quinones. Now they begin to see that it isn't true. The real cost to them of the scheme is becoming visible, and they remember all over again that they have no reason to trust the Quinones family. The Rosarians were Republicans almost to a man, you must remember; people like the Mayor have only come here since the war.'

'And Pablo's father not only fought for the Reds but spent half his life in exile afterwards. The present battle begins to look ugly, doesn't it?'

Don Alberto hesitated for a moment. 'There's one more complication you may not know about. I learn from Edwina Marriott that a ... a close relationship is developing between her niece and Manolo's younger son. I fear the strain this quarrel must be imposing on *them*.'

There was a small silence in the room before his visitor answered. 'I did know about it. But Felipe is a Quinones – a born survivor in other words – and *she* is...'

But he seemed to have lost interest in what he was going to say next and Don Alberto had to prompt him. 'She is ... what exactly?'

'Oh, very skilled at getting men to eat out of her hand – even customers as difficult as my uncle was, and no doubt Manolo Quinones still is! We needn't add to our problems by worrying about Venetia.'

He smiled as he said it, with a kind of bitter humour that seemed directed at himself. Puzzled by it, Don Alberto dragged them back to the main problem. 'What is to be done?'

'Pablo Sánchez will sabotage Quinones in any way he can – inflame feelings in the *pueblo*, remind men of the past, especially try to dissuade them from working at the site. Manolo may not realise it yet, but he's up against an *andalúz* quite as tough and determined as himself.'

'And the *andalúz*, I think, has Ian Gilmour on his side, which makes him still more formidable,' the priest put in quietly.

He was offered a rare, attractive smile. 'I'm the voice of reason, *amigo*, that neither

358

of them wants to listen to! I've asked Quinones to meet us, to discuss, not fight! Rather to my surprise, he's agreed. I thought you'd feel happier to know that, but right now I must be on my way while I can still see the track up to El Perdido.'

The priest waved him off, feeling indeed better now; things were less likely to get out of hand with his Scots friend back in Rosario.

The subject of the proposed meeting cropped up again between the Mayor and his sister. He sounded excited at the prospect, already anticipating the rout of those lined up against them. Ian Gilmour's public attack on him hadn't been forgotten and he relished the prospect of seeing the foreigner and his troublesome friend made to look fools this time. Consuela, who always listened carefully to the gossip in her shop, advised him to wait before counting his chickens.

'The man Sánchez is not a fool,' she insisted calmly, 'and his friend nearly won the *pueblo* over once before. Don Manolo's hotel isn't safe yet.'

Don Ramón was accustomed to heeding his sister – with two years' seniority and a nice little fortune won by her own shrewdness, she merited humouring – but this time he was confident.

'They're too late, Consuela, and for a change we even have the law on our side!'

She considered it for a moment and eventually had to concede that indeed it made a useful difference this time.

Twenty-Two

Felipe drove alone to Rosario, leaving Venetia to follow by bus when Friday came. The problem of where they should stay had loomed over them until the last minute; then, to ward off a disagreement, she'd suggested that they might pitch a tent half-way between Las Cuadras and La Paloma, to establish impartiality. As usual when she tried humour as a help in time of trouble, Felipe remained grave.

'It's not a very useful idea, *querida*,' he pointed out sadly. 'I think we should go on as before ... just for the moment. Of course, I shall come down and visit you, and your aunt and uncle.'

'You *must*,' she insisted with a smile. 'It's their birthday on Saturday.'

He'd kissed her tenderly and driven away, leaving her to reflect that she'd been madly over-optimistic with Ian Gilmour. The truth was that she and Felipe were still far from being sorted out, and even the weekend ahead looked fraught with anxieties.

William was waiting for her at the bus station, and at least there was nothing but pleasure in seeing *him* again.

'Everything all right?' he asked casually after a glance at her face.

'Everything's fine, but Felipe thought it best to stay at La Paloma after all.' Then she hurriedly changed the subject. 'How is Rosario?'

'Tense ... unhappy,' William had to admit. 'It's only being kept under control by Ian's sheer force of character, but we can't expect him to stay for ever, keeping opposing sides from brawling with each other. He's suggested a meeting with Manolo, to prevent the Guardia Civil having to be called in.'

It seemed shameful the following day, given the connection between them, that a family birthday lunch should exclude Felipe's father, but Venetia told herself that a strained pretence at cordiality was no way to enjoy a celebration. She was talking to the Marriotts' other guest, Don Alberto, when Pablo Sánchez walked into the room clutching an enormous bouquet of flowers that he must have ransacked Ubrique to find. Venetia shot a reproachful glance at her aunt – with Felipe there, it was embarrassing to have Pablo also invited to the party –

but Edwina offered her sunniest smile in return, knowing that there was one more guest still to come. A moment later he strolled into the room.

He found his voice first, but didn't move forward to hold out his hand. 'This is either Edwina's little surprise, or she just forgot to mention that you'd be here.' Then Ian Gilmour acknowledged Felipe's presence by nodding to him. 'I'm not sure of the rules governing these things – am I to congratulate you and Venetia?'

Before the question could be answered she turned to the man beside her with a bright smile pinned somehow to her mouth. 'Darling, you haven't met Señor Pablo Sánchez, the owner of El Perdido. But I think you do know already that he doesn't like the idea of your father's hotel at all!'

She had, she realised, unfairly passed her awkwardness on, like the baton in a relay race she was desperate to get rid of. But Felipe didn't let her down; he offered his graceful bow and even smiled at the two men watching him. 'Fortunately we're here to celebrate a birthday, not to argue about a difficult matter.'

On cue, William opened champagne more noisily than usual, and the worst embarrassment seemed to be over. They could remember the reason for the gathering, and drink to the health of their host and hostess.

The party was even going quite smoothly when Encarnita, apparently under the impression that she was ushering in another late guest, appeared in the doorway with Fernando Quinones beside her.

This time even Edwina looked momentarily aghast, Venetia wasn't sorry to notice. This was no little surprise of her own arranging; this was Fate at work, unforeseen and malicious. But she pulled herself together and tried to smile at the newcomer.

'A birthday celebration for my brother and myself ... join us, won't you?'

Reduced to the role of onlooker, Venetia could have sworn that Fernando, at least, was enjoying himself. He glanced round the room, shot a faintly questioning smile at his brother and then advanced to shake hands with William and Edwina.

'My congratulations, of course, but I'm afraid *I'm* expected up at the house.' Again his glance wandered round the room, as if assessing who was present. 'My reason for calling was to fix the meeting tomorrow that concerns us all.' He looked at William. 'Would you like to suggest a time, *señor*?'

William answered as calmly as he could. 'Shall we say at noon tomorrow?' No one seemed prepared to disagree, and William turned again to Fernando. 'Where do you suggest we meet?'

Venetia stifled an insane desire to offer the middle of the drive again, and heard Fernando make his own obvious suggestion instead.

'We shall expect you all at La Paloma. Until tomorrow, then.'

Another smile and he was gone, leaving a deafening silence behind. It was Encarnita who reassembled the party by returning to announce that lunch was ready, and Ian Gilmour who suggested with a surprisingly biblical turn of phrase that they would enjoy it more by shelving the topic of the meeting, sufficient unto the day being its evil thereof.

But it had to be mentioned as the party broke up and Felipe got ready to return to La Paloma. 'It served my aunt quite right that your brother should decide to turn up then,' Venetia said to him quietly, 'but I'm afraid it makes things awkward in just the way you didn't want.'

Felipe gave her hand a little pat. 'Not as awkward as all that, because I decided to tell my father beforehand about the lunch party! Fernando probably guessed who else would be invited. Walking in like that was just the sort of tactic that would appeal to him – military men call it seizing the high ground!'

Venetia digested this in silence for a moment. 'What are we going to do about the meeting?'

'Attend, of course, even if we don't take part.'

'Our part, I imagine, will be to keep them from each other's throats!' But her smile went awry and, understanding the extent of her worry, Felipe spoke gently.

'Listen, my love – this is not a full-scale war breaking out! It's a small incidental dispute in a matter that already has the approval of the *pueblo*. There will be whatever adjustment is possible over a problem that Pablo Sánchez is probably using to settle an old score; then, when honour is satisfied all round, my father will resume his favourite role of generous host, and that will be that.'

She thought the chances were that he was wrong, but it seemed pointless to go on saying so when they could do nothing to influence the outcome one way or the other. 'Well, I shall be glad when the meeting is over and we can go home,' she murmured instead.

But even that was tactless, she realised when she saw him frown. La Paloma was still *his* home, however uncongenial she found it herself; and it was where most of his work had to be done.

The following day, as noon approached, the meeting convened. Manolo's other supporters proved to be the building engineer in charge of the project; the Mayor, wonder-fully brushed and turned out for the occasion; and the provincial official whose signature had first given the project permission to go ahead. He looked quite as smooth as Don Ramón, and Venetia dis-trusted him accordingly.

Being mere women who didn't count, she and Edwina were placed at the foot of the table, but it was a vantage-point from which to observe the men who confronted one another: her uncle, Ian Gilmour and Pablo Sánchez ranged against Manolo, Fernando and his acolytes, while Don Alberto, at the head of the table, was given the unhappy role of referee. Felipe was missing, but he walked in at the last minute and seated himself with only the merest hesitation beside his father and brother. But where else *could* he have been expected to sit? she asked herself: he *was* a Quinones, and what did it really matter where a chair had been left for him?

Manolo invited the engineer to speak first. With the aid of plans spread out in front of them, he explained the layout of the site – the hotel buildings themselves, the new approach road, car parks and ornamental gardens. There was bound to be mess while work was in progress, he admitted, but when it was finished no one would have cause to complain; it would all look beautiful.

Next, the official confidently confirmed that the plans matched those submitted to the *ayuntamiento* – all was in order and Don Manolo had been given full permission to proceed. That, his tone implied, should really be the end of the discussion.

Venetia watched Pablo Sánchez, half expecting him to shout that the *ayuntamiento*'s approval had undoubtedly been bought. But he was looking at his friend, obedient to some instruction he'd been given.

'Enlighten me, *señor*,' Ian Gilmour said affably to the official. 'Has new legislation been passed abolishing the *cañadas reales*? If not, one of them lies directly underneath the new road Don Manolo's men are already at work on.'

His victim smiled ingratiatingly. 'No new legislation, but in this case what would be the use to anyone of a drove road that will only lead in future to private grounds and a hotel?'

'At this moment I don't know, and nor do you; but the appropriation of what is common land remains, does it not?'

He suggested it almost gently, but they were all aware that the man wouldn't be let off the hook he was caught on. Venetia nearly found it in her heart to pity him, so quietly implacable was the angler reeling him in.

The official fell bravely on his sword. 'In

the circumstances we considered the infringement merely a technicality; objection to it was waived.'

William now entered the fray, pointing at the engineer's plans. 'The gardens, attractive though they may eventually be, will replace what *naturally* clothes the sierra, the habitat at the moment of many animals and birds. Was this another objection that you decided to waive – in contravention of Spain's acceptance of EU conservation laws?'

Despising the official as a broken reed, Manolo took up the fight himself. 'Your concern for birds and flowers is well known, Señor Marriott; my own concern is for the people who belong here ... for the majority of the *pueblo* who made *their* choice some months ago.'

Ian Gilmour ignored him and spoke again to the official. 'Another infringement, *señor*, or do we only *imagine* that these laws exist?'

'They exist, of course ... in principle, that is. But local economic factors must be allowed to override them occasionally ... Let us admit the truth – we are still Spaniards, as well as Europeans!'

His honesty earned him a charming smile. 'And Señor Marriott and I are not – the point is taken! But my other friend here *is* a Spaniard, much concerned with economic factors since his land will be the first to be ruined in order that these delightful gardens can be laid out and the hotel water supply assured. He isn't only anxious for himself, however; others will be affected as well.'

Manolo shook his head, as a horse might try to dislodge a troublesome fly. 'There can be no infringement because I am not breaking the law,' he pointed out, resisting a strong desire to shout. 'I am entitled to the water which falls on my land; I'm not proposing to take anyone else's.'

Pablo stared at him across the table, eyes now blazing. 'You're proposing to keep for yourself what would otherwise flow down the hillsides, benefiting everyone else. In better times than these there *were* once laws regulating how much a man might claim from what God sent down from heaven. It was not to be more than he needed, and never at his neighbours' expense.'

'Moorish laws!' Manolo said contemptuously. 'We live in today's world, Sánchez, not in the conditions of five hundred years ago. If a few vines and vegetables and olive trees wither, that's the price of progress. *You* weren't here when Rosario voted in *favour* of what I'm prepared to do – at great personal expense. The task is presenting technical problems enough without a handful of trouble-makers causing more obstructions. The *pueblo* voted for a hotel, but even I cannot establish it without water.'

'Nor can you establish it,' Pablo insisted, 'without men willing to build it and women prepared to work in it. I can tell you that even those who voted for it three months ago are fast changing their minds.'

They had reached the heart of the matter now, and for a moment everyone present acknowledged the fact by waiting for whatever must come next. Venetia watched Fernando, who had said nothing since the meeting began; her hope, too fragile to have been shared with Edwina, was still that *he* would decide the issue by persuading his father to some kind of compromise. As if he felt her eyes pleading with him, he suddenly looked in her direction, but his face was expressionless as he began to speak.

'The men are less willing because you've been talking to them, no doubt, raking over a past they should have been allowed to forget. For us, it doesn't matter – if *they* won't work we shall simply bring in the men and women we need from outside; they'll be grateful enough for the chance.'

'But then where will the *pueblo*'s economic advantage be that we're told so much about?' Ian Gilmour queried gently. 'For Rosario there will be only loss.'

Fernando gave his little shrug. 'That's its choice, I'm afraid – it can enjoy the benefits of collaboration or see them go elsewhere.'

It was time for hope to die. She'd been a fool to think she might have influenced him a little; he remained what he was – Manolo's son. The man she *ought* to be thinking about was Felipe, hunched in his chair and no doubt wishing more than anything else that he wasn't there at all. She could guess his discomfort easily enough, and the fault was hers. She'd persuaded him that they must be neutral, however uncomfortable it might be; he'd known all along, probably, that the suggestion was not only shameful but impossible.

She smiled at him with lovely, warm encouragement, waiting for him to say what must be said, just as he'd bravely done at the public meeting. Fernando's solution to the problem had to be refuted, and it needed to be done by a Quinones before Ian Gilmour did it himself. But although Felipe met her glance, he gave a barely perceptible shake of his head. Suddenly feeling rather sick, she looked across the table at her uncle – an elderly man risking eviction from his home in a battle he could have claimed, more easily than Felipe, wasn't his to fight. Scarcely aware that the words were in her mouth, she addressed Fernando herself in a cool, clear voice.

'What you've just suggested has historical precedents, of course; it was the tactic the Fascists used when they brought the Moors over from Africa to win the Civil War. Bring in a little army of your own by all means, but you should understand your countrymen well enough to know that it will cause still more resentment and bitterness.'

Even as she spoke she knew it for the one accusation that Manolo would never forgive. No one was allowed to remind him of the days when his family had taken part in bloody reprisals against the Republicans. He'd made an apologia for them only once himself, saying that the church burners and priest slayers on the other side had deserved their punishments. Brought up in the Church's same persecuted faith, she'd come close to agreeing with him then.

He looked down the length of the table, smiling dangerously at Edwina. 'Venetia seems to have deserted the family I thought she now belonged to! Would *you* like to say something on our behalf, señorita? If not, you might both prefer to leave *us* to finish the discussion.'

Edwina glanced composedly at her niece. 'Don Manolo would like us to go; I think we should, don't you?'

They walked to the door, and found Ian Gilmour there before them, waiting to open it. He half smiled at Edwina, but merely stared at the white-faced girl beside her; he could see no way in which a friendly gesture from him would help the trouble she was

372

in. Outside in the hall a servant hovered, waiting to serve wine, but she went away when Venetia shook her head.

'I expected Felipe to do something – speak himself, or walk out with us,' she said in a voice that trembled on the edge of tears. 'Stupid of me – just about as stupid as telling him that we needn't take sides.'

'Neutrality, in Spain?' Edwina considered the outlandish idea, then shook her head. 'Perhaps ... when "fishes flew and forests walked and figs grew upon thorn"; but not in human knowledge, I'm afraid.' Her expression grew sober at the sadness in Venetia's face. 'My dear, I'm sorry, but you have to be fair – consider the trap that Felipe is caught in.'

'We're both caught in it,' Venetia said with the calmness of despair. 'He loves this house, needs it to work in, and also – for the first time in his life – has managed to reach some kind of understanding with Manolo. I feel stifled here, and in any case want to go on working in Seville; on top of that I've just heaved a brick through my own fragile relationship with his family!'

Edwina baulked at asking outright the only question that now seemed to matter. Instead, she approached it crabwise, wishing that she'd had more practice in such matters.

'Forget Pablo's olive trees, and even William's precious eagles – there are enough of us to fight for them and lose if we have to. Think of how and where *you* can best be happy.'

Venetia looked at her aunt, knowing her for the fierce, forthright, but kind woman she was.

'For once you're not asking the question in your mind,' she said gently, 'which is, I think, why am I sharing my life with Felipe when there seem to be so many difficulties in the way? Well, it's true that so far we haven't been hugely successful as lovers, but that may be partly my fault, and left to ourselves I think we can get better at it! But we are, in any case, the best and dearest of friends. Without him I'm very lonely, and he needs me – he says so and I know it's true. It ought to be enough, don't you think, to see us through our difficulties?' She smiled at her aunt, trying to look cheerful. 'I thought Ian Gilmour and his troops did rather well – he's an impressive man in action. But I pity poor Don Alberto; there doesn't seem to be the slightest chance that he can wring a compromise out of the single-minded die-hards gathered in there.'

'And Ian won't be here much longer to keep Pablo Sánchez in order.' Suddenly Edwina's face looked old and very sad. 'I'm afraid Manolo's wretched hotel has murdered our contentment. Even if he doesn't throw us out I doubt if William will feel happy to stay.'

'Well, what shall we do now?' Venetia asked. 'Wait here like naughty children sent out of class, or go home?'

'Go home, I think – where at least we can drown sorrow in our own fino.'

A message was left with the servant for Felipe, and then the two of them walked back along the drive.

'Nobody really wins in a fight like this,' Venetia finally said. 'Perhaps Manolo will realise that and suddenly become sweetly reasonable.' Looking at her niece's drawn face, Edwina for once strove to be tactful by saying nothing at all. They smiled at each other, but walked on in silence after that.

Twenty-Three

The men they'd left behind walked in half an hour later but, judging by their faces, the meeting had been a failure. Venetia supposed that Manolo had remained obdurate, Fernando unhelpful and Felipe as uninvolved as possible.

'Don Alberto not with you?' Edwina asked. 'Man of God though he is, I'm sure *he* needs a glass of wine as badly as the rest of you.'

'I think he needs his church more,' William suggested quietly. 'The poor man now sees prayer as Rosario's only salvation.'

'The "adjustments" Felipe hoped for couldn't be made?' Venetia asked in her turn.

'They weren't even considered, and I'm not sure we ever thought they would be. Manolo has an *idée fixe* where his hotel is concerned.'

'Where his personal profit is concerned, you mean,' Pablo said bitterly.

Handing round the wine that William was pouring, Ian Gilmour frowned over Pablo's remark. 'That's the maddest part of the whole mad business. Quinones won't live long enough to even see his investment back. He's going to have to pour money into the venture, and for at least half of every year his expensive white elephant will be closed or running at a loss.'

Edwina was getting impatient. 'We still don't know what happened. Will someone tell us, please?'

Gilmour smiled at her. 'A stand-off is the correct term, I believe! We warned them that every legal objection we can find will be used to delay the work; a little less legally perhaps, Pablo hinted that the men whose crops are threatened will talk to anyone still ready to sign on with Quinones. Fernando seemed to sneer at both suggestions, but I can't help feeling that he knows the bottom-less pit of trouble and expense they're digging for themselves.'

'And you also can't help feeling,' Venetia put in again, 'that he – and Felipe, of course – should have the courage to tell their father the truth. Well, it isn't a lack of courage. They've both explained to me that this is Manolo's dream – the last challenge of his buccaneering life. They aren't going to spoil it for him.'

She spoke calmly, but her pale face showed the effort she was having to make. Ian watched her, knowing that he had to make an effort of his own. He'd got Venetia Marriott labelled, he thought – misleadingly kind to her aunt and uncle but otherwise a beautiful fraud. Quietly and gently she'd gone after what she wanted and succeeded very well. But the label refused to stick now; she'd come close to wrecking her own future for their sakes this morning, and his heart knew her for the girl she was.

Unable to say so, he spoke in a voice that sounded detached to the point of indifference. 'Then we must manage without Manolo's sons ... and without *you*, too, I suggest. Why make life hard for yourself?'

A smile touched her pale mouth for a moment. 'Or, put another way, why don't I at least stay loyal to the side I'm supposed to be on? Thank you for the reminder.'

An uncomfortable silence was broken by Encarnita bustling in with a tray of tapas dishes. Like Josefa in Seville, she loved preparing these small delicacies – the more colourful and varied the better – and in the quantities she provided they constituted a meal in themselves.

The impromptu spread was almost over when Encarnita reappeared, bringing coffee this time and a note for Venetia, brought by a servant from 'the house'. She opened it, registered its signature first, and then read the message itself.

Dear Venetia,

Forgive this note, but you abandoned us unnecessarily – my father only meant you to leave the discussion, not the house.

We have since been plunged into the greatest anxiety, because he was very unwell at lunch; it's the slight heart attack that the doctor had warned him about. He shouldn't have been upset as he was this morning. Fernando has business meetings he must attend on the coast, so I am clearly the one to stay here. There seems little point in asking you to stay with me, and in any case I know how anxious you are to get back to Seville.

I'm afraid it means a tedious return journey for you on the bus; forgive me, please, for that.

Ever yours,
Felipe

She read the message through again, wondering whether Manolo had dictated its terse phrases from his sickbed. Only the apologetic closing sentence sounded like Felipe. All along she'd clung to the belief that he was different from the rest of his family, and in many ways he *was*. But she couldn't reasonably blame him if, when the Quinones were under attack from outside, he became more, not less, one of them. She'd told Edwina, with a kind of mad

379

optimism, that difficulties musn't be allowed to matter – assuming that, even if he
didn't say so to Manolo, it was how Felipe
would feel as well – but she was much less
sure now. With the note crammed in her
pocket she turned to face the others.

'Felipe is having to stay on up at the
house,' she said with heroic calm. 'His
father has had what they think is a slight
heart attack, and Fernando needs to leave
for the coast. They rather blame us, I think,
for upsetting Manolo this morning.'

'He should blame himself for having eaten
and drunk too much at lunch,' Pablo suggested. 'By the look of him, he always does.'

'Perhaps,' Venetia agreed, 'but at least
admit that we didn't help!' She turned to
look at her uncle. 'I was going to drive back
with Felipe this evening. Can you bear an
early trip to Ubrique in the morning, so that
I can catch the first bus? Now, I've work to
prepare, so if you'll excuse me I'd better go
and make a start on it.'

She smiled cheerfully at them and went to
her own room, thankful to be alone at last.
But although tomorrow's lectures needed
thinking about, so did her own stupidity. Ian
Gilmour had once – a long time ago, it
seemed now – asked if she could stomach
the Quinones family, and she'd said she
didn't have to, that only Felipe mattered. It
had been her first mistake. But Felipe

380

should equally have asked himself whether he and his family could stomach a girl whose views were always likely to differ from theirs in every important particular.

Determined to lay bare the skeleton of the problem, she finally uncovered what she thought was the truth. Luc had spoiled her for other men and, dishonestly but unconsciously, she'd settled for a kind, attentive companion who wouldn't blot out his memory.

Felipe's dishonesty had been of a different kind. He'd wanted it known that he wasn't lacking Fernando's masculinity, had even seemed very inclined for love, but it had been meant to be only in principle, she now realised ... rather like the official with his conservation laws! Passion would always be kept for his music; the possibility that a woman might have needs of her own was *not* what he'd anticipated. Born out of his time, Felipe would have made the perfect medieval troubador, ready to sing his lady's praises. To treat her as a real woman, or fight for views she wasn't supposed to have, was not in his scheme of courtly love.

Sad but clear-eyed at last, she finally abandoned the pretence of working and went back to her aunt's sitting-room. The autumn evening had turned raw and wet, prompting William to light a fire, and she smiled gratefully at the sight of it.

'Lovely, Uncle Will; just what we needed. Warmth and the lovely smell of juniper and vine clippings!' She knelt down by the hearth, holding out cold hands to the blaze. 'Why don't you both think of spending Christmas with me in Seville? If Encarnita has no relations to go to you could bring her as well.'

Edwina considered the implications of this suggestion before answering. 'You and Felipe will be expected at La Paloma, surely?'

'The family always goes to Madrid, to stay with Blanca and Rodrigo. That might depend on Manolo's health this year, but in any case I'm sure I shan't be needed.' Their anxious faces made her go on. 'The tea-leaves in my cup tell me that my connection with the Quinones family is probably over – or it will be when Felipe braces himself to come and admit the fact!'

'My dear girl, it's nothing of the kind,' William protested fiercely. 'He will have understood that you were simply supporting us this morning – which of course you shouldn't have done.'

Venetia shook her head. 'What he understood was that I should always support you against his father; even if Manolo hadn't pointed that out, Felipe would have seen it for himself. I'm afraid it's something we can't get over.' She smiled faintly at them.

382

'Now, may we talk about you instead, and give up pretending that magnanimity is Manolo's long suit? At the public meeting he wanted to be seen as a generous winner, but there's nothing to be gained by behaving nobly in private.'

'Our rental agreement is due for renewal at the beginning of the new year,' William said calmly. 'We'd supposed it to be a mere formality, but that probably isn't the case now. I'm fairly certain he will ask us to leave – sad, but not nearly the loss that yours has been.' He looked across at his sister. 'We'll move nearer Seville, my dear; then Venetia won't have so far to travel!'

She realised that it was all he would say on the subject – anger or recrimination were equally pointless because, having chosen a course of action, they must accept what it led to without complaint. It was an unfashionable code in a world that always now looked for someone else to blame, but it was William Marriott's and would be until he died.

She threw more twigs on the fire and watched the flames dance before asking her next question. 'Ian Gilmour spoke of delaying things, but that can't go on for ever. What will Pablo and the other men do – hang on for as long as they can?'

'Of course; this is *their* place, not to be given up without a last-ditch struggle, and that's something Andalucíans are very good at. It was the case again and again in the Civil War – they were disorganised and often ineffective in attack, but brave and stubborn defenders. Manolo isn't out of the wood yet, and Fernando at least certainly understands that.'

'Will the bitterness *ever* die?' Venetia asked slowly. 'Will Spain ever be able to become one country?'

'Juan Carlos is still called King of all the Spains, I believe,' William pointed out, 'so perhaps he isn't any more sure than you are; but in the end the war *will* become just another episode, bloodier than most, in this country's tormented history.'

After that they agreed to talk of other things and the long, strange day drew to an end; but, kissing her aunt good-night, Venetia insisted that there was no need for her to rise with the dawn. 'I'll just make coffee; then Uncle Will can breakfast with you when he gets back from Ubrique.'

But the following morning, in the kitchen together, Venetia and William were startled by car headlights shining in the dimness outside. A moment later Ian Gilmour appeared at the door.

'Thought I could save you a trip,' he said to William. 'I have to go into Ubrique.'

'At seven in the morning?' Venetia asked in open disbelief. 'Nothing's open except the

384

bus station.'

'What I have to do there is my concern – it needn't bother you. Now, do you want a lift or not?'

Feeling, as always, that this unmanageable man was bound to win because he simply ignored the rules of normal behaviour, she admitted with dignity that she would be glad to save her uncle the drive. But, installed in the car a moment later, she found an objection that she might have used before.

'Are you sure it's safe to leave Pablo Sánchez on his own? He might decide to burn La Paloma down while your back is turned.'

'The Civil War ended sixty years ago,' he answered with unimpaired calm; 'my friend is well aware of that.'

'All right – so it was a silly thing to say,' she admitted after a small silence. 'My only excuse is that you bring out the worst in a woman.'

'I know,' he agreed. 'Look where it got me!'

Silenced by the tactlessness of what she'd said, she stared silently out of the window until they rounded a bend and had to come to an abrupt halt. In front of them a milling herd of goats was making use of the tarmac until it suited them to abandon it for a track leading down into the valley. The river of white, fawn and brown creatures, wickedly yellow-eyed and viciously hoofed, flowed all round them – the true familiars of ancient Spain, part of its landscape since prehistoric times. They jostled one another, but they were in no hurry to move on, and the warmth and smell of the car were things that apparently had to be investigated.

Feeling tension screw itself a little tighter round her tired brain, she was shockingly tempted to wind down the window and scream at them. She gripped her hands together in her lap, fighting the temptation, and suddenly felt the warmth of Ian Gilmour's hand covering her own.

'I'd almost swear they're *enjoying* the knowledge that we must wait for them,' she said unsteadily. 'Goats have been old in wickedness since the world began.'

'They'll go when it suits them, but we're in plenty of time.' He released her fingers – too soon; she would have liked the comfort to last longer – to wind down the window instead and shout a greeting to the goat-herd, now prodding the last lingerers across the road with his stick.

They had too much time in hand, it seemed, when they arrived in the town a few minutes later. The bus station still looked nearly deserted, and there was nothing to suggest that a bus would soon be ready to leave for Seville, or indeed for anywhere else. Only a solitary individual, unenthusi-astically sweeping up the previous day's layer of cigarette ends, answered her en-quiry for the 7.30 a.m. bus.

'Leaves at nine o'clock now,' he corrected her almost with pleasure. 'Seven thirty's the first bus in the *summer*.'

Almost weeping with vexation, she went back to where Ian Gilmour waited by the car. 'I should have checked the winter *horario*,' she said, trying to sound uncon-cerned. 'When I've brought Encarnita to catch the bus before, it was always in the summer. It doesn't matter – the coffee shop across the road will soon be open; I can go and sit in there.'

'And I can read timetables – there's one hanging up on the door! Get in, Venetia – you can't hang about here until then.'

'Nor can you drive me all the way to Seville, if that's what you're thinking of doing. The thing's *absurd*,' she almost shouted at him, self-control slipping at last. 'It won't be the end of the world if I'm late back, and in any case Pablo will wonder where on earth you've got to.'

'Pablo and I can talk to each other on a splendid modern invention called the mobile telephone! Just get back in the car and hush your tongue, woman, while I speak to him.'

Had the coffee shop been open, she would

have stalked across the road and taken refuge in it. But to cling to the door of the empty bus station and refuse to be parted from it did not seem, even in her present disintegrating state, the behaviour of a rational woman. She got back into the car and, after a brief conversation with Pablo Sánchez, he did the same. But before starting the engine he turned to look at her, noting the signs in her pale face of a troubled and probably sleepless night.

'Relax, Venetia,' he said gently. 'Don't worry about Manolo and his bloody hotel, and don't imagine for a moment that you need worry about Felipe, either. He'll be in Seville soon enough, to make his peace with you. Now, go to sleep while I drive *ventre à terre*, as they like to say in France, for Arcos – we'll be needing our breakfast by the time we get there.'

His kindness threatened her composure, but it wasn't the moment to try his patience by having a weeping woman beside him. The only comfort she could cling to was that at least he didn't know what she'd told William and Edwina. She'd admitted even more than that to herself, knowing finally that she and Felipe were bound to have failed in the end, even without the complication of his father's hotel. But the man beside her had jeered too often at her mistake; she couldn't admit now that he'd

388

been right all along.

Arcos was waking up as they arrived, but the Plaza del Cabildo in the centre of the town was pleasantly empty of cars, and they were made welcome in a *parador* not crowded with summer visitors.

The dining-room offered its usual, beautifully presented display of food, guaranteed to meet the breakfast requirements not only of Spaniards but of every known foreigner under the sun. Venetia declined the porridge, sausages, bacon and eggs that Ian Gilmour's eye lighted on, but she was suddenly aware of having eaten very little the day before, and helped herself to fruit, rolls and coffee.

Appetite blunted at last, Gilmour regretfully refused a fresh supply of toast, but accepted more coffee. 'We shall be in Seville by noon if we leave in half an hour – is that early enough for you?' he wanted to know.

She agreed that it was, wishing she could insist that they must set off at once. He could be gentle when he chose, but her heart was too sore for anybody else's touching, and rather than talk about it she turned the conversation to himself.

'I assume you won't stay much longer at Rosario. What will you do instead?'

'Since I'm part of the way there, immediately I shall do what I intended doing before Pablo's SOS deflected me – I want to

389

see the Río Tinto mines before they close for good. Then perhaps I can begin to make sense of all that Duncan wrote about them.'

'While I was staying with him he spoke a lot about his childhood and his working life there.' Venetia's face was suddenly shadowed by the memory of listening to his quiet voice. 'He was proud of the engineering achievement, even though he admitted that the miners' working conditions were brutally hard.'

'As they were for anyone below ground, here or anywhere else,' her companion observed. 'It's only in recent times that our collective conscience has become tender about such things.'

'Are you going to do something with Duncan's memoirs – publish them perhaps?' she asked.

'I'm certainly going to make use of them – but I've got a rather more ambitious book in mind: half a dozen key places, remembered as I saw them years ago and compared with the way they look now. The differences should say quite a lot about what has happened to Spain.'

She considered him for a moment – gaunt but no longer haunted, reticent but not embittered, with some kind of acceptance of grief achieved after a private battle that would have destroyed most men.

'It sounds fascinating,' she said after a

pause, 'though not perhaps what your publisher would expect from you.'

'He doesn't have to take it; I'm doing it mostly for myself.' He glanced at her face, aware of the sadness she tried to conceal. 'What else is bothering you, apart from my publisher?'

She offered him part of the truth. 'My aunt and uncle, mainly. They pretend to be calm about losing Las Cuadras, but I know they aren't – they love being there too much.'

Her companion drained his coffee cup and slowly replaced it on its saucer. 'Aren't you all despairing too easily? Manolo enjoys sudden rages, and certainly doesn't like anyone standing in his light. But even he can see the difference between fighting the Pablos of this world and taking out his spite on a couple like Edwina and William, who also have the advantage of being closely related to *you*. In a fit of temper he may be tempted to forget what charming tenants he's got, but you and Felipe will be able to talk him round.'

She gave a little nod, meaningless because for once it was he who was wrong; more meaningless still because it had nothing to do with the fear that suddenly filled her mind. His idea for a Spanish book *was* interesting, and she clung to it with desperate insistence, so as not to have to admit to something else: she simply couldn't bear the thought of losing track of him as he wandered about the country; they might need him again, not knowing where he was. He had no right to make them dependent on him and then disappear like the genie in Aladdin's lamp. She fought her way out of that drowning wave of panic like a swimmer gasping for air, and managed, somehow, a fairly creditable shrug.

'We'll call in reinforcements if we have to ... Blanca has the reputation in the family of being able to keep her father in order even if Fernando refuses to help.'

Ian Gilmour's glance wandered over her face again for a moment before he answered. 'I don't think he'll refuse – not if *you* ask him. Now, shall we be on our way again?'

She nodded, unable to say that she'd already asked and been refused.

By the time he'd paid the bill and walked outside she was at the far side of the square, looking up at the Gothic faade of the Church of San Pedro. It was built vertiginously on the very edge of the gorge that fell away to the Guadalete River and, as always, its intricately carved stonework told all manner of biblical stories. She would have liked to stay and read them, but she had to remember she was being delivered to Seville. Her chauffeur would be anxious to deposit her and move on, thankful that her muddled life was really no concern of his. She swung round to go back and found him a few paces away, engaged in conversation with a wandering minstrel earning his living with a guitar. A stray shaft of sunlight slanting through the overcast sky illumined them, youth and man apparently finding something worth talking about together.

But the golden beam of light showed her more than that. She was seeing Ian Gilmour steadily and seeing him whole for the first time in their chequered relationship. There'd been fleeting glimpses before of the man he truly was, but she'd swept them aside and wandered blindly into the Quinones camp instead. The truth was in front of her now, complete and unavoidable.

He saw her standing there, and smiled – glad, she thought, that the journey could be resumed. Pleased with herself, she was able to smile in return, but when they were back in the car she suddenly asked him not to drive off immediately.

'I know Rosario isn't your problem,' she said, 'but will you still be able to keep an eye on Pablo Sánchez? He's like most Spaniards – contemptuous of the officials who are supposed to govern them.'

'I realise that. I'll do my best to keep him, however marginally, on the side of law and order.'

Calmly she went on with what else filled her mind. 'If Duncan had known that you meant to stay and work in Spain I think he'd have willed his house to you, and it seems right that it should belong to a Gilmour. As long as you'll agree to keep Josefa and Aurelio on, I'll gladly make it over to you.'

She made the offer quietly, as if it was a small keepsake she was suggesting he might like, but his own voice was rough when he finally found something to say.

'As a paid-up member of today's army of tough, self-regarding womanhood, you're a disgrace, you know. Even if you have other homes to go to, giving this one away would be an insanely generous gesture.'

'You won't accept it?' Her eyes were luminously bright with disappointment.

'Certainly not – I've no fancy to be haunted by Duncan's ghost, rising from his grave in protest!' But she didn't smile, and something in her face made him speak in a different tone of voice. 'My dear girl, feel no guilt towards the Gilmours. I'm quite certain that Duncan's only wish was for *you* to live there and be happy. That's all you're required to do.'

'Oh, easy then – no sooner said than done!' she agreed with an odd smile. 'I can start now.'

No more was said until he stopped the car outside the house. Then, without warning, his hand beneath her chin tilted her face to meet his kiss. It lasted only a moment and she had to suppose that the earth didn't *really* shift under her feet for the fraction of time it used up.

'You looked sad,' he said a little unevenly. 'Imagine that was Quinones *in absentia*! *Vaya con Diós, amiga.*'

Unable to say anything at all, she waited for him to drive away, but when Aurelio opened the front door he wondered why she stood there blindly staring at the empty street.

Twenty-Four

She went back to her students, trying to remember Fiona's recommendation that, when all else failed, work was the thing. She would expunge – she liked the word and kept repeating it to herself – the memory of Ian Gilmour's farewell kiss; it had meant nothing. Worse than that, it had been *kindly* meant, and, as kisses went, what could be more lowering? He'd set off alone on his Spanish adventure, and the truth that had to be faced was simply this: he had learned to become, more likely had always been, a solitary man. That she could admit to; but something else, too painful to contemplate, had to be buried in the deepest, most secret corner of her heart. If she allowed herself to understand the significance of that moment in the square at Arcos she would know finally and for ever what had now been lost to her.

Felipe came to Seville on a morning so cold and wet that Andalucía seemed to have drifted northwards and anchored itself somewhere between Galicia and Cornwall. He walked in looking miserable, and she felt deeply ashamed to realise how little she had missed him.

'You look tired,' she said gently. 'Have things been very difficult at home?'

'Difficult, but they're getting better. My father had enough of a fright to listen to his doctor for once; it won't last, but for the moment he's still obeying orders.'

She led him into what had been Duncan's study – apart from the courtyard, her favourite part of the house; it smelled always of flowers and now of the aromatic twigs as well that crackled on the hearth. With none of La Paloma's luxury, it was comforting and full of grace – like its new owner, he thought. More than anything he wanted to go back to the time when they'd been together in Madrid, but that sort of perfection couldn't last. He'd known all along in his heart that he couldn't make it last.

Venetia saw his sadness and felt responsible for it. 'I'm sorry things went so awry last weekend – it was mostly my fault, I'm afraid.'

He made his familiar gesture of ruffling already untidy hair. 'Your only fault was to forget what you'd said: we weren't to get involved in Rosario's problems ... don't you remember?'

'Yes, I remember, but *that* was my mistake.' Resentment darkened his face, bringing a fleeting look of his father, but she hurried on. 'Felipe, please try to understand. I dislike La Paloma not because it's too ornate but because it's built on the proceeds from a ravaged coast; that matters, I'm afraid. And if the water tanks your father now insists on building drive men from the land, that matters too. I pretended that we could separate ourselves from those things; the idea was not only dishonest but unworkable.'

He stared down at his hands, not surprised to see them trembling a little. Manolo had warned him that she wouldn't change, and he was probably right, but one last effort had to be made.

'It's *you* who don't understand. The *pueblo* will benefit handsomely in the long run, but for now a few people have to get hurt. Dislike Fernando's clients if you must, but

397

Spain desperately needed the foreign money their developments brought in. For that it was worth putting up a few buildings your aunt and uncle don't like.'

She lifted thin hands as if to ward off what he'd said. 'I hear Manolo talking! You won't admit that he might be more reluctant to ruin Rosario's men if their fathers hadn't fought the Nationalists sixty years ago. "A few buildings" scarcely describes the ruination of a once-beautiful coastline.' He didn't answer at once, and she added one more reproach. 'It's agonising, having to take sides – but you did speak for Juan at the public meeting.'

Felipe looked at her with sad, honest eyes. 'Because I wanted *you* to think well of me, after I'd been such a fool about Fiona. Fernando never expected that I'd be able to keep you. He doesn't say so, but I know what he thinks – our trouble has more to do with *me* than Father's water tanks. I'm sure my brother's right – he always is about women.'

'For once Fernando is wrong,' she lied steadily. 'Manning different barricades is hard enough, but we've had another problem as well. I thought I was cured of loving a ghost, but it was another of my mistakes. I can't replace what I lost ... I should never have tried. It was all *my* fault, not yours.'

Felipe smiled at her with some of his old

sweetness regained. He felt anguish still, but it would grow less; and suffering was probably good for his music. He would continue to love her, of course, but at a distance, and *that*, all in all, might suit him very well.

'Shall we still be friends ... when all this hotel nonsense is over? Will you promise me that, Venetia?'

She nodded and smiled, not inclined to mention that the hotel 'nonsense' might end the Marriotts' connection with Rosario.

'Then I shall be able to manage,' he said finally. 'Now I must go, I'm afraid – my father hates being alone at the moment.'

She wished him a safe journey and closed the door behind him. Tiredness and relief fought for the upper hand, but there was something else as well. She insisted to herself that the house only felt empty because she knew that Josefa and Aurelio had gone out; the future looked too uncertain only because she was anxious about William and Edwina. But when she walked back into the study to find that the fire had almost burned away, she began feverishly to coax it into flame again. The wood refused to catch and as she watched it go out completely she knew what she must do without – not Felipe, not even Luc, but a different man, who'd made up his mind that he preferred to travel alone.

She resisted the temptation to go to Las Cuadras the following weekend, but William reported on the telephone that the situation was worsening. 'There was an unpleasant fight again in Luís's bar. It was settled without the help of the Guardia Civil at Ubrique, thank God, because even now that would probably have meant a beating for the offenders, but I'm afraid the trouble won't stop there.'

He sounded so woebegone that Venetia spoke more cheerfully than she felt. 'Don't anticipate it, Uncle Will – a handful of bored young men have let off steam and probably feel much better for the exercise! I suppose it's too much to hope that Pablo Sánchez wasn't involved?'

'He was – but only to help break up the fight. As Luís said, "The man is as strong as an ox, *señor*. If we all have to pummel one another before we're done, I'm glad I'm on his side"'.

'We've done our best–' William went on, 'begged the authorities for a delay to be imposed while our case is being studied – but Manolo is pressing on, of course, while he can. Thank God the weather has been against him – it's the wettest autumn for years.'

'He really *has* been unwell, it seems,'

400

Venetia reported. 'I was inclined to agree with Pablo – too much food and wine on top of too much ill-temper! But when Felipe came here I could see what a worry it's been.' She hesitated and then went on. 'He and I have agreed, by the way, *not* to be an item after all.'

'I'm *sorry*, my dear,' William said miserably. 'Divided loyalties are the very devil. Poor Felipe, too – torn between keeping you and perhaps killing off his father with a more serious heart attack.'

'It wasn't even as simple as that. He'd come round to Manolo's way of thinking – the hotel *was* going to be worth the trouble it was causing.' She changed the subject abruptly. 'Did Ian Gilmour tell you what *he* plans next – a personal view of Spain spanning the last quarter of a century?'

'He mentioned it – ambitious, but very interesting,' William agreed. 'We could do with him here, though, at the moment.' Aware of sounding depressed, he tried again. 'We shall feel better when the weather improves – our poor expatriates on the coast must be wondering why they didn't stay in Manchester!'

But that night, when he came in from locking up outside, he predicted to Edwina a change in the weather. For the first time in what seemed like weeks he'd seen patches of clear sky through the thinning pall of cloud, and even the glimmer of a star or two. By morning his forecast was confirmed: the day broke clear and bright – Andalucía was its early-winter self again, serene and crystal-skyed.

Rosario itself was anything but serene; Don Alberto came to report that the talk was of a busload of strange workmen building a dam across Pablo's little river, which was now threatening the construction of the new road.

'It's on Quinones land – just!' Don Alberto admitted. 'But by holding the water there Manolo will get *all* the advantage of it higher up, and no danger to the road in future.'

'But Pablo will get none, nor will the men who use the water further down,' William said sharply. 'He's *goading* them to violence – can't he see that?'

'He's seeing only what he needs – what he's convinced himself Rosario needs. Don Ramón is busy on his behalf, of course, and the *pueblo* must either fall in behind *him* or Pablo and his friends. I pray at night for what remains of the castle to fall down, but even then I'm not sure that Manolo Quinones wouldn't build it up again.'

'I just pray that the Office of Public Works might awaken from its habitual sloth and procrastination sufficiently to answer our appeals,' William said with rare bitterness.

402

'No wonder Spaniards are cynical about their bureaucrats.' Then he smiled apologetically at his friend. 'I expect you're going to tell me this is a vast country and they have much to do.'

'No – I was going to be a cynical Spaniard,' Don Alberto said calmly, 'and tell you that Rosario is a long way from Madrid!'

He walked home deeply anxious for his flock, and aware that even a brief visit to his friends would have been noted; there would be one or two communicants the less at Mass on Sunday, because the Mayor's supporters would spread the word that he was on the wrong side. Partisanship was an insidious evil, seeping into every nook and cranny of *pueblo* life – even the children were beginning to follow the attitudes of their parents and spit threats at one another.

The violence erupted two days later; the dam workers arrived to find the site occupied by a crowd of angry, determined men. The foreman called the Guardia Civil to quell the battle that broke out, and they assumed that the law breakers were the Rosarians – which technically they were, Pablo admitted when he'd been released and Edwina was attending to his cuts and bruises.

Suspecting him of having enjoyed the fight, William spoke very firmly. 'My friend, one more disturbance like that and you'll all find yourselves in gaol. Perhaps you can afford it, but Pedro and his sons, and Miguel and Angel can't – they must get their olives in and pressed.'

'The last they'll have if we *don't* stop Quinones,' Pablo insisted stubbornly. 'It would be different if those lazy sods in Madrid lifted a finger to help us, but they won't. We *must* fend for ourselves.'

He was right, William admitted when he'd gone home, but as things stood the law was on Manolo's side. The Guardia would be watching for the next sign of trouble, and their ways were not gentle when a warning had been ignored.

Edwina stared gravely at her brother. 'Will dear, I know you wanted *not* to embroil Ian in our troubles again, but I think you must now. If you don't, I shall – before someone gets seriously hurt.'

He let out a long, troubled sigh. 'Yes ... I'm afraid you're right. I'd better go and try.'

At his third attempt to ring the mobile phone number he'd been given contact was made, and Ian Gilmour's voice answered him.

'It was a short conversation,' Edwina said when her brother returned and she'd failed to listen through the door.

'Short but satisfactory. Ian is taking the AVE to Madrid. He'll camp outside the *aparejador*'s office until someone attends to our appeal, and then come straight back. Now, I must walk up the hill and persuade Pablo to hold his fire until Ian gets here. After that we can only pray for the Office of Public Works to put a brake on Manolo. If not, even our Scots friend will be unable to keep war from breaking out.'

Ian Gilmour returned to Rosario two days later with something concrete to report. The Guardia Civil at Ubrique had confirmed that serious trouble was brewing, and the authorities in Madrid proposed to override the provincial officials by sending their own inspectors to settle the dispute. In the meantime work must halt, and so must the disturbances.

'So far, so good,' Ian said to William, 'though God knows what will happen if the inspectors in their infinite wisdom decide that Quinones can be allowed to resume operations. We'll cross that bridge when we come to it.' William's troubled face prompted another question. 'What of your own future – any word about that?'

'No, Manolo's been genuinely unwell. But Edwina passed him in the drive this morning and they exchanged frigid nods. She swears she could see him framing the letter we shall receive after Christmas, inviting us to leave.'

'Where will you go?'

'Somewhere nearer Seville.' William hesitated a moment. 'Venetia is another casualty – she and Felipe have parted company, and I feel much to blame. Edwina pretends that they weren't well suited, but she has no way of knowing that, being rather inexperienced in such matters.' William brushed the painful subject aside and tried to smile at his friend. 'We're immensely grateful to you, but now you'll be wanting to get back to your own work.'

'Not until we hear what the inspectors say. A verdict against us, and Pablo will probably start assaulting the Mayor – he'd do it now for two pins. I must stay at El Perdido for the time being.'

He was on his way out when Edwina returned from her afternoon walk, frowning slightly. 'I met Felipe on my way in. His father doesn't feel like travelling to Madrid for Christmas so the Estebans are coming here. I can't help thinking it a pity – Juan might have been spared the knowledge that his grandfather is destroying Rosario.'

'Blanca won't want him spared,' Ian pointed out. 'What better moment to wean him off his appetite for country life than to see this unhappy place as it is now? But even at that she might be disappointed – he's a stubborn little cuss.'

Work went on while they waited for the men

from Madrid to arrive. Ploughing had to start as the floods subsided and the land dried out; the olives had to be harvested for the village presses. Don Alberto continued to preach tolerance and neighbourly love, even if no one listened to a word he said, and as Christmas drew near the women made their usual preparations. But the impression remained that Rosario held its breath, waiting for the strangers who – knowing nothing of the place or its people – had been given power over their lives.

The inspectors came at last and were inspected in their turn by a battery of suspicious, watchful eyes. William pitied them – the opposing hazards of Scylla and Charybdis seemed slight compared to the task in front of them. But they trudged the hillsides, measured water levels, and asked questions that the Rosarians deeply resented.

To spare his father exertion, it was said, Fernando arrived back from the coast to conduct the inspectors around Quinones land. They also called on the Marriotts and Ian Gilmour, but only to point out politely that, owning no land, their opinions carried little weight in the matter. At the end of a tense week the *pueblo* was at least united in being thankful to see them go, but William seemed pessimistic when he reported to Venetia over the telephone.

'The worst thing is that, if they decide in favour of Manolo, *nothing* will convince the men here that Fernando didn't bribe them. But the painful truth is that he had no need to. The economic arguments in favour of the hotel are probably overwhelming, set against the wishes of a handful of ageing peasant-farmers.'

'Suppose Manolo wins,' Venetia suggested, 'and he does nothing about evicting you ... will you want to stay?'

'No ... I don't think so.' William's answer came slowly. 'If I could continue to stomach my landlord, which would be difficult enough, I could *not* shake hands with the Mayor! What would Don Alberto say to that, I wonder?'

'He'd say you're human after all,' Venetia suggested calmly, 'a sinner like the rest of us! Now, let's talk about Christmas. If you'd rather stay where you are, may I bring Josefa and Aurelio to swell the party?'

'My dear, of course. Edwina will want to swell it more by inviting Pablo and his guest.'

'His ... his guest?'

'Ian Gilmour is still at El Perdido while we wait to hear from Madrid, and thank God he is. There's a malevolent atmosphere hanging over us at the moment, like an unwelcome ghost from the past.'

Venetia was silent, trying to work out

whether any part of Christmas spent in the company of Ian Gilmour would be more strain or more joy than she could bear. That word 'joy' rang in her mind like a golden-voiced bell, the very sound of the season they were to celebrate; but after it would surely come worse desolation than she had ever known.

'Venetia ... are you still there?' William's plaintive voice sounded in her ear.

'Yes ... yes, I'm here.' What had they been talking about? She flogged her chaotic thoughts into some kind of order. 'When ... when do you expect to hear from Madrid?'

'Soon, because Fernando will have put all the pressure he can on them – his workmen have had to be sent away for the moment. But I can't imagine that we shall have heard anything by the time you get here; the bureaucrats are probably already packing up for Christmas.'

But in this William did them an injustice. The inspectors' decision reached La Paloma and the Mayor and the Captain of the Guardia Civil in Ubrique two days before Christmas Eve.

Twenty-five

Felipe collected Blanca and Juan from the station in Seville for their Christmas visit. Back at La Paloma, Manolo inspected his grandson, then claimed with pride that he'd grown since the summer.

Juan's shy smile agreed. 'Two centimetres ... well nearly, Mamá says. But my friends at school are still taller than me.'

'Taller than any, you'll be, and cleverer too, *nieto mío*.'

'Perhaps – if he does what he's told and works hard,' Blanca put in, 'otherwise he'll be much like any other child.' But she didn't believe it, any more than Manolo did. This child she and Rodrigo had begotten *must* be exceptional, because after a miscarriage five years ago there had been no others. She put the grief aside and smiled at her father. 'You're looking better than I expected, but Felipe says you're already disobeying the doctor's orders. That won't be allowed while I'm here.'

Manolo's plump hand dismissed the doctor. 'The man means well, but he's a fool. I just got a little *inquieto*, that's all – stupid people here were making difficulties.' He glanced at his son's face and hurried on. 'Happily, over and done with now, though; the decision we've been waiting for has come through. Fernando knows, and so does Ramón Perez – he's posting a notice on the church door.'

'He couldn't wait until after Christmas, of course – not the Mayor!' Felipe's voice was sharp, but he saw Juan prick up his ears and managed a smile. 'Come with me, Juanito – I've work for you to do.'

It was Blanca who broke the silence when they'd gone. 'I heard about Venetia on the way home. I'm sorry; I should have liked her in the family.'

Manolo shrugged, but looked uncomfortable. 'I should have been more tactful just now. All the Marriotts were involved, of course, so you'd better tell Juan not to keep visiting them while he's here – they won't be happy that the inspectors' decision has gone in our favour.'

'Will there be more trouble when you start work again?'

'No ... the Guardia will see to that. There'll be some ill-will of course for the time being, but it will die down if it's allowed to. The worst trouble-maker is Pablo Sánchez, up at El Perdido. Luckily

Juan isn't going to be roaming the hills in the middle of winter or I'd *insist* that he doesn't go up there – he certainly wouldn't be welcome.'

'It's not only the ill-feeling, is it?' Blanca suggested gently. 'I know from Fernando that the whole venture is proving far more difficult than any of you ever thought it would be.'

Manolo smiled at her. 'You're being *very* tactful, *querida*, and trying not to suggest that I'm no longer able to cope with difficulties! What you don't understand is that if it were easy I wouldn't have wanted to do it at all. Now, when are we going to see that wandering husband of yours? I thought he was coming with you.'

'So did I,' she agreed wryly, 'but at least he's in Spain for a change, and he promised by all he holds dear to arrive not later than Christmas Eve; with that I have to be content. When do we see Fernando?'

'This evening, with a girl *he* swears is not only beautiful but unboring. I hope she is – he's been unlike himself recently. I don't know why ... he usually thrives on problems, the same as me.'

Blanca chose not to explain what ailed her brother, and merely said instead that it would seem strange not to be on friendly terms with the *ingleses* at Las Cuadras.

'Their fault,' Manolo said testily. 'They're

stubborn people – don't know when to give in.'

She didn't irritate him further by pointing out that sometimes in the past this English failing had proved a good thing. Instead she recommended a little rest while she saw to their unpacking; but she went away wondering how she was supposed to make an eleven-year-old child understand that his dear bird-friend might no longer want to see him.

She did the best she could; and the next morning, given the task of entertaining Fernando's glamorous guest while he and his father shut themselves away to talk business, she assumed that Juan was with his uncle in the music room. Only when Felipe reappeared alone at lunchtime was this shown not to be the case.

'The wretched child will have gone to Las Cuadras after all,' Blanca complained; 'so much for too-subtle hints that he wouldn't be welcome, but I was trying to make as little as possible of our disagreement with the Marriotts.' Then she looked at her watch. 'It's unlike them not to have sent him home by now ... but why should they want to be helpful!'

Felipe shrugged the comment aside. 'I'll walk down,' he suggested, 'and probably meet him scurrying back.'

But Juan wasn't in the drive, or at Las

Cuadras itself. He'd certainly called, William said, a couple of hours ago, but they hadn't seen him since. If he'd spotted Ian Gilmour somewhere about, it was likely that he'd gone up to El Perdido.

'I *said* he wasn't to go up there,' Blanca commented when Felipe got back to the house. 'But if anyone had told me that his friend "Yan" was around, I'd have known that he'd go anyway, unless I tied him to a chair.'

'Well, he can drink his soup cold when he comes in,' Manolo snapped. 'We're not waiting any longer.'

The leisurely meal came to an end and there was still no sign of him. Blanca told herself that anxiety was absurd; whatever ill-feeling there might be, no one in Rosario was going to hurt a child. The hillsides were vast and empty, but Juan knew the tracks better than most of the village people did, and he'd made the climb to El Perdido dozens of times. Even so, she smiled gratefully when Felipe got up from the table saying that he would go and fetch the truant home.

At the *cortijo* he found Juan's friend, retrieving parcels from the Land-Rover parked at the door. 'Good-afternoon,' Ian Gilmour greeted him. 'I've already seen the notice on the church door, if you came thinking to break the news more gently.'

414

Did contempt or pity lurk in his glance? Felipe could never be sure but as always he felt himself to be at a disadvantage ... unable to say that he would have liked to be a friend, not an opponent. 'I've come looking for Juan,' he finally explained. 'He should have been home for lunch a couple of hours ago. William Marriott thought it likely that he'd walked up here.'

'I only came back myself ten minutes ago ... You'd better step inside.'

Pablo glared inimically at a Quinones entering his kitchen, but he answered Ian's question. 'Yes, a child came to see you ... said he'd helped plant the trees here, so then I knew who he was. He kept staring up at the ruin – did I know it was where the eagles lived? I said they'd probably moved away, not liking the commotion going on up there nowadays. He looked upset, but said good-bye politely enough when I told him he ought to be getting home ... seemed a nice child altogether, considering where he comes from.'

Ian Gilmour ignored the shaft aimed at Felipe. 'How long ago was this?'

'He was here soon after noon ... I was pouring my usual glass of beer.'

'Three hours ago,' Felipe said, speaking for the first time, 'time to walk to Ubrique and back, much less reach La Paloma. I should have come sooner, but he's so used to roaming these hills...' Polite like his nephew, he remembered to thank them, but his face had grown white with anxiety. 'I'll start looking now. Juan wouldn't be lost – he knows the route blindfold; he must have had a little accident of some kind.'

'But you didn't come across him on your way up,' Ian pointed out briefly. 'If he's out looking for his eagles, as I suspect, God knows how far he's wandered – so he might well be lost.' He frowned at Pablo's kitchen clock, then made up his mind. 'I'm afraid we can't wait, with only an hour or so of daylight left. *Amigo*, will you take the Land-Rover and round up all the men you can find in the village? They'll need to bring torches or lanterns. When you're ready to start, work up the hill from that side while Quinones and his people tackle it from theirs. I'll begin at the top, although I never knew Juan to go that far by himself.'

Pablo nodded ... collected torch and jacket, returned for his mobile phone and then disappeared. As the sound of the Land Rover died away, Felipe spoke in a hoarse voice. 'It's a fool's errand you've sent him on. Everyone will have read the notice by now. Why should men who hate my father lift a finger to help us?'

'Perhaps they won't – in which case we shall have to manage by ourselves.' Ian Gilmour was pulling on boots as he spoke.

416

'How many men can *you* muster?'

'Five of us – myself, my brother, two servants and the gardener; *not* my father, of course, provided we can keep him chained indoors.'

'Better try, I think! Go and get started – we'll meet somewhere on the hill.' He led the way outside, then smiled briefly at his companion. 'Don't despair! Children are usually tougher than we think.' Felipe nodded and set off at a run down the track; then he turned uphill himself, trying to believe what Ian had just said.

There was so much unusual mid-afternoon activity in the streets of Rosario that Venetia feared yet more trouble, especially when she saw Pablo Sánchez gesticulating in the middle of a knot of men. It seemed a sickening start to the Christmas season; but when she'd delivered Josefa and Aurelio into Edwina's welcoming hands, William put a different interpretation on what she'd seen.

'It's not what you're imagining, I think. Pablo called in on his way down to say that Juan Esteban has gone missing. The men you saw were probably forming search parties – good of them in the circumstances.' He watched his niece buttoning up her jacket again and shook his head. 'No, my dear ... they won't want *you* on wet and slippery hillsides; my own services have already been refused. We shall be more useful as a listening-post here, apparently.'

'Quite right too,' she agreed, 'but I'm only going to La Paloma. Blanca will be trying not to run mad with anxiety.' She half smiled at William's worried face. 'It's all right – if I'm not welcome I'll come home again.'

A red-eyed maid at the door led her to Blanca, who was pale but composed.

'I don't suppose there's anything I can do,' Venetia said quickly, 'but I was afraid you might be left alone here with your father.'

'He's watching a film I told him Juan particularly wanted to see, while the nice girl Fernando brought for Christmas holds his hand! I know exactly what's going through his mind. If only he can *make* himself follow that damned film, his grandson will come home safely, expecting to be told about it!'

Venetia nodded, thinking it an attitude her uncle would applaud. 'I expect you know that search parties from the village are getting under way.'

'Organised by Pablo Sánchez!' Blanca's mouth twisted wryly, '...Something this family must accept with grace.'

'Something to prove to us all that Don Alberto is right,' Venetia suggested. 'We can oppose but still not hate each other.'

The too-taut face watching her didn't

relax. 'I expect you know that my father has been given permission to go ahead. Fernando doesn't say so, but it isn't what *he* was hoping for, and, with a different verdict, Juan mightn't have set out to say goodbye to his eagles, or ... or whatever insanely foolish thing it is my ... my only child is doing.' Her level voice broke at last and, forgetting that this was Blanca Esteban, self-assured, sophisticated and super-cool, Venetia wrapped warm arms about her while she wept.

Calm again at last, Blanca looked sadly at her comforter. 'I know we disagree about a lot of things, but I can't help feeling we should not have let you go.'

Venetia smiled at her. 'Will friends do? It's what Felipe and I hope to settle for in the end. Now, if you can really manage here with the help of your nice guest, I'll get back to William – he's manning what he calls the listening-post.'

Blanca walked with her to the front door, but stopped to unburden herself of her worst anxiety. 'Felipe said that Ian Gilmour had chosen to search the castle. I saw Fernando's face at that moment, and although he denied it afterwards he suddenly looked very afraid – as if there was something wrong up there.' She stared at Venetia's suddenly sheet-white face, understanding why Felipe hadn't been able to keep her. The girl in front of her was looking at a world that might not include Ian Gilmour, just as she herself was staring at one that might not include her son. 'I keep trying to pray,' she muttered, 'although I can't think of any reason why God Almighty should bother to listen to me – I never thank Him when things are going well.'

'Keep praying all the same,' Venetia insisted desperately, unable to voice the thought that hammered in her brain. Ian Gilmour wouldn't foolishly throw his life away, but if laying it down could save Juan he'd offer it without hesitation: the guilt of the past finally wiped away to ensure that this time something precious wasn't wasted.

Above the belt of woodland the slopes of the sierra became a harsher place, gorse and scrub barely concealing the slatey grey rock underneath. The surfaces were still slippery with running water, and at this height the wind blew very coldly. In the fading light the ruin looming above him looked so intimidating that no effort of imagination could convert it into a welcoming, luxurious hotel. It also looked too desolate ever to have tempted a child to go inside, but he went through the echoing, empty chambers all the same, calling Juan's name.

The castle sprawled over a ridge linking several hills. At its far end was the Moors' finishing defensive touch – a tall, octagonal tower, crenellated and arrow-slitted. It had looked less forbidding in the golden days of spring, but there was another difference now as well: added to the reek of violence and cruelties long past was a more immediately pungent smell of decaying mortar and ancient brickwork collapsing into dust.

He stepped through the hole where a door had once been, and almost fell headlong over the pile of rubble at his feet. Even in the dim light it was obvious what was happening. The outer wall, of massive blocks of stone, still looked as if it could stand for ever, and the stairs cut into the stone still clung solidly to the wall; but the tower's inner shell of brickwork was disintegrating. Either a thousand years of weathering had been too much for it, or the engineers' recent drilling on the site had weakened it to the point of collapse. Already the first twenty feet of inner wall no longer protected the stairs; it had now become the rubble piled over them and the brick-dust thickening the air.

About to turn and leave, he glanced upwards and felt his heart stop beating for a moment; lying awkwardly huddled round the angle of the stairs was the boy he'd come to find. Beside him the still-standing wall seemed to be trembling. There was no answer when he dragged enough breath into his lungs to call Juan's name. He stepped outside and forced his shaking fingers to tap in Pablo's number on his mobile phone.

'We're climbing up steadily – no sign of him so far though,' his friend's voice answered immediately.

'He's here in the tower, unconscious; I haven't been able to get to him yet. Send someone to warn Quinones. We'll need a stretcher, and an ambulance as near as it can get. Don't bring a lot of men up here, and move about quietly when you come. The bloody thing's falling to pieces inside.'

Then he rang off, confident that he could rely on Pablo Sánchez. For himself there remained only the problem of reaching Juan and getting him down that all-too-exposed staircase before the rest of the wall fell in.

How much later he didn't know – it became a span of time lost and agonising – he staggered out of the tower coughing dust out of his lungs, with the child in his arms. Unable to trust himself to carry Juan down the treacherous slopes, he sat propped against a wall that mercifully felt firm; breathed in cold, fresh air; and waited. With his hands bleeding and filthy, he couldn't be sure of the pulse he felt for; he simply cradled the child's thin body against the warmth of his own and prayed to the God that Venetia believed in. If she knew their need, *she* would be praying too – there was comfort in that, and in the knowledge that, as soon as anyone humanly could, Pablo would arrive.

Rosario took time to recover from that night. The men bringing the stretcher down perilous mountain tracks retold their story afterwards in Luís's bar, but what they kept remembering most was the sight of Manolo Quinones' sons embracing Pablo Sánchez – *hombre*, now that *was* something to marvel at! The wounded *forastero* – a brave man, it was noted approvingly in passing – wasn't embraced, but it was well known that his race behaved differently at moments of high drama.

By the morning of Christmas Eve the whole *pueblo* was in possession of certain facts. Though concussed and with a broken arm and ankle, the child they'd searched for was safe; but the *moros*' castle was now considerably more of a ruin than before. Another fact was only given to them when Don Alberto addressed a packed church at Midnight Mass and read out Don Manolo's message. He thanked his dear friends for their kindness to his grandson, and wanted them to know that he'd decided to abandon the hotel project. A buzz of comment hummed round the church, but the congregation were obedient to the priest's raised hand and he was allowed to go on.

The plan had been beset with technical

problems, but its worst effect had been to damage the peaceful atmosphere of the *pueblo*. Don Manolo would now discuss with his sons what should be done with the sierra, but it was already agreed that the castle ruin would be rendered safe and then left to history.

'A nice touch,' William commented as they walked home afterwards, 'and I'm bound to say the Mayor's smile scarcely wavered.'

'Because his son will be handsomely paid off,' Edwina pointed out. 'The Perez family won't lose by it, though a few others with rosy expectations might, I suppose. Still, we have God's infinite mercy to thank that the tower began to collapse without killing Ian and Juan – I don't think we could have recovered from that.'

William nodded, then gestured in the direction of Venetia and Felipe, walking home behind them. 'No more opposing sides – does that solve *their* problem?'

'Perhaps,' his sister said briefly, unwilling to ruffle his contentment by admitting that she hoped not.

Suspecting that what William had suggested might be in her companion's mind as well, Venetia spoke of impersonal things. 'Rosario felt a happy place again tonight – the men who opposed your father readily joined in the search, and the men they were fighting a week ago know that; it's been important for the future of Rosario.' Then she risked a question. 'What made your father suddenly change his mind – Juan's passionate attachment to the sierra?'

'That might not have been enough, but there was something else as well,' Felipe answered. 'He's still a simple, superstitious man at heart, and he became convinced that he was being warned not to go on with his dream. When Fernando went up with the engineers this morning they found that still more of the inside had caved in, and the staircase where Ian Gilmour found Juan had been completely buried in rubble.'

She said nothing, and after a glance at her face Felipe spoke more cheerfully. 'Our Scots friend is something of a hero – he'll be greeted as such when he shows himself in public.'

'He won't – show himself, I mean,' she said, making it a statement of fact. 'He'll hide until he's fit to travel, and then ... just disappear.'

'You seem very sure!'

'Yes ... yes, I am sure. It's how he is – proud and solitary.' She imagined that she explained this calmly, until Felipe halted in his tracks to stare at her in the moonlight. Then, afraid of having given herself away, she tried to smile. 'Blanca seems to think that Fernando hasn't made a mistake this time ... hurrah for him at least!'

Felipe accepted with his usual grace the lead he'd been given. 'Yolanda is beautiful, as all my brother's women have to be, but the surprise is that she turns out to be kind as well. Manolo is very pleased with her and already anticipating the grandsons she will produce for him! Even Fernando sees her, I think, as a wife he might at least manage to put up with.' Felipe's smile was suddenly very rueful. 'It's what we all seem to be doing ... not getting what our hearts were set on, but just managing!'

'Our hearts will have to learn to lump it, I'm afraid! But it's Christmas morning already, and Juan is safe; so we'll count our blessings and not complain. *Felices Pascuas*, Felipe!'

He kissed her on both cheeks and solemnly returned her greeting, and then they went on walking home.

Twenty-six

In the kitchen at Las Cuadras Encarnita and Josefa added up in conversational terms to considerably more than the sum of their separate parts; and even Aurelio, inspired by Encarnita's willingness to laugh at anything he said, had grown talkative.

There were visitors in the drawing-room as well, Felipe bringing peace offerings from his father of hothouse fruit and wine, and Fernando with the beautiful, smiling Yolanda in tow, to meet people he'd promised her she would like but completely fail to understand. Looking at her, Venetia reckoned that Manolo's expectations were sound – here *was* his perfect daughter-in-law. They explained that Blanca and Rodrigo had returned from the hospital, where Juan was fully conscious, and already pleading to be allowed to come home. He remembered slipping and falling down the tower staircase, but nothing of Ian Gilmour's struggle to get him safely outside.

Their next visitor was Pablo, surprisingly *en route* for La Paloma to answer an

427

invitation from Manolo.

'How is Ian?' Edwina asked at once.

'Irritable, *señorita*! His broken ribs pain him a good deal, and his hands are bandaged so that he can't do anything.' Pablo brushed aside the memory of the nightmare journey down the mountain and grinned at them. 'When we got back from the hospital yesterday evening I was just in time to squeeze into the church. We aren't safe yet, of course; but nothing Quinones thinks of next can be worse than the hotel, so we've plenty to celebrate today, thanks be to God.'

'Don Ramón's notice was removed from the church door very quickly,' William said with a smile. 'It won't be long before he's convinced himself that he foresaw the difficulties of his *patrón*'s castle extravaganza all along!'

Edwina mused over this for a moment. 'We've overlooked something – with Rosario *not* to be on the tourist map after all, the Mayor might decide it's too cramping for a man of his business abilities and go elsewhere.'

Venetia, watching the expression on Pablo's face, chimed in next. 'I hope he does; otherwise the *pueblo* might have to brace itself for fresh hostilities.' She smiled at her aunt and uncle. 'What will you bet me that Pablo isn't thinking of running for Mayor himself?'

428

Pablo placed a finger along his nose in the time-honoured gesture of a man who wasn't telling what he knew, but Edwina smiled at him approvingly.

'It's an excellent idea, provided you marry into Consuela's family first, to keep *her* in order. I believe she has a niece who's quite presentable!'

Amid shouts of laughter the prospective bridegroom buried his head in his hands, and suddenly it felt like Christmas morning. Joy was incomplete because Ian Gilmour wasn't with them, but Venetia wasn't surprised to hear Pablo say that he'd chosen to remain at El Perdido. The role of hero wasn't one he would play; as soon as he was well he'd walk away from them, self-sufficient and content. She must travel on herself without him, but it wouldn't be like losing Luc. This time she had almost nothing to forget: a handful of meetings, only a little understanding sometimes reached, no promises exchanged at all.

Pablo agreed to look in on his way back from La Paloma, then asked Edwina to accompany him to the front door. When she returned she was frowning a little, and spoke abruptly to Venetia.

'Something to show you; come with me please.'

Mystified, Venetia did as she was told, and was led into the familiar, friendly muddle of her aunt's studio. Spread out on the table was a wonderful assortment of what the Spaniards called *belenes*, or Bethlehems: all the traditional components of the nativity scene realised in small, beautifully painted clay figures, but now surrounded as well by the traditional characters and animals to be found in any Spanish village. Each tiny piece had been fashioned by some unknown potter with such verve and sure precision that together they made a rustic master-piece.

'Wherever did you find them?' Venetia asked wonderingly. 'Everyone buys plastic ones nowadays, these have become collec-tors' items.'

'Ian found them,' Edwina explained, 'in a junk shop in Huelva, about to be thrown away. *There's* a comment on our mad, modern society for you.'

Venetia ignored a favourite hobby-horse that her aunt was always ready to mount. 'It was a generous gift; these things are valu-able, as well as very beautiful.'

'Ian asked me to renew some of the paint on the figures where it had got worn away. It was a lovely task, but the *belenes* were never intended for me, they were to be his Christmas offering to *you*. He said you'd cherish them as they deserved.'

There was silence in the room for a moment while Venetia stared at what she

430

could no longer see for the tears that filled her eyes. 'But he changed his mind?' she asked unsteadily, '...decided not to give them to me after all?'

'Well, everything got disrupted, of course, by Juan's accident. By the time it was over we knew the hotel war had been called off, and Ian assumed that your problems with Felipe were solved as well. He gave Pablo a message for me – I was to forget about the crib figures; they'd just be an embarrassment to you now.'

Venetia smeared away tears, needing to focus on her aunt's intelligent, horse-like face. 'But you didn't do what he asked ... Why not?'

'Because I watched you waiting for news two nights ago. I'm not experienced in these matters, but even I know agony of mind when I see it. In any case I've understood all along that Felipe wasn't the one for you.'

Venetia answered by wrapping her in a ferocious hug. 'We'll share the *belenes*,' she said hoarsely afterwards, 'since I know very well that you love him almost as much as I do.'

And there, with what Edwina afterwards claimed to William was heroic self-restraint, she managed to leave the subject of Ian Gilmour alone, even when Venetia suddenly announced that she needed to take a pre-luncheon walk.

431

She hoped she was observed to select a track that didn't lead in the direction of El Perdido, but not observed a few minutes later when she suddenly made up her mind and veered off it on to one that did. Stupidity and blindness might be forgivable; cowardice was not. She arrived at Pablo's *cortijo* determined but pale, and well aware that this might be the worst of all her many mistakes.

Ian Gilmour fumbled to open the door, then stood there staring at her. Apart from bandaged hands and tiredness in his face, he looked the same withdrawn and private man who'd brought Edwina home the day of their first meeting. Saving Juan's life hadn't changed the way he saw himself; the changes were all in her. She struggled to find something commonplace to say.

'You ... you look in quite good nick, all things considered.'

'Thank you, I am – though not able to do much embroidery at the moment, as you can see.'

It was an unpromising start, making her flounder. 'I was p ... passing by ... taking a little w ... walk.'

His eyes wandered over her. 'It seems to have been rather strenuous – perhaps you'd better come in and sit down. If coffee is needed, I'm afraid you'll have to make it yourself; I'm clumsy at the moment. Pablo's answering a royal summons from La Paloma but I pleaded decrepitude.'

She shook her head at the suggestion of coffee but collapsed gratefully into a chair at the kitchen table. He sat down as well with due care, but seemed disinclined to help the conversation. 'I wasn't just out walking,' she admitted. 'I came to thank you for the loveliest present I've ever been given – except that you *didn't* give it to me; Aunt Edwina did. She ignored the message Pablo brought, you see.'

'I do see,' he said grimly, 'but there was no need to trudge all this way – a few old-fashioned clay figures don't merit that amount of gratitude. A convent upbringing has left you ridiculously determined to be polite.'

It seemed the right word – ridiculous was probably what she was, and ridiculous was the belief she'd clung to on her walk that the *belenes* had been important.

'I came to say something else,' she went on doggedly. 'You were right – I couldn't hope to separate Felipe from his family, and should never have tried.'

'Never mind – his brother is waiting impatiently in the wings, I'm sure.'

Not intending to hurt, he merely sounded so detached that she could swear the conversation bored him, but she'd come this far and must go on now to the bitter end.

'It's too late; Fernando looks like being settled with someone else at last. I *was* once tempted to accept what he offered, but I was afraid that sex without love might be even more unsatisfactory than Felipe's preference for love without sex.'

Ankles neatly crossed, hands folded in her lap, she felt for all the world like the convent pupil he'd accused her of being, come to confess some small sin to Mother Superior. But having made the admission, she was strongly tempted to burst into tears. The last few days had been over-full of emotion, and she'd capped them with this absurd and quite pointless interview. Her final humiliation would be to have him laugh at her, but she could scarcely blame him if he did.

'Juan's making good progress,' she said, unable to go on talking about herself.

'I know ... Pablo rang the hospital this morning.'

It was like trying to find a hand-hold on smoothly polished rock. Defeated, she still managed to smile at him. 'The Marriotts are basking in your reflected glory – rather unfairly, but at least it means that William and Edwina can stay where they are. I suppose it's also why I came ... to thank you for that. I'd better go back now, though. Josefa and Encarnita were very merry in the kitchen when I left, and lunch may never get cooked.'

What she needed now was some merry little quip to see her safely to the door, but while she was still flogging her brain for it, Ian Gilmour spoke himself.

'Are you going to stay in Spain – make your home here permanently?'

At least it was a question she could answer calmly. 'Yes, I am. *Not* what I bargained for when I set out for my grandmother's funeral, but the past year seems to have taught me that this is where I belong.'

He stared at his bandaged hands resting on the table in front of him, and she was free to look at his face ... to commit it to memory, if she could, for the long, lonely years ahead. His greying hair showed a rebellious tendency to curl, she noticed, and the scars on his face were only noticeable now as faint, pale lines on the brown skin. She would have liked to touch them, smooth away whatever pain they still represented. She wanted to stay with him for ever, not to be left behind. The futility of it would be something to face when she was on her way home, but he'd begun to talk again and she must listen to his quiet voice.

'I'm not the young Frenchman you loved so well; I've no desire to be the gentle friend you found in Felipe; and to date my record as a family man has been disastrous. All in all, I can think of no reason on God's earth why you should let me share your life, but it's what I'd very much like.'

Had she really heard him say that? It seemed so, because his expression was grave. Over the obstruction in her throat she strove to answer. 'I'm afraid you're prepared to carry kindness much too far. I can manage well enough without Luc now, and Felipe will remain a friend. It's absurd for *you* to pretend that a companion is something you miss.'

A faint smile lifted the corners of his mouth. 'I was thinking in terms of a *wife* – a revolutionary idea in this day and age, but I'm not young enough for more flexible arrangements.'

She was silenced again; either she'd gone quietly mad and was imagining this conversation, or there was only one other explanation.

'I suppose I gave myself away by coming here,' she said finally. 'Or perhaps it was that morning in the square at Arcos. Whichever it was, I refuse to have you think I need salvaging.'

His mouth twitched again, but he shook his head reprovingly. 'Churlish, my dear love ... *not* the way to respond to a proposal, even if you're determined to turn it down!'

She ducked her head for a moment, made dizzy by the endearment. Then she managed to look at him. 'Did you mean what you just called me?'

His bandaged hands reached out to cover hers, and his face answered before his words did. 'Oh yes, I meant it ... I could expound, enlarge, elaborate almost indefinitely, but it will do to be going on with! All the time I was trying to get Juan down that damned rubble-bombarded staircase it was the only coherent thought in my mind. I couldn't die there, not without you knowing that you were meant to wait for *me*, instead of cluttering up your life with the Quinones family.'

She was beginning to believe it ... already she could hear the horns of elfland faintly blowing; no, not fairy horns ... golden trumpets blazing out a message of hope and joy. But with happiness transfiguring her face, she still tried to sound rational and calm.

'We've barely managed to be civil to each other up till now. Shouldn't we try something less ambitious than marriage to start with?'

He shook his head, trying not to smile. '"A man's stretch should exceed his grasp, or what's a Heaven for," said Robert Browning, and I agree with him!' Then his face grew serious again. 'Our timing is deplorable, I'm afraid. Unfair persuasion is beyond me at the moment, and although I should strive with heart and body and soul to make you happy, I can't *promise* to succeed ... I can only promise that you'd be truly loved.'

Tremulous but sure now, she was able to answer him. 'The unfair persuasion would have been enjoyable, but it's not essential, and you've given me the only promise I need.' She got up and walked round to his side of the table. 'Would a small, *chaste* kiss be acceptable in your present weakened state, or reckoned too unsettling?'

'Weakness being so fast recovered from,' he murmured unevenly when his mouth finally released hers, 'that full manly vigour will soon be restored. But the best I can do for the moment, my heart, is to escort you decorously down the hill.'

She swathed a coat, cape-fashioned, about his shoulders, kissed him again to spur vigour on, and then smiled ruefully. 'I suppose you know that Aunt Edwina will be insufferably pleased with herself. There've been heavy hints already that she knew where I was going wrong.'

He nodded, eyes suddenly brimming with laughter while he tried to look woebegone. 'I was a marked man from the day I brought her home. Even then I remember there was mention of a charming niece – a trifle headstrong and wilful, perhaps, but...'

Her hand closed firmly over his mouth, stifling the rest of it. He kissed her fingers instead, then smiled at her again. 'I shall tell

Edwina that I couldn't get Duncan's house on easier terms – that ought to put her in her place, don't you think?'

Still laughing, they set off down the hill, decorously as befitted Ian's battered ribs but filled with deep and shared delight.

At Las Cuadras Edwina watched them approach, met them at the door to be sure of what she saw, and then called to her brother.

'Will, dear ... I think we need champagne!'

They were in the act of drinking it when Pablo arrived back, and stared accusingly at his friend.

'In *far* too much pain, you said, to go with me to La Paloma, but I find you here, gaily swigging wine.'

'Venetia called unexpectedly, and I felt obliged to totter back with her, that's all. The wine is restorative.'

Pablo examined the bottle more carefully, then looked at them again. 'Something else has happened. *Dios mío*, I leave you alone for a moment and at once you get into fresh trouble.'

Smiling broadly, William put a glass in his hand. 'Join us, anyway, my friend, in drinking to their happiness.'

Pablo did as he was told, but the expression on his face made Venetia say sympathetically, 'Look on it as losing a troublesome lodger and gaining a friend!'

Pablo glanced nervously in Edwina's direction. 'It feels more like losing a lodger and gaining a wife I don't want.' But fortified with another sip of champagne, he suddenly smiled at them. 'No, I've remembered that I shan't have time for one! Leaving aside the business of becoming Mayor, I'm going to be *muy ocupado* in future.' He paused a moment to heighten the suspense. '*Now* shall I tell you what is to happen to the sierra? Don Manolo's new plan is to make it into a nature reserve ... a properly tended, natural mountain wilderness, in other words. After giving it some thought I had to admit that I liked the idea.'

'With *you* doing the tending?' Ian hazarded a guess.

'Who else? I shall be its official warden, assisted in the school holidays by the *señorito* himself – Juan Esteban!'

William, also liking the plan very much indeed, nevertheless looked anxious. 'You came back here to tend your own land, my friend. Can you do that *and* Manolo's job as well?'

'I can do whatever needs to be done – just by working harder,' Pablo said simply. 'But Rosario has to be involved as well, because there'll be a great deal of work to do. The bored young men who were going to become hotel waiters will be offered a different future from the one Ramón Perez suggested. If they are lazy or stupid enough to turn it down then I shall know that Spain itself also has no future.' He lifted his glass and smiled at them. 'It's a risk, of course, but here's to hope, *amigos*!'

They drank to his toast, and then settled down to discuss the scheme until Encarnita appeared to say that lunch was served.

William had already made it plain that she, Josefa and Aurelio were expected to sit with them at table today, and for the entire company it became a celebration to remember. Encarnita, a little flown with wine, repeatedly assured her host that there had never been such a Christmas Day; and William as repeatedly smiled and agreed with her.

Afterwards, when the servants had retired to the familiar comfort of the kitchen and the others were settling down again in William's study, Ian drew Venetia aside.

'You're looking pensive. Tell me what's bothering you, please?'

She smiled but didn't deny what he'd said. 'I was wishing we could have shared that happy meal with the people at La Paloma.'

'Perhaps we can in future,' he said gently, 'or is it really the *future* that is worrying you? It doesn't look uncertain to me, my love; does it to you?'

'At eighteen it wouldn't have done,' she

441

admitted; 'approaching thirty I'm more faint-hearted!'

'Then pity me – considerably more than thirty, and much more accustomed than you to snares and pitfalls!'

She looked at him with troubled eyes. 'Ian, will it all work out? Will the nature reserve be something that Rosario can take pride in? Can Spain prosper without losing its soul? Shall *we* be able to stay here for ever and be happy?'

He smiled at her and touched her cheek with gentle, bandaged fingers. 'The reserve will succeed because Pablo and Quinones together won't let it fail. It's not, by the way, Manolo's own idea ... I'd stake my life that Fernando and Felipe combined to talk him into it – their gift to *you*, I suspect, rather than to Rosario!'

She was so touched by the idea that her voice became unsteady. 'All right – Rosario and the nature reserve will live together happily. What about Spain, to which we've committed ourselves so thoroughly?'

'Spain is simply Rosario writ large, and infinitely more varied. Pablo doesn't really doubt its future any more than I do, and for a very good reason ... he knows it rests on people like himself.'

She nodded, remembering the simple kindness of the woman on the train coming back from Madrid. 'Which leaves *us* as the only uncertainty, despite Edwina's conviction that all we've got to do is apply ourselves to the serious business of living together!'

He did his best to look grave. 'Well, I've been assured by Josefa and Aurelio, separately and together, that I'm exactly the *señor* you need, so I don't really see how we can fail!' He kissed her and then smiled. 'We *aren't* eighteen-year-olds, thank God, starting out, with all our mistakes still to make. We've got the past along with us as baggage whether we like it or not, but without it we wouldn't be here, ready to set forth together.'

Venetia nodded, suddenly content. 'I've never been able to join my life up before – it always seemed as if bits of me were in separate little boxes that had nothing to do with each other. But I do believe I'm continuous at last ... rather like Arabic calligraphy!'

'Beautifully cursive in fact!' he managed to agree solemnly. 'It's a pity we can't, as Edwina would say, apply ourselves at once; but we *shall* soon, and then I defy you not to find the past put to rest at last and the future full of delight and certainty.'

She smiled whole-heartedly then, knowing that it was quite safe to believe him.